D1414352

# And Abram Journeyed

BY THE SAME AUTHOR

Under Strange Skies
Jewish Notables in America 1776–1865
Jewish Participants in the Civil War
Saga of American Jewry 1865–1914
The Chosen One

# And Abram Journeyed

Harry Simonhoff

South Brunswick
New York · Thomas Yoseloff · London

Library of Congress Catalogue Card Number: 67–10814

Thomas Yoseloff, *Publisher*
Cranbury, New Jersey

Thomas Yoseloff Ltd
18 Charing Cross Road
London, W.C. 2 England

6563
Printed in the United States of America

To My Brother
Samuel

Whose criticisms and
suggestions have been
extremely helpful

# Contents

# And Abram Journeyed

# Ur of the Chaldees

# 1

# The High Priest

THE TEMPLE OF NANNAR, DEDICATED TO THE MOON GOD, was the foremost sanctuary in the old city of Ur, which for a time had been the capital of the Sumerian empire. It was in the late afternoon of the New Moon festival and worshippers were still bringing offerings and sacrifices for the various gods. The high priest, his assistant, and eight of the elder ministrants had gone to a celebration in honor of the god Nannar at Erech, a city that was perhaps older than Ur and also mentioned in the Book of Genesis. A young priest of high promise named Sabbattu was in charge of the temple.

A man about forty years old, along with his daughter, approached Sabbattu. The daughter, Anunu, a very pretty girl of about sixteen, would be presented to the temple. The father made his seal upon the soft clay tablets in cuneiform figures which set out the formalities necessary for a woman to become a permanent votaress. The paganism of *Circa* 2000 B.C.E., saw nothing unseemly about a priestess offering her body to any man who could pay the required fee to the temple.

That same night Sabbattu the priest took Anunu into

his own bed to consecrate her as a *kedashe*. He found she was no longer a virgin and suspected the father of deflowering her. There was something guilty about his manner; it was a manner that betrayed an intimacy other than filial. The daughter, too, whenever she looked at her father, seemed to look at him with a kind of reproach. The priest concluded that perhaps the man's wife resented the relations between her husband and her daughter. Probably the girl was the child of his concubine whom he either divorced or perhaps sold. Such triangles, not uncommon, were often the causes that prompted fathers to dedicate their daughters to the service of the temple.

Anunu had to go through a period of probation before final acceptance. She was observed, studied, and tested as to her fitness for the calling. To become a hieyodule, a girl or woman had to demonstrate the ability to attract admirers and to wheedle larger sums for the temple than the stipulated fee. Anunu was carefully taught the nuances in the art of love. The teachers also paid attention to qualities that would enable a *kedashe* to serve in other capacities when no longer attractive or useful in the profession. The temple was a large institution and required an organization to fulfill its many labors and duties.

One morning, while receiving instruction, Anunu became nauseated and she vomited. The instructors immediately concluded that she was pregnant. This created a problem. Priestesses in certain categories were not permitted to have children. If a *kedashe* conceived in the usual course of her duty, then she remained and the child was raised either in or by the temple. But pregnant women were not admitted. Sabbattu was informed that his ward would not be accepted until after the child was born.

Sabbattu recalled that Anunu's father had disclaimed all further responsibility for her the moment he delivered his daughter to the priest. It now became obvious to the priest that she was brought to the temple because her father had good reason to suspect that she was or might become pregnant. He could have been forced to take her back, at least until the child was born. But Anunu refused to go back to her home. To further complicate matters, Sabbattu had become extremely fond of her. He simply could not get enough of her caresses. The girl threw her arms about his neck and kissed him, but she refused to give herself to him any more until he promised to carry out her request.

"And what is your request?"

"Get Harran the weaver to house and feed me until I give birth."

"And why Harran the weaver? I can place you in a better home."

"Because Harran and his wife are decent. They are Arameans and among such people a father does not sleep with his daughter, nor does a brother lie with his sister. They are very strict about adultery or incest."

"But, Anunu, our laws are strict about adultery and incest. They sometimes punish such crimes with death. I don't understand."

"Well, I do, my beloved," and she sealed further talk with kisses.

The next day Sabbattu called at the home of Harran, son of Terach, the image-maker. Harran had attempted to follow the profession of his father but showed neither interest nor skill in making idols. His wife, Davarah, skillful in weaving wool and flax, finally induced her husband to set up a small weaving establishment for themselves. She also wanted her own home since she did not get on well with her mother-in-law. She prevailed upon Harran to lease a house with seven rooms and a court below for weaving. Davarah had trained her female slave to be a competent weaver and had hired two other slave women from their masters. She began to weave cloth and soon had accumulated more than she could sell. The house was filled with woven material for which the merchants offered much less than what it cost Davarah to produce.

It was at this critical period in the affairs of Harran that Sabbattu introduced himself as the newly appointed overseer of woven products in the temple of Nannar. Harran had felt it useless to attempt to sell his wares to the temple since he heard that it had a big stock on hand. He knew, as did everyone else, that the sanctuary had a large retinue to clothe, and he also had heard that the temple sold vast quantities of cloth locally and throughout Sumer and Akkad. He therefore felt dubious when the priest asked to see samples and prices. When Harran furnished the required information, Sabbattu stated that he would consult his subordinates since he was unfamiliar with the weaving industry.

When the two finished talking business, Harran offered the priest some date wine, a courtesy approved by established custom. The priest sat on the divan and Harran crouched down on his haunches. The talk drifted to the different national groups that lived in Ur, and the priest casually mentioned a bothersome task that had been assigned to him. He had to place a young girl for about nine months or less in the home of some Aramean.

"Who is the girl?" inquired Harran.

"Anunu, daughter of . . ."

"Of course I know her. She is a friend of my daughter Milcah."

Harran begged to be excused. In another room he consulted his wife and impressed upon her the importance of gaining the good will of the priest, who could if he wished take over their entire stock. Harran would even sell at cost since the temple silver would pay all his debts and enable him to make a fresh start. On his return, Harran declared, "Adoni, it would be our great pleasure to invite Anunu to make her home with us."

When the priest asked the charges, Harran replied, "The honor of serving you is compensation enough."

The next day Harran and his wife welcomed Anunu into their home. Sabbattu came to see her quite often and became friendly with Harran, who succeeded in selling his entire stock to the Temple of Nannar at low prices, yet above his cost. Harran continued to supply the temple with a goodly part of his production until his death. He had introduced his father Terach to the priest who had quickly recognized an opportunity to benefit by the new connection. He induced the high priest to give the image-maker the monopoly of selling idols in the Temple of Nannar. This raised the prestige of Terach as both artist and business man. Soon customers from the city and the adjacent country came to buy statuettes at his shop. It did not take long before he was unable to supply the demand; this forced him to buy the idols of his less successful competitors. Yet Terach could never get rich. The book-keeper and agent "recommended" by the priest relayed, to his secret chief, the earnings of the business as well as the gossip and information gleaned from the customers who patronized the shop.

As the months moved slowly on, Anunu evinced emotional instability. She became sad with the premonition of early death. Sabbattu could do nothing to cheer her up. Anunu became convinced that the gods were punishing her for her incest; that they sent evil spirits to plague her. She was frightened, insecure, and knew that a demon entered and distended her body. No amount of reasoning could convince her otherwise. In one of her hysterical seizures she told the priest that she would never survive the birth of her child. Nearing the day of delivery, she made Sabbattu take an oath to Nannar, Enlil, Nergal, and Irnina that he would induce Harran and Davarah to rear the child as their own.

About seven months after the priest first saw Anunu, she lay writhing in birth pains which lasted more than a day. She had no further strength left when the baby's cry reached her. Harran's wife raised it so that the mother might see her child. Immediately she fell asleep and never awoke. Sabbattu prevailed upon Harran to bury Anunu under the chapel vault beneath his house, in accordance with the prevailing custom in Ur. Her child, Zirru, was reared by Harran and Davarah as their own. When Zirru was eight, Lot was born and she regarded him as her brother. She was much at home in Terach's house and began to love his son Avram at an early age.

## II

Sixteen years later Sabbattu was high priest of the Temple of Nannar. The hierarch had assembled his fellow priests to discuss the opposition that had arisen against his proposed erection of a statue to the moon god. He made no statement himself but simply asked why anyone present resented the idea of honoring Nannar, the patron deity of their ancient city.

There was silence until an old priest spoke up. He thought that the question concerned the competence or artistic skill of the sculptor. The older priests favored Terach, who continued to fashion gods along the stylized convention that had been practiced in Ur for more than a millennium. A neophyte with artistic proclivities declared, "After all, Terach is but third rate. He certainly is not in the class of those new artists springing up in upstart cities such as Babylon or even Mari."

He was seconded by a priest who had traveled on a boat as far as Egypt. Vain of his worldly knowledge, he ventured, "I consider him inferior to the sculptors of Egypt, who can make life likenesses out of granite or the black basalt dragged from the Libyan desert."

The second ranking priest, Hunate, had overheard his chief telling the son of Nahor: "If your workmanship will do justice to our puissant god, the statue will be placed in a prominent spot of the temple court, even where a human sacrifice might be offered should the occasion arise for placating the wrath of Nannar or Enlil or Irnina." Proud of his Sumerian blueblood, Hunate hated Akkadians, Arameans, Egyptians, and especially anyone of Semitic blood. Unable to restrain his resentment, he burst forth:

"Terach is neither a Sumerian nor even an Elamite," as he suddenly recalled that the high priest was of the stock of Elam. "He is an Aramean whose father came from Aram Naharaim and always spoke our sacred tongue with a thick, gutteral accent. No worshiper of Marduk or Baal can sense the nobility of our Nannar, or estimate the cosmic power of Enlil. Nor can he comprehend the noble passion that surges in our Irnina. She is our beloved goddess and even other nations worship her as Ishtar, or Ashtoreth, or Astarte. No other goddess endows lands with such fertility as our crops produce in Shinar between the two rivers. Can anyone not a native of Sumer comprehend the wisdom of our sea god Ea?"

The high priest was rapidly losing patience. As a final fling to silence the criticisms that he felt were directed towards himself rather than against Terach, or any other foreigner, he declared with a certain asperity, "If you know anyone superior to Terach in craftsmanship, then produce him. If he can be found in Ur, I shall immediately engage him even if his skill only matches the workmanship of Terach."

At this stage Khar-Sak, a teacher in the temple school and noted throughout Sumer for his learning and clarity of thinking, arose and said, "There seems to be here either a strange confusion in thinking or some are purposely trying to muddle the waters, as the saying goes. As far as I can see the issue runs deeper than the skill of the sculptor. Our lord Sabbattu has made it clear that he will accept any image-maker who is more competent or better endowed than Terach. But you are silent and that means that this simple solution is not what you really want."

"Let's get down to basic issues. There are two fractions here: those who are satisfied for things to remain as they are, and those who want changes. The first group holds that what was good for their forefathers should be good enough for them. The opposition maintains that such a state of mind prevents growth, development, expansion. It is the stagnant as against their own progressive attitude. No one, oh Sabbattu, is against honoring our great Nannar. The issue involved is whether the statue of Nannar should be carved on a flat wall, known in technical language as bas-relief, or should be round, visible on all sides, and without the support of a wall or anything else. This statue, they maintain, should stand on its two feet unaided, like a human being."

Khar-Sak received a round of applause.

After complimenting Khar-Sak for the wisdom and clarity of his presentation, Sabbattu went on to say, "Brother priests, let me call in our official sculptor who will explain our transaction and answer such questions that you may have."

Terach, son of Nahor, informed the gathering, "One day when on business in the temple I stopped to pay my respects to adon Sabbattu, and he called attention to the drab appearance of the wall opposite his study. He asked what I thought of a carving on the wall of Lord Nannar sailing a ship inside a large quarter moon. I thought it splendid but suggested something new in art. Instead of a carving in bas-relief, why not follow the example of the Egyptians and do a statue independent of any wall. His eminence rejected the suggestion and ordered me to make a sketch of the god sailing in the moon. Several days later his Lordship sent word that I should work out the statue idea and prove to him that it was feasible. I am working on it now."

"Did you ever do a large statue before?" asked Hunate, the second ranking priest.

"The largest round statue I ever did before, your worship, was two cubits high. These I sell to householders for their prayer chapels."

"Then why do you think you can do this one?"

"This principle I work on is the same. It is only a matter of proportion. I tested out a four cubit image, the size of a fairly tall man, and it stood on its own feet very well. Then I tried six cubits and it was satisfactory. Now I am working on eight cubits, about twice the size of a man. I feel confident that it will stand the test."

"Suppose this statue does not turn out well. What then?" inquired Khar-Sak.

"Then it will be turned back to clay and I shall not require payment."

The high priest knew that he was not liked by his sacerdotal colleagues who felt resentful that an Elamite should be their superior. The Sumerians prided themselves on the high culture which they believed was older and greater than those of all other lands including Egypt. They enjoyed reminding travelers or strangers that their ancient city of Ur existed long before the great flood destroyed all living creatures, except those saved by Ut-Napishtim in his ship that floated on the waters until the flood subsided. But the great day of Sumer's military prowess was over. The Sumerians had known the humiliation of defeat; they had been conquered and ruled by the neighboring kingdom of Elam. Though Ur had finally regained a measure of independence and was now enjoying a spurt of commercial prosperity, a new fear was gnawing at Sumer's vitals. The Amorites in the north had made Babylon into a mighty city and the most powerful fortress in all of Mesopotamia. Everyone knew that the capable Hammurabi had slowly extended his dominion over neighboring cities until he ruled most of Akkad. Many were also aware that he did not rely solely on military power. His wisdom, wealth, and shrewdness brought many cities and entire districts into his expanding empire.

The people of Ur could not help wondering how long their proud and cultured old city might resist the encroachment of this Amorite ruler. Pride gave way to fear and when the old high priest died, the king, his councillors, the priests, and nobles thought it politic to select his successor from the Elamite group which resided in Ur and had intermarried with the native Sumerians. In the event of invasion, the Urites, needing the help of the Elamites, consciously chose the priest with the strongly scented Semitic name of Sabbattu, which meant a weekly day of rest. Yet as time went on the younger priests never became reconciled to the domination of a foreigner descended from their conquerors and theoretical rulers.

The high priest asked whether there were any further

questions and hearing none declared in a peremptory voice, "The meeting is closed."

III

Slaves were scouring the oven-burnt brick on the paved court that comprised the bottom floor of the 14-room house occupied by the image-maker Terach, son of Nahor. This court opened into the narrow unpaved Street of the Ancients winding through the heart of Ur. Near the front door a tiny lobby with a drain in the floor invited the visitor to wash his hands and feet. Brick stairs led to the upper floor where lived the family, its servants, and slaves. Some of the rooms were used for spinning, dyeing, or the kneading of clay for the numerous statuettes which the head of the house made and sold. Behind the stairs was a lavatory with its terra cotta drain. In the kitchen, consisting of a fireplace and stone grinders, food was prepared for the household.

The entire family, the servants, and slaves were making the court fit for the reception of Sabbattu, the high priest, who had sent word the day before of his intended visit at noontime. He wished to inspect the statue of Nannar while in the course of construction. Sabbattu was curious about the size, height, and workmanship of the tallest image he had ever seen, one that would stand without any support. This statue would occupy a prominent spot on the terraced roof of the Temple of Nannar, the largest in the city, with the exception of the Ziggurat which was reported to have been built shortly after the great deluge. The legend was still alive that its builders had planned to scale and storm the heavens.

The sun shone directly overhead in almost a perpendicular line when Sabbattu, accompanied by five priests of the upper echelon, together with six temple *kadoshim* (holy castrates), entered the cleanly swept floor of Terach's patio. After a most respectful greeting Terach knelt, kissed the extended hand, then led his exalted visitor to a throne-like chair, the only seat on the floor which also contained the showroom of the idols on display for anyone to purchase. On this afternoon only the exceptional creations of Terach's craftsmanship were displayed. The commanding figure of Nannar stood out high above the rest, the white alabaster gleaming in the noonday light that spotted mottled sunbeams here and there.

The image, hardly more than half finished, revealed sufficient head, face, eyes, and beard to apprise the visitors of the conventional features accorded to the moon god on almost every icon in the temples or houses of Ur. The craftsmanship was hardly above mediocre, yet there lingered in the face a suggestion of character and vitality that denoted a limited artistry. When asked how he produced such an effect, Terach answered, "When the gods are pleased with my efforts, they enter the figure and a portion of the divine remains in the statue."

After inspecting the incompleted statue of Nannar and trying to read the thoughts of the priests and *kadoshim*, Sabbattu remarked quite casually that he wished to see Terach's workshop. Since the priest had seen the workshop before, the son of Nahor sensed that Sabbattu had something to say in private. Nannar's high priest often had requests which never failed to benefit himself and prove burdensome to his image-maker. The holy man was directed up the brick steps into the reception room on the second floor. This time Sabbattu did not complain about the heavy expense of operating the temple; nor did he suggest a "loan" that would make Terach gasp and beg for its reduction to about one-half, the amount he knew the priest had contemplated to begin with.

To the surprise of Terach, this time the hierarch merely asked whether he could make a good image of the queen. When he recovered his breath, the idol maker replied, "I could be inspired by such a commission, but it would be necessary to make a close study of Shub-Ad's beautiful face. Of course, the queen of Ur would hardly deign to honor my humble workshop with her presence and it is doubtful whether a lowly sculptor would be allowed sufficient time in the palace to catch the head contour, the subtle smile, the grace and charm of the most beautiful woman in the world."

"I believe it somehow can be arranged," assured the priest of Nannar. "Either you can go sometimes to the palace or she might come masked and disguised to your studio. I know that Queen Shub-Ad is greatly beloved by our glorious Irnina. The great goddess actually told me so in a vision. The goddess had said, 'Shub-Ad is the most beautiful queen that ever appeared among mortals and I would have her likeness stand close to mine.' "

Terach bowed in submission. He felt beaten since he knew that the high priest usually succeeded in getting whatever he went after. The image-maker also knew that he would never receive a shekel for so difficult and trying a commission. He wondered why ironically people envied his "good fortune" of having the sole right to sell idols in the great Temple of Nannar. Everyone assumed that it was a profitable concession and entirely due to the patronage of the high priest who alone had the power to bestow such largesse.

Now the time had come for questioning. While in no sense a spy, Terach knew that he was expected to keep his patron informed as to what was going on in the world. The large display of idols attracted many people to his shop which had become a sort of meeting place not only for the purchase of images but also to chat, to argue, and even to exchange views.

"Have you anything of interest to tell?" questioned the priest. "Nothing in particular, Adoni. The usual grumbling about high taxes to the king and tithes to the temples."

"Give me more in detail," commanded the priest, showing a slight irritation at Terach's reticence. He suspected that the image-maker had much more to relate than he revealed.

"Some are bothered by Hammurabi's growing power. They wonder whether he has spies or trusted agents in Ur. One farmer living close to Nippur said something rather bright attributed to the Amorite king: 'It is easier to take a fortress with a single ass carrying a bag of gold than with ten thousand soldiers bent only on pay for drink and women.' "

"Nothing else?"

"A merchant who makes regular trips to Damascus by caravan said that the people of Amuru are watching our kingdom closely. They always want to know what taxes were paid in or by our provinces. He feels that the Hittites are in league with the Kassites and have an understanding with the Elamites and some of the subjected people."

"And where does Hammurabi fit into this conspiracy?"

"The consensus is that the king of Babylon is not involved. He has his hands full consolidating his conquests and integrating his empire."

"What have people to say about the gods? Do they question their might, their justice, or their unlimited powers?"

"The usual argument centers about the superior strength of the individual god. Is the moon god, Nannar, more powerful than the sun god, Utu? One traveler observed the other day that the gods of the different nations are the same but with different names. Irnina is the same as Ishtar. The people of Canaan call her Ashtoreth; the Syrians, Astarte. The Egyptians worship her as Isis. He had a long written list and identified our gods with those of other nations. He named gods unknown to me and worshipped by people I have never heard of."

"Tell me, do people question the goodness or the cruelty of the gods? Whether they show compassion and mercy? Does anyone complain about the injustices of the gods towards men?"

"Yes, your eminence. Those who suffer often complain bitterly. They declare that the invisible demons all about us seem to possess greater powers than the gods themselves, for the evil spirits afflict men, women, and children far more than the gods benefit them." And Terach touched the amulet suspended to his neck by a leather band and quietly uttered a prayer.

Sabbattu seemed absorbed and after a short silence resumed his questions.

"Did anyone ever talk about a secret god, a god who has no form and therefore cannot be seen? His followers are forbidden to mention his name; they simply refer to him as Adon, Lord. No graven image portrays him, yet his small sect maintains he is either the only god or perhaps that he is mightier than all other gods; I don't know which. His worshippers believe that he alone created heaven and earth and all things therein. They appear certain that he can hear from the heavens the prayers of all persons in the world at the same time. They brag that he is justice itself. Have you ever heard of him?"

"No, Adoni," answered Terach.

The high priest then asked Terach about his children. "Yes, your holiness, my son Nahor lives in a city up north not far from the Naar Purattu. As you know, his brother

Harran is dead with only a widow and son left; but my youngest, Avram, lives with me."

"Let me see him. I may confer Nannar's blessings upon him."

Terach opened the door, clapped his hands, and ordered the slave to summon his young master. A young man of eighteen came into the room and bowed low. The priest eyed him and exclaimed, "What a handsome youth, tall and strong! He would make him a fine *Kadosh* for my temple."

Terach became alarmed. While a believer in Sumer's gods, he was too much of an Aramean to relish the notion of his son being castrated and wasting away his life in a temple. He declared rather hastily, "My son would never do for such a service. He asks questions about the gods which I find it difficult to answer. I might say he lacks the feeling of piety. I, myself, wonder how firm is his faith."

Nannar's representative smiled sardonically and said, "He should then make a good priest. Are you training him in your craft?"

"No, Adoni, he shows neither skill nor interest; nor has he any emotional depth to express feeling for the godhead."

"Has he had any schooling?"

"Yes, your eminence. He has attended all the grades that Ur has to offer. His teachers say he would be a good student if he applied himself. He is equally skillful with the stylus on the clay tablet as with a reed on papyrus in the Egyptian manner."

"What does he do to occupy his time?"

"He works, after a fashion, selling my statuettes."

Terach feared Sabbattu. He thought he had underplayed his son sufficiently for the priest to lose interest in him. He was therefore startled to hear him say to Avram,

"You can join the priests' college in my temple on the first day after the new moon festival. Take this and present it to Khar-Sak, who is the best teacher and the most learned priest in all of Akkad and Sumer. He will clear up your doubts and fill you with adoration for the gods."

And the high priest handed a small seal to Avram who was about to leave but remained at a sign from his father, who then asked smilingly, "Would my Lord care to see his daughter?"

"Daughter? Oh, I forgot. Well, is she out of her swaddling clothes?" The priest raised his hand to his mouth as if to stifle a yawn.

"Zirru is stately as a palm tree and graceful as a gazelle!" exploded Avram, his eyes shining, his fervent words and look of adoration revealing an emotion not at all in keeping with his father's analysis.

"Now, Avram," exclaimed Terach flabbergasted, "don't forget you are in the presence of the holiest man in all Sumer and Akkad. Run along and bring Zirru so that she might be blessed by the high priest of Nannar."

Avram bowed and hurried off without giving the slightest intimation that he was awe-stricken by the man of god. "I hope your holiness will pardon my impetuous son," apologized Terach. "He is a good example of the rising generation which has neither the manners nor the filial respect of the youth in my day."

Sabbattu's long vulpine smile had neither warmth nor humor. It seemed to denote a rather bored interest when he remarked somewhat casually, "The young colt is evidently enamored of my little girl."

"It is common knowledge, Adoni, in my family and among my relatives, that he is deeply in love—"

"Oh, puppy love," interrupted the priest. "He will get over it when the next girl comes along."

"They both talk of marrying," ventured Terach rather timidly. He favored the idea of becoming related to the most powerful person in Ur, not even excepting the king. Sabbattu controlled the wealth in the temple and would no doubt give a handsome marriage portion with his daughter. Moreover, he could most certainly give Avram a post of honor and trust in keeping with his own high rank. The priest wore a contemptuous expression and his upper lip began to curl. But before he could say anything, the boy and girl entered the room.

Avram remained near the door while Zirru advanced hesitatingly, her eyes downcast. Slowly she knelt and kissed the hem of the priest's robe. Sabbattu looked piercingly at the tall, well-formed girl dressed in a simple shift of linen dyed in a bright shade of blue, with sandals to match. She appeared well-groomed despite the simplicity of her garment which displayed the outlines of her slim yet rounded figure quite effectively.

"It seems uncanny!" commented the priest in a low voice; "the very image of her beautiful mother!"

Zirru smiled and her entire face seemed to light up. Her greenish-brown eyes sparkled, her mouth assumed an eloquent cast forming her lips into a bow, and her dimples enhanced an already natural charm.

The priest was fascinated. He closed his eyelids, lifted both hands, and prayed, "Oh, Irnina! Thou goddess of beauty, love, and fertility. Give this child your favor and protection. Let her receive grace from the gods, love from men, friendship from women. Preserve her health and beauty. Grant her happiness and the good things in this life. Spare her sickness, pain, sorrow, and poverty. So be it."

He extended his hand and gently drew the girl towards him so that she sat on his knees. He kissed her on the cheek and she encircled one arm about her father's neck. Sitting thus, he fell into a reverie which reverted him back to that New Moon festival day when he was a young priest in charge of the temple for about ten days. A man brought in his daughter to become a votaress of the temple. Anunu was young and very pretty. He recalled how he fell in love with her. He wanted her near him constantly. He could scarcely perform his duties. How tragically death came in her early youth when she appeared most beautiful.

Sabbattu awoke from his reverie as from a trance. His eyes had been closed and Zirru assumed her father to be asleep. She gently removed her arm from his neck and shifted from her sitting position without disturbing him. When the priest became conscious, he saw Terach standing near him while Avram and Zirru were whispering at the far end of the room. Zirru approached and smiled when she heard him say, "I saw your mother as if in a vision. She was indeed beautiful." When he noticed her bewitching smile, he gave her a ring and said to Terach's son, "Avram, when you go to Khar-Sak's class on the day after the new moon, be sure to take my daughter along. This ring will admit you both anywhere in the temple. As for you, Zirru, you must on the same day have the afternoon meal with me. But first, see what interests you in the Temple of Nannar."

# 2

# The Lovers

THE PATRON OF UR WAS THE MOON GOD, NANNAR. CONSEquently the birth of each new moon called for joyous celebration. The feast began the moment the high priest detected the arrival of the thin crescent in the heavens. Up to that moment the temple as well as the entire city was clothed in total darkness. The high priest stood on the open second platform of the terraced sanctuary surrounded by the priesthood including the *Kadoshim* and the entire female contingent from the first lady, the bride of Nannar, down to the lowest category of *Kadoshes.*

Assembled on the ground level stood men and women listening to the hymns chanted by the priests and followed by the music of cymbals, harps, tamborines, double-pipes, drums, citharas and trumpets. A priest then led the multitude in prayer. More music was followed by an orator who recited passages from the *Epic of Gilgamesh,* the sacred poem of Sumer.

The orator was interrupted by seven trumpeteers who blew three long blasts. Then the high priest pronounced the birth of the new moon. Quickly, priests produced small fire pots and, while pronouncing the blessings of

Nannar, lighted the candles, lamps, or torches held by the people close to them. The lights spread rapidly as the men and women lit each other's combustibles repeating the blessings of the moon god. Soon the sky seemed all aglow. At the highest point of the temple, on the square pyramidal platform that supported a small shrine to Nannar, a huge caldron filled with the fat of sacrifices burned a flame that was visible throughout Ur and the surrounding flat countryside.

Residents, visitors, and guests in the city houses as well as the retinue of the royal palace were eagerly watching for the light in the temple to apprise them of the new moon's birth. All adults as well as slaves and teenagers over thirteen had been fasting all day. The burning caldron gave the signal to light up and start the feast for which the population was hungrily waiting. Soon the city was illuminated by the many bright lights visible on the flat roofs of the houses in which the families and invited guests were eating at joyous feasts. The festival that began with the new moon lasted until the following sundown.

On the next day the public celebrated the holiday by attending the temple in droves. Many devotees came who were unable to come on a work day. Some brought offerings; others had sacrifices performed. The devout came to pray or receive the blessings of the priests. Sick people prayed to one or more deities to cast out the demon that had them in its toils. Others supplicated that they be protected from the evil spirits which pervaded the darkness or even the shadows.

The temple was not only a religious sanctum where the faithful could pay meet adoration to the gods, but in addition it served as a market, a bank, a trading center, a mart for the barter of animals, commodities, or merchandise. Devout souls believed that anything bought, traded, bartered, or exchanged in the sanctuary had the blessings of the gods. Some merchants would consummate an important deal only in the temple and immediately make a votive offering.

On this festive day Terach, his wife Emtelai, and his widowed daughter-in-law, Davarah, came to the Temple of Nannar, each to make an offering to the priests for the gods and to breathe a silent prayer that Nannar and Irnina bring about the marriage of their son Avram with their adopted child Zirru, daughter of the powerful high priest. While the three stood in the long line awaiting their turn to reach the altar and sacrifice Terach's goat, Emtelai's lamb, and Davarah's turtledove, the eight-year-old Lot impatiently tugged at Zirru's dress to take him to the top of the shrine where the burning caldron of the night before was still smoking. Little Sarai, the half-sister of Avram, seconded her cousin's plea. Zirru would rather have been with Avram but she could not ignore the wish of Lot whom she considered her brother, nor of her cousin Sarai, in whom she sensed a certain hostility. When Avram told Zirru to take them, as he wished to inspect the busy scene without being annoyed, Sarai felt hurt for she loved Avram and was jealous of the beautiful Zirru.

The eighteen-year-old youth wandered about watching the people haggling, the priests receiving offerings and repaying the rich with smiles and prayers, the poor with frowns or slurs. He stopped to see buyers inspect his father's idols, for which some were making offers and receiving counter-offers from the clerks. He stood at the stall that sold his sister-in-law's woven cloth. A busy market-day atmosphere prevailed. He saw a pickpocket snatching a woman's purse and helped to catch and hand him over to the ba'iru (the royal police).

Avram found himself carried along in a stream of young men going in a certain direction towards the southwest corner of the compound. The group was stopped in a narrow lane by a crowd who watched an exhibition near the opening that led to a section of the outer temple wall. Several girls standing on a three-foot elevation, transparently dressed, were swaying their bodies seductively while shaking tamborines and clashing cymbals. Another girl ascended the elevation and began dancing slowly, swaying her hips, shaking her breasts, and writhing her arms. Her pace accelerated as she moved her body more rapidly. Her movements became an exciting rhythm of aggressive sensuality when she fell into the arms of a young man who stood near, evidently prepared for her fall.

Following, or rather pushed along in the crowd, Avram struggled through the gateway and reached a group of men clustering about an elderly woman garbed as a priestess. She sat in the open doorway of an anteroom behind a table with a large and small scale on it. A rustic looking man gave her a bundle of grain which weighed about four measures. She shook her head affirmatively and gave him a small tablet of baked clay incised with the seal of the temple. He went to a large veranda with an awning overhead that was a protection against sunshine or rainfall.

Girls and women were on the porch. Some, partly clad, were reclining on large pillows. Others stood talking to each other at the same time looking over the men who came into the enclosure. One woman, almost nude, leaned against a square pillar supporting the awning. She carried a brazen air and stood winking at the rustic who was holding the small tablet with the temple seal. She laughingly invited him to come over as he had nothing to fear.

He gave the tablet to another elderly woman wearing a priestess' garb and walked behind the bold-faced woman through the door and into a house that had a number of rooms.

Another man, apparently looking for a girl, called her by name. She arose from her reclining position, ran up and kissed him, then they both went through the portal into the large house behind the wall. A middle-aged man coming out of the house shouted excitedly that he had been robbed. He had had silver worth two shekels in his script but it was no longer there. A husky, brutal-looking eunuch swinging a leather thong went up to the man and demanded, "Do you accuse these holy women, dedicated to the goddess, of stealing?" The man answered, "But my money was stolen in that house." The eunuch raised his whip and cut him with a lash that swished loud enough for everyone to hear. The man cried out and fled from the enclosure. One rather good-looking, self-satisfied man stalked with a jaunty air. A girl ran up, threw her arms around him, and called him by name. Another girl, somewhat older, rushed up and said to the girl, "Take your hands off him. He is my man." The younger woman paid no attention to her rival who grabbed her gown and tore it off her body. The two began to claw at each other, scratching and biting. They were soon rolling on the ground, each beating the other. The eunuch watched the fight for several moments, then raised the leather whip and began lashing the girls. They screamed with pain and ran into the house behind the canopied wall.

Leaning against the sun-baked brick wall near the room in which the elderly priestess sold or traded the sealed tablets for intercourse with a *kadoshe,* Avram could not but hear the chaffering that went on. The fixed minimum price in silver was half a shekel. But most of the younger men, having no silver, which was by no means plentiful, brought along farm products such as grain, corn, dates, figs, or small animals, articles of cloth, clay, wood, stone, or metal. The men tried to get the tablets for as little as possible while the priestess, a shrewd bargainer, was bent on making the best possible deals. Four youths from a farm near Ur brought a little lamb. After much arguing she would only give three tablets in exchange. Five teen-agers, age fifteen to eighteen, produced a spear with a copper tip fastened on an oak pole. They said it had belonged to the father of three of them and he was dead. It had been taken from an Amorite when Hammurabi invaded Nippur. They maintained that it was valuable and worth at least ten tablets. The priestess wanted assurance that it was not stolen. After much bargaining with all five boys, she finally gave each a tablet.

For reasons he could not fathom, Avram felt depressed. Evidently there was something wrong about the scene he witnessed. Why should the goddess Irnina demand the sacrifice of a girl's virtue? The girl might be guided by the best intentions to devote her life and service to the goddess, yet he felt that as time went on she would become degraded. There appeared to be little justice, certainly no chastity or decency in the operation of this establishment. The women were at the mercy of a detestable eunuch who could whip a priestess as if she were a slave girl. They seemed to have little or no protection from his brutality. And the middle-aged man who said he was robbed evidently had little chance to obtain redress to his complaint. He might appeal to the civil judge but the eunuch seemed quite assured of his actions.

He knew that the sleep of few Chaldeans was disturbed by the institution of the *Kadeshes* serving their god and his temple by submitting their bodies to anyone who had the price. But wasn't this practice, the people argued, old and time honored in the ancient city of Ur which, he had been taught, was the oldest settled place in the world? Besides, it was approved and maintained by the priests themselves; and who was wiser or better qualified than the priests of Nannar to know the wishes of the gods? Didn't the gods often appear and speak to their favorite ministrants?

Yet such pat arguments did not satisfy Avram. But who was he to question divine wisdom or justice when such able people all about him accepted the direction of the gods without protest. After all he was immature, ignorant, and perhaps stupid. He knew that his mother loved him yet regarded him as quite naive. His father tried to teach him the craft of fashioning images out of clay but gave up the task as a hopeless and showed disgust at his son's ineptitude. Terach would display impatience at such questions as who created the gods. The answer that they were always there did not convince the teenager. "But there must have been a time when they were not here." Terach would invariably close the questioning with the dictum: "You must not ask such questions. Do what everyone else does and believe what everyone else believes. After all, we are getting along quite well in a land that is not our own. What would happen if I should question, criticize, and express doubts of the established religion? First of all I would immediately lose my profitable connection with the temple. Then I might even be expelled as an alien. Do you know that the punishment for blasphemy or heresy is burning in the lime-kiln of the temple?"

For the first time Avram felt a mild enthusiasm at the thought of attending the class of Khar-Sak. He would no doubt have true answers to the problems vexing him from the renowned sage who prepared students for the priesthood. Engrossed in thought Avram had been meandering about absent-mindedly in the temple compound, through the large gateway, then up the long, high flight of brick steps that reached to the top platform upon which stood Nannar's shrine. Halfway up he met Zirru, Lot, and Sarai who were coming down.

"Uncle Avram," exclaimed Lot enthusiastically, "I saw from up there, the river, a ship, and a big animal with big long teeth coming out on the sides of his mouth. He walked from the ship on dry land. Is this animal a demon? Does he bite and eat little children?"

Before Avram could answer or before Sarai was able to comment on her observations, Zirru spoke:

"Now, let us go down. Mother, Grandfather and Grandmother are waiting to take us home for the afternoon meal. I am starving and I know you are also hungry. You can talk all you want in the house. Let me see you children run down."

Zirru held Avram's hand and both walked down the straight flight of steps. They found Terach at the image shop. Emtelai waited at the cloth stall while Davarah was checking the number of her woven pieces sold that day.

The evening meal was still part of the festival and some of the dishes were peculiar to the occasion. Breads baked in hard, flat, crescent-shaped wafers were dipped in honey to symbolize a coming sweet month. The head of the house poured wine over a statuette as a libation to the moon god. Nor were other gods neglected. Incense was burned to Irnina, goddess of love, fertility, and queen of heaven; to Enlil, the mighty storm god; to Ea, the friendly god of wisdom and the sea. Nor was Ningal, the goddess wife of Nannar, overlooked. The festival ended with a prayer from Terach that the entire household including everyone present be at the same table to celebrate the next new moon.

While Emtelai and Davarah were directing the slaves in cleaning up after the feast, Avram and Zirru sat on the open roof looking at the numerous stars twinkling in the black skies without moonlight or clouds. The spring air was mild and the atmosphere pleasant. Zirru remarked, "One would think that the stars are little holes that reveal the bright light through the floor of heaven."

The Sumerians were the first to develop a study of astrology out of which evolved the science of astronomy. Avram had studied that science in school and imparted to his beloved some of the knowledge acquired:

"The stars are very large. They seem small because they are so far away. Many have names and their courses have been charted. The priests know the movements of some planets and have marked out certain groups such as the little bear, the big bear, the dipper, and other constellations."

"You are so wise, my beloved. You simply know everything. I do feel proud of you, Avram. I am so happy. Oh, how I enjoyed this day at the temple. You know, when we got to the top of the steps a man, a *kadosh*, I suppose, stopped us and said, 'you are not permitted here. The shrine of Nannar is holy.' I drew myself up proudly, pulled out father's ring and said as haughtily as I could, The lord Sabbattu is my father. See this! He looked at me, than at the ring and said, 'I believe I saw you recently at the house of Terach, the image-maker. A group of us accompanied the lord Sabbattu to inspect the statue which Terach was making.' Oh, he was very nice. He pointed out many places in the city and out in the country. Among them was the Ziggurat which, he said, was the oldest building in the world. It was built at least a thousand years ago, right after the great flood. He showed me the royal palace. I would love to see Queen Shub-Ad and how her court ladies are dressed. But you are not listening . . ."

She waited, then called out, "Avram!"

He started as if suddenly waking up. "Yes, Zirru."

The girl looked intently at him in the darkness and said, "You seem to be unhappy. Is something bothering you? I am looking forward to visiting my father and eating with him. You know he is a great man. I am proud to be his daughter. I thought you would share my happiness. What is wrong?" She swallowed hard and ventured timidly, "Perhaps you don't love me any more," and tears welled up in her green-brown eyes.

He moved closer, took her in his arms and kissed her eyes, her cheeks and her mouth. "Of course, I love you, sweetheart. But you know, I am subject to moods. I often feel depressed."

"But there must be some reason for your sadness."

"I don't know. I feel uneasy as if something bad will happen."

"I know. A demon has gotten into you. Did you pray at the temple?"

"No, I didn't. Somehow I never have the urge to pray any more. I don't know why."

"I know what I am going to do. I will ask father to chase the demon out of you."

From below, Davarah called out, "Zirru, it's time to go home. Lot is falling asleep."

Terach and Avram lit torches and accompanied Davarah, Zirru, and Lot to their dwelling. In the dark, narrow, winding streets of Ur it was dangerous, for women especially, to walk at night unattended. Some vicious house dwellers thought it fun to throw garbage upon pedestrians. Others eagerly seized the opportunity to pour slops upon their heads. But when they saw torches they refrained, fearing to be hauled up by the ba'iru to answer charges. The laws generally were strictly enforced in the ancient city.

The lovers said good-night and squeezed each others' hands. It was bad form to kiss before their elders.

## II

On the following day in the forenoon, Avram and Zirru set out for the Temple of Nannar. The depressed mood had left Avram pretty much as a fog lifts over land or sea and vanishes in thin atmosphere. The lovers were in a buoyant, jovial frame of mind. Suddenly, they changed their course. Having been in the temple the day before, they decided to wander about the city and then go to their destinations in the sanctuary.

First, they proceeded to the royal palace. They stood outside the walls at a respectful distance from the large gateway guarded by four soldiers carrying long, copper-tipped spears and short bronze swords in leather scabbards. They watched the Lugal of Erech dressed in royal garments, attended by retainers and slaves, coming at the invitation of the king. The Patesis of several cities rode in red and green chariots of painted wood held fast by copper bands and rolling on four spoked wheels. The Patesis stood in the war chariots alongside their drivers who cracked their whips urging greater speed from the two asses hitched to each vehicle. Ladies dressed in the height of fashion, their headgear of wreaths made from lapis lazuli and carnelian and hung with golden rings, willow leaves, and golden flowers, came to lunch with Queen

Shub-Ad. Each hour a cordon of armoured guards with bronze-pointed helmets, leather jerkins, daggers, spears, swords, and circular shields made the rounds about the periphery of the palace walls.

Turning from the palace they decided to inspect the waterfront. As a little boy, Avram loved to linger near the river Purattu which later the Greeks made famous under the name Euphrates. But he had been forbidden to go near the docks after some sailors tried to kidnap him. His cries brought the ba'iru who rescued the boy from being dragged on board by some rascally seamen, perhaps pirates, to be sold into slavery in some distant port. Yet, it always fascinated him to watch the unloading of merchandise, animals, or birds from far away lands. He then dreamed of one day traveling to see for himself foreign cities, strange people, curious buildings, and unfamiliar ways of living.

While looking at a boat with a large square sail which supplemented the labors of galley slaves plying their oars, Avram noticed large slabs of rock, shoved, rolled, and heaved upon round wooden poles and stacked about fifty cubits from the river. It was not surprising to see rock and stone imported from far away. Lower Mesopotamia had no rock whatsoever in its earth, which was formed by the water of heavy rains flooding the banks of the rivers and depositing silt, sand, and mud that stretched the mainland further and further south along the Purattu and Tigris Rivers. The soil, barren of rock, produced a fertility greater than in any other place outside of the Nile Valley. The stone and rock slabs were heaved from the boat to the shore by a troop of asses helped by a gang of hired slaves.

Two young men in foreign kilts passed, talking Aramean, which Avram, and Zirru to a lesser degree, understood.

"Shalom Aleichem," greeted Avram.

"Aleichem Shalom," answered one of the young men, who appeared several years older than Avram.

"Whence come ye, strangers?"

"We loaded our cargo in Etzion Geber on the tip of the Sea of Reeds."

"In what land is that?"

"Canaan."

"You are natives of Canaan?"

"My friend is but I am from Damascus and my name is Eleazer."

"I am Avram, son of Terach, the image-maker for the Temple of Nannar. The damsel is my niece and my betrothed."

Eleazer seemed about twenty years old, thin, of middle height, and with a light brown complexion; he had dark brown honest eyes and seemed completely trustworthy. Avram continued:

"This is the first time I saw a cargo of rock. Does it pay to transport it such a long way?"

"Perhaps not, but we believe we can sell rock in a land that has none of its own. But we intend to profit by our return cargo."

"To whom do you sell this rock?"

"To temples, to the royal palace, to rich merchants for their houses."

"Have you the proper rock for statues or monuments?"

"Yes, we have some limestone, alabaster, sandstone. We have granite but it is too hard to chip. The black diorite is better."

"You might try my father, Terach the image-maker. His house and workshop is on the Street of the Ancients that winds through Ur. It starts over there at the big dock."

"I shall see him. Thank you for the information."

"I am often at the workshop or in the showroom. Please ask for Avram. Farewell."

"Farewell to you both," answered Eleazer, bowing respectfully.

"You know, Avram," remarked Zirru, "he looks very honest. I would trust him with anything. He might buy some of mother's cloth to take with him."

"I will tell him about your mother's weaving establishment, although I don't know if he has the power to buy or sell. He looks quite young."

"Then what was your reason for wanting to see him?"

"Well, I want to ask about the lands he has visited, about the ways of their people, and about their gods."

"You with your gods," and she gave him one of her bewitching smiles. "Why don't you leave the gods alone? What do you care about the gods of strange people far away? Haven't we got our own gods who are greater and better than the gods of any other people?"

"I imagine," responded Avram, "those other people say the same about their gods."

"Avram!" rebuked Zirru, as if shocked. Yet her serious tone was not in keeping with her laughing eyes. "I sometimes wonder how you will get on in the world. I feel nervous about your attitude toward the gods. Somehow you always have questions about them. I think you are too critical. Today you will go to the school for priests. I wonder what they will think about your questions. It seems to me that you should accept the teachings of the priests without trying to air your views. I want you to be a priest and I would be proud to be the wife of a priest.

They walked along the river, then stopped near an enclosure surrounded by a wall of mud brick that had been baked by the sun. The elephant that Lot saw the day before stood near the wall. It was guarded by a dark man, almost black, who held in one hand a metal prong and in the other a hempen rope that was tied to the beast's foot. A mat of plaited reeds hung over the wall's opening and a dark man wearing a turban sat at a table which held scales, a yardstick, and several clay containers of various sizes. Avram and Zirru could hear people laughing and applauding behind the wall.

The man sitting at the table responded to Avram's question that the performance was well under way and that it would be necessary to wait for the next one to start. Avram opened his scrip and showed the dried figs and dates in it. The man shook his head affirmatively, accepted the offer, and said something to the elephant keeper who held up the mat over the gateway so that Avram and Zirru could enter the enclosure.

The midday audience of more than two score were standing about a wooden cage in which a lion was reclining. A strong-looking dark man wearing a turban and swinging a whip opened the cage door and entered quickly. The lion growled and stood on its four feet. The man said something in a strange language, walked up to the beast, and continued talking. He put his hand on the lion's head, caressed the mane, then gave the beast a hunk of meat which it began to devour. The man opened the door and quickly left the cage.

The lion tamer walked towards the wall to a shallow pool beyond a low wall of mud brick. He approached the water and with a rod nudged a black mass which moved and turned out to be an alligator. The ugly animal moved to the water's edge, and the man held a piece of meat on the rod close to the monster's now opened mouth. Immediately, the man thrust a wooden peg into its mouth which now could neither close nor open. He then placed a wooden pole under the scaly body. Both front legs grabbed at the wood and held it tight. Suddenly the man made a quick twist and turned the beast over on its back. The man massaged certain nerves on its scaly belly and soon the animal fell asleep. Then with a quick wrench he pulled the wooden peg out of the alligator's mouth. It quickly turned over onto its feet and made for the water. This was the climax of the show.

The audience broke into small groups. Some looked at the camel, kneeling to let a man get on its back. The camel then rose with its human load and walked across the compound. Others watched the antics of several monkeys loosely tied to each other with ropes made of hemp. A group looked with interest at a peacock all puffed up and were curious about the conduct of a rooster with several hens. They had never seen fowl of the bird kingdom and were puzzled about the egg which one hen laid before their eyes. When the rooster crowed some were frightened and wondered if it was not an evil spirit. The largest party looked with fear and astonishment at a dark turbaned man sitting on the ground with his feet drawn under him playing a flute which caused four cobras to slither out of a wicker basket and stand up half their length and sway their heads to the rhythm of the music.

The lovers moved about slowly, gazing at the animals, which they could not imagine existed in the world they lived in. A striped ass and a big-horned cow with a hump on its back looked especially strange. The elephant walked into the big yard with a man sitting on its head holding a metal prong. On its back rested a howdah gilded and dyed in purple, red and green shades, holding several men richly clad in foreign costumes.

"I wonder who formed these animals and what was the purpose of their creation," mused Avram. The show had put him in a thoughtful mood.

"Who could create these animals but the gods?" declared Zirru, feeling that he expected some kind of answer. She went on: "If the gods created people, why couldn't they also create these ugly, filthy beasts?"

"How do you know that the gods created men and women?"

"I was always told that the gods created people to serve them and honor them with sacrifices."

"Of animals?"

"Even with men, women, and children if such is the will of the gods," affirmed Zirru with conviction.

Walking slowly and hearing someone speaking to about a dozen people, they stopped at a corner of the lot and heard:

"Your king was gracious enough to grant our rajah asylum until we find it practicable to go back to India."

"How is it you talk our Sumerian quite well?" asked a bystander.

"I have been to Ur before. We, living in Cochin on the Malabar coast, have been trading with your city for many, many years."

"Why did your ruler have to leave?" he continued.

"That is a long story. To make it short, our land has been invaded for about a century or much more by foreigners from the East who call themselves Aryans. They are white in color, tall in stature, physically strong, and extremely cruel. Our land is very great, about ten times as large as your Shinar between the two rivers. These Aryans came from time to time, not in great hosts, but in small caravans except they ride in wagons drawn by oxen and bring their wives and children along. They come in peacefully enough and settle between our cities. Others come later, and when they are numerous enough they take over the surrounding lands including villages, and sometimes even large cities. You probably know that India is no single great empire. We have a large number of city-states that are often enemies to each other. When the Aryans make war on one city, they often have the help of other city-states. Thus they have taken over a great part of our country and are ruling it."

"Does it make much difference who rules as long as you have peace, security, and good business?" interposed another bystander.

"That is exactly what we lose when our enemies rule over us. You cannot imagine how these white fiends hate the dark-skinned people. First of all they disarm us, then take over the best land and the profitable trade. Those that they do not enslave they reduce to a low social level. They have instituted what they call castes, and that means all social, commercial, intellectual advantages are denied to us. Each person is put in a class, so-to-speak, out of which he can never emerge. The son must follow his father's occupation. No one can marry outside of his tribe or caste as they call it. Life in India has become hateful to the conquered or submerged classes."

"How did you manage to get away?" asked another Sumerian.

"The Aryans were spreading far and wide. Soon Cranganore, our neighboring state, was taken. We knew that our turn would come next. Our rajah decided to leave while it was possible. He is now negotiating with our confederates to expel the invader from the west coast we call Malabar."

"In your haste how did you get the animals and the ships away?"

"The ancestors of our rajah have been collecting animals for more than a hundred years. They were kept in a garden we call the Zoo. Our city Cochin is on the great sea in front, with a body of water in the back. On this bay we have been building ships for many generations. Our rajah loaded three ships with food and things of value. He took along as many animals as he could."

Several people left and made room for Avram and Zirru who found themselves facing the spokesman. They noticed an old man with a full white beard sitting on his crossed legs on a wooden divan about a cubit above the ground. He had sharp piercing black eyes that seemed to penetrate through the person he looked at. Avram inquired,

"Do you have gods in your country?"

"Oh yes, many."

"How many?" pressed Avram.

The spokesman bent down, said something in a foreign language to the old man who appeared to answer him.

"Thirty-three higher gods, of which 11 dominate the heavens, 11 the earth, and 11 the intermediate region. But we have many more besides."

"Who created them?" continued Avram.

Again the spokesman talked quietly with the sage and then declared,

"The gods were never created. They are emanations out of the Supreme Spirit, the Lord of the Universe, the God above all gods who created the earth, the heavens, the waters."

"Did your great number of gods help their worshippers in their day of trouble, in their time of great distress?"

"This question I won't answer," responded the spokesman somewhat caustically, after consulting the man of wisdom.

The white bearded sage stood up and faced Avram. His eyes seemed like burning black coals. His look became concentrated as if he would bore through Avram's eyes into his brain. Avram began to feel as if he were losing consciousness, as if his mind, his will, his emotions were becoming suspended under the compelling control of the Indian sage.

Zirru became frightened. She pulled Avram away with the pleading words, "Avram, it is getting late. You must go to the priests' class and I must hurry to my father."

# 3

# The Temple School

THE SON OF TERACH SAT AMONG THE STUDENTS WHO aspired to the priesthood. He had just left Zirru and the depressed feeling came back. She was no doubt with her father, probably eating the afternoon meal. What were they talking about? Zirru would no doubt tell him about their love and her desire to marry. Would the priest object to the shiftless son of an Aramean image-maker, who owed his success to priestly influence? The high priest might say that he could get her a better husband, a member of the Amelu, the Sumerian highest aristocracy.

The musings of Avram were interrupted by a student reciting a memorized passage out of the *Epic of Gilgamesh,* which describes the passion of the goddess of love, Irnina-Ishtar for the great hero:

"Amid the Dud'im plants he now reclines,
And to his welcome fate himself resigns;
The lovely queen beside him now doth lay,
And leads his soul along the blissful way
That comes to every heart that longs for love,
When purest joy doth bless us from above;
From her soft liquid eyes the love-light speaks,

And her warm hands she lays in his and wakes
Beneath her touch a thrill of wild desire,
Until his blood now seems like molten fire.
Her eyes half closed begat a passion wild,
With her warm breast, her loves hath beguiled;
She nearer creeps with hot and balmy breath,
And trembling form aglow, and to him saith:
'My lips are burning for a kiss, my love!'
A prize like this, a heart of stone would move,
And he his arms around her fondly placed
Till she reclined upon his breast, embraced,
Their lips in one long thrilling rapture meet."

The glowing passion of the goddess affected the students to such a degree that the teacher could hardly get a sensible answer to his questions about the archaic words in the poem. He, therefore, left the room to get a drink of water and invited his pupils to do likewise. But they did not leave. Some whistled their admiration for the goddess. Others imitated the lovers in the paroxysm of their excitation. One rather noisy student, who passed for the wit of the class, playfully embraced a somewhat effeminate boy and got down on his knees supplicating him, as a loyal worshipper of Irnina, to relieve his burning love.

Avram was in no mood to fall in with the jollity of the students. He felt as if some misfortune was overhanging his Zirru. He feared that in some way his beloved would stir the wrath of Irnina. Familiar with many incidents current about the goddess, he felt a revulsion at the cruelty displayed toward anyone who attracted her love or stilled her unquenchable lust. He wondered why Irnina-Ishtar could never feel compassion or show kindness to those men who had excited her passing fancy. Her young husband, Tammuz, later known in Syria and Greece as Adonis, was killed by a wild boar apparently at her instigation. The sheperd king Tabula, who appeased her love for a time, she transformed into a hyena to be torn into pieces by his own dogs. Isullanu, the uncouth laborer, who burnished her metallic vessels, had his eyes torn out when no longer useful in assuaging her passion. On refusal to eat her poisoned food he was turned into a pillar of stone.

Ishtar did not even spare animals. She tore the wings off her favorite Allala and the eagle fell to the earth dead. A lion attracted her love and in fierce delight she plucked out his claws unheeding his piteous cries. She next tried a powerful stallion and exhausted his strength. She rode the glorious war steed for 14 hours without food or drink until he sank to the ground before his waiting mare, his head drooping and spirit broken.

Two words slowly emerged out of his subconscious: cruelty and licentiousness. Were these two attributes inherent in the gods or were they the result of their actions or conduct?

While Avram was ruminating Khar-Sak had returned and began commenting on phases of Sumerian theology. He noticed the distraction of the new student and in a mild voice asked him a question without receiving a reply. He touched the student with the rod he always held. Avram started and when he heard the class laugh he realized how far away he was in his abstraction that he never heard the funny remark the teacher evidently made at his expense. He was wide awake and attentive when the teacher asked, "Does any student know the story about the revolt in heaven against the Supreme God Anu?"

Everyone kept quiet and Avram finally summoned up enough courage to raise his hand.

"The new student? And what is your name?"

"Avram, son of Terach."

"State what you know. But first tell us the source of your information."

"My father, Terach, the image-maker, has his workshop and display room on the Street of the Ancients. People come to buy, to inspect, and chiefly to talk. We hear some interesting and often instructive talk, sometimes from caravan travelers and more often from men who come in on ships. Since I was a child I love to listen. Years ago, when a little fellow, I heard a visitor tell this story which I never forgot. Shall I start with your permission?"

"Yes," answered the priest.

"Long, long ago, when the god Anu created this world, there was great rejoicing in heaven. I still remember the words the man used: 'The morning stars sang together, and all the sons of God shouted for joy.' All the five thousand gods were up there in honor of the Supreme God. Music and song came from the choral band of one thousand. All the gods joined in the hymns. Suddenly there appeared a dragon who had seven heads and his tail drew a third of the stars and cast them down to the earth. At the same time loud cries of contempt broke out spoiling, confusing, and confounding the hymn of praise to Anu. It was a planned revolt by a thousand gods who were envious of Anu and sought to displace him. They shouted evil blasphemies when a trumpet blast sounded loud enough to wake up the dead. The god of divine speech expelled the thousand wicked gods who immediately began to fall headlong to our earth. They fell for nine days. The wicked, fallen, expelled gods remained on earth without power to return to heaven. To fill the void created by the loss of so many gods, Anu, with the help of Ea, created man. The fallen gods became the deities of many among the new race of human beings. Some became demons and evil spirits. Others instituted cruel forms of worship such as casting babies and children in the fire to honor them. There is eternal enmity between our gods of light and the dark, rebellious, wicked demons of darkness."

"Well spoken!" exclaimed Khar-Sak and the students applauded with their hands.

"Is all this true, or only a myth?" questioned a student from Nippur.

"It is difficult to say," responded the teaching priest. "It is not as well known as the great flood. But this tale is very old. Its origin is unknown. I tried to trace the source but did not succeed. I did run across an old clay tablet in Erech, which city some claim is even older than Ur. But I had great difficulty making it out. Some of the cuneiform figures are hardly legible. And there were words which neither I nor anyone else could explain. I cannot pass judgment on this epic. But it is magnificent poetry."

"Couldn't the same be said about most stories affecting the gods?" persisted the skeptic.

"No, not necessarily," assured Khar-Sak. "There is no doubt about the great flood. Let's go over it now. Has anyone prepared it on a tablet?"

A student from Erech raised his hand and the teacher nodded his head for him to go on.

"The great hero Gilgamesh had become dangerously sick and thought he would soon die. He decided to find his remote ancestor, Ut-Napishtin, whom we in Sumer call Zi-u-sud-ra, and inquire of him how a man may attain immortal life. After a perilous journey under great difficulties, he reached Ut-Napishtin who informed him that immortality was not for man. This was a surprising answer from a man who was now immortal. The divine man told the hero the following: "The greater gods were assembled and decided to send a flood to destroy all men. Ea, the god of wisdom, heard the decision and whispered to the hut of reeds, 'Oh, hut of reeds, reed hut. Oh, wall, wall. Oh, reed hut, hearken, oh wall attend. Oh, son of Ubara-Tutu, pull down thy house, build a ship, forsake thy possession. Take heed of thy life! Bring living seed of every kind into the ship." The mortal said to the god, "Thy command, oh my Lord, I will honor and fulfill. But how shall I make answer unto the city, the people and the elders?" Divine Ea answered, "Thus shalt thou answer and say unto them: 'Because Enlil hates me, no longer may I abide in your city nor lay my head on Enlil's earth. Down into the deep sea must I go with Ea, my Lord, to dwell.' Ut-Napishtim built a barge and on it he set a house 120 cubits high and divided it into six stories of nine rooms each. He daubed it outside with bitumen and the inside he caulked with pitch. When the ship was ready he carried into it all the gold and silver he had and filled it with living seed. He then brought his family, his household, cattle and beasts of the field. The sungod Utu said to him, 'At eventime the lord of darkness will send a heavy rain. Then enter the ship and shut thy door.'

"At eventide the lord of darkness sent a heavy rain. Ut-Napishtim was afraid to look upon the storm. He entered the ship and shut the door and committed the floating palace and all therein to the sailor Puzur-Amuvis. The storm burst. The Anunnaki lifted up flaming torches that lit up the entire earth. The whirlwind of Ramman mounted up into the heavens and all light was turned into total darkness. A whole day the tempest raged and the waters rose on to the mountains. In heaven the gods were afraid. They drew back and climbed up into the heaven of Anu. The gods crouched like dogs; they cowered by the walls. Irnina-Ishtar cried out like a woman in travail. 'Let that day be turned to clay when I commanded evil in the assembly of the gods for the destruction of my people. That which I brought forth where is it? Like the spawn it filleth the sea.' The gods of the Anunnaki wept with her, the gods were bowed down; they sat weeping with lips pressed together.

For six days and six nights the wind blew and the deluge overwhelmed the land. On the seventh day the tempest ceased, the sea grew quiet and subsided. Ut-Napishtim opened the window and the whole world was sea. When the light fell upon his cheek he wept bitterly. After 12 days the ship landed on a mount and held fast. He waited seven days and sent out a dove. It flew hither and thither, found no resting place, and returned. He then sent out a swallow which found no resting place and also flew back to the ship. He waited, then sent out a raven which did not return. He then assembled wood on the mountain top and offered a sacrifice. The gods smelled the sweet savor and gathered like flies about the offering. The queen of Heaven came also and said, 'Let all the gods come except Enlil, who took no counsel, sent the deluge and destroyed my people.' But Enlil did come and when he saw the ship he became enraged against the gods for allowing anyone to escape, and declared, 'No man shall live after the destruction.' Ninib said to Enlil that only Ea could have thought of saving anyone for he knows everything. Ea rebuked Enlil for sending the deluge and said it was he who sent a dream and revealed the purpose of the great gods. Thereupon Enlil relented, went into the ship, took Ut-Napishtim and his wife, made them kneel and declared, 'Hitherto hath Ut-Napishtim been a man, but now let him and his wife be like unto the gods, even as us, and let them dwell afar off, at the mouth of the river.' "

After complimenting the student who read the tablet he had incised, Khar-Sak went on:

"There are many questions one can ask. Yet it is not easy to answer them. But I would like to hear some comments."

"My difficulty is to understand the reason that prompted the gods to bring on the flood," stated the reader of the story. "My reading only disclosed the fact of the flood and not the cause."

"I see some inconsistencies," stated another. "At the beginning the gods seem to agree in council to bring on the deluge. After it is over, only Enlil is blamed for not taking counsel or listening to advice."

"It seems strange to me that only the god Ea should foresee the destruction and try to guard against total annihilation," observed another student.

"The most difficult thing for me to comprehend is the divine lack of compassion," revealed Avram. "Irnina-Ishtar merely regrets the loss of her worshipers. Nothing is mentioned, before or after the flood, about the pain, suffering, terror, or fear that human beings—men, women, and children—endured. The gods seemed quite callous."

"It seems to me the poet who wrote the *Epic of Gilgamesh* shows scant respect for the gods. Expressions like, "The gods crouched like dogs or they cowered by the walls" actually reveals hatred," further ventured the Nippur skeptic.

"I could make a similar observation about the gods smelling the sweet savor of the sacrifice and gathering like flies around the offering," seconded the Erech student.

"The conduct of Ishtar," added Avram, "shows a marked difference from her usual attitude. There are incidents in this epic that depict her cruelty and even ruthlessness. It is strange to hear that Ishtar cried out like a woman giving birth. This comes ever more strange from the goddess who was present and who agreed to send the deluge. Couldn't she know what the flood would do to her votaries?"

"I won't attempt to answer the questions raised here this day," declared Khar-Sak thoughtfully. "May I remind you that in this life there are no answers to certain questions, or solutions for every problem. There are mysteries all around us, and not all deeply imbedded; they are on the surface in the world about us. Is there any explanation to the mystery of life and death, to light and darkness, to space and time without beginning or end, to the sun, moon, and stars, to the process of birth, to the unfolding of understanding in the child? If we cannot fathom these enigmas that confront us each day, then why do you expect to solve the profound mysteries that are wrapped in the godhead?"

When the teacher priest was silent the Nippur student resumed the questioning:

"I believe you stated before that while there might be doubts as to the revolt in heaven, there could be none about the deluge. But why couldn't the same objection be applied to both?"

"This question has been discussed and argued thoroughly by the sages," replied Khar-Sak. "First they point to internal evidence. This epic quotes the actual language of Ut-Napishtim, who was son of Ubara-Totu, king of Erech. He repeated to Gilgamesh the very words that the god Ea spoke to him. Look how rich these expressions are in atmosphere, how these idioms, now archaic, are fresh and reflect the living spirit of long, long ago. 'Oh, hut of reeds, reed hut. Oh, wall, wall. Oh, reed hut, hearken, oh, wall attend.' No poet could have imagined such expressions. They are the original words of the god of wisdom."

"How do the sages account for the disrespect to the gods in this narrative?" queried a student from Lagash.

"That is an important point and I am happy you thought of it," answered the man of wisdom. "The contemptuous attitude to the gods proves how genuine the whole account is. A poet would not have dared to take such liberties. But Ut-Napishtim could and did. Remember that he felt no love for the gods, who had destroyed the world—his world. It was only due to Ea that he remained alive. Ut-Napishtim could revel in his emotions to get even with them. With what zest he declares, 'The gods were afraid. They drew back and climbed up into thy heaven of Anu. The gods crouched like dogs; they cowered by the walls.' Remember he was now immortal and the gods could do him no injury. He spoke out of bitterness, out of antagonism as he recalled the indescribable catastrophe of the deluge."

"Does any physical proof of the flood exist today?" asked a middle-aged resident of Ur who recently had felt the call to serve the gods.

"Yes, we have such proof; in fact I saw it myself. About a decade ago or more we had a drought, just as we are having today. The shortage of water became acute. The king ordered his overseers to seek underground springs. The priests of the Ziggurat informed him that they had records to prove the existence of a well which had become filled with all manner of rubbish. The king sent slaves to clean the deep shaft. As you probably know, the Ziggurat is our oldest structure and the ground within the enclosure is about three cubits lower than the level of the ground outside.

"The slaves removed all the rubbish but could not locate any spring. It had either dried up or the waters had been diverted elsewhere. They went on cleaning up the debris, an accumulation of centuries. About ten cubits below the surface they discovered a vein of clay, about four or five cubits in depth. The clay was unusually compact, clean, and free of dirt, sand, or branches. Clay quarries are never found in that condition. In spots they discovered house utensils, stone vases, and several spears with flint points.

"The king consulted his soothsayers, magicians, overseers, and sages. Their general opinion was that during the great flood clay floated about in grains stirred up by the turbulent water. Gradually when the waters calmed down the grains of clay, being heavier than water, sank first to the bottom. The pressure of the water packed down more and more clay until the vein reached about four or five cubits high. The weight of the water pressed the grains together and forced all mud, sand, and silt out of the clay, which is today as clean as when the great flood formed the vein. So you see, several leagues from here we have positive proof of the great deluge that destroyed all mankind, save the single family of Ut-Napishtim."

Khar-Sak looked through the open window and saw the declining sun about half an hour from the horizon. He dismissed the class and Avram rushed out to meet with his beloved.

## II

Upon leaving Avram, his beloved Zirru wandered about the temple grounds viewing the articles for sale as well as the clerks and the purchasers. She was stopped by a male in priestly garb whom she quickly recognized as the *kadosh* who had permitted her, Lot, and Sarai to mount the straight line of steps leading to the Shrine of Nannar, the highest point in Ur. He greeted her and said the Lord Sabbattu was in his chambers expecting her. She took the holy castrate's arm and followed him to the quarters reserved for the priesthood.

The high priest embraced the girl warmly and kissed her on the forehead. A *kadoshe* served fermented date wine while they sat side by side on the soft-cushioned divan. The talkative teenager regaled the priest with the sights on her morning tour, dwelling mainly on the strange animals. The priestess directed two slave girls, who carried in a table and brought fruits, lentil soup, crescent-shaped cornbread baked for the new moon, and broiled lamb sacrificed the day before as an offering by a pious votary. When the table was removed citrus juice squeezed from the ethrog distilled in water, and nuts, raisins, sweetmeats were left for dessert on small round tripods.

The talk drifted to her upbringing. Mother Davarah was very good to her but strict. She would never permit her to play with the boys in the neighborhood; in fact Avram was the only boy she really knew. She loved him dearly. He was kind but too self-centered. Sometimes while she was talking he would become lost in his thoughts and forget she was there. When he attended school he would tell her what he learned that day and expected her to remember. She looked forward to living happily with Avram as her husband. Now being fully grown she was old enough to marry.

Sabbattu put his arm around the girl's waist and drew her closer as she sat next to him on the divan. He looked into her eyes, kissed her mouth and said, "Zirru, I want to tell you something that very few girls are privileged to hear. You are most fortunate and blessed. When you were standing high up near the top shrine of our temple the Lord Nannar was inside. He saw you and selected you to become his bride."

Her beautiful eyes opened wide with fright. The ready smile froze into a frown. Her heart beat violently and for several moments she could hardly breathe. When she regained her breath she burst forth, "But I don't want to be the bride of a god. I am a simple girl and am happy to be Avram's wife and bear his children."

"My daughter, I am afraid you don't understand. When a god selects we have no choice. You were not asked, you were chosen."

"So I can never marry Avram?"

"I am afraid not. The gods do not share their women with men."

Zirru got up from the divan and began pacing the room. Like a bird trapped in a cage she moved back and forth in her agitation, which seemed to increase as the understanding of her predicament became clearer. In desperation she cried out, "Suppose I refuse. What then?"

"The god Nannar has the power to turn you into a stone pillar," answered the man she considered her father. "In a similar situation your mother, who was then only a little older than you are now, rebelled and spoke of the gods with disrespect. The Lady Irnina punished her. She died the moment you were born."

In her grief she scarcely knew where she was going and suddenly fell on the divan. Burying her face in her hands she moaned, her entire body quivering with her sobs. Sabbattu was stroking her head, his hand caressing her long, dark-brown tresses. When she finally quieted down, he spoke:

"My dear child, you don't seem to understand the great honor conferred upon you. The bride of Nannar walks next to the queen in all royal processions. She ranks first among the priestesses and is queen of the temple. This distinction is eagerly sought by princesses of royal blood. The present bride of Nannar is the daughter of the Lugal Kudur-Mabug, king of Larsa."

Two elderly priestesses came into the room. They raised Zirru from the divan and led her through the long narrow hallway into the compartments of the priestesses.

## III

While waiting for Zirru's return from the living quarters of the high priest, Avram took his stand at the stall of images operated by his father. The sun looked like a large ball of fire as it descended imperceptibly towards the horizon. He watched the western sky which also seemed afire as the declining sun lit up the light thin clouds that flecked the inner orb of the heavens. An incident of childhood came back to Avram which shut out for the moment all the sights, thoughts, and ideas that made the day eventful.

When eight years old, he was stricken with a disease. He could still recall the sensation of freezing to death. His mother and the servants covered him with woolen cloth while his teeth chattered violently. Then the excessive coverings made him so hot that he thought he was burning up. The temple priest recommended bathing with an image of Enlil, metal or stone, in the tub and declared that the god sent this punishment because the household did not sacrifice to him or bring offerings to his temple. The priest ordered the boy to be kept in total darkness so that the invisible *shaidim* that flutter about in the sunlight would not see him; for when they see someone afflicted by the gods, they enter his body to carry off his soul and make a fellow demon out of him.

For weeks he lay in bed. Finally, he got better; so the priest gave permission to have Avram carried to the flat roof early in the morning. Avram watched the rising sun and thought it the most beautiful sight in all creation. He was certain that the sun was the greatest of all the gods.

He prayed with all the fervor in his weak body and worshipped the sun with a grateful heart. Towards midday his mother came up and thought it was getting too hot. Not a breath of wind was stirring the tree leaves. But Avram begged to remain on the roof. The newly discovered sun god took complete possession of him, body and soul. He wished to lie on the roof forever and pour out his deepest feelings to the majestic, benign god that filled him with warmth, kindness, and joy. The sun rays would never get too harmful, for nothing about this god could ever be evil or harmful.

The brilliant sunlight began to pall and a certain uneasiness tugged at Avram's heart. Dark clouds were rising on the horizon in the east. The sun orb had passed the meridian in the sky and was beginning its descent. A long, black cloud that resembled a mountain was rapidly approaching and bringing on a shade that resembled twilight. Soon the sun was no longer visible and the sky became overcast. The slaves rushed to the roof and carried the convalescent boy down to his room on the second floor. The window on the west remained open and streaks of lightning appeared to cut lines of fire in the black clouds. Thunder crashes seemed to fall near enough to strike Terach's house. The household welcomed the heavy downpour and even enjoyed the hail that pattered like pebbles dropped by a host of boys. Everyone, including the slaves, agreed that the rain was long overdue. A water shortage was menacing the city and the drought threatened the crops that were not fed by the dried-up canals.

Avram's heart sank. To the fevered imagination of the boy the glorious sun had fled from the storm clouds. Was it possible that the winds and the thunder-lightning were more powerful than the orb of light and heat that brings happiness to the heart of man? So the sun is not the all powerful god who vanquishes all opponents and is stronger than all other gods. With the approach of the tempest the sun seemed to have run for protection and left the field completely to the enemy. The sun, therefore, is but a minor god and is not to be worshipped as the Supreme Being.

His retrospections were interrupted by a *kadosh* who asked whether he was Avram, son of Terach the image-maker. On hearing the affirmative, the castrate declared, "Adoni Sabbattu desires to inform you that your half-sister Zirru has been greatly honored. She was selected the bride of Nannar and will not return home."

Avram was stunned. The world turned black. He staggered and was supported from falling by the temple under-priest. He finally managed to inquire whether he could speak to her.

"It is forbidden for commoners to converse with god's chosen bride even if they be relatives. Her life is henceforth dedicated to the Lord Nannar and his holy temple."

Slowly Avram shambled out of the temple compound and wandered through the district known as the Temenos area until he reached the long winding Street of the Ancients which runs through the entire city. In his dazed state of mind Avram, instead of keeping to the right, staggered to the left and continued in that direction until he reached the river front. By this time the twilight was merging into darkness. He passed the animal show but paid no attention to the individual stragglers walking or standing near the spokesman of the morning who, under a huge torch, was barking out his invitation to see the wonderful display of India. Two of the ba'iru armed with daggers and clubs standing near the barker under torchlight watched Avram and came to the conclusion that he had been drinking or was drunk, and was wending his way home.

Out of the ship that carried rock from Etzion Geber came Eleazer of Damascus and his Canaanite companion heading towards the Indian circus. Eleazer came near Avram, recognized him, and said "sholom uvracha" but received no reply. Puzzled by this coldness, he remarked to the Canaanite, "Strange. You recognize the young man, don't you? Remember we saw him this morning with the very pretty girl. I believe he calls himself Avram ben Terach. I wonder why his walk is so unsteady. Is he not well? I am curious."

"Drink, no doubt," suggested the man from Canaan without interest.

"I like this fellow," continued Eleazer "and would not want him to meet with foul play. Let's follow him."

The Canaanite expressed dissatisfaction but went along. They followed Avram from a distance as he wandered in the direction of the sandalmaker's lane that began at the water's edge not far from the bad smelling tanneries. About 30 paces in front of him walked two burly ruffians, apparently seamen, who from time to time looked back towards Avram to see if he was following. It became quite dark and after a short space of time Eleazer lost sight of Avram as he wandered into the sandalmaker's territory.

"Let's hurry up. I don't want to lose sight of him. This is rough waterfront territory where many crimes are committed. Keep your hand on your dagger," commanded Eleazer sharply, sensing the unwillingness of his comrade, who mumbled, "I don't see what concern this is of ours to get mixed up in a business that might turn out dangerous."

They reached the sandalmaker's lane and by the dim lights in open doors they could see or hear cobblers hammering leather strips over wooden sandals. As the two men passed one open door, two slightly clad women, almost nude, invited them to come in. With the passing of each minute Eleazer was becoming more and more alarmed. Then he beheld two men carrying a body, one holding the feet and the other the armpits under the shoulders. He recognized the two seamen and felt certain that they were dragging Avram.

"Halt in the king's name!" cried out Eleazer in seamen's argot understood on all waterfronts and containing words from Phoenicia, Aram, Elam, Amuru, Canaan, and including Cretan, Egyptian and Sumerian idioms. Several more doors opened and some cobblers held up torches and lamps. By their lights he recognized Avram and exclaimed, "I know this youth. He is Avram, son of Terach the image-maker for the Temple of Nannar. . . ." Before he could say another word the ruffians laid Avram down and fled. Eleazer bent down, felt his pulse, and listened to the heart beat. By the increasing number of lights he could see a gash in Avram's head from which blood was trickling. He stood up and said, "Would one of you men call the ba'iru. They are standing near the Indian animal show, right under the torchlight."

No one stirred.

"Then I will go myself." Addressing several men he continued, "Will you two please remain with my comrade who cannot speak your language?"

A sandalmaker's apprentice offered to go if he would receive a quarter epha of barley.

"I will give you half an epha if you act quickly."

The ba'iru soon arrived. They examined Avram and said that since his skull was not cracked he would recover.

Eleazer gave them Avram's name and parentage. The policemen stated, "We know Terach, the image-maker; he is on the Street of the Ancients." Then addressing the residents that had swelled into a small crowd, the ba'iru asked if anyone had a reed stretcher. Everyone remained silent. "We won't confiscate it; we just want to borrow it to bring the injured man to his home. We are sure the imagemaker for the Temple of Nannar will reward you handsomely."

The resourceful apprentice offered to borrow one from his master if the reward would be sufficient. Upon Eleazer's assurance the boy ran off, then produced a stretcher of reeds tied together with strips of leather and sewed onto two wooden poles. The two ba'iru placed Avram on the stretcher and together with Eleazer and the Canaanite held the ends of the poles and walked away followed by the apprentice carrying a lighted torch.

Loud knocks shattered the quiet on the Street of the Ancients. From the open window on the second floor Terach shouted, "Who is it?" The ba'iru answered that they brought his son who was hurt. Terach hurried down the stairs, unbolted the door, and by the light of the apprentice's torch saw Avram lying on the stretcher, his head covered with blood. The four men entered bearing the stretcher. The ba'iru assured Terach that his son's condition was not serious; that he be put to bed, his head washed clean and bandaged; that some strong wine would restore his senses.

By this time the entire household stood in the court patio. Under Emtelai's direction slaves carried her son on the stretcher up to his room on the second floor. They bathed him, washed his hair, dressed his wound, then tied a linen cloth about his head and the upper half of his face. In the court below Terach ordered full goblets of wine for the four men and the apprentice. While sitting on benches and drinking in the patio, Eleazer spoke in Aramean about his meeting with Avram in the morning and the happenings that evening. Davarah inquired anxiously about her daughter Zirru but the man from Damascus could only answer that he saw a beautiful girl with Avram in the morning and knew nothing more.

The ba'iru rose to go saying that it was a great privilege to visit such a distinguished host but excused themselves that they must go back to duty. Terach gave the police two jugs of wine and each a container of nuts, figs, and raisins. To the apprentice he gave a similar gift and in addition a full measure of barley. He invited Eleazer and the Canaanite to remain overnight and eat breakfast in the morning with him. But Eleazer refused on the ground that he and his comrade must stay on board to keep the first and second watch. He thanked Terach and asked permission to come and inquire about his son. Terach ordered his two slaves to carry back the stretcher and help them with the containers.

Terach went upstairs and found Avram asleep. He tried to give his son wine but Avram did not open his mouth and the liquid spilled on the bed and on to his nightshirt. Seven-year-old Sarai brought in her pillow, spread her bedclothes on the floor, and insisted on watching over her Avram. She soon dropped off to sleep and did not wake even when the concubine Shuah lifted up the girl and put her to bed.

# 4

# The Most High God

THE NEXT MORNING AVRAM LAY IN HIGH FEVER AND APparently in a state of coma. Terach hastened to the Temple of Nannar to offer the sacrifice of a young buck, to give a liberal donation of five shekels in silver, but mainly to consult with the high priest. Sabbattu replied by messenger that he was too occupied to see him because of the visiting high priest of Babylon, which country was rapidly becoming the leading world power; but if Terach would confide in the confidential messenger he would be advised what best to do. Terach informed the priest's representative about Avram's condition and of the family's anxiety over Zirru's disappearance, about which they were in total darkness.

Sabbattu answered that he would immediately send the temple's doctor, the most skilled physician in Ur, also a priest to invoke the gods for Avram's recovery, and the *Ashipu* who would utter incantations that would ward off the *shaidim* that haunted a sickroom and whose intent would be to do harm to the invalid. He would even do the unprecedented and send along the five sacred figurines of the moon: the crescent, the quarter, half, three-quarters, and full orb which would place the invalid under the special protection of Nannar. "As for Zirru, do not worry about her. She has attained the highest distinction that could be reached by any female. She was selected by the Lord Nannar to become his bride."

By the time Terach returned home the physician was already there. He washed Avram's head, then cut off all his hair and covered the wound with a hot poultice of pig's meat moistened with cow's urine and saturated in olive oil. Then he bandaged his head with white woolen cloth. Unable to rouse his patient, the doctor prescribed a bath of warm water containing poppy seeds and ground sunflower for the invalid as soon as he regained consciousness. He could not make Avram swallow any wine so he ordered Emtelai to prepare broth of veal, honey, a bit of wine, and goat's milk, and if possible to get from the Indian ship on the waterfront some of the hard black beans which they called pepper. They were quite expensive, but seemed to be the best medicine for any kind of sickness. She should pound about five pepper beans into a fine powder and sprinkle it on the hot soup. This spice had great healing power.

For four days Avram lay in a coma; at times he was very hot, then he would cool off until he felt ice cold. On the fifth day his eyes opened but he did not speak. Emtelai rushed to the kitchen to heat the broth which she had already prepared. She had even purchased at a prohibitive price some peppers from the Indian ship. Emtelai fed her son with a spoon until he dozed off again and slept for another day. The next morning he awoke refreshed, elated, his eyes shining, his spirits high; he ate a hearty breakfast. When Terach was alone with him, Avram asked, "Father, was I here all night?"

"Of course. Where else could you be? You were sleeping all the time. Thanks to Nannar and all the gods, you have recovered."

"Father, are you sure that I did not get out and rise high, high into heaven?"

Terach felt a sinking sensation in his bowels. He rose, went to bed, put his hand on his son's cheeks, then felt higher up as far as he could under the woolen white cloth. He looked into the shining eyes, the flushed face, and said, "It seems strange. You have no more fever. Yet your eyes and cheeks would indicate that you are still sick."

"Am I sick?" He became aware of the cloth about his head. He touched it and said, "Then what's wrong with me? Why is my head bound up?"

"I'll tell you later, when you are stronger."

"I am strong enough now." He tried to get up but fell back on the pillow. "Did you hear a voice speaking to me?"

"No, but this morning I heard you moaning and mumbling words that I could not make out."

"Is it possible that it was only a dream?" asked Avram in evident disappointment. "Yet, it looked and sounded so real."

"Tell me about it," requested Terach, his curiosity aroused; "that is if you feel strong enough."

"I felt," began the invalid, "I was ascending, rising higher and higher into space. Bands of red, green, blue, gold, yellow, purple, and silver seemed to be encircling me, quite close to me. At times these rings were separate and distinct; other times they merged into each other, mingling together like a rainbow of many colors. I was going ever higher without the aid of anyone or anything. The atmosphere became clearer, purer, more and more rarified. Everything seemed strangely quiet; not the slightest sound marred the stillness. The light became extremely bright as if powerful rays were sent out of somewhere, yet neither sun nor moon nor stars were visible. Then I heard a voice that I cannot describe. It was stern, clear, strong, commanding, yet agreeable and kind. I heard it say, " 'Avram! Avram!' "

"I answered, 'Here I am.' "

" 'I am the Most High God, Creator of Heaven and Earth!' "

"I knelt, covered my eyes and fell on my face."

" 'I am the God of your forefathers, of Enoch, Noah, Shem, Eber, yet your father Terach knows me not!' "

"I said, 'he serves Anu, Nannar, Ea, Irnina, Enlil, Ningal.' "

" 'They are false!' thundered the voice."

" 'Might I know thy name, Oh Lord God, that I may serve thee?' I trembled waiting with fear, but the dread voice spoke no more. The bright atmosphere began to dim and I had a sinking sensation as if I were slowly descending. I must have fallen asleep."

Terach was visibly shaken. He shuddered, then trembled. After a pause he spoke more to keep up his own courage than to say anything to his son.

"Well, after all, it was only a dream." He thought awhile, then asked himself: "But which god sent this dream? Was El Elyon angry with me? I wonder if it is a bad omen." He touched the amulet that hung suspended from his neck and uttered a silent prayer. Perplexed by the beatific look on his son's face he wondered if Avram was in his right mind.

"Father, did you know about the Most High God?"

"My father, Nahor, mentioned several times that his ancestors worshipped El Elyon, the Creator of Heaven and Earth."

"Did he speak of his forebears?"

"Yes, he mentioned the same names, Eber especially, and some others. He said that one, whose name I cannot recall, lived 969 years. He thought that was an exaggeration."

"Did he say why he ceased to worship El Elyon?"

"Well, it seems that Father Nahor grew tired of living in tents. He decided to give up the life of a nomad for the big city. He tried Haran and married into the Reuel clan who were also Arameans. But he moved to Ur, being the largest city in Chaldea, and with better opportunities. He struggled in poverty and finally went to work for Ur-tan-tu, a well-known sculptor in his day, and sold images for him. When father noticed that I was fond of fashioning figurines out of clay, he apprenticed me to Ur-tan-tu who taught me his craft. This is how I became a sculptor, which the Chaldeans usually designate an image-maker."

"But you did not answer why you gave up El Elyon."

"Well, you see, Father believed in being like the people around him. One time he gave me a long lecture on living right. He said that as soon as he settled in Ur he decided to do what the Sumerians did, live like them, worship like them, and be in every respect a good Sumerian. For instance, he thought that there was little sense in serving gods who were defeated and whose statues were carried away in captivity. Every god, he said, had power in his own land only. When a man's country is conquered then it was only sensible to worship the conqueror's gods, who proved stronger than the native gods."

"Am I to understand that Grandfather's ideas and beliefs are also yours?" asked Avram apprehensively.

"In substance? Yes."

Avram's face registered disappointment. His elated expression faded away but did not show unhappiness. He shut his eyes for a time, then asked, "Did Grandfather tell you about his ancestors?"

"When he got old he would talk a great deal but I seldom listened. I thought they were foolish stories and therefore was just not interested."

"Tell me some of them," begged his son.

"Let me see if I can recall any. Father Nahor said that when he was a boy he often slept in the same tent with his great-great-grandfather Eber. You know, people lived very long in those days. Eber was a very old man and he liked to tell stories over and over again so Father simply did not listen. But when in turn my father became old, he regretted not paying attention to Eber whose memory went back hundreds of years."

"Hundreds of years? Then how long did Eber actually live?" questioned Avram with astonishment not free from skepticism.

"Father said more than 500 years; he did not know exactly."

"And Grandfather knew him? It sounds incredible. I am now more curious than ever to hear some of his stories."

Terach thought a while and said, "Father used to spin an incredible tale about a great flood that rained 40 days. All life perished except his ancestor whose children started life anew on earth. You don't expect me to believe such yarns, do you?"

"This is truly amazing!" exclaimed Avram. "Only yesterday we studied this story in class. You say our direct ancestor and his family were the only ones saved. Tell me, if you remember, what was his name?"

"I believe Father said it was Noah."

"Now would you believe it that in Babylon he is call Ut-

Napishtim and the Sumerians know him as Zi-u-sud-ra. They are very proud of possessing this tale as you call it. Let me think. Noah? Noah? Why in my vision Noah is among the followers of the Most High God. You say he worshipped El Elyon. Then both must be the same god. I wonder whether he is the same person as Ut-Napishtim who survived the flood. Do you recall anything else about him?" questioned Avram excitedly.

"I believe his son's name was Shem."

"Shem also served the Most High God and El Elyon. And was it he, you say, who started life again on this earth?"

"So Father said, not I. To me the whole yarn is rubbish. I don't see any reason to get so excited," pooh-poohed Terach. "Besides, the story is old and antiquated."

"The teacher-priest, Khar-Sak, who has a truly great mind observed only yesterday that old stories are very significant," quoted Avram. "The older the tale the more important it might be. There must be a good reason why it has escaped oblivion. A fable might sound absurd," he said, "yet it usually contains a moral or it has imbedded some deep meaning. Old stories should be saved by all means."

Terach ruminated for awhile, then said, "If you think so much of these old, grandmothers' tales, then listen to this one about the Garden which has just come back to me. Eber told Father about his ancestors of long, long ago, one thousand or perhaps two thousand years back. A man and wife lived in an orchard that was the most delightful spot in all the world. It never became too hot or too cold. They simply wore loin aprons woven out of fig leaves. The owner, a magician named Shadai, if I remember right, placed them there to take care of his garden. Their duties were light and the animals, all tame, helped them to remove broken branches or twigs. Springs furnished cool water for the couple as well as for the animals. The fruit on the trees was copious, tasty, satisfying, and ample for all, the couple and all the living, creatures or birds. But such happiness was too good to last.

"A serpent also lived in the orchard. He walked on two feet, had two hands and a penis. He could talk and was very subtle. The woman was young, extremely beautiful, and the serpent desired her. He often begged her to lie with him but she refused. 'Why?' he would ask. 'Because it is forbidden,' was her steady answer. The serpent planned to trap her. There was a tall apple tree standing in the center of the orchard, and Shadai had forbidden anyone to eat of its fruit. The man and woman were led to believe that the moment they touched the tree, death would come. They were careful to stay away.

"One day the woman was passing and saw the serpent coiled about the trunk of the tall apple tree. 'That's forbidden!' she exclaimed. To which he replied with the question, 'What happens if I eat the apple?' plucking one from a branch. 'Why you will surely die,' she declared horrified. He began eating and taunted her. 'Well, you see I am not dead. It is very tasty. You must eat one also. Let me get you a good apple.' And before she could say 'No' he plucked a large red juicy one and tried to hand it to her. She refused. 'Now you must eat it. I insist,' he commanded. 'Suppose I don't?' she questioned. 'Then I will tell your man that you lay with me every afternoon while he slept.' Too frightened to think she took the fruit and ate it. Immediately her eyes were opened and she realized that she was duped.

"What should she do now? Tell her man that she had eaten the forbidden fruit? She could never explain the reason why. He would never understand, nor forgive her stupidity. The serpent suspected her dilemma. Her husband must commit the same offense or he would have dominion over her and him. 'Now take another apple and bring it to your husband and see that he eats it,' ordered the serpent, feeling now he had the upper hand and that she would obey him in everything, including the enjoyment of her body. She was now really afraid of him. She plucked a large apple and went looking for her man. He would no doubt be resting after completing his morning task.

"She found him sleeping on the leafy bower under the large oak tree where the couple usually took their afternoon nap. She woke him and seeing her alluring smile he was seized with desire and reached out for her disengaged hand, the other grasping the apple which she held behind her back. 'No, not now. Eat this delicious fruit first,' and she held the apple for him to take.

" 'It is forbidden to eat these apples and you know it,' " he exploded angrily.

" 'Nonsense,' " she smiled with all her charm. 'I ate an apple and the serpent ate one, yet no harm has come to either of us.'

"He cried out in alarm, 'Now you will surely die.'

"She then said laughingly, 'So you will die with me. Surely you do not wish to live without me.'

"He hesitated, then said, 'I suppose not.' He took the apple, ate it and declared, 'This is the most delicious fruit I ever ate.' Wild passion gripped them as they satisfied their desires in each others arms and then fell asleep.

"In the cool of the evening the magician walked to inspect his orchard and noticed the three apples missing from the large tree. He wandered through the garden and found the lovers fast asleep in the leafy bower under the oak tree. Near them lay the core of the eaten apple. He woke the man with a touch of his wand. 'What happened to this apple?' he demanded, pointing his wand to the ground. Frightened and obsessed with a feeling of guilt which blurred his mind, the man blurted out, 'The woman gave it to me and I ate it.'

"By this time the woman was wide awake. Her apron of fig leaves lay on the ground. For the first time she felt ashamed at the awareness of her nakedness. She bent over and grasped her knees. The magician said to her, 'What is this you have done?' Her head down and looking at the earth she replied, 'The serpent beguiled me.' The magician demanded, 'How so?' She hesitated a few moments and declared, 'He said he would tell my husband that I tried to tempt him to lie with me. Of course, this is not true. He lied.'

"The serpent had seen the magician walking in the garden and sensed that something was brewing. He followed, stood near, and listened to what went on. He was preparing to say something when the magician exclaimed, 'Silence! You shall speak never more! Nor will you ever eat fruit again. Hereafter you will crawl on your belly and eat dirt all your days.' He waved the wand three times. The serpent's hands, legs, and penis came off. His teeth fell out; the wide mouth narrowed to a point; the tongue shrank to a thin needle. 'There will be everlasting hate between you and the man. His seed will crush your head and your seed will poison his feet. Begone, Serpent!' And the snake slithered out of the garden.

"The magician turned to the woman and said, 'You have sinned this day. Your act proved that you are not the equal of your husband. Therefore, he shall rule over you and your desire will go out to him. Nine moons hence you shall give birth in pain, sorrow, and anguish and will be the mother of all living.'

"To the man, Shadai said, 'There is no excuse for your guilt. You heard from my mouth that eating of that tree was forbidden. You were not content to live in peace and with little labor or pain. You are, therefore, banished from the most pleasant garden in all creation. Henceforth you shall labor until sweat covers your face. Thorns and thistles shall grow together with herbs of the field. Bread you will eat with sorrow all your days. When you die you shall return to dust.'

"The magician then said, 'Stay until I return.' The man and woman put on their aprons of fig leaves. Just then a lion strayed into the open space. He had been friendly and seemed to enjoy being patted on the head and mane by the woman. Now when he passed he let out a roar which they never heard before. It shook the trees and for the first time both were frightened. Then passed the large dog that always accompanied the man and carried branches in his mouth to throw away into the ravine which bordered a part of the orchard. When he saw both, he barked viciously and would not approach them.

"Shadai returned carrying skins of animals made into coats. 'Take and wear these skins covered with fur to protect you from beasts and keep you warm especially in the night. Come!'

"They followed the magician to the edge of the orchard. 'Go, and never return to my garden.' The woman began to weep and the man put his arm around her as they left and walked 100 cubits from the garden. Turning to look at their blissful abode for the last time, they beheld white, shining creatures with wings guarding the entrances. A great flaming sword moving and turning in every direction gave warning to everyone not to penetrate the sacred ground."

Affected by the moving story, the most touching and

beautiful he had ever heard, Avram lay silent, his eyes closed. Terach thought the strange tale had put his son to sleep and left the room. Excitement was gripping him as he became certain that it was not simply a dream in which he heard the voice of a deity. The conviction grew momentarily that the Most High God actually spoke to him. And everything seemed to confirm this conclusion. The very words of his matter-of-fact parent produced additional evidence. In fact, the skepticism of his unimaginative father was stronger testimony than blind uncritical faith. It thrilled him beyond measure to know that the El Elyon of his forefathers was the Most High God who spoke to him. And it was El Elyon who saved his ancestor Noah and family from the destruction of the flood.

But the most remarkable of all was the garden story. It whipped up additional excitation in his breast. Intuitively he felt the story to be basically true, even if errors and changes had crept in with centuries of retelling. Were this man and woman of the dim, long forgotten past also his ancestors? If not, how was it that the story was preserved and handed down generation after generation in a single family? The serpent was, in doubt, a symbolic figure meant to represent a fiend, a demon, the power of evil. But how could a human magician have such great power? Suddenly, a thought came flushing to his brow and made his heart beat excitedly. Was it possible that the magician Shadai was in reality El Elyon in human disguise? Only a god could perform such wonders. Then another intuitive thought made his heart virtually stand still for a moment. This man and woman were probably the first couple on earth, created by the Most High God, called El Elyon by his ancestors.

His pounding heart almost stopped his breathing. Worn out by the almost unbearable excitement, he lost consciousness and slept continuously for another day and night.

II

In her room in the compartment of the priestesses Zirru felt isolated, depressed, and frightened. Was there any use in appealing further to her father? Slowly a suspicion crossed her. Was he really her father? Mother Davarah had always kept a discreet silence. Coming to think of it she never referred to him as her father. Nor did she ever share Zirru's respect for his greatness as a man or his holiness as a priest. Perhaps Davarah knew more than she would disclose. After all, he had never come to see his daughter. Nor did he ever inquire about her. He finally did see her but only at Terach's prodding. Feminine instinct subtly intimated that his glances were not altogether paternal; his look seemed tinged with desire, almost like the look she was accustomed to get from most men. His kiss was far more warm than Terach's grandfatherly, kind, dutiful peck on the cheek. Zirru suddenly felt uneasy, a victim of doubt, suspicion, and distrust.

Reclining on a large couch, the only bed in the room, she recalled the depression felt by Avram. Were the same *shaidim* warning her of some pending disaster? Wondering when she would see Avram again she wept softly altogether unaware that she had a visitor. A woman almost twice her age, slightly above middle height, was scanning her closely. She was olive-complexioned, neither pretty nor homely, with cold gray eyes, more angular than curvaceous in figure, yet neither. Her expression suggested firmness of character, and her speech, movement, and carriage seemed to indicate a deliberate, calculated intention to impress one with her regal bearing.

"Welcome to the new bride of Nannar from the one you

are replacing." Zirru sat up ready to stand but the visitor waved her hand and continued: "Please do not get up. Just resume your relaxed position. Please. I am sorry to see you unhappy over the great honor conferred upon you. Don't take it so tragically. It is not as bad as all that."

"But I don't want to become the bride of Nannar. I am happy to marry my beloved Avram, son of Terach, the image-maker for the Temple," cried Zirru. "Can't anything be done to release me?" And the flood gates opened with tears flowing copiously. The visitor sat on the couch, took Zirru to her bosom. Kissing and caressing her she replied, "I am afraid not. I heard it said that Adon Sabbattu is your father. Is that true?"

"So I have been told," answered Zirru as she became calmer.

"What was your mother's name?"

"Anunu."

"I know about her. She died a short time before I came here from Larsa where my father was king."

Zirru opened her eyes wide. They had more than their usual sparkle by reason of her tears. "And the king, your father, was unable to save you?" she asked in surprise.

"It was not my wish to be saved. I wanted to come."

"Didn't you want to marry the man of your choice?" asked Zirru.

"Actually no man of my choice showed up. You probably don't know that we princesses of the blood have no free choice. We can only marry royalty. The available men were not attractive to me. Perhaps I did not attract them. I, therefore, decided to remain single and serve the gods."

"I thought one has to be chosen by Nannar to be his bride."

"It is so refreshing to find anyone in Ur so fresh, naive,

and charming. Oh, I can just love you," she said, kissing her more warmly than before. "The bride of Nannar is in a position of responsibility and trust. Her power among women equals the high priest's among men. The god does not always choose his bride. Sometimes he has one in each of several temples. If the position is open then the priests select her. I am not beautiful like you and consequently was never chosen by any god."

"Will I be burdened with trust and responsibility? I don't know how to do difficult things," confessed Zirru apprehensively.

"I will keep my post as head of Nannar's priestess division with its administrative labors. You will only comfort his bed while you are young and toothsome," she said playfully biting Zirru's neck.

"Do you resent me for pushing you out of this post?"

"My dear, you had nothing to do with it. I see how anxious you are to be relieved from it." It was quite dark and light came through the window from the moon. "I must go now. I have many chores to do before I retire."

"Oh, please do not leave me alone. I am awfully lonesome and frightened," wailed Zirru, "and please tell me your name."

"Zur-na-na. This was given to me here when I was consecrated. Your name will also be changed. If you wish I will come later and spend the night here."

"Oh, please do," and Zirru kissed her cheek with gratitude.

Left alone, Zirru began to cry. She felt deserted, neglected, and afraid of the *shaidim* that lurked in dark places. The elderly priestess came with a lamp, a nightshift, and offered to bring her something to eat. She refused since the afternoon meal ended shortly before sundown. But a slave did bring a goblet of mild date wine which Zirru emptied, then dozed off. She slept until she found herself in the caressing arms of Zur-na-na. The king's daughter brought along a jug of excellent wine, the best in the Temple cellars. Slowly she sipped about half while urging Zirru to consume the rest. The young girl's spirits began to rise as fear and depression evaporated. She began to feel towards Zur-na-na as to a man whom she could look to for guidance, help, and protection.

"Don't you find the confined life in the Temple boring?" she asked her companion.

"Not quite. I have many duties to perform, religious and administrative."

"What is there for fun or excitement? Do the men help you?"

"We really haven't enough men here for our needs. The *kadoshim* are useless to us. Actually these castrates dislike us. The priests are too few and most of them too old. Besides, their world is open and they can take their pleasures where they find them."

"So you do find things monotonous?" asked the young girl to whom fun and excitement meant life.

"No, not really. We have resources within outselves."

"Sewing, knitting or sitting and talking?" Zirru's cheeks were glowing, her eyes were now bright. The wine was having its effect.

"We have love," declared the princess with quiet emphasis.

"But for love a man is necessary," stated the girl, equally emphatic.

"My lamb, how innocent you are. You have much to learn. Men do not understand love; they only know brutal lust, like animals. The delicate nuances of love escape them entirely." With these words Zur-na-na finished her wine with a gulp.

"Please tell me more. I am so ignorant."

"True tenderness, real delicacy is possible only between two women who love each other. Selfishness, the joy of inflicting pain, heartless cruelty are natural to the brutal male. Kindness, heartfelt consideration, compassion are practiced only by women in love. But you will only understand all this in time and only through experience."

A wild urge to dance came over Zirru. She slipped off the couch and began to swing about the room. She had been taught the art but not for professional purposes. All girls of the upper or middle class, who could afford the luxury, received instruction. While the dance of Asia or Egypt was basically sensual, the respectable girls were taught to refrain from excessive hip swaying.

Her movement slow and graceful at first began to quicken until she was whirling around the room, at times scarcely distinct in the uncertain, failing lamplight. She would become more visible when nearing the open window with the moonlight streaming into a part of the chamber. Zur-na-na removed her own dress and while dancing together succeeded in pulling Zirru's nightshift over her head. Both in the nude they danced apart, then circled about the room with their arms around each other. The tempo became so rapid that they fell breathless upon the couch.

Zur-na-na kissed her on the mouth, a long passionate soul kiss. Then her lips were moving over Zirru's body, sometimes softly and gently, at other times biting her tenderly. Zirru's spirits were rising, then soaring, and she felt as if she was losing consciousness. Pleasure and pain were commingling and reaching an acute state that was becoming unbearable, when climactic liberation came. Zirru cried out in breathless relief.

Sha lay with the arms of Zur-na-na about her. When

able to breathe more easily, she whispered in the ear of the older woman, "Is this what the god Nannar will do to me?"

"I don't know," laughed Zur-na-na. "Each man treats his woman in his own particular fashion."

Zirru's steady breathing showed that she had fallen asleep.

## III

On the following afternoon all the female priesthood of the Temple, including those *kadoshes* who were not on duty serving men, assembled at the hall of the goddess Irnina. The chamber that could hold about 200 was approximately three-fourths full. The decor of the room illustrated and symbolized the functions and powers of the love and fertility goddess. In the southeast corner stood a huge phallus carved out of alabaster. At the opposite northeast corner stood the torso of a nude woman revealing her genitals. On the wall, figures of nude men and women in bas-relief or incised on sheets of alabaster, sandstone, clay, or diorite related to the love act between the sexes and its processes from procreation to birth. At a prominent place a full-size bas-relief of Irnina holding a child in her arms symbolized and emphasized the mother-goddess.

On a raised dais of about two cubits from the floor sat Zur-na-na on a large chair suggesting a throne. The chair next to her was vacant. Hunate, the assistant high priest, sat next while several other chairs were occupied by priestesses of rank. The rest of the women sat on the floor or on cushions. Matters affecting the women's division had evidently been discussed and completed. Zur-na-na announced her readiness for the consecration of the next bride of Nannar.

The four ranking priestesses left the dais and returned with Zirru in their midst. They stood facing the dais and at a sign from Zur-na-na disrobed Zirru of her dress and sandals and immediately wrapped a purple sheet about her. A priestess rolled the dress and sandals into a bundle and placed it on the altar standing on the dais. The assistant high priest uttered a prayer to Nannar and Irnina to show their favor to the new bride about to devote her life to their service. He and the priestesses resumed their seats leaving Zirru standing alone.

The audience together with the dais was waiting in tense silence for the miraculous to happen. If the bride was acceptable to the moon god and met with the approval of the love goddess then a fire would start automatically on the altar and consume the dress and sandals of the neophyte. If no flame sprang up by itself, without the aid of human hands, then the neophyte had been rejected by both or either of the gods. Everyone in the hall waited breathlessly.

The tension suddenly snapped. On the altar smoke was seen curling upwards, then a number of small, scattered flames arose. From many throats a shout broke forth: "Hail, bride of Nannar, blessed among women." Hunate approached the altar and sprayed incense over the small fires and on Zirru's dress. The little fires burst into a roaring flame that quickly consumed the dress and sandals. Some of the younger women felt disappointed. They expected a flash to burst out of the sky and consume everything in flames.

The four elderly priestesses stepped from the dais and surrounded Zirru. They removed the purple sheet and dressed her in a white gown of silk from India, a white veil and wreath of white roses on her head, white sandals clasped to her feet with strips of leather covered by silver. Hunate pronounced the blessings of the gods and ended with, "Today you are born a second time. Hitherto you were Zirru, daughter of Harran. Hereafter you shall be the priestess Keturah. The former Zirru passed out of existence with the burning of your clothes. The pure white raiment you now wear ushers in your new existence as the bride of Nannar."

She was conducted to the vacant chair on the dais and seated next to Zur-na-na while the assembled women chanted in chorus, "Keturah, bride of Nannar, long life, health, and happiness to you."

The four priestesses accompanied Zirru-Keturah out of the Irnina hall and led her through a long corridor into a bathing chamber which contained a large pool surrounded by divans and benches. Six nude young women and two eunuchs were there ready to prepare the bride to share the couch of the Lord Nannar. They undressed the neophyte and all the girls dived into the warm water. After a short swim she was placed on a divan. The two eunuchs washed her thoroughly, then rubbed her with a lotion that had a pleasant fragrance. The girls applied a thin oil and massaged her entire body. Their deft, experienced fingers awakened certain nerves that stimulated desire until her flesh throbbed and her body ached with passion. Again a lotion was applied that contained musk. She was given a goblet of wine sprayed with a mild aphrodisiac. Again they dressed her with the white silk gown, the veil, and silver sandals. The priestesses conducted her out of the bathing chamber into a corridor that led to steps where Zur-na-na joined them.

Two slave girls brought four clay lamps burning oil. Two they gave to the priestesses and one girl, lamp in hand, guided the group up the dark steps, while the other closed the procession in the rear holding up her lighted lamp. On reaching the head of the steps they walked through a long, circuitous corridor until they reached a door that opened into a chamber. The lamp lights disclosed a well-furnished room with a luxuriant couch, curtains draping the walls, a thick rug on the floor, carved tripods that held decanters of wine, fruits, sweetmeats, cookies, dates, nuts, and figs. A smaller door opened into a washroom in which stood bowls of water, a tub, a rack with towels. A terra cotta pipe for draining water perforated the blue glazed brick wall.

After examining the room and the bed, Zur-na-na dismissed the priestesses and slave girls, who left their burning lamps.

"I feel nervous," whispered Zirru-Keturah. "Will these lamps remain burning?"

"No," answered the older bride of Nannar undressing her younger colleague. "It will be so dark that you won't be able to see your male lover. Do not talk to him. I doubt whether he will say anything to you."

"I am curious to see what he looks like."

"He does not come in his divine form," stated Zur-na-na, putting the nude young girl in the bed. "Chances are he may assume the human shape, perhaps some priest of the temple. If he says anything it will be with a human voice, probably someone you may know whose voice you will recognize."

Embracing and kissing her she whispered, "Do not be frightened, my darling. No harm will come to you. I shall be waiting outside. When he leaves, open the door and call me."

Zur-na-na blew one lamp out, took the remaining lighted one in her hand, opened the door, walked out, then closed it.

In the total darkness lay Zirru-Keturah, a prey to mixed feelings—virginal fears, a sense of isolation, curiosity, and passion aching to be assuaged.

# 5

# Eleazer of Damascus

EARLY THE NEXT MORNING AVRAM OPENED HIS EYES AND called for food. The excitation of the day before had calmed down into a more even and less dithyrambic elation. The dream was gradually sinking into the recesses of his consciousness and becoming an integral part of his psyche not to be disturbed, exalted, or depressed by hourly or daily incidents. An abstract, imageless concept of the Most High God was gradually taking concrete form and hardening into a settled conviction, not to be unsettled by emotional upsets.

While eating, Avram inquired why he was in bed with his head bandaged. Terach explained as tersely as he could that he had been hit over the head a week before by seamen intent on taking him on board a ship to be sold, no doubt, into slavery. It was a common practice in all ports and harbors, he added. How did he escape from them? He was miracuously saved, first by the help of the gods, then by Eleazer of Aram Dameshek, who has since been coming almost every day to inquire after him. "I don't want to miss him next time he comes," commanded the convalescing youth.

"Why doesn't Zirru come to see me?" he suddenly asked. It was then that Terach, with all the enthusiasm he could muster, stated that Zirru had received the highest honor allotted to any woman; she had been chosen the bride of Nannar. At this moment the recollection came back of waiting at the image stall in the Temple and the statement of the *kadosh* that no one could see Zirru since she received the high elevation. Avram's eyes filled as he turned his head to the wall muttering, "Nannar can be unjust."

The physician came accompanied by the priest. He removed the bandage, declared the wound to be healing rapidly, and discarded the woolen cloth tied about the head. Instead, he recommended one of those new-fashioned turbans which had become all the rage since the Indian boats docked in the harbor. All the tailors and seamstresses were occupied filling orders of men and women for the new-styled headgear. The priest thought it was time to take back the five ancient figurines of the moon, sacred to Nannar, and which for the first time, to his knowledge, had been removed from the sanctuary. The doctor suggested that while the patient needed plenty of rest, it might be well for him to move about more. He even recommended that Avram be helped to the top flat roof so that he could benefit from the sun's rays to a limited extent.

Terach and Emtelai assisted their son in his climb up the steps though he protested that he was able to walk unaided. When comfortably installed on a soft divan under an awning that shaded the sun, a pattering of small feet announced little Sarai who exclaimed breathlessly that the man from the ship came again and asked about her Avram. Emtelai went down to invite Eleazer to the roof but informed him that her boy, while much improved, had become depressed a little while ago upon learning about his beloved Zirru. She warned the stranger that her moody son might have little to say.

Avram returned the visitor's greeting absentmindedly, while Terach carried on the conversation.

"Are you leaving soon?"

"My ship will sail in several days, perhaps a week, depending on the wind. But I will not return to Etzion Geber."

"Will you remain here?"

"I am planning a project that might take me to India."

"To India? That sounds interesting, even exciting. You have aroused my curiosity. Are you in a position to tell me what it is all about?"

"Why not, dear sir? On the waterfront I became acquainted with some of the Indian seamen who invited me on their ship. We spoke about different lands and I learned a bit about India. They come from the seaport Cochin on the Malabar coast, as they call it. The pepper plant grows there profusely and is very cheap. In Ur, pepper is in great demand and very dear. My objective is to buy pepper cheaply in India and sell it here at the market price."

"That sounds very interesting," remarked Terach, his curiosity and cupidity aroused. He had a strong acquisitive instinct and was ever ready to increase his substance. "But, I suppose you have many hurdles to overcome before you attain your goal?"

"Yes, dear sir, many, too many. Sometimes I think the difficulties are too great to surmount," confessed Eleazer disconsolately.

"I can name a few myself. Where will you get a ship? What will you use as export cargo in the empty boat going to India?" questioned Terach, his interest mounting.

"Here is my plan, complete," explained Eleazer. "The Indian captain told me that his rajah would consent to supply a ship, crew, and food for half the profits. The population of India is large and food for all the people is a great problem. They need what you have here in excess, such as grain, barley, and corn. These products would fill the outgoing vessel and pay for a return cargo of pepper and other such necessities as can be used here. Do you know they have a winged feathered bird that cannot fly? It is delicate food. The female hen, as they call it, can lay an egg every other day. This egg can produce another fowl or it can be eaten. This fowl can live and fatten on your corn and multiply without limit. Do you realize what this fowl could mean to Ur and the entire land of Shinar between the two rivers?"

"All this sounds reasonable enough, my young friend," observed Terach. "But how far have you gotten with your project? What's holding you up?"

"My plan is complete," replied Eleazer. "But I need the people to venture it, men who can furnish the products to launch it."

"Have you anyone who would start this venture so that others would be encouraged to follow his lead?"

"You, sir, are the only native I know in Ur."

Little Sarai came pattering up the steps again and called, "Father, someone in the workshop wishes to talk to you."

Terach excused himself, but before going told Eleazer that the project met with his approval; that he would think it over and see what could be done. Perhaps something might come out of it.

Emtelai declared that the person waiting to see him had no business of any importance. She sent Sarai to get her husband off the roof so he would leave the youths to themselves. Avram needed at this time the friendship and understanding of a companion, someone of his own generation to talk with and receive consolation.

"Emtelai, I also want to talk to you. I believe Eleazer is unusually capable and should be helpful to us and to Avram especially. That young man has the particular kind of capacity, merchant ability, they call it on the Temenos, that our son, I am afraid, hasn't got. This fellow plans a commercial enterprise in all its details while Avram is finding fault with the gods. His ship will sail shortly, perhaps in a week, but he does not intend to go back to Canaan. I think we should invite him to stay in our home. At this time, in particular, his influence over our son will be very wholesome, I am sure. Before he leaves you must invite him."

When Terach left the roof Avram said to Eleazer, "Why is it you don't want to go back to your own country?"

"It's a long story and telling it might weary you."

"No, it won't. I am certain it will interest me very much. Please do," urged Avram, and listened intently.

The uncle of Eleazer was a priest in the Temple of Baal at Aram Dameshek, known in history as Damascus. His father served as a functionary in the temple and was useful in various capacities. Eleazer never knew his mother who was possibly a *kadashe* in the same temple. He attended the temple school and was a good student until about fifteen, when the Hittites raided the city and captured much booty, including men, women, and girls who could be sold into slavery.

The people were taken by surprise. Those who resisted were slain immediately. Eleazer assumed that his father was among the dead. He himself was taken captive by a Hittite soldier. His lot was not too bad. There was little to do beyond accompanying his captor and taking him back to the camp when drunk. The Hittite proved to be an inveterate gambler and soon lost, in dice, most of his booty. In desperation he frequented a house patronized by well-to-do adventurers who made their living in games of chance. A group surrounded the table watching the pot as the bets multiplied until they became a sizeable sum. The winner, anxious to scoop in a big pot, raised his bet to 50 shekels of silver. So large an amount scared off every one of the players. The Hittite soldier saw his opportunity to recover all his losses and a tidy sum besides. He accepted the challenge and sang out he would cover the 50 shekels. At the throw of the dice he lost and had no silver to pay his bet. The military police were about to incarcerate him as a defaulting debtor when a Phoenician, residing in Tyre, offered to give him 50 shekels for the young slave. The deal was consummated and Eleazer changed masters at the twinkle of an eye.

The Phoenician, a crafty, unscrupulous speculator who followed armies with the intention of buying plunder and captives, brought Eleazer along with his other slaves to Tyre, a small city which showed great promise of becoming a rising mercantile power. Wherever he went Eleazer accompanied him as guard, servant, or attendant. In Tyre the speculator became love-smitten for the young wife of a trader who was absent at sea. The woman, whom her husband had purchased in Gaul, was fair-skinned, had corn-colored hair, and eyes the shade of a cloudless sky during sunshine. Among the brunette women of Tyre, she was considered an exceptional beauty and much sought after by the lust-bitten young blades. The speculator visited the blond who found him quite detestable. In order to get rid of him she agreed to let him into her bedchamber in return for the young slave he brought along. He remained all afternoon in her bedroom and Eleazer found that he now had a mistress over him instead of a master. He did various chores about the house with the other slaves and did not think that the blue-eyed, corn-haired beauty paid the slightest attention to him when one night he received an order from an old slave woman to come to the mistress's bedchamber. While he hesitated the slave came with a whip and said her orders were to lash him if he delayed any longer. He had hardly fallen asleep when a key opened the door and in walked the trader who had just come from the ship which had docked about midnight. Instead of punishing his unfaithful wife, he seized the whip, scourged Eleazer, and sold him the next day on the slave market.

The buyer was another Phoenician, a merchant of Sidon, on his way to the annual fair at Knossos, the capital of the great sea power in Crete. All manner of merchandise, farm products, artifacts, and slaves were on display. It was a known fact that pirates brought to sell their captured prizes of varied articles including human cargo and could easily compete with all merchants and even the Cretan government which traded its own manufactured items. The Phoenician took Eleazer wherever he went either as a bodyguard or to display his riches.

Eleazer could then see the marvel of Knossos at its peak of prosperity. The white palace, perhaps the greatest single building in the world, covered more than five acres and was said to have a thousand rooms through which no one could ever find his way out. Called on the street the Labyrinth, it was said to contain a monster, half bull and half man, whose chief delicacy was young maidens. Sophistication in Knossos was best revealed by its women who dressed in gaily figured gowns, ruffled and slit in front, ornamental helmet-like headgear, high stiff collars yet the breasts fully exposed. The climactic event that capped the week of chaffering, bargaining, pleasure, and debauchery was the perilous combat between a huge bull and acrobatic youths together with dancing girls. A young man, scarcely more than a boy, stood in the arena. The bull rushed over to him, He lowered his head about to gore the boy, who grabbed the horns and held tight. The bull's head jerked up and tossed him backward. In a split second the boy let go and deftly landed on the bull's back with feet foremost. Then he nimbly jumped to the ground. A deafening cheer went up from the applauding spectators. The next round was between the bull and a young girl. This time the dancer slid off the back on the opposite side. Her friends were not there to catch her. She fell and the bull's hind leg trampled on her. She died that afternoon.

The merchant of Sidon stayed with his retinue of slaves in the largest hostelry of the city, not far from the great palace. During the busy week the inn was crowded with strangers, travelers, merchants, questionable characters, gamblers, and painted, over-dressed women. Eleazer having few duties would wander off on the main street not too far away or remain near the tavern watching the stream of passing faces. A well-spoken man with the flashy clothes of a Cretan and familiar with several languages often spoke in a friendly manner to Eleazer and even invited him into the tavern for a goblet of wine, but the innkeeper would not permit anyone in slave dress to mingle with the free men. The stranger would talk about different cities he had visited and was quite cordial. Smoothly he ferreted out of Eleazer the name and occupation of his master and learned that he owned his own ship. He soon knew the ship by sight and its destination to the Philistine port of Askelon where the cargo of goods and slaves would bring better prices than in highly competitive Knossos.

After the hectic week the guests began to leave. Each day fewer and fewer people milled about the inn. One day Eleazer was scurrying about hither and thither, preparing to leave. While rushing by the well-spoken Cretan stopped him and asked, "Why so busy? Getting ready to leave?" Eleazer replied, "Yes, sir, we pull out tomorrow if the wind is favorable." The Cretan said, "Good luck to you. I believe you will need it." In his haste, Eleazer did not stop to inquire the meaning of the last words.

The next day promised to be ideal for sailing and the ship captains competed with each other to be among the first to leave the crowded harbor of Knossos. It took skill to steer the boats, especially around the large naval fleet stationed by the Knossos rulers to maintain order among the varied domestic of foreign craft and be on the alert for sea robbers. The Phoenician ship managed to get through and since the eastern breezes blew briskly enough to billow the lone rectangular sail, the galley slaves were relieved of the back-breaking toil of plying the oars.

The boat sailed steadily for two days and continued until darkness set in on the second evening. Following the north star, the captain noticed another boat gaining steadily, shortening the distance between the two crafts. By midnight the pursuing ship sailed alongside, grappled the hull, and its seamen expertly boarded the deck. They quickly overpowered all opposition by killing the armed guards. A burly, scar-faced sailor mounted the poop and ordered the entire crew to assemble by torchlight. Next to him stood the flashy dressed Cretan who had spoken to Eleazer at Knossos. He told everyone to continue their work as if nothing happened if they valued their lives.

The next day both ships docked in the Philistine port of Askelon on the coast of Canaan.

The Cretan pirate, suave and unctuous, understood navigation, merchandise, and the value of slaves, but above all he knew how to deal with the royal or priestly rulers of petty city kingdoms. He invited Achimelech, king of Askelon, and his court to be guests on the captured vessel. A sumptuous repast would be prepared on its deck. The king accepted and came with a chosen number of men whom he wanted to favor, but did not neglect to bring along a cordon of troops which were stationed partly on board and the rest on the dock. The Cretan knew he was running the danger of arrest but he also knew that Achimelech was not averse to getting a share of the captured booty. As for the danger of protest from Erbaal, king of Sidon, who had a right to be incensed over the capture of his subject's ship, the pirate had heard that the neighboring king was guilty of similar practices. Besides, he was on bad terms with Achimelech. In fact, most of the cities on the sea or on trade routes had rulers who kept their tiny kingdoms alive by barter and trade. It was an open secret that such kings were not above being in league with pirates who helped to bolster their shaky economy.

At the table sat a Canaanite who told the Cretan pirate sitting next to King Achimelech that he was in charge of a large caravan which took long journeys; that he was in need of a slave who could read, write, and keep accounts of the different travelers, paying for the protection, water, and provisions he furnished. Looking at the king, who nodded, the Cretan surmised that Achimelech was interested in the caravan either as owner or partner.

"I have the ideal man for you," declared the pirate. He is quite young, but intelligent, well mannered and from

Aram Dameshek. You will do me a great honor if you accept him as my personal gift."

"That's kind of you, but I would like to look at him first," asserted the cautious Canaanite who had evidently never heard the maxim of the wise that one does not count the teeth of a gift horse. Of course, he knew that the present was for the king and not to him. The Cretan signalled to a seaman and commanded, "Find Eleazer and send him to me."

When the Damascene appeared the Canaanite asked his age, birthplace, and when he ascertained he had studied in the temple of Baal he said to the Cretan, "I accept him with many thanks."

The Cretan now knew that the king was his man. He informed the Canaanite that he could take Eleazer along after the repast was over and could sign the legal document the next day.

For four years Eleazer worked hard on the caravan. He experienced every kind of labor from feeding the camels to purchasing supplies. It was his responsibility to watch closely the dwindling supply of food and water towards the end of a journey. He had to know in what town or farm it was better and less expensive to buy grain, corn, barley, fresh, or dried fruit. Also which cities offered the best values in tents, garments, sandals, and weapons for ready use or resale, what articles were in demand in distant places and which could be purchased because the market was glutted. Prices varied as to time, place, or special circumstances.

The caravan visited far and near from Carchemish, the Hittite outpost, down to Memphis, the royal Egyptian city surrounded by temples and pyramids. A number of times it passed through the Philistine cities adjusting themselves to the Bronze Age. The caravans avoided Phoenicia, which land did not look with favor upon traders competing with her own acute and expert merchants of Tyre, Sidon and Byblos. Passing through Sodom and Gomorrah the Damascene found these degenerate places too scandalous and loathsome even for the loose morals that were rife in Canaan. Jericho, the high-walled city in the low plains near the Salt Sea, was already ancient with its palm and date trees. In Salem on a mountain he found that its priest-king worshipped the Most High God in a shrine. The caravan had need for a strong detachment of armed guards furnished by King Achimelech to ward off the attacks of robbers and especially the Habiru, those fierce and hungry nomads who had forsaken the sun-drenched deserts of Arabia to find food in a more fruitful land.

These and many other places were interesting enough but after four years Eleazer grew weary of seeing new and different sights. In addition, being a slave was by no means pleasing even if he could not complain of harsh treatment. He had done every kind of work and was more competent to direct caravans than the Canaanite manager representing the king of Askelon. Stopping at Etzion Geber, the port on the Reed Sea, the manager decided to rest for several days before taking on more supplies and water.

The next day Eleazer went bathing at Elath on the Sea of Reeds; then he stood watching a long, flat, Egyptian boat with a long rectangular sail. He was moved to ask why they were loading large, flat-hewn rock.

"We are sailing for Ur of the Chaldees," said a seaman who turned out to be the captain. "You will ask what everyone else does, why of all things are we loading stone? Well, the land of Shinar between the two rivers has no rock. They will buy all we bring."

Looking closely at Eleazer, he remarked, "You look like

you would like to sail the sea." Hearing no answer he went on: "If you can read, write, and keep accounts, we can use you." Lowering his voice he continued, "If you decide, come when you can, day or night. We expect to pull out early tomorrow if the wind keeps brisk."

The captain evidently had had experience in luring dissatisfied men onto his ship. He could work them without pay.

In the third watch that very night, Eleazer slipped on board and sailed away at sunrise.

## II

The troubles that visited the family led Terach to fear that in some way his household had incensed the anger of the *shaidim;* it couldn't be the wrath of the gods, for the sacrifices and offerings he brought so steadily to the temple were sufficient to mollify them. Yet with the recovery of Avram he was getting over his apprehension, and the fact that Zirru had been chosen bride of Nannar was evidence of the favor rather than the anger of the gods. Still, Avram's dream was disconcerting. Was it possible that El Elyon had begun to revenge himself for his and his father Nahor's defection? Both he and Nahor had believed that El Elyon was powerful in the desert but hardly in Chaldea which had a pantheon of the most powerful gods of any land or people. He felt it necessary to consult Sabbattu about this disturbing matter.

The project of Eleazer, now his house guest, would also be a topic of discussion with the high priest. Terach saw great possibilities in a steady export-import trade with India. He would like to be in the enterprise but it was beyond his means. It could be launched by a group but he did not have such connections. Sabbattu was the proper person with the influence to form such a combination. In fact, he commanded the resources to handle it either for himself or for the temple. Terach hoped to benefit in some way by bringing it to the priest's attention; he might become a partner or possibly obtain a position for Avram. Eleazer would certainly go along and might somehow get Avram in. Such a trip would benefit him greatly. It might even make a merchant out of him, something his father desired to see most ardently. Incidently, it might be well to discuss his son with the high priest, who could in his wisdom find some way to divert him from El Elyon and bind him more firmly to the gods of Sumer.

After waiting for quite a while, Terach was finally admitted into the presence of Sabbattu who immediately inquired after Avram. The image-maker thanked him profusely for his kindness in sending the doctor, the priest, and the exorciser, all of whom brought a quick healing to his stricken son. Then he went into the trade project. The high priest said that trading with India was not a new thing. For centuries there had been considerable importing and exporting between the Sumerians, or even the Elamites, and the Indians but it was interrupted by the disturbances resulting from the invasions of the white barbarians. The proposition had merit and could, no doubt, be profitable but the stringency of farm products throughout the land between the two rivers was becoming desperate. He went on to say, "The drought is simply destroying the countryside. Canals are drying up and cattle are being slaughtered because water is lacking. The shortage of grain will, the gods forbid, bring on a famine. Thus it would be highly impractical to send out a shipload of grain, oats, corn, or barley when many people will soon be reduced to starvation. May the gods be merciful and prevent this. In fact, I took up the matter with the high priest of Babylon when he visited recently to worship in our temple. I asked him to enlist the aid of King Hamurabi. In fact, I am thinking of sending a messenger to urge his help. I will, however, give your proposal about exporting and importing to India full consideration."

"One more matter, if I may take up Adoni's valuable time. I am concerned about my son's attitude towards the gods." Terach told of the dream and its effect upon his son. As a father he would want Avram to have the proper adoration for the gods and feel towards them as a good Chaldean should. He feared that this critical attitude was not healthy for the family and might make the gods angry.

"When your son is completely healed, why not let him come back to the advanced class for the priests. I will ask Khar-Sak to set aside a time for a private talk. I may be present, if not engaged."

Several days later Avram came back to the class and Khar-Sak welcomed him, hoped he would meet with no further misfortune, and then addressed the students:

"Strangers, travelers, and occasionally our own countrymen criticize our institution of the temple priestess. They say these consecrated *kedashes* are no better than prostitutes because they will lie with any man who pays the sanctuary fee. Now, in your capacity as priests you will, no doubt, be challenged to explain or even defend this practice. It will, therefore, be necessary for you to understand the fundamental reason behind this institution. I, therefore, selected the incident of Irnina-Ishtar's descent to the dark underground Aralu and her emergence thereform. Will the student who has this assignment read his clay tablet."

"Irnina-Ishtar, the goddess of love, passion, birth and war, becomes deeply enamored of the youth Tammuz, called Adonis in Syria and Canaan. He goes out on a hunt and is gored to death by a wild boar. The goddess mourns, grieves, and cannot be consoled. She determines to go down deep into the earth to Aralu, the land of the dead, ruled by Ereshkigal, who hates and resents her sister. Ishtar resolves to bathe the wounds of her beloved in the waters of a spring that contains life-restoring elements. She presents herself before the gates of Aralu and is told by the keeper that she can only enter the realm of the dead completely nude.

"At the first gate her crown is removed; at the second, her earrings are taken off; at the third, the warden takes her necklace; then at each successive gate her garments, ornaments, girdle of many jewels, spangles from hands and feet are given up. She is finally left with only a loin cloth, but this she must also surrender. When she enters the land from which no one returns, Ereshkigal commands her messenger to inflict upon her the disease of the eyes, feet, heart, head, and sixty other sicknesses. Ishtar is detained by her sister, the goddess of Aralu.

"Meanwhile, life on the earth above virtually ceases. Nothing grows, no one plants. The bull does not mount the cow, the ass does not approach his mate. Men do not go near women, neither on the street nor in bed. All the ways and arts of love are forgotten. The population starts to decrease and the offerings of men to the gods shrink to the vanishing point. The gods were going hungry and they commanded Ereshkigal to release her sister. But Ishtar refuses to move unless she could take the resurrected Tammuz with her. She also insists on the return of all her ornaments and garments. As soon as she appears on earth vegetation grows, plants bloom, food becomes plentiful, animals start reproducing their kind, and love returns to the gods and to men."

Before starting his comments, the priest-teacher asked

for questions or comments. None came except from Avram.

"My question does not relate to the central theme but to a side issue. I am intrigued by the resurrection of Tammuz and his return from the lower region back to life on earth. This incident reveals the power of the gods to restore life to the dead. Is there any teaching in the wisdom of Sumer, Akkad, Assyria, or Babylon that promises a final resurrection? Or will the great heros, the good and just who dwell in Aralu, ever rise from the dead and resume their lives on earth?"

"I am not aware of such a doctrine. But the gods in their own good time may come to such a decision," answered Khar-Sak, and hearing no further comments, continued:

"Great wisdom is concentrated in this saga which is no doubt true, for a number of nations of various faiths have it in substantially the same form. One is almost tempted to say that if it did not really happen then a fable of like occurrence should have had to be invented out of sheer necessity. The importance of this adventure in the subterranean region is of great significance. It brings home to the most learned sage, as it does to a child, the great yet simple truth that the world cannot go on without passion, without the copulation of the sexes in man, in animals, and even to a degree in plants. Our religion thus teaches that passion, the central force that governs the world, is something truly divine. Passion is not merely symbolic of Irnina-Ishtar; it is divinity itself. The goddess of love, passion, birth, and war not only injects this vital force into all living creatures and plants but it is in the very nature of which she is a part. This is what our religion stands for: that there is a strong human element in the gods and that the godhead itself is part and parcel of all nature. Thus the gods are in everything and all nature is in the godhead.

"There are people, and women in particular, who are repelled when they enter the hall of Irnina in our temple and see the phallus and the vagina carved in alabaster or stone. This attitude is nothing else but a mistaken and erroneous sense of false modesty. Are we to ignore the most important thing in our lives, the power to procreate? What is there more beautiful, more vital, or more exciting than the act that creates living men and women? Our religion, I am proud to say, strips away all hypocrisy and reveals the true and the beautiful. It is liberal, tolerant, and truthful. It stresses the essential and ignores the irrelevant when we pay tribute in our temples to passion without which life disappears and the earth becomes a desert. We pay homage to the goddess of love and passion which produces motherhood. She is often carved on rock as holding a babe in her arms. She is the mother-goddess, our noblest conception.

"Thus, to sum it all up, we pay special honor to Irnina-Ishtar by glorifying love and passion in our sanctuaries. Sacrifice is a noble thing, for by this act we demonstrate our complete submission to the gods. The man is called upon to sacrifice his substance, yea even his life for divinity. Women or girls must sacrifice their most precious possession, their maidenhead, their virtue to the goddess. Those who serve the goddess, but not by force or duress, demonstrate their devotion by offering her greatest gift to mankind, love and passion, to male worshippers who come to her shrine. It is their mark of loyalty and adoration to the great glory of Irnina-Ishtar."

The priestly sage asked whether anyone had further questions or observations. The astute student from Nippur, whose mind was active and searching, observed,

"The devotion to the goddess would sound more convincing if the *kedashes* gave themselves out of devotion and not for compensation."

"This is an obvious and quite common criticism," declared Khar-Sak. "If the services of the priestesses were free to all comers, then the temple precincts would be overcrowded from early morning to midnight. The same men would come in daily to satisfy their lust. Payment keeps away the undesirables and attracts only the more worthy males. But even more important is the practical consideration of food, clothes, and other necessities for the women. Who will supply them? Obviously not the temple which is unable. Only fees can make the system work."

"Aren't these women being idealized when called priestesses?" questioned the middle-aged man who felt he had a call to serve the gods. "Do they serve the goddess or themselves? They do no physical work; they escape the cares and duties of a household; they present no problem of support for their families. Nor are they compelled to seek work for themselves. It seems to me they enter the temple to seek an easy livelihood."

"Such criticism," replied the teacher, "might be leveled against the priests of the temple, soldiers who enlist in the army, or workers of any civil, religious, or governmental institution. There are, to be sure, always some careless, lazy, unworthy individuals in any group. But an institution must be taken as a whole and not judged by its worst members. The question is whether the *kedashes* as a whole are beneficial or detrimental. I believe the system in its entirety is good rather than bad."

"It would seem," observed Avram, "that being a *kedashe* should bring about a marked degeneration in a healthy, normal, well-intentioned girl. After all, she does come into most intimate relations with some repulsive characters. Youth is marked by eagerness, enthusiasm, idealism, religious fervor, and personal friendships. If one watches the priestesses as they are being selected by lustful brutes, one cannot detect these qualities in them."

"But these same transformations take place in other occupations as well," disagreed the priest. "It takes little time to lose youth's freshness, its attractiveness, its finer attributes in facing the world or in doing menial tasks. It even takes place in marriage when the young woman is faced with raising a brood of children."

Khar-Sak dismissed the class and said to Avram, "If you have nothing to do on the forenoon of the New Year, come to this room. I would like to speak with you."

# 6

# Events Foreshadowed

THE EVENING MEAL WAS OVER AND THE SUN HAD SET. AS A rule the high priest took a short nap before going into the chapel for the night prayer to the moon god. Sabbattu tried to lie down but could not relax. Instead he walked up and down the chamber deeply engrossed, his hands clasped behind his back.

"Has the time come for action?" he ruminated. "Hammurabi is about to begin his campaign against the Lugal Rim-Sin, king of Larsa. His city may be attacked at any time. With the fall of Larsa the road will be open to Ur. Our King Ibi-Sin is in the provinces ostensibly inspecting the dried-up canals and looking for underground springs. Actually, Ibi-Sin is watching the movements of Hammurabi and collecting troops in the countryside. I feel a suppressed tension in the air. Some of the more aware people are wondering if Hammurabi is contemplating the invasion of Ur. I wonder do people suspect their high priest?

"But the public is far more concerned with the drought from which there seems to be no relief. In Ur proper the situation is not quite so bad. The warehouses have enough grain for the time being. As for drinking and cooking water, the cisterns that catch the rainfall are low but not dry. For washing and cleaning purposes people go to the Purattu River. Women wash clothes on its banks and bring water home in jars. A new business has sprung up. Owners of carts drawn by asses are peddling river water on the streets in buckets, tubs, or containers."

The high priest was a personage whom few could comprehend. He assumed a serene and reasonable air that misled the people who considered him generous, soft, yielding, and pious. In a sense, he was all these and few could suspect a hard streak in him that was capable of callow ruthlessness. Yet he was no conscious hypocrite, even when he employed guile or duplicity to cover his objectives. In truth, he had a split personality. At times he seemed to act with kindness and consideration; at other times, when governed by passion or opportunism, he could carry out a cold and calculated plan of action that might bring death and destruction to multitudes.

His most obvious vice was sensuality, which he neither tried to control nor even sought to conceal. If a woman appealed to him he simply reached out to get her, without weighing the consequences. When he saw Zirru he immediately desired and planned to have her. As it happened she was not his daughter and he was quite sure of it. But even if she were it would not have altered his determination to obtain her. He even had designs on Queen Shub-Ad and slowly schemed to possess her. Ordering Terach to carve a statue of her in alabaster formed part of his design.

As it happened Sabbattu was in a most strategic position in Ur, which was at this time in a peculiar situation politically. In theory, Ur was a feudatory of Elam, the kingdom east of the Tigris that had a century earlier subdued the southern portion of Sumer. But Elam, also on the decline, did not enforce her prerogative too strictly. Ur could throw off the suzerainty of Elam but preferred to pay a nominal tribute for her own protection. Everyone feared the evergrowing might of Hammurabi who was extending and consolidating his power over the entire Shinar territory between the two rivers.

Ibi-Sin, the nominal king of Ur, also recognized for his own safety his kinsman Rim-Sin of Larsa as the over-all protector of the Sumerian cities. It was becoming clearer every day that Rim-Sin would soon clash with the wise and ambitious conqueror, Hammurabi, who raised the city of Babylon into its preeminent position and who was considered a match even for the Pharaohs of Egypt.

In this jittery state of affairs the power and influence of Sabbattu spiraled upward. No one made the slightest attempt to mitigate his ascendency. In fact, the nervous tensions abated somewhat in the public mind with the consciousness that being of Elamite descent the high priest would as a matter of course bring pressure upon Elam to send help the moment Ur was attacked. Actually, the king himself contributed to Sabbattu's prestige by showing him a certain deference. While Ibi-Sin, like all kings, was jealous of his own royal prerogatives, he would do nothing to undermine his shaky throne by antagonizing the powerful priest.

The high priest himself had his own methods of reckoning. More clear-sighted than his colleagues or contemporaries in the city, he saw with prophetic clarity that neither Ur nor the rest of unconquered Sumer could withstand the invincible King of Babylon. Hammurabi could take over Ur whenever he saw fit. Then what was the best thing to do? Oppose him? When not swayed by passion or lust Sabbattu could act with cool detachment. Opposition meant his personal extinction. And he had little desire to join the endless dead in Aralu.

It was not difficult to open negotiations with the priests of Nannar who resided in Babylon. Communications became quite frequent and finally the high priest of Nannar's temple in Babylon came to Ur on a visit. This was nothing remarkable since it was known throughout Mesopotamia that Ur was the favorite city of Nannar, who was her special guardian. In fact, the people including the priests felt rather encouraged by this friendship which seemed a sort of tie between the two cities; it might even lead to an alliance. When the matter came up for discussion in the temple Sabbattu deprecated the possibility of strife or warfare and said, "Hammurabi is the greatest king who ever appeared in Sumer, Akkad, and all the rest of Shinar between the two rivers and even beyond. He excels Sargon of Agade in warfare, Dun'gi in wisdom, Gudia in justice, Ur-engur in patience. Most conquerors are satisfied with the mere capture of a city, a province, or even an entire land. After their death the results of their efforts dissipate and melt away. The conquered cities either go back to their former rulers or the successors quarrel among themselves and divide the territory between them. But see how different this statesman acts. Conquest is only a beginning. He spends years of patient effort in consolidating his gains. He establishes peace, brings prosperity, and promotes the general welfare of the conquered. He now is drafting a code of laws that will excel all previous codes compiled anywhere. And all this is for the benefit not only of Babylon itself but for the entire empire. See how it has become an integrated unit. One would think it had been formed centuries ago. Yet Hammurabi recently celebrated the close of the third decade of his reign. One must go back more than a thousand years to find his equal in the mighty Nimrod, the great hunter, builder, and empire maker."

"Would the adoni high priest advise that we send the keys of our city gates to the Amorite King of Babylon and declare our ancient Sumerian capital his possession and dependency?" asked the assistant high priest with obvious irony.

"I did not say that at all," answered Sabbattu, sensing the hostility wrapped up in the question. "What I am concerned with is the safety of our city and the welfare of its people. I would welcome an offensive and defensive alliance with Hammurabi that would bring us into a federation with Babylon. Such an alliance would protect us in war and insure our prosperity in peace."

"And why should this wise monarch take on the burden of protecting us without some benefit to his growing empire? He has enough cities to defend now," returned the skeptical Hunate.

"It would be only just and fair to contribute a fair share for the protection and benefits that will accrue to us," replied the high priest.

"In other words," flung out the assistant priest, "we shall pay tribute to Babylon as any other conquered or subject city."

"It is no tribute if we give it voluntarily for protection that benefits us," declared Sabbattu. "It is contributing our share in the cost of government. But it is already past the time to begin our night service. Incidentally, we must prepare for the New Year. Does anyone know the time for the *moled* of the new moon?"

The priest whose function it was to investigate the exact moment when the new moon would rise stated that the next birth should take place some time after midnight, which could be in the second watch.

## II

After the night prayer the priest went back to his room. He sat looking at the moon as it was visible from the opening high on the east wall, which served as a window and at the same time ensured full privacy. His thoughts went back to the previous discussion with the priests. On the matter of alliance with Hammurabi the group seemed by its expression and manner equally divided between himself and Hunate. The assistant high priest was obviously inimical. He, no doubt, wanted the high priesthood for himself. There's no telling how far he would go to attain his goal. In a troubled period when a drastic shake-up was possible, he might cause plenty of trouble. He might be trying to promote strife between Sumerian and Semite. To Sabbattu the assistant high priest spelled evil and was an additional reason to forge the links with Babylon so firmly that nothing could break them. Of course, the matter of alliance did not come from Hammurabi himself. The king did not as yet reply to the suggestion Sabbattu made to the priest from Babylon on his recent visit to Ur.

While thus engrossed he did not see Zirru-Keturah slip into the room. He became aware of her presence when she sat on his lap and kissed him lightly on the cheek.

"How is my *yeddidi* (beloved) this evening?" For a month the girl had been in the temple. She had learned a great deal from the older priestesses who had been giving her instructions in the art of love to a degree that her actions were losing their natural spontaneity and becoming artificial. For instance, she was instructed never to reveal strong affection for any man. She should hold back her emotions and only exploit them in a moment of climax. If she wanted something of the man, she should wait until he was sufficiently aroused before making her request. When she came into a man's chamber she might sit on his lap but give him a light, almost imperceptible kiss on his cheek. She might kiss him passionately on the mouth only when she wanted to awaken his passion.

Her conduct, bearing, and manner of speech were undergoing a change under Zur-na-na's tuition. The former princess drilled it into her to remember at all times her pride and dignity as the bride of Nannar. She must maintain her reserve with men and never permit any familiarities. With women, priestesses, and the *kedashes* in particular, she should cultivate a haughty air and make them feel far beneath her but not alienate them completely. Women are an important source of information and the *kedashes* could keep her amused with their stories about the friends and families of the men who had intercourse with them. Her inner attitude was changing with her outer bearing. Under the influence of the temple milieu she began to use the formal, pretentious language of the ritual and sacerdotal idioms. But she also picked up the argot of the temple prostitutes who heard and adopted the jargon of their lovers. Among themselves, the priestesses used the slang of the market place and waterfront, words never used and hardly understood in respectable society. Many expressions handed down from generations of *kedashes* had the effect of double talk understood by the craft exclusively.

"How is my *yeddidi* (beloved)?" she began, putting one arm about his neck. "What's bothering my lover? He seems to be distracted and in a serious mood. He will have to snap out of it." By this time she knew that he was not her real father, and that knowledge relieved her from the guilty feeling that she might be committing incest.

"Oh, in my position one has many responsibilities and

must make important decisions, which are not always easy." He put one arm about her waist then reached for a goblet of strong wine and gave her several sips as he emptied the rest. "My sweet *tinuki* (child)," he murmured in her ear, warming up as he kissed her on the mouth. She responded this time with more warmth but as he attempted to carry her to the couch she stopped him.

"No, not so fast. I have a request to make," kissing him with the art of a trained practitioner in the temple of love.

"What is it, my little witch?"

"I want to see my beloved Avram and mother Davarah."

"You cannot. It is against the law."

"But you are the law here, my old lecher. You take the place of Lord Nannar in diddling his bride."

"What you ask is impossible, so forget it, you little minx. You are rightly named a water nymph (Zirru)."

"You should know. You made a harlot out of me. And I thought you were my father, you old fornicator."

"Now, take it easy! Don't lose your temper and you will remain my sweetheart. I forgive your nasty words."

"So when will I see my mother and Avram?"

"No, that is strictly forbidden."

"Then let me go." She wrenched herself loose out of the sitting position with his arm around her waist. "You will have no difficulty in finding another nymph, you old libertine." She walked out and slammed the door.

He sat alone, disturbed and disheartened. His little Zirru now Keturah had unknowingly insinuated herself into his affections. It was painful to give her up. Yet he must not give in to her. First of all, it would give her complete domination over him. When an older man becomes infatuated with a young girl, he is at a disadvantage. He feels strong affection while she remains indifferent and perhaps resentful. She, therefore, has the advantage. She can toy with his feelings, retain her serenity, and perhaps enjoy his anguish. Yet at this time it would be particularly dangerous to let her talk with her closest connections. There is no telling what she would say. It was no secret in the temple that the high priest had the privilege of sleeping with the woman who is supposedly the god's paramour. But such gossip should not get out on the street. His prestige in the political arena would immediately be impaired, especially after Hunate and his henchmen would give the proper twist to such misrepresentations.

His regrets and anxieties were drained off with several goblets of wine. Again his thoughts turned towards the political horizon clouded by the armies of Babylon. It was probably time to take a public stand, for when Hammurabi captures the city he could ask what else did Sabbattu do other than talk secretly with some priests of Babylon. It might be practicable to advocate an alliance with Hammurabi openly and before a large gathering on the New Year festival. If Hunate insisted on talking, as he most certainly will, then he should speak first and Sabbattu last.

The birth (*moled*) of the New Year would take place after midnight. Like on all new moon festivals, the temple should be in darkness until the *moled* is announced by the trumpeteers. It might be well to end the fast by sundown and permit the New Year feast to begin throughout the city with lights on. There were precedents for such procedure if the *moled* was too far from sundown. But the temple must be kept in darkness. How would the crowd be entertained? With choral singing and instruments playing, prayers intoned by the priests with the multitude joining in, poetry read and speeches made. It would, however, be more effective if he delivered his own speech in the daytime.

Suddenly a thought lit up his brain. It would create a splendid impression if the beautiful queen, Shub-Ad, could also appear the same night. She would be announced to the great crowd as coming for the specific purpose of appealing to Nannar in his own shrine to end the drought that was afflicting the land. She would mount the long, straight steps and enter the shrine in darkness. She could offer in the very presence of the god her willingness to make any sacrifice for and in behalf of her people. Then in the dark chapel the god would tell her what sacrifice he required. Sabbattu's face glowed with exciting anticipation.

## III

The high priest sent a message asking permission to pay his respects to Queen Shub-Ad. This beautiful woman, who adopted the name of a former queen who had lived about a thousand years or more earlier, sent a gracious invitation for him to call at the noon hour of a certain day. She rose to receive him in deference to his rank and served burnt almonds, dried fruit, and a luxury recently introduced—wine with shrimps boiled in salt water. The salty tang of the shrimp produced additional fillip for the wine.

After the social amenities the queen asked the occasion for the honor of this visit. He expressed deep concern about the future of her kingdom and more especially for the immediate distress caused by the drought which was increasing daily. The priest wondered whether the gods were angry; if so, they should be immediately appeased. She asked what could be done. He really did not know but the great festival of the New Year was approaching. He thought that on the holy night the king and queen might visit the temple and enter the shrine of Lord Nannar. The god would probably be there on this important occasion. The royal couple might plead for their subjects directly. He might perhaps answer their prayers. There was nothing to lose since conditions were getting desperate.

The queen replied that she was ready to make any sacrifice for her people. The king was in the provinces raising troops, examining the canals, reviving the depressed spirits of the people, and searching for springs and underground wells. He may not arrive in time for the festival, but she herself would gladly come and lift up her voice in supplication to the gods in general or to Nannar, the guardian and protector of Ur.

The priest explained that the *moled* of the new moon would happen long after midnight. He would, therefore, make a special concession and permit the people to light up their homes and start their feasts after sundown. But the temple must be in utter darkness until the trumpets announce the arrival of the new moon. The priests would, of course, maintain their fast and continue the service throughout the intervening time. As for the royal entrance into the temple and the shrine, it would be better if it were done under the cover of darkness. There was always danger in a large multitude especially at night. Often there were strange characters around. Some might be afflicted with madness by the *shaidim*. There could possibly be spies from hostile kingdoms ready to destroy the lives of royalty. Deranged people either for notoriety or for reasons that are strange and unknown to normal people were ever ready to destroy the prominent.

IV

Two hours after sundown Queen Shub-Ad and seven of her ladies-in-waiting accompanied by ten armed guardsmen came to the gate of the temple which stood like a mountain against the black sky. A *kadosh* immediately notified Sabbattu, who hastened to greet the queen. Two *kadoshim* carrying bronze lamps walked up the brick steps, followed immediately by the high priest and the queen to his right, then came the seven ladies. The guards closed the procession. In the darkness the two lighted lamps moving up the steps were visible to those assembled on the ground and to those taking part in the ritual. Immediately the news passed by word of mouth that the queen was going to the top shrine and would appeal to Nannar for the relief and help to all her subjects. This information had a heartening effect upon the people.

The procession, on reaching the seventh step of the Ziggurat, watched the lights burning in many, but not all, of the houses in the city where the New Year's feast was being celebrated. A large concourse was on the temple grounds, some going and others coming to take their places. It was not totally dark. Although no moon was yet visible a limited light radiated from the stars which no cloud obstructed. The voices of the multitude in prayer and song created a pleasing sound of pious hope and devout expectation. The harmoney of instruments mingling with the chanting induced a comforting sense of consecration and reverence.

The high priest unlocked the door of the shrine. He took one of the lighted lamps, then dismissed the attending group. They waited at the head of the straight line of steps below the platform on which the sanctuary stood. The cordon of soldiers guarded the entrance to the steps below preventing anyone from encroaching. Sabbattu opened the door and with a bow invited the queen to enter. He followed and closed the door. The light from the lamp, which burned olive oil, displayed the chamber containing a long table filled with decanters of wine, fruit, and a large silver dish of hot roasted beef emitting an appetizing and steaming odor. The priest explained that the roast came from the sacrifice of a stag offered by the queen that very afternoon. This food was reserved for the god should he be hungry after the strenuous labors performed that day. A couch covered with white flaxen sheets partly hid the rich carvings of the wooden bedstead. A washroom smelling of frankincense contained pitchers, bowls, a large tub, and a drain of glazed terra cotta dipped in Tyrian purple. Carpets evidently woven in India with geometric designs of squares, triangles, circles, and cubes interspersed with figures of animals covered the walls.

Sabbattu suggested that the queen take off her formal official clothes and relax on the couch since there was no telling when the god would appear. He might not come at all, since he would probably visit some of his other temples. The priest left the lighted lamp on the table telling her that when she would be at her ease to knock on the door for him to remove the lamp. The chamber must be completely dark when Nannar arrives.

"Will I be left alone? Where will you be, Adoni?"

"I shall be in the other room lying on the divan. Tap on the door whenever you want me."

"Have you ever seen the Lord Nannar? I wonder how large he is."

"No, your majesty. I have not. Whenever he appears I fall into a deep slumber. But I understand that he assumes human form when he visits on earth."

The queen divested herself of her stiff garments and felt more comfortable. She knocked lightly on the door. The priest came in and removed the lamp. She lay on the bed for half an hour, a prey to nervous tension uttering such formal prayers as she knew. She heard no sound of anyone moving or any door opening when a voice declared, "My loyal follower and servant, Shub-Ad, Queen of Ur. I greet thee."

"Hail to thee, my God Nannar, Lord of the Moon and one of the hierarchy in heaven."

"Thou comest with some request? State thy wish!"

"My Lord, send us rain lest my people perish from the drought which is destroying our kingdom."

"Any other desire thou hast?"

"Yes, Lord Nannar, protect us from any invasion contemplated by the King of Babylon for the conquest of our land and cities."

"What sacrifices hast thou brought or art thou ready to make?"

"My Lord, I have this day offered a stag which is ready now for thy consumption. It lies on the table over there. As for sacrifice, I am ready to offer my body, my soul, my life unto thee."

"Art thou willing to remove thy garments, stand nude before me, and give thy body for my pleasure?"

"I am, my Lord God."

She stood nude in the darkness. A man moved about first touching her side. Apparently he was unable to see her. Then her body felt the embrace of a man, short, stocky, with a sizable paunch. It was hot and she felt the perspiration oozing from his pores, emitting an unpleasant odor. His breath virtually stank and he burped. She shuddered and suddenly a suspicion assailed her. Was the being embracing her truly the God Nannar? She thought of Sabbattu and fury seized her. Enraged she broke away and exploded imperiously, "You are not Nannar, the god. I have been duped. You are some man. I believe the high priest. Away from me, you wretch!"

The voice answered slowly and deliberately, "Thou has offended me. Thy supplications are in vain. Thou wilt suffer grievously for this insult. Thou wilt experience the wrath of a god."

She heard the door shutting. Everything was dark and silence seemed to hang over the chamber like a pall. She trembled while dressing in the dark. When fully clothed she saw a flash of fire through the vents high up in the openings in the wall for the admission of fresh air. Was it lightning? Perhaps the rains will descend. Perhaps the drought has ended. She tapped on the door but heard nothing. Opening the door and by the light of the lamp she beheld Sabbattu lying on a divan apparently fast asleep. She called to him, then touched him but he lay in deep slumber. The queen went into the washroom, dipped a towel in water, and applied it to the priest's face. Slowly he opened his eyes, yet appeared to be in a daze.

"Please don't strike me. I shall never do it again," he pleaded, then opening his eyes wider he asked, "Where am I? Who are you, woman?" Then yawned.

"Don't you know where you are and who I am?" the queen asked with the usual authority in her voice and hauteur in her manner.

"Oh, your majesty," he arose and muttered. "I must have fallen asleep. I went back to my childhood in Elam. It all seemed so real."

"Didn't you hear a voice speaking to me?"

"I heard my grandfather scolding and striking me."

"Did you see a flash of fire, as if lightning?"

"I did not, my queen. Now things are coming back to me. You, my lady, were in the other chamber awaiting the arrival of Lord Nannar. I remember nothing else. The god must have put me to sleep. Did he speak to you?"

"Yes, he did indeed. He embraced me and wanted to lie with me. I refused and the god became angry. He seemed quite wrathful," and the queen felt a cloud of uneasiness descending upon her.

"Did he agree to lift the drought or protect us in the event of war?"

"No, he did not!"

"May I advise, your majesty, that this unhappy incident be kept a closed secret. Should it reach the public, fear and panic would break out among the people with evil consequences to everyone."

The queen became silent and preceded the priest out of the shrine into the night air. On reaching her ladies in attendance, she maintained silence. No one had the courage to question her. Everyone including the soldiers followed her down the steps. Reaching the Temenos she got into her sedan chair carried by four men. Her women crowded in three chariots drawn by asses. The soldiers went in front and in back of the procession, which took on the gloom of a funeral cortege.

## V

The turnout on New Year's Day at the temple was quite large, in fact larger than usual. New Year, the most solemn festival on the Sumerian calendar, began technically with the *moled,* primarily a moon celebration. While some who attended the night service came the following day, the great majority were those coming out of respect for the festival itself and those who did not want to miss at least one meeting on the temple ground floor.

The public mind was disturbed by the drought and fear of invasion. The visit of the queen to the shrine of Nannar spread throughout the city and the silence that followed the visit did not ease the tension. The people were anxious to hear some public discussions while the news that the high priest or his assistant would speak about the state of the nation helped to swell the crowd of eager listeners.

Renate spoke first. His weltanschauung was what several milenniums later became known as racial-national. To him, of equal importance with religion, the gods, or the temple, were the Sumerian people, the oldest, greatest, noblest, bravest, wisest of all times or places. It was an evil hour that brought Akkadians, Amorites, Arameans, Kassites and others upon the holy soil of Sumer. Now the lesser breeds demanded not only equal rights but were actually pushing aside the ancient stock whom with polite condescension they termed "natives."

"There are people who advocate a close union with Babylon. Would anyone say honestly that such a union would be a free and equal partnership? Has anyone ever seen a partnership in which one was not a senior and the other a junior? Such an alliance would result only in our abasement to ultimate serfdom if not to outright slavery. Because Hammurabi has conquered the Akkadians, an inferior degenerate tribe, these alliance seekers advocate what is virtually an abject surrender to Babylon. Do people forget how the Akkadians, another horde of Semitic barbarians, treated all cities or peoples they subdued? With what savagery, cruelty, and ruthlessness Sargon subjected everyone he ruled?"

He went on to paint a detailed, grim picture of the vanquished and concluded, "They say that Hammurabi is a wise king. He must be, for he is too wise to attack us. He never has and never will. Because if he is truly wise he must know something of our history and great accomplishments. We are the greatest, oldest, most creative people in all history. Hammurabi should know that we were the first people in the world to make chariots and train asses to draw them. We were the first to use armor of bronze for our soldiers. We invented the wheel without which the wagon would never have been. Before anyone else we fashioned vessels, jewels, rings, and vases of gold and silver. We made the strongest weapons and enclosed them in sheaths of gold or lapis lazuli. Who could ever rival our seals whether of metal or precious stone? We first built the Ziggurat which the Babylonians copied in their temples and the Egyptians utilized when they set up their pyramids.

"Whatever of value Babylon may have they derived from us. They took over our pantheon of gods and changed the names into their Semitic tongue, yet retained Sumerian as the sacred language of prayer. Our Irnina became their Ishtar. Anu they transformed into Marduk and made him the ruler of all the gods. Hammurabi is drawing up a code of laws by copying the codes of our Kings Dungi, and of Ur-engur, who was the first ever to codify the laws and statutes of any people. We were the first to form a state and our King Ur-engur was the first to organize an empire. We were the first to dig canals to irrigate land, the first to develop writing with the stylus on clay. What writings of any people can compare with our poetry and literature? We first founded schools and libraries of clay tablets. We were the first to build palaces and temples, and to discover the arch, the vault, the dome, and the column. We have an old culture superior to that of any people on earth. Now I ask you, fellow Sumerians, is it dignified or fitting for us to knuckle under Hammurabi and beg him to take us under his wings?"

"Nay! Nay!" came from many throats. But an equal number shouted, "Yea! Yea!" Clearly there was division in the public opinion of Ur.

The high priest then stood on the podium. He had neither the fanatic demagoguery, the narrow articulate sweep of the spellbinder, the emotional intensity that drew strength from and imparted inspiration to the masses. His approach was rational, matter-of-fact, logical, and convincing to the intelligent. He agreed with all that Hunate had to say about the Sumerian greatness but reminded the listeners that they no longer played the dominant role of rulers or conquerors in the land of Shinar between the two rivers. The great days of the Third Dynasty were over. Ur had been conquered and was at this time paying tribute, a nominal sum of course, to Elam, under whose protection the city had prospered. But Elam itself was trembling at the prospect of invasion by Hammurabi. There was no sense in imagining that the halcyon day of the great kings Gudea, Urukagina, Lugal-zaggisi, Naram Sin were still here. The power and dominion of Ur were in the past and there was no use in shutting one's mind to an obvious fact. Like individual men, nations enjoy their periods of growth, strength, power, and expansion. Then comes age which brings decline. This is not confined to Ur. The great kingdom of Egypt, upper and lower, was overrun and conquered by Semitic tribes which more civilized nations might call barbarians. Yet today mighty Egypt is ruled by the Hyksos and not by native Pharoahs, descendant of Amon Ra, their supreme god.

"We must not act according to our emotions but by the dictates of reason. And reason points to an inescapable conclusion. It would be ruinous to engage in armed conflict with Babylon. Perhaps we should bear in mind the aims and objectives of Hammurabi. He evidently envisions a united Mesopotamia that will include Sumeria, Akkad, Amuru, Ashur, Mettanni, Shinar, Maharina. With such an empire he can spread in every direction. He can move westward and take Syria and Canaan. He can reduce the Philistines and capture the rich Phoenician trading cities. He can then conquer the remarkable island of Crete, the greatest sea power the world had ever seen. He could then invade Egypt and make it a tributary.

"Do you realize what it would mean to us to be a member of such an empire? Its trading power would be without limit. We would benefit enormously by its wealth and expand our prosperity to hitherto unknown heights. But all this is contingent upon entering this Babylonian league voluntarily. The choice is ours to make. Do we wish to become honorable members of a great empire, the greatest of all time? Or shall we be forced to carry out the mandates of a conqueror under whips and scourges?"

Pandemonium greeted these words. The din of the shouting, yelling, screaming mob made it impossible to proceed further. Clearly public sentiment was divided. It was obvious that Hammurabi had many adherents prepared to enter the impending strife. Only the presence of the temple guards, the ba'iru, the king's militia, averted bloodshed.

# 7

# Polytheism

AT THE NEW YEAR'S GATHERING IN THE TEMPLE, AVRAM and Eleazer were together. Since Avram's illness the Damascene accompanied him everywhere at Emtelai's insistence. Eleazer could not understand much of what either speaker said so his companion gave him a succinct summary of their speeches. Eleazer observed that once Ur was tied to Babylon it would become subservient, despite all assurances of the high priest. Such was the fate of the weak on becoming a satellite of the strong. When the violent dissension arose between the opposing factions the two walked away and wandered over the temple compound.

The splendor of the temple astonished Eleazer who had seen the sanctuaries of Tyre, Sidon, Carchemish, Knossos, and lesser fanes from Damascus to the large black Kaaba worshipped in Mecca and surrounded by the idols and altars of numerous gods. The most magnificent were, of course, in Egypt, yet the Temple of Nannar compared quite favorably even with imposing edifices in Memphis or Sakkara. He looked with interest at the various stone slabs covering the exterior walls of burned brick and their carved bas-relief friezes inlaid with semiprecious material portraying some of the famed kings in respectful postures before the greater gods, their battle scenes and sieges, their conquered graveling while others were being flayed alive. The walls adorned with copper entablature rested on columns and were covered with enameled or glazed tile of deep blue. The interiors were panelled in cedar, cypress, and other rare woods inlaid with agate and gold, onyx, marble, and alabaster. The statuary of gods and heroes, bulls, and animals did not have the finish or beauty of Egyptian sculpture yet were powerful figures revealing a plain and blunt vitality.

When the sun arrived directly overhead the young men knew it was noon and time to go to the classroom. They waited almost an hour before Khar-Sak came in and excused himself for being late. He had listened to the two speeches, then watched the wrought-up factions ready to tear each other into shreds. On becoming aware of Eleazer's presence he looked inquiringly at Avram. The latter explained that his friend who had probably saved his life on that fateful night was from Aram Dameshek and knew but few Sumerian words.

The teacher-priest said that adon Sabbattu would probably drop in for a while; he had taken several goblets of wine to calm his excited nerves after the hectic morning. The high priest had informed him of the dream and the strong impression it left. Perhaps a discussion might clear up certain difficulties that were troubling the young student. Avram repeated the "vision" word for word and its effect upon him.

"You use the word 'vision.' Wouldn't 'dream' be the proper term?"

"To me it was no dream. I am unable to convey the sound of that voice, which I cannot forget. Every word sank deep into my heart. They will always remain with me."

"Do you really believe that the Most High God spoke to you?"

"Absolutely."

"Strange. He gave you no instructions, nor did he command you to serve him. He would not even reveal his name. You saw neither face, nor form, nor figure. Yet you are ready to forsake your father's gods and the deities of your birthland for a voice that sounded agreeable. What makes you so certain? Have you spoken to any worshipper of the Most High God?"

Avram told of his father's revelations, of the deeply impressive stories about the flood and the orchard, of his own deductions that the El Elyon of his ancestors and the Most High God whose voice he heard were one and the same. As for being certain he went on:

"I cannot explain this change that has come over me. Something has happened to me. I firmly believe that El Elyon sends me these thoughts. He has implanted in me an everlasting faith that nothing can change or destroy. I believe in him with all my heart, my soul, my might. If I receive a message from him I will carry it out regardless of the cost. I will sacrifice my life if he orders it. Tell me, Adoni, do you deny the existence of El Elyon?"

"No, my young friend. His existence is quite possible. If there are so many gods why can't there be another one? But then you answer me a similar question. Do you deny the existence of our gods, the pantheon of Sumer, Akkad, Elam, or Babylon?"

"No, I do not deny their existence," answered Avram.

"Then would you make any sacrifice, say your life, if Lord Nannar requires it?" questioned the teacher.

"No, I would not."

"Why not?"

"Because Nannar is neither just nor merciful. I have served him faithfully in childhood. When I grew up I selected him as my guardian. Yet he did not hesitate to take Zirru from me or from her mother merely for his own pleasure. I loved her deeply and wanted to marry her. Yet Nannar disregards the pain and suffering he caused all of us including Zirru. I am sure she is unhappy and wishes to marry me instead of being a temple priestess. May I ask adoni Khar-Sak whether he ever heard of El Elyon? He is a great sage, very wise, and learned. He seems to know everything."

"Yes. As a matter of fact I have. While classifying the mass of clay tablets to form the temple library, as they call it now, I ran into some old records, very old ones, which seemed to imply that long, long, long ago all people served but one god. I seem to recall the name El Elyon but I can't remember in what connection. Then as the population multiplied and spread far and wide, different languages arose and new gods appeared. Since many new lands were settled and people set up kings, these new gods came and selected certain territories as their own regnancies. But I never could ascertain which land El Elyon chose as his habitation."

"Does that mean that you did talk to people who served the Most High God?"

At that moment Sabbattu came in. The young men rose to bow but he waved his hand for them to sit down and told the teacher to go on and disregard his presence.

"About ten years ago or longer three men came to this temple. Adon Sabbattu called me to sit in on the discourse. The men, fine types to be sure, but completely one-sided, fanatic one might call them, set out to convert us, that is the priests who were present, to their single

Most High God. They expected courteous, respectful attention from us but when Adon Sabbattu requested them to hear about our religion they refused to listen and put on horror-stricken faces. They left us as if we were trying to poison them. I believe they said their temple was somewhere in Canaan, some tiny city-kingdom ruled by a king-priest whose name I can no longer recall."

"I believe," declared Avram, "my friend Eleazer, who has traveled far and wide, has seen this place. Shall I ask him about it?"

"By all means," asserted Khar-Sak.

"Our caravan," related Eleazer in Aramaic, "was proceeding south from Dameshek to Jericho, Sodom, Hebron, down to Etzion Geber, also known as Elath, on the Red Sea. We stopped in the midday heat on a hill called Har Hazophim overlooking a most beautiful view. On the right of us a deep valley emerged to a hill they call Har Zion or some similar name I cannot recall. It was probably not too high up but from the low valley it looked like a mountain. I spoke to a peasant living in a hut nearby and he pointed to a rather small shrine made out of unhewn rock on the mountain top, without a roof, and open to the sky. Nearby stood an altar and curiously the smoke seemed to ascend straight to heaven. Of course, it might be that no wind was blowing at the time. The peasant said that nearby on the hill stood a small city named Salem, which means peace. It had no wall, no jail, no soldiers except some armed guards to protect the inhabitants from robbers. The king of Salem, Melchizedek, which means *my king is righteousness,* is a priest of the Most High God. I asked whether this god dwelt in Salem or in the shrine and the peasant answered that the heaven above was the dwelling place of El Elyon who created heaven and earth; that the Salem we were looking at was always a most holy place and always will be to the end of time. I would like to have found out more but our caravan began to move in order to reach Jericho, which is very low, and could only be traveled comfortably at night by moonlight. When the sun is shining the road to Jericho is excessively hot and a rest is necessary."

A *kadosh* walked in and reported that the Adon Hunate required the help of Adon Khar-Sak. The staff on hand was not sufficient to cope with the great numbers who, imbued with the spirit of the holiday, were ready with offerings and sacrifices. There simply were not enough priests on hand to relieve the pressure. The high priest excused the teacher and decided to carry on the discourse himself. He spoke in Aramaic for the benefit of Eleazer who evidently would as time went on wield strong influence on Avram, in whom the priest had become interested.

"You might wonder why we, who were occupied with important tasks on the most solemn festival in our calendar, take up our busy time with a single student. It is because we consider this discussion quite important. Firstly, we want to clarify the truth and banish errors and misconceptions which from time to time plague the minds of even our most brilliant students. Secondly, I consider Avram promising priest material and wish to guide him on the right path. Thirdly, we regard the issues he raised vital to our faith and want to analyze them thoroughly. Is there any special question that you have or shall I go on from where the sage, Khar-Sak, left off?"

Avram remained silent.

"Today you, no doubt, heard my assistant Hunate glow over the great achievements of the Sumerians. I agree thoroughly with his summation. Only he did not dwell upon the time it took for such creativity to develop and expand. Some of our legends maintain that Sumer is at least 241,200 years old and perhaps older. I cannot determine the antiquity of our history. I can only state that it is old, very old. It takes a long time to build up a culture. Let me tell you that the issue you raised today has been raised before. Nothing that anyone can say is really new. It has been argued, threshed out, dissected time and time again by thinkers of many generations and our best minds have come to some definite conclusions."

"Your eminence, I am not aware of raising any issue at all," objected Avram. "I came here because I was told to come."

"I know you are not aware of it. You haven't as yet thought it through. Yet what you intimated, unconsciously perhaps, is of the highest importance. It might some day become an issue of the greatest moment. It is the idea of belief in one god as against the worship of many gods."

"But I never maintained that the Most High was the only God in the world," said Avram intuitively apprehensive of antagonizing the most powerful person in Ur. He began to feel uneasy about the consequences to which this discussion might lead. After all, he was too young and not sufficiently experienced to argue with so high an authority. Besides, he had not as yet given the matter of his dream sufficient consideration. Who could have told the high priest about the vision? Was he laying a trap for him? Instinctively, he felt a distrust and could not banish some nervous twinges.

"I said you did not. So please don't interrupt unless you have a serious question to put!" The priest obviously was getting impatient but he went on. "Without being exposed to the teaching of the Salem shrine in Canaan, you nevertheless talk their language. Khar-Sak told you of the three who came to convert us. I was curious to know more so quietly I invited them to come back. I entertained them for a whole day and believe I exhausted all their knowledge of their Most High God, which is little enough. In fact, they knew nothing other than feeling a fanatical belief in Him. It might be true that they did not deny the existence of our pantheon but they never recognized nor affirmed our gods. I got the impression that they hated all the gods except their El Elyon. They said that belief in Him has existed since time immemorial. But when I challenged them to name a land or a people or a city except Salem that worships Him they were silent. There is, I believe, a good reason for the world's indifference or perhaps resentment to this religion. Just what have these followers of one god, the monotheists, to use the new term coined by the Babylon intellectuals, to offer the polytheists, another expression of the same coinage? What possible attraction could this dour, somber, repressive, gloomy creed have for the free, untrammeled, gay extroverts of our joyous polytheism?

"Now I behold a phenomenon which I frankly do not understand. A young man, born in a city with a ripe and lofty civilization, raised in the shadow of our temple, taught to venerate the gods, suddenly rejects a universal religion because of a dream. After all, you know nothing more about the Most High God other than that he dwells in the clouds, is aloof, unknowable, untouchable, removed from men and their life on earth. There is something impious and even arrogant about this ignorant appraisal of the gods worshipped by all the people in the world. This exclusive reverence for an unseeable, unapproachable abstraction of divinity is not only offensive, it breeds disgust in us and even engenders hatred.

"The differences between us might be summarized in

two words: intolerance and liberalism. We say let us know about this Most High God, the creator of heaven and earth so that we can include him in our pantheon. I would then send for your father and order him to make a statue of Him and place it in our temple among the other gods. This is a fair, just, and liberal attitude, to my way of thinking. But you won't do that; you will no doubt say, first remove and destroy all your idols and then you can worship our god who has no eyes, ears, hands, or feet. He is supernatural; he is above nature and will not mingle with common gods made of clay.

"Another thing of great importance you overlook. You are too young to understand the consequences of drawing away from the faith of your fathers. This act will cause resentment in the temple which is the center of our religious, social, and political life. From the temple it will reach out to the people in the city and they will not make fine distinctions between monotheism and the worship of many gods. Rumors will spread that you are worshipping a demon who will bring misfortune to everyone. You will find yourself isolated, with all avenues to success and advancement barred. Merchants will believe it unlucky to deal with one who has angered the gods. The odium might also attach to your family and particularly to your children, who will find themselves aliens in the birthplace of their forefathers. Have you the right to bring contumely and disgrace upon your descendants? Now reflect what this rejection of the gods implies. I am sure you have not realized it.

"I also feel quite sure that you fail to grasp the similarity between what we have and what you advocate. You don't seem to realize that Your El Elyon is virtually the same as our most high Anu, the god of heaven, who rules the hierarchy under him. All other polytheistic religions have similar systems. The Babylonians recently elevated Marduk to the highest place among the gods of Shinar between the two rivers. The same is true of Baal in Syria-Canaan and of Ammon Ra in Egypt. The Indian sage in our harbor told me that Brahma is the supreme god of the Indian pantheon. I was also informed that among a far away people called Achaeans or Hellenes or Ionians the chief deity named Zeus is the father of gods and king of men. When I asked the Salem missionaries whether El Elyon rules the entire world alone, they answered he is assisted by *malachim,* which word could be translated as messengers or angels. What are supernatural angels but gods with wings carrying out the mandates of their lord and master and are hardly to be distinguished from the lesser gods obeying the behests of Anu, Marduk, Zeus, Baal, Brahma, or Ammon Ra."

The high priest asked rhetorically whether the people of the world would be better off if they worshipped one god. This was purely hypothetical since it seemed far-fetched and highly improbable for polytheism ever to disappear or give way to the monotheistic belief. Monotheism, he argued, carried within itself the seeds of fanaticism which leads to persecution. He compared it to monogamy as against polygamy. The single wife is bound to display jealousy whereas many wives in one house learn to adjust themselves to each other and live amicably together. It is in the nature of things that a sole deity becomes jealous of his prerogatives and resents fiercely the intrusion of another god with whom to share the worship and sacrifices of his votaries. This is also true of a king who would never brook the presence of a rival to dispute his rights, his powers, or his privileged position. Thus it is in the very nature of monotheism to be intolerant, to persecute, and even to exterminate any group that might adore other gods.

"On the other hand," continued the high priest, "our polytheism is liberal, tolerant, and flexible. We do not pretend to have the whole truth about the gods. There may be others that we know not. Our temple astrologers maintain that there are numerous stars which are never seen. Every now and then they discover some unknown star or planet and bring it into their constellations. This is our attitude toward the gods. When we discover a new truth we adopt it. Thus, if we recognize merit and worth in a new god we admit him into our pantheon.

"In our way of life we practice the same open-minded tolerance. Our gods are identified with the forces of nature all about us. We see the divine in the sun and the moon that course through space by the force of energy without end. We regard them as part and parcel of the sun and moon god. The puritanical monotheists of Salem pretended to be flabbergasted on seeing the *kedashes* in our temple. They simply shut their eyes to the miracle of sex which is the greatest gift that the godhead can give to man. The procreation of a newborn babe is to us an event of the greatest joy. The pleasure it gives is certainly nothing to be ashamed of. In fact, it is the key to our mental and spiritual attitude. We are here to enjoy life to the fullest, for we know nothing of the beyond except unverified fables. Our faith just didn't come overnight, willy-nilly, without rhyme or reason. Our polytheism is the result of the life, experience, pain, joy, and thought of untold centuries, possibly millennia. What possible objections can you or anyone else raise against our true, just, liberal, and tolerant religion?"

"Your Eminence," responded Avram, "does not take into account the lack of kindness in the gods. They practice cruelty to each other on occasion and to mankind in general. The religion that permits licentiousness leads to downright sensuality. The gods are neither moral nor just.

Yet I firmly believe that El Elyon is the god of justice and righteousness. A religion lacking morality, purity, and righteousness is, to my way of thinking, worthless."

The priest drew a deep breath, then released it. This gesture might have designated patience or the intention to control his feelings. He did, however, say that this discussion could be continued but he was too occupied with many matters on this busy holiday. He then addressed Eleazer:

"Are you the young man who proposed trading our commodities for Indian pepper? Your scheme has merit but as you saw today we are in a troubled period; besides, the drought is becoming more serious daily. But when the situation clears I may use your services. Meantime I have an assignment for you both. I want to send a message to Babylon reporting fully today's discussion on the temple grounds. I can supply two asses with saddles, and requests to the temples all the way to Babylon and back, to take you in, house, and feed you while traveling. The stay in Babylon might take a little time. I will furnish you with a limited weight of silver. All this must be kept strictly confidential, although what took place today is far from a secret. Tell me within a fortnight whether you accept this mission. You may now go with the blessings of the gods."

## II

The companions walked towards the Terach stall expecting to meet members of the family who usually came to the temple on high holidays. As soon as both arrived the *kadosh* who had previously delivered the news of Zirru's selection approached Avram and stated that someone wished to see him. He followed the castrate through a corridor and stopped before a chamber. A knock at the door and a voice which sounded artificial and unfamiliar answered, "Come in." There sat Zirru, her face and hair made-up, garbed in the finery befitting the bride of Nannar, and beautiful.

The door closed and Avram stood breathless when Zirru sprang up, ran and threw her arms around him. She kissed him several times and wept softly. She then led him to the couch and sat alongside.

"Here you are at last. I disobeyed orders in sending for you. Let them punish me but I just had to see you." She kissed him again, then asked about mother Davarah, her "brother" Lot, and each member of the family, including the servants, the slaves, and the dog.

"I trust you are not unhappy here," ventured Avram not knowing what to say.

"Well, what do you think?" Her eyes welled up. "But tell me about yourself. I am dying to hear your voice."

"But first you tell me how did you know we were here?"

"I saw you in the crowd while the speeches were going on. We were behind the speakers and could see everyone. Yet I doubt whether you could see me in the center among all the priestesses."

"But that was some time this morning. How did you know where I would be?"

"In the temple everyone knows what is going on. This is a world all its own. I asked the *kadosh* to be on the alert for you. He could undergo punishment if the authorities knew that he brought you here. But he has always been very friendly. I suppose he believes that I have influence and can help him. Now go on and tell me everything that happened since I saw you last. It seems so long ago."

She listened intently to every detail of his recital. While the adventures of Eleazer were not of particular interest, she hung on to every word. It was thrilling to listen to her

Avram's voice. She smiled ironically when he related how helpful the high priest was in sending the temple doctor.

"Now you tell me everything about yourself since I saw you last," demanded Avram.

For a moment she smiled bitterly, then sat up straight, stiff, and imitated, in mock seriousness, the tone, accent, and manner of Zur-na-na. "I am the bride of Nannar and am not permitted to disclose anything said or done in this sanctuary." She winked slyly and gave him her most alluring smile. "And here you are kissing and caressing a holy priestess." Again she reverted to the formal, stilted manner of the former princess, "Are you sure that you know me? It is strange I cannot recall your name. Where did you meet me?" Unable to keep up the banter she laughed rather brittlely, then went on. "I am so happy to see you again. But let us celebrate this grand occasion with sacramental wine." She poured out of the decanter two goblets and handed him one. "To the next time we meet," was her toast.

"Would you mind if I removed this heavy stiff raiment for public occasion? It is awfully hot and uncomfortable. After all, you saw me many times in a shift." She removed the formal garment of a high-ranking priestess and stood before him in a thin, blue underdress. "I remember you once came into my room unexpectedly. I was completely nude. I so wanted you to stay and see my body, which is supposed to be perfectly proportioned, but you ran out as if I were an archer ready to let fly a shaft at you." Her laugh somehow conveyed a slightly coarse timbre.

She sat on the couch facing him, sipping the wine slowly, her head somewhat lowered, giving the impression of eyeing him archly over the goblet. He had raised his goblet to his lips during her toast and instantly laid it down on the tripod. He looked at her with too much affection to be consciously critical yet he became vaguely aware of some slight transformations. Her shift accentuated the roundness of her figure. Did she put on any weight? Slim and curvaceous as before, she somehow gave the impression of increased fleshiness. A dash of ruddiness in her clear brunette complexion betrayed a *soupçon* of sensuality, invisible yet vaguely perceptible. Her manner of speaking had undergone some slight changes even when she did not imitate scoffingly the high-falutin vocality and intonation of the princess. In her air and manner a slight hauteur seemed to indicate some growing sense of power and importance. Where these blemishes always there or were they due to her associations in the new environment?

Zirru finished the goblet and reached to take the one which Avram barely had touched. Watching him apparently in thought she asked, "Now what are you thinking about, my sweet dreamer?"

"You," he started, as if roused from sleep. "I am thinking that you drink too much. At home you scarcely touched a drop."

"Wine does wonders in relieving the boredom in this place. Incidentally, what did you talk about so long with the teacher Khar-Sak and the high priest?"

"How do you know I was with them?"

"I told you we know everything that goes on. Besides, I wanted to see you so badly that I had you shadowed. Come to think of it, our meeting here would make some juicy gossip."

"How do I get out of here? I don't know the way."

"I have someone watching, silly. The door is locked and no one can come in. You see how I think of everything. Yet you never considered me smart." She hiccoughed, then ordered, "Here, finish this drink. I believe I have had enough."

She took the emptied goblet and laid it on the tripod.

Then she stretched out on the couch with her head resting on his lap. "This would make a good story for the gossips, male or female. The bride of Nannar entertaining her sweetheart in her bedroom." She laughed in a lower key than before she entered the temple. This time her laugh jarred Avram.

"Now you did not tell me what the priests and you were talking about."

"The merits of polytheism," answered Avram with a smile.

"The merits of wha-a-at? Why do you use such long words? No one can understand them, my turtledove."

"That means the numerous gods you serve."

"I serve? How about you?"

"I worship the Most High God who spoke to me during my recent illness."

"Now, Avram, my sweet boy, you don't expect me to believe such tripe. I always thought you naive but it looks like the older you get the more foolish you become. Now forget all such nonsense and kiss me." She drew his head down to her lap and kissed him with all the force of her recently awakened passions. She continued, "I worship the goddess of love and passion, the high-breasted, hip swinging Ir-ni-na with her lustful womb."

It suddenly became apparent to Avram that a wide chasm separated Zirru from him. How was it that he never suspected it before? He felt he must point out this difference.

"The Most High God I serve wants his worshipers to be clean, pure men and chaste women."

"Oh rubbish," and she laughed in the manner that was irritating Avram more and more. "We don't hear that kind of stupidity here in the temple from anyone. Forget such imbecility, will you? You better start loving me while you have the chance. Many a man would give his right eye to be where you are, judging by the way they look at me."

Again she kissed him in the titillating fashion taught her by the love experts. She whispered in his ear. "Do you happen to know, my love boy, that I am no longer a virgin? Come take your clothes off."

"She arose and slipped off her shift. Avram also rose out of his sitting position on the couch but moved nearer the door. Zirru-Keturah stood before him, a choice morsel, irresistible in her youthful naked beauty.

"Why don't you remove your clothes? Come to my arms and I will shower you with such bliss as few men ever tasted." When she tried to embrace him she heard him say, "It is not pleasing to my God for a man to lie with a woman unless they are married to each other."

"Oh what a drivelling idiot!" she cried in anger and disgust. "Here I am offering, nay begging to give him the most thrilling pleasure that a man can ever experience and this solemn ass is hesitating. I will not keep on . . ."

"Farewell!" interrupted Avram, as he opened the door and stepped into the corridor.

She fell on the couch sobbing and when the priestess who guided Avram out of the deserted female compartment opened the door, she found Keturah lying face downward beating the pillow with closed fists.

"Now my beautiful lamb, what went wrong?"

"Everyone says I am beautiful," she sobbed, "yet here comes my beloved who wanted to marry me, gets me as hot as a lime-kiln, then leaves me. He actually refused to diddle me." Another outburst of tears. "Did he say anything?"

"Nothing. He looked sad and somewhat grim. Let me suggest that you take a dive in the pool. It will make you feel better." The priestess Tar-tu-khu picked up the blue underdress from the floor, hung it up in the clothes press and took out Keturah's bathrobe.

"Here, my gazelle. Put this on and let's go to the pool. Come!" She took the girl by the hand and drew her off the couch. Keturah swam for a while, then Tar-tu-khu began drying and rubbing her with some bath towels, starting at the head and working down gradually. She got down on her knees and while rubbing the legs she put her arms about the lower part of the body and kissed her below the thigh. Anxiously looking up to watch the effect, she saw the "bride" turn her head as if looking in the distance. Then the girl laid her hand on the priestess' head. Neither saw Zur-na-na open the door, look in, and quietly close it.

Tar-tu-khu led Keturah back to her chamber, locked the door but forgot to leave the key in the keyhole. She took off the robe and laid the girl on the couch, then began to fondle and caress her. Suddenly Tar-tu-khu let out a shriek after feeling several lashes on her nude body. She turned and saw Zur-na-na swing a green switch, exclaiming, "This will teach you not to corrupt my young charge." Tar-tu-khu grabbed her clothes and rushed out of the room.

"Now I will teach you a lesson for being unfaithful, you little whore," and she began to flog Keturah with her green switch. The girl screamed, "Please stop it. Please don't hit me. I am not unfaithful. I'm not a whore." The priestess went on lashing and seemed to enjoy the yells and screams of her charge. Her eyes glinted and a cruel smile played about her hard, set mouth. The moans and the screams of the girl seemed to stimulate the flogging until the princess's face assumed a repulsive expression of sublimated lust. She then threw aside the switch, took Keturah in her arms, which hardened into an iron vise. When her passion cooled, she appeared to relax and spoke more gently. "I am sorry this happened but I hope you will see to it that this occasion will never again recur."

The girl would not utter a word. The princess began to wonder whether she had not been too harsh. In a physical way she had become enamored of Keturah and had not the slightest intention of giving her up. Was it possible that she had to win her back again? A strongly self-centered nature hardly ever realizes what goes on in another person's mind. She took it for granted that Keturah felt a similar affection for her.

"Keturah, my darling. Do you realize how much I adore you? I could never act as I did if I did not feel an overpowering love for you. I was simply burned up with jealousy. Now tell me, sweetheart, that you forgive me and that all will be as before."

There was no answer. Suddenly a fear came over her that Keturah might tell Sabbattu of this unfortunate incident. All she had to do was to show the welts on her body and all the prestige of the princess would vanish. Uneasiness was taking possession of her when the realization came that the girl might be in pain.

"Darling, are you in pain?" No answer. "I will bring you a lotion that will give you immediate relief." She got up, dressed, and left the room. When she returned the door was locked with the key, this time plugging the keyhole. Zur-na-na knocked and knocked but received no answer.

# 8

# Babylon

THE TWO YOUNG MEN INFORMED SABBATTU OF THEIR READINESS to take up his assignment. Eleazer had investigated the best means of locomotion and decided that travel by donkey was impractical. In fact, caravans were postponing their journeys for more propitious times. The scarcity of water and the growing shortage of provender made an expedition over land most inadvisable. Investigation disclosed that boats were sailing up and down the Purattu which flowed by and even through Babylon. It would be cheaper, less dangerous, quicker, and more pleasant to take a boat to and from the great city. While it was true that Hammurabi's river boats, which carried 90 people, were no longer visiting Ur, smaller craft were available. The high priest was pleased to obtain the services of so skilled a caravan operator for his important tasks.

The priest decided that written papyrus was easier to carry than clay tablets. But the travelers had to memorize the contents lest the script be lost or stolen. The Aramaic script was in code so if captured or stolen the contents would make little or no sense. The messengers had to memorize the script and repeat the scrolls by rote, without understanding their meaning. The priest furnished silver for expenses and gave them letters to the temples of Nannar to grant them food, rest, and assistance in whatever city they visited, including Babylon itself.

The boat moved slowly. At times no wind billowed the sails and the seamen had to use their oars to glide up the Puratttu River. This was not too difficult for the strong tide flowed down the river only in the spring. The slow progress enabled the travelers to scan the countryside. Numerous canals crisscrossed the terrain, but they were dry because of the drought. The skipper informed his passengers that normally the water in the canals irrigated the fields and one could see numerous sailboats hauling merchandise, metal, timber, stone to and from the cities, some coming from distant points. The normally busy highways treaded by asses pulling their loads were virtually deserted. Unless rain came the skipper did not know what would happen.

The boat made numerous short stops at towns and villages. The first city was Eridu, about 15 miles south of Ur. This place was revered as sacred and generally considered the oldest upon the earth. Its patron was Ea, lord of the sea and the god of wisdom, who invented handicrafts and the art of writing. In the temple, Ea was represented holding a vase from which flowed two streams of water while fish were swimming up and down in the stream. Eridu had a population of about 20,000.

About 65 miles north was Erech, mentioned in the Bible as having been ruled by Nimrod, "a mighty hunter before the Lord." Erech was very old and according to the legends of Sumer its 12 kings ruled for 2310 years after the flood. It was the birthplace of Gilgamesh, the great hero who freed his city after it was captured by Elam. While walking the streets of the ancient city, Avram recalled lines from the great Sumerian poem, *The Epic of Gilgamesh,* which was the *Iliad* and *Odyssey* of Chaldea:

> Oh Erech! dear Erech, my beautiful home
> Akkadia's pride, O bright land of the bard,
> Fair land of my birth, how thy beauty is marred
> Gone are her brave heroes beneath the red tide
> No more on the river her pennon shall ride.

Travel was a new experience for Avram who had always been interested in foreign lands and their people. His reactions were twofold. No two persons were alike, yet in the mass people were quite similar, even if dress and costumes varied the farther away he got from his birthplace. Each city had a different atmosphere. The Sumerian dialect spoken in the various places differed more or less in accent, pronunciation, street expression, or in idioms used. Yet, basically all cities were alike, at least to the superficial observer. He recalled the well-worn adage: "All the world is one city." The temples varied in size, yet mostly of the Ziggurat design but in different heights, dimensions, and number of terraces leading to the shrine at the peak.

Sitting at night in the boat under moonshine or starlight, Avram found Eleazer most interesting. He never tired listening to him of the places seen, the ways of the people, or the manners and customs of remote lands. Eleazer had observed the religious practices in various countries as a curious traveler rather than as the probing thinker searching for causes and meanings. The most impressive land was Egypt, not only because of its magnificent temples and palaces, the sphinxes and pyramids, the statuary and wall paintings but because of the high civilization attained by its people. There was widespread learning in the priesthood, a high standard of living, the manners of the nobility seeping down to the middle class. The physicians, dentists, and surgeons were the very best. The living comforts and good administration of law and government denoted a civilization that took long to develop. Yet Eleazer could not square the learning of an intelligent priesthood with the childish notions that prevailed in religion. "How can a highly cultured people, the heirs of an old civilization, worship the Cat of Bubastes, the Bull Apis, the Cow Hathor, the Crocodile Sebek, the Baboon Thoth, the Ram Ammon, the Hawk Horus? The most beautiful women are forced to have sexual intercourse with a 'divine' goat."

This led the discussion into the realm of the gods, all of which concerned Avram profoundly. What was the divine responsibility? Should the gods by their actions set the example for men to follow? Could man be expected to act higher, kinder, nobler, more generous or just, than the godhead? But the mind of Eleazer was pragmatic and utilitarian. He had never thought in terms of abstract morality. For the first time he was subjected to a theological discussion when he listened to Khar-Sak and the high priest. Like Sabbattu he could not conceive of a better world under monotheism. He heard what Avram said without that comprehension, that intuitive grasp which means real understanding. Obviously something was wrong with the world but he could not make any contribution to the problem that was stirring his companion.

At Kish, the youths got off the boat ready to see the very old city when a bearded armed guard halted them and wanted to know their destination and their reason for traveling. He returned them to the boat and told the skipper that since they were in Babylonian territory and since a state of war had been declared, he was posted to watch for spies. What did he know about these men who looked quite young to be entrusted with important messages from the high priest of Ur to the Temple of Nannar in Babylon? When the skipper assured him they were trustworthy and not spies, the guard replied that he could not take chances in wartime. The skipper must not let them out of his sight but keep them under arrest until he turned them over to the waterfront guard in Babylon. He need not keep them chained but he would be held responsible for them.

## II

As the boat approached Babylon the travelers could see the shrine at the peak of the ziggurat 650 feet above the flat earth of the city. The skipper informed them that the shrine high up contained a massive table of solid gold and a wonderfully carved bed to which a woman came every night to give pleasure to the god. This ziggurat was the tallest building in all the world and rose as a mountain of masonry in seven terraces with glazed and gleaming tile enameled of several brilliant colors. This was the "Tower of Babel" from which the early men attempted to storm the heavens. Eleazer looked up with astonishment and admiration. "This surpasses anything in Egypt. The tallest pyramid looks small alongside of this temple. There is nothing like this anywhere."

The skipper pointed to the magnificent double portal covered with tile of the most brilliant green, adorned with colored flowers and vital animals that actually seemed to move. "This is the Ishtar Gate at the end of the Sacred Way." The Sacred Way was wide and spacious, paved with bricks of asphalt over which were laid limestone flags and breccia consisting of various fragments of red rock cemented together. The holy avenue contained a number of temples on both sides of the wide street. In the center of the way and south of the ziggurat stood the enormous Temple of Marduk, recently made the chief god of Babylonia. From this temple spread the city proper in wide avenues spaciously laid out and crossed by canals and narrow winding streets where many bazaars served the constant flow of crowds in thoroughfares winding, narrow, and filled with garbage and people. Such was the greatest city in the world under the conqueror, builder, and lawmaker—King Hammurabi.

The young men carried their own luggage after being told by the guard who directed them that the porters were not always trustworthy in spite of the protective laws. They walked from the riverfront across a long bridge and reached the Sacred Way. The broad avenue lined with tall palms and temples on both sides was an imposing sight. Babylon did indeed differ from Ur and other cities. The clean-shaven men of Sumer wearing kilts were rarely seen. Most men wore long beards, curled, oiled, and platted. Their long garments made them appear taller than they were. Numerous soldiers walked with their armor clanging, bearing the air of conquerors. Eleazer remarked that Egypt did not have the same feeling of power in the air as was felt in Babylon.

The Temple of Nannar was not nearly as imposing as the one in Ur, which was famous throughout the land of the two rivers and even beyond. Yet it was smaller and seemed quite inconsequential alongside the gigantic Tower of Babel or the magnificent Temple of Marduk on the same avenue. But it had prestige since the moon was an integral part of the star worship strongly imbedded in the theology of Babylon. The waterfront guard turned them over to the assistant high priest called by the Semitic term, the *Sagan,* and demanded his receipt for the two prisoners. The *Sagan* listened to the youths and requested to see their papyrus script. On being informed that the Adon Sabbattu had instructed them not to deliver their written messages to anyone but the high priest in person the *Sagan* sent a message by a *kadosh,* who returned with the answer that the men be given a room in the temple compound and fed the noon meal; that he would receive them two hours after the sun passed the highest meridian.

The high priest asked whether they had any verbal messages and Avram answered that they had something written in code that was no doubt in the papyrus. He asked them to repeat what they memorized and checked the papyrus word for word in Sumerian and in Aramaic. After appearing satisfied that they were authorized messengers, he requested the *Sagan* to have the papyri decoded. He then asked whether they had anything further to say. Each gave his impression of the speeches delivered on the New Year and the popular reaction. The high priest told them to remain in the temple until the return message would be ready, that if they needed silver to pay expenses they should let him know. He then ordered the *Sagan* to put someone at their disposal for them to enjoy their stay in Babylon.

A temple *kadosh* showed them the city to much better advantage than they could have seen by themselves. He took them to the Tower of Babel and from the top terrace they got a splendid view of the city and its environs. The immensity of Babylon and the surrounding country was simply breathtaking. The *kadosh* said that the city was surrounded by a wall 56 miles in length and wide enough on top for a four-ass chariot to pass over it. The walls enclosed an area of 200 square miles. They could see the Purattu, with trees shading both sides, running through the city and spanned by a graceful bridge. The glazed tile that covered the walls of houses and buildings was enameled in blue, white, and yellow shades and adorned with animals and plants that glistened in the bright sunlight.

The *kadosh* enumerated for the benefit of the strangers all the holy places in Babylon. They were amazed to hear about the sanctuaries which seemed numberless. He could count 53 temples. There were 55 shrines to Marduk, 350 to divinities on earth, and 600 to heavenly gods like Shamash, the Sun-god. The goddess Ishtar had 108 altars devoted to her, and 108 to Nergal of the underworld and to Adal the god of divination. Even the minor gods had 12 altars. Altogether in Babylon there were 1080 sanctuaries. He reminded them that these fanes were set up to the gods worshipped in the whole empire.

It was a festival day and in the charge of a *kadosh*, the two Urites were admitted into the royal grounds in time to see King Hammurabi and his queen leaving for the Temple of Ishtar. The royal couple, clad in gorgeous raiment, accompanied by courtiers, priests, patesis from conquered cities, and high military officers, were passing through the "gates of the yellow lions," another name for the celebrated gateway of the fertility goddess. The enclosed grounds about the palace were covered with green foliage, bright-colored flowers, trees and exotic plants, all watered by the Purattu River. On leaving the royal precincts they strolled on the Sacred Way, then along the broad avenues that separated the city into squares and rectangles. They beheld numbers of worshippers, mostly women, carrying gifts, birds, images to the Temple of Ishtar. Then followed a procession of priests attended by singing males and females, accompanied by the music of cymbals, trumpets, and tambourines.

From the broad avenues the three turned into the narrow, unpaved lanes, which contrasted sharply with the wide highways. Here traders from foreign lands mingling with native hucksters were bargaining, chaffering, arguing, some shouting, others gesticulating. On one of the better narrow streets under awnings they saw the famed excellent cloth made in Babylon. On display were pottery, jewels, articles of brass and leather, silver-banded sandals, weapons, in fact almost everything that the best artisans in the world could make. They stopped to buy a drink called beer fermented from barley, and also tried the wine from the palm. In one lane all varieties of foods including fish, vegetables, fruits, cheeses were hawked and traded. Crowds were staring at the fortune-tellers sitting in booths, their heads covered with peaked hoods and garbed in black with white figures of the moon and stars sewed thereon.

Tired out by the heat, the smells, the noise, and dust, the sight-seers stood on the bridge spanning the Purattu and got relief from the breezes wafted by the water. Eleazer looked with interest at each bale of merchandise, bound and sealed with bills impressed by the stylus on clay tablets tied to each package. These bales were carried to the huge warehouses along the river waiting their turn to be delivered to boats or caravans bound for Aram Dameshek, Phoenicia, Canaan, the Hittite country and Egypt to the west, and Elam or the Persian plateau on the east. Hungry and weary they trudged their way to the temple and came in time for the evening meal.

The temple had numerous attendants and the big dining hall adjoined the kitchen in which large stoves out of clay bricks, that became harder after each fire, cooked the food. The meals were served in three categories. The top echelon of priests, astrologers, diviners of the future, and important visitors ate first. In the next shift were the *kadoshim,* students, guards who protected the treasures and maintained order, chanters of the divine service, the exorcists of demons out of the sick, musicians and travelers. The last class to receive food were the petty officials, brewers, makers of bread and ceremonial cakes, confectioners, cooks, servants, and slaves attached to the temple.

The hungry feeders stood in line each holding a clay plate with a wooden spoon. The cook ladled into each plate hot barley soup in which swam pieces of beef. This was an unusual luxury due to the holiday. The offerings and sacrifices were quite generous and meat spoiled quickly in the hot climate. The priest in charge sent the oversupply to the kitchen rather than to the garbage pails. Thus when Avram and Eleazer were going to the dining hall in answer to the bronze gong, the priests were coming out. On seeing both travelers the *Sagan* stopped and asked whether they would care to attend the king's feast on the coming day of the sun in the royal palace among the high priests' retinue.

"This would be a high honor as well as a great pleasure," beamed Avram, "but we haven't the proper garment for the king's palace."

"I believe it could be managed," declared the *Sagan*. Just at that moment the chief tailor passed and the priest asked if he could fit the young gentlemen with suitable clothes for the occasion. The tailor answered in the affirmative and both strangers were thrilled at the prospect.

## III

The next morning the *kadosh* informed his two charges that he would take them to a place where they would find great enjoyment. In one of the courts of Ishtar's temple, he explained, it was the custom, long sanctioned by use, for every native woman once in her lifetime to have intercourse with some stranger. Once she seated herself in the temple court wearing a crown of cord around her head, she must follow the man who dropped a piece of silver in her lap. She became obliged to lie with him and thus discharged her obligation to the goddess.

"Are men obligated to have intercourse with these women?" asked Avram, who immediately felt antagonistic to this practice.

"He is under no compulsion," answered the castrate. "But Ishtar is pleased when he does."

"Is everyone admitted regardless of who he is?" queried Eleazer.

"Not everyone. He must pass the inspection of the overseeing priestess and has to be properly vouched for."

"Who is vouching for us?" questioned Avram.

"I am," replied the *kadosh*.

Avram's first impulse was to let Eleazer go alone, but on reflection decided to see for himself the wickedness prevalent in the greatest city in the world. It was necessary to witness further indications of the basic immorality inherent in the gods.

They passed through the splendid gate of Ishtar with its beautifully enameled tile and entered the temple complex. A crowd of men gathered outside the sanctuary wall evidently unable to gain admittance. The old priestess scanned the two youths, looked at the *kadosh* whom she obviously knew, and nodded. The guard opened the gate for their admission.

The courtyard was filled with women sitting on the grass or on the cushions or rugs they brought along. Trees or curtains shielded them from the scorching sun. The roped-off lanes leading in all directions enabled any man to go through the yard and pick out the woman that appealed to him. Theoretically it was a democratic system in which all the women had equal status and equal chance of being selected. Actually, stratification prevailed. The rich or powerful or prominent came in covered wagons and monopolized certain favored spots that rendered them virtually inaccessible to the inquisitive male who came to select either beauty or rank or nobility. The choice corners enabled the votary to remain concealed in the midst of numerous retainers or servants. If a plebian insisted on his right to inspect the female aristocrat, he saw the apparently humble servants transformed into armed guards uncovering daggers that threatened reprisals after the "ritual" would be consummated.

"What happens if a woman is not selected?" questioned Avram.

"She comes back and waits patiently until she is chosen."

"How long is she required to wait?"

"Some of the repulsives or deformed are known to have come back for a period of four years. But why don't both of you go through the lanes and inspect them at close range."

Avram went through the lanes and saw all manner of women, from young girls to the middle aged, some pretty, some ugly, dark or light, tall and short, slim or obese. He stopped near a short deformed female in her late thirties. Her features were sharp and her face lined. Clearly life had rejected her time and again. Her expression was both pathetic and resentful. The milk of human kindness had long dried up in her. Sensitivity had given way to a kind of fanatic religiosity which sustained her conflict with life. After a moment's hesitation Avram dropped a silver piece in her lap.

Her face registered surprise. A faint smile spread over her features which seemed to imply: So you see, someone finds me attractive. A woman might know that she is not pretty yet finds some consolation in the thought that she is not so ugly either. No woman however homely feels that she is not completely without attractions. Avram's act of charity helped for a moment to bring assurance, if not confidence, to her blighted existence. When she got up and looked around she could see the derisive smiles and hear the jeering laughs of the sitting women whispering loudly enough for many to hear. "Well, you never can tell. No accounting for tastes. He must be very hard up. No one should ever despair."

The hunchback followed by Avram moved through the lane to a gate in the wall which was opened by a priestess. She knew the name without asking, took the silver offering, then marked something on a clay tablet with a stylus, and gave the deformed woman a small square seal stamped "The Gate of Ishtar." The two, now outside of the temple compound, walked a short distance to a house of burnt brick with many cubicles inside. A rather youngish priestess at the door took the seal and pointed to a numbered room several paces away.

The woman brushed aside the reed curtain over the doorway, walked in, and began to take her dress off. Avram remained standing in the corridor and heard her ask, "Why aren't you coming in so I can close this curtain?"

"Don't bother to remove your clothes," he stated. "I am leaving."

"Leaving?" and her happy expression froze into the glowering frown. "Won't you enjoy what you paid for?"

"My enjoyment is the thought of your release from sitting and waiting . . ."

"So that's your game," she interrupted scowling. "Making sport of my deformity; telling your friends how you outwitted a poor wretched creature so they could laugh with you."

Looking miserable and feeling guilty he managed to stammer, "I thought you would be happy to end the nightmare of hearing those malicious remarks of the women about you."

"You feel quite virtuous, you son of a donkey."

The priestess walked up and asked whether anything was wrong.

"Yes. Plenty is wrong. He refuses to lie with me. This eunuch gets his pleasure in making a woman miserable."

"Well," laughed the callow priestess, "no one can blame him for not going to bed with you. But why should that bother you? He has liberated you and now you are free to do as you like and go your own way."

"But I am not free. I have not discharged my obligations to my goddess."

"Don't worry about the Lady Ishtar," counseled the priestess. "I assure you she is not bothering about you. My record shows that you are discharged. So run along and count yourself fortunate."

The poor deformed creature went away scowling. Avram was about to go when the priestess held his arm.

"What's your hurry, handsome? Stay and talk to me," urged the priestess. "When you get older you will learn that people resent those that help them. Come into this room and I will show you a nice time."

She tried to embrace him but Avram drew away and said politely that he had to go to friends who were waiting for him.

Unable to get back into the yard where the women were sitting, Avram waited outside the temple compound. The *kadosh* had evidently gone back to the temple. Finally Eleazer came out, gay and in a cheerful mood. Avram remained silent and both returned to the Temple of Nannar.

IV

It was evening of the day to the Sun-god when Avram and Eleazer were walking in the retinue of the high priest on their way to the royal palace for the feast given by King Hammurabi. The priest seemed pleased with the appearance of his young protégés garbed in the splendid clothes of a merchant prince's two sons who had been drowned in the Persian Gulf while on their father's ship bound for Egypt. The youths became even more nervous when their host made the observation that the king welcomed guests from other cities and sometimes was even gracious enough to ask them questions.

The party entered the great hall redolent of incense and bedecked with banners of conquered cities. On the dais sat the mighty king on a throne of gold resting on lion's claws of ivory in the midst of his favorite wives and surrounded by princes and concubines. At another table on the dais were top military commanders, *lugals* and *patesis* of conquered cities and high officials from Amuru, Akkad and Assyria. Another table held high priests of the large temples, top astrologers, master magicians, soothsayers, and wise men of the East known everywhere as Chaldeans. The king's table was fanned by ladies-in-waiting waving fly swatters made of peacock feathers.

Below on the floor of oven-baked bricks were long tables occupied by priests, wealthy merchants, public officials, and prominent out-of-town guests who could report to the folks at home the power, wealth, and magnificence of the great king. The tables were stacked with trays of nuts—ripe, baked, or salted. Slaves kept filling up the wine cups of gold, silver, or bright-hued clay which were glazed and enameled. The waiters served appetizers of heavily spiced beef with vegetables. Roasted lamb and calf meat held on skewers, and fish fresh from the Purattu cut into small pieces were served in generous portions. The rare delicacy of roasted pheasant was eaten at the king's table only. The guests handled the food with their fingers even though bronze knives and spoons lay on the tables. Forks had not yet been invented. While everyone ate with his fingers, the well-bred could display superior breeding on the agility and ceremony with which they picked gobs of meat off the plate and put them in their mouth.

The long banquet was interspersed with entertainment between courses. The music of the harp, flute, psaltery, sackbut, tambourine, and cornet soothed the excitable or roused those who were made drowsy by the strong wine. Girls with and without clothes danced about between the tables. Humorists and clowns amused the worldly while poems out of the national epics elevated the sensitive. But the high point in the annual feast was the chief astrologer's newest prediction of what he read in the stars.

Astrology, born in the Plain of Shinar among Sumerians, was taken over by the Babylonians, who thought they perfected star gazing and divination into a science. They scanned the heavens to predict the course of events since each planet was a god who could determine or forecast the future. This star gazing led to the science of astronomy and established the names of our week days. Nor did the Roman Church with all its hostility towards paganism ever change the names dedicated to the Sun-god or Moon-god or the five other gods later transformed into their Latin or Teutonic equivalents.

The king's herald announced the chief astrologer, who

rose, walked over to the royal table, bowed low, and exclaimed, "Oh king, live forever! The stars have their message in the skies but its meaning is not easy for us poor mortals to decipher. As far as our college can determine, the message of the stars is, *Ke m'ur hakevusha yetzai hamevaser shehimlich El Elyon leolmai ad b'urushalem.*"

"Now, what does that mean, adon astrologer?" demanded Hammurabi.

"Your sublime majesty, as far as we can ascertain, the meaning is, Out of thy conquered Ur shall come he who will proclaim El Elyon the Eternal in the City of Peace."

"Will you repeat the original message?" ordered the king.

*"Ke m'ur hakevusha yetzai hamevaser shehimlich El Elyon leolmai ad b'urushalem."*

"What have you to say, my priests, soothsayers, or Chaldean men of wisdom?" inquired the king.

Each group stood up and their spokesman responded separately but with the same meaning: "We would beg to be excused so we can consult with each other." The king dismissed them and the entertainment went on. In less than an hour, all had returned. The high priest of Marduk's temple declared, "Oh divine majesty, when thou shalt conquer Ur there will be peace in the world. Then, thou, oh king, wilt proclaim Lord Marduk the ruler of the universe."

The chief of the soothsayers ventured with less confidence. "Babylon, oh king, is and will always be in the hereafter the city of peace. After thou shalt conquer Ur, thou wilt become El Elyon and reign eternally in the heavens above."

The chief Chaldean informed the king that his group could not add anything to what the wise men have already said. King Hammurabi appeared not satisfied. He thought for a while, then instructed the herald to ask whether anyone of the guests could explain the message of the stars. There was silence and finally Avram rose and said to the herald, "I believe I have the answer." The herald looked at the king, then said, "Come up on the dais." Bowing low as he saw the others do, Avram addressed the king:

"Your most gracious majesty, Uru-Salem is a city in Canaan which has a shrine and altar to El Elyon. Its king, Melchizedek, is the priest of the Most High God."

"Have you seen it?" questioned the king.

"No, your majesty, but my companion sitting over there has seen it."

"Why is one so young as you interested in such matters?" asked Hammurabi.

"Because, oh king, the Most High God has spoken to me."

The conqueror and empire builder who drafted the great code of laws looked sharply at the youth, then asked, "What did He say?"

"He said, oh king, that He was the god of my forefathers back in the days of old but my father knew Him no longer."

"Who is your father? Where do you come from? What is your occupation?" inquired King Hammurabi.

"My father, oh king, is the sculptor for the Temple of Nannar at Ur. I am a student at the temple and brought a message from Adon Sabbattu, the high priest of Ur, to the high priest of the Temple of Nannar in Babylon."

"Do you worship the Lord Nannar?" pursued the great lawmaker.

"Your gracious majesty, I serve El Elyon, the Most High God."

A slight frown clouded the thoughtful face of the king

when he dismissed Avram, who went to his table. The feast was breaking up and groups were forming to leave the great dining hall. Everyone was staring at Avram and the high priest seemed displeased because the king did not speak to him.

# 9

# The Return to Ur

EVERY DAY THE TWO ROAMED THE STREETS OF BABYLON, which was a constant source of interest and wonder. Eleazer was attracted by the outer manifestations of pomp and grandeur. He never became weary of gazing at the great buildings, the thriving commerce, the traffic, the great concourse of people, the clang of armored soldiery. Here was the greatest agglomeration of military power, of wealth, of orderly government he had ever seen or could even imagine. Evidently this city was greatly beloved by the gods generally and by Marduk in particular. Eleazer had heard people say that the great King Hammurabi was divine and should be worshiped with the other gods.

Was the vast city, wondered Avram, indicative of the preference which the gods displayed for its people? Was it due to more faithful worship, to greater offerings, or more choice sacrifices that Babylon rose to be the queen of cities? Avram failed to see in what respect the Amorites of Babylonia were more faithful or brought better sacrifices than the Sumerians of Ur. Ur was great and respected before there was such a place as Babylon. But Babylon was growing ever greater and more powerful while Ur, the former seat of a great empire, was declining perceptibly. Yet both served the same gods. Then why should the gods, if they were just or righteous, make a favorite of one people and deliberately disparage another just as worthy?

While absorbed in such reflections they reached the Ishtar Gate and though Avram was not especially keen about the goddess, he desired to see how Irnina, as they called her in Ur, was regarded in Babylon. He found her temple unusually magnificent and in keeping with her station in the pantheon of Babylon. She appeared second in the godhead, next only to Marduk. The first sight that greeted the visitors was the bas-relief plaque of the mother goddess holding a male child at her breast. There were scenes of domestic happiness incised on diorite, of a happy family sitting together at a meal in harmonious accord, of a bedchamber with a young husband and wife lying in a heart-to-heart embrace. Painted in gay colors on walls were dairymaids milking large cows, peasants working in fields, rural scenes of bursting green crops ripe for harvest, trees shading peaceful farmhouses, sheep covered with thick wool ready for shearing, lovers sitting by the light of the moon holding hands and eagerly awaiting their wedding day, youths and virgins dancing at a rustic feast, elders sitting in a farmyard drinking wine with their guests. All seemed quiet and peaceful enough. Removed from such domestic scenes stood a wall painting of unclad women embracing men in frenzied passion while Ishtar, the protector and guardian of harlots and prostitutes, looked on approvingly. A most striking plaque in white alabaster on a startling background of black diorite displayed a nude Ishtar embracing with passionate tenderness her young lover, the newly resurrected Tammuz near the life-giving spring in the nether regions of Aralu.

Turning to Eleazer Avram remarked, "Here they play down the goddess of war and her many cruelties and crimes to those men or beasts who for a while basked in her love. This entire conception of Ishtar is a tribute to, and a glorification of, woman. The great mother and homemaker, with her passionate nature fertilizes man, beast, and the earth. This concept is too placid or domestic for divinity. I prefer my God, El Elyon, who, standing above in heaven and beyond nature, not only created all things but directs the universe and all life therein with justice and righteousness."

Next they proceeded to the temple of the war god, Nergal. The plaques in bas-relief on stone, or the painted scenes in vivid colors, celebrated the ruthless god of terror, his blood lust for inflicting human suffering. Avram could almost hear the drunken shouts and laughter that greeted the wailing or dying victims in the seething panorama of fiery destruction. Clearly visible were the armies storming the ramparts, hurling blazing torches onto temples and cities; conquerors setting fire to buildings, houses, and even huts, hacking off the legs and arms of the defeated while flaying alive the more robust; blinding the captured kings before the eyes of their wives and children; thrusting princes and captains in boiling oil; dragging women by the hair to lead lives far worse than death in Aralu. "Is it such deities that men are taught to revere and worship?" asked Avram. After gazing at similar scenes the companions left the broad avenue for the side lanes to buy fruit and drink.

Feeling refreshed Avram noticed on the same lane a shop displaying idols, which he scanned to compare with the craftsmanship of his father. He started a conversation with the shopkeeper and told him that the sales of his father's display room would hardly support the family;

were it not for his monopoly at the Nannar temple they would have starved. The owner then explained that his chief income was derived from selling clay tablets of literary works produced by the advance guard of rising intellectuals who were making Babylon a cultured center equal to if not surpassing Memphis or Thebes in Egypt.

While waiting for Avram and looking at colored tile in another shop, the Damescene heard, "Eleazer. Here you are, and I have been waiting for you to come and see me. What are you doing here?"

He turned and saw a comely woman, brunette, with dark flashing eyes, black hair, and a figure still slim but beginning to show roundness. She was the woman he had enjoyed in Ishtar's temple.

"I am waiting for my friend," he answered, pointing toward Avram.

"Well, he is better looking than you, but I like you all the same. Now both of you come to my house. I have a girl friend I think he would like. I know she will go for him."

"Avram doesn't pay much attention to girls. He is a student and serious, a thinker, you know.

"Oh bosh. They all act the same in bed. He does not look like a eunuch to me. Oh yes, tell him I have a very important piece of news that will interest him. Call him over."

"Howdy, good-looking. Let's all go to my house. It is not too far from here. As I told Eleazer, I have something highly important to tell you."

"Tell it now," demanded Eleazer.

"No. If he is not interested enough to come with us, I just won't tell him. I don't care for these stuck-up people anyhow."

"What important matter could this woman have on her

mind?" Avram asked himself. "This is, no doubt, one of her wiles to get men into her house. Why should I go along and spend the afternoon talking nonsense when the shopkeeper who appears intelligent can tell me about the intellectual life in Babylon?"

"I am sorry, madame, but I can't go along. I was interrupted in the midst of an interesting conversation. But you can go without me, Eleazer. I shall see you in the temple for the evening meal. Farewell, madame."

"Now you have aroused my curiosity," declared Eleazer. "Tell me now, Shoshana, about this very important matter."

"So you can leave me and go back to your catamite? No. I want you this afternoon for myself. I will tell you that news when you are about to leave me. Come and don't waste time talking here if you want any loving today."

The shopkeeper pointed to clay tablets that treated of history, religion, law, poetry, medicine, astrology. Avram asked whether thinking people were questioning the justice or goodness of the gods. The owner thought it rather strange for one so young to be concerned with so baffling a topic. He took out two clay tablets and said, "Here are the complaints of one, Balta-atrura, who is quite critical of the gods. He alleges that he had never failed to carry out their wishes or obey their commands and yet he has suffered virtually every kind of misfortune from the loss of his parents to the destruction of his property. He had little enough left when highwaymen robbed him of what remained. He complained bitterly to his friends and they thought the gods punished him for his misdeeds, for insolence, for the arrogance that wealth brings. They assured him that these apparent ills were often blessings in disguise, for the gods will do no wrong. In the end he will be rewarded and his enemies punished, if he only continues to call on the gods for help."

"Was he eventually helped?" asked Avram.

"There was evidently much more to this fragment, but all I could ever assemble are these two, and the second one ends too abruptly."

"Who wrote it?" questioned Avram.

"I don't know. I had them translated from Akkadian. They seem to have been written when the great King Sargon ruled in Agade. But here is a much better poem on the same theme written by an Amorite who lives in Babylon. He comes here quite often. In fact, a group of these intellectuals assemble in the room above. They sip wine or drink fruit juice mingled with water and discuss by the hour everything under the sun. Here, glance at these outside while I attend to the customers who just walked in."

The poem was allegedly composed by Tabi-urul-Enlil, supposedly a former king of Nippur. He had sacrificed, made liberal offerings to the gods, and never failed to invoke the goddess Ishtar at every meal. He prayed constantly, taught his subjects to honor the gods and goddesses, which he thought should please them. Then troubles fell upon him by the bushel. One day he was strong and alive when suddenly he felt crushed and overtaken with grief. His eyes went bad and his ears would not serve him. His genitals became diseased. He lay in dung like an ass, and mixed in his own excrement like a sheep. His bowels swelled, pained, and his entire body felt as if death was upon him. He could not sleep by night or walk by day. His limbs seemed all dismembered. From a king he changed into a slave. His boon companions maltreated him as if he were a madman. Why did such misery overwhelm one who had been so good and pious? It was simply impossible to understand the actions of the gods. But suddenly things changed; a mighty storm drove the demon of disease out of his body. A spirit appeared and cured him of his ailments. He offered up sacrifices and praised Marduk, then called upon everyone never to despair of the gods.

When Avram brought in the tablets he wanted to know if the gods were ever reviled or blasphemed. The shopkeeper replied, "Here is a tablet recording a dialogue between the young Gubarru and a wise old Chaldean who admits the shortcomings of mankind. He goes on to say that people exalt the great who are skilled in large scale murder. They justify the wicked rich and disparage the poor who are just and who seek to carry out the will of the gods. Yet the wise Chaldean advises not to offend the gods but rather carry out their wishes. But Gubarru answers that the gods and the priests are always on the side of the greatest wealth. They favor the rich in noble words and help those who need no help. They maltreat the poor man like a thief and extinguish the weak like a flame. Gubarru will have no part of the gods or the priests."

People began coming in and walking up the brick steps. The storekeeper asked whether he wished to go up to the room above and listen to some sophisticated talk. Avram wanted first to complete the purchase of the tablets they had discussed. They were too heavy to carry and the dealer offered to have a slave accompany and help Avram whenever he decided to leave. He introduced the student from Ur as a youth eager for knowledge and ripe for unconventional discourse. One of the older men asked whether he was the young man who at the king's banquet answered a question that puzzled the priests, astrologers, soothsayers, and the wise Chaldeans. He added that it took courage to impart information displeasing to the king and his top advisers before the highest gathering in the land.

The discussion centered about the code of Hammurabi which had just been completed. Approximately 300 laws were incised on a black diorite stele somewhat less than eight feel in height and placed at a prominent spot in the Temple of Marduk for everyone to see and read. An objection came from a temple student preparing for the priesthood. He thought the figures appearing at the head of the stele showing Hammurabi as standing before the Sun-god Shamash impious in that the king and the god were virtually on an equal footing. One was as tall as the other. The king was undoubtedly a great and wise ruler but should not be classified among the gods. He for one objected strenuously to the rising tendency of deifying kings and worshiping them as gods.

Another objector considered it in bad taste for the king to utilize the stele for fulsome self-praise. No one should say of himself, "I, Hammurabi, am the King of Justice to whom Shamash committed law. My words are choice; my deeds have no equal; it is only to the fool that they are empty. I wrote my precious words on my stele and in the presence of the statue of me, Hammurabi, the devout, god-fearing prince."

A student whose father held a profitable post as overseer of roads and canals stated that it was easy enough to find fault but no one should forget that the Hammurabi code was the greatest, best, and most beneficial in the memory of man. "What other body of laws ever insisted upon justice to the widow, the orphan, the poor. Punishments are no longer left to the gods or to avenging relatives but must be enforced by the state with physical or financial penalties that are just.

A critic pointed out that according to the stele King

Hammurabi seemed to consider his code as his personal wisdom. His statement, "my words are choice; it is only to a fool that they are empty," would imply that these laws came out of his own head. "But it is a well-known fact that there are at least three other codes in existence. About 150 years ago Lipit-Ishtar, king of Isin, drafted a set of laws which according to a clay tablet in the Temple of Marduk library, 11 by 9 inches, has ten columns on each side. Most of these laws appear in our king's new compilation. Anyone who will take the trouble can find in the code of Hammurabi about 50 laws copied out of the collection of King Eshnunna written about a century ago. Then there are the laws of Ur-Nammu, the founder of the great Third Dynasty of Ur. He lived more than 300 years ago and his prologue states that he instituted such reforms so that 'the orphan was not given over to the rich, the widow to the powerful, the man of one shekel to the man of a mina (60 shekels).' Codes do not just spring up in the heads of the wise. Laws are tested out for generations and finally, if found useful or beneficial, are compiled into a permanent code. What I mean to say is that Hammurabi has incorporated in his code the laws and customs which the Sumerians developed and lived under for many centuries."

"We are grateful," commented the poet of Gubarru, "to our wise king for retaining many laws of the older codes that are sound and have been tested by time and experience. But it is regrettable that he did not see fit to eliminate such barbaric laws that belong to a primitive society. For instance, he could have left off the stiff punishments for the clearly innocent. I understand that he has retained the provision that if the son of a householder is killed because of faulty construction, then not the builder but his son must suffer death. If a temple priestess walks into a wineshop she shall be burned. If a woman neglects her house or humiliates her husband she shall be thrown into the water. If a man kills a girl then not he but his daughter must be killed. If a plebian strikes one of his own class he is fined ten shekels but if he strikes a signeur or a man of property he must pay 60 shekels. If a patient loses an eye as the result of an operation, the surgeon will have his fingers cut off. A woman accused of adultery must prove her innocence by leaping into the river. If she can swim she emerges innocent; drowning is proof of her guilt. A sorcerer goes through the same test. If innocent he receives the accuser's property. If he drowns then the accuser receives the sorcerer's property."

The discussion absorbed Avram until he happened to look over the railing above the inner court and saw the sky darkening. The sun was no doubt setting and he had promised to meet Eleazer at the evening meal in the temple. He therefore made haste to depart and the shopkeeper sent a slave along to carry the tablets. Eleazer was anxious and wondering whether he had lost his way in the narrow, uneven, and winding lanes. Both managed to get enough food despite their late arrival. The *Sagan* had informed Eleazer that the message was ready and a boat would leave the next day for Ur.

Avram had forgotten all about the woman and Eleazer quickly informed him of her important piece of news. He had met her in the Ishtar temple. She was the widow of a petty officer who had been killed in action. That very day she had a sudden visit from her dead husband's friend who wanted to marry her. He came to Babylon with a cordon of troops to deliver Ibin-Sin, the king of Ur, whom he had captured while on a scouting mission. He delivered the king to the royal palace and was told to keep this capture a secret. Capturing a king was a feather in his helmet and he expected a promotion that would enable him to marry and support her.

Both agreed that this was serious news and portended an attack on Ur by King Hammurabi. They decided not to tell anyone until they first informed Sabbattu. The next day they boarded the same boat with the same skipper who had brought them to Babylon.

## II

On the return journey Avram read his clay tablets all day and at night relived with Eleazer the experiences in the big city. He could hardly find the right words to shade the differences between Ur and Babylon. His companion considered age the determining factor. In Ur he felt the same as in Egypt. Many generations have a way of leaving their impress upon a city. It was almost the difference between an old house and a new one. One is a home and the other simply a house. For one thing the pace was faster. There was an exuberance about Babylon that was lacking in Egypt or in Ur. Avram wondered whether religion was a determining factor in the life, the attitude, the atmosphere of a place. Eleazer felt that basically people were the same regardless of the gods they worshipped. He repeated Sabbattu's dictum that the world would be no happier under one god than under 50 gods.

"For instance," commented Avram, "I saw something unusual in the auction of wives. You were not with me that day. A number of unmarried girls or women are assembled. The most beautiful is offered in marriage first to the highest bidder. Then the next in beauty is put on the block, so to speak. She brings a lesser sum. This goes on until all the pretty ones are sold. A considerable sum is realized. Then a homely one is offered with a slight bonus to the prospective husband. The uglier they come the more money goes with them. Larger and larger sums are given with the repulsive or the deformed. This goes on until all the girls or women are disposed of. When the auction was over I listened to the comments of bystanders. Nearly everyone thought it a wise procedure."

"This might not be a perfect device," stated Eleazer, "but it does have certain advantages. It may not be useful to the wealthy or the beautiful, for they have no problem in satisfying their desires. But it is an advantage for the homely women who can't get husbands or to the impoverished men who can't support wives."

"What you say might be true," admitted Avram, "but in every arrangement, even in the bad ones, some are benefited. Yet is that the way to measure the worth of a system? As I watched the auction I felt something wrong in this plan even if it does help some. I could not help thinking of the newly married couples going to their homes. What follows? Each, no doubt, felt bound to a person he or she did not know. The first thing they did was to go to bed. But is marriage simply a device for men and women to sleep together? If so then prostitution answers their purpose."

"What purpose is there in marriage other than begetting offspring?" asked Eleazer.

"That is an oversimplification of the most important institution in life," replied Avram. "The home and children are the basis of society, of life itself. Therefore, there should be a relationship, an understanding, a rapport between man and wife. There is something sacred in marriage or adultery would not be a capital crime punishable with death. It was, therefore, disturbing to watch the holy institution of wedlock decided on the auction block. Isn't there something offensive, not to say criminal, in selling women to men or men to women as if they were cattle? And even cattle breeders are careful in selecting proper mates for producing better stock."

"It is strange," smiled Eleazer, "how the gods twist people about. Here you and I are evidently misplaced in our ways of thinking. You were born and raised in fortunate circumstances. You have a nice comfortable home with all your wants provided. You received an excellent education. Your future is assured either in the priesthood or in the government service with good chances of advancement. You have never known sorrow or misfortune except in the recent incident. You of all people have reason to be satisfied with life. Yet you are not only discontented; you are restless with the desire to eliminate the evils of this world and bring about a better life for everyone. On the other hand, I never knew a mother's love. For the past five years I have been tossed about from pillar to post as a slave. I should be the dissatisfied one. Yet I do not rebel against fate. I try to come to terms with life. I accept what the gods have in store for us."

"*What the gods have in store for us,*" repeated Avram. "Now you touch on the evil that underlies the entire fabric of our existence. How can our lives be tolerable if the gods who direct our fates are not motivated by goodness, justice, or mercy. You saw the plaques and paintings in the Temple of Nergal, the Babylonian God of War. We are merely playthings knocked about helter-skelter for the amusement of such gods."

"What can we do about it?" questioned Eleazer.

"We can reject them and work to bring about the rule of a just, compassionate, and righteous god."

"And that God is?" asked Eleazer, who knew the answer.

"El Elyon, the Most High God, creator of heaven and earth and everything therein."

## III

The return to Ur was faster than the ascent to Babylon up the Naar Purattu. While the downward current was not as swift as during the spring, it nevertheless carried the boat at a fairly rapid speed. Nor was there too much traffic to impede the craft's progress. The passengers were told that the farther south they proceeded the more visible would become the ravages caused by the drought. Dead carcasses or skeletons of oxen, cows, sheep, goats, and even asses would lie about on farms, fields, or highways, dead from lack of water. All this might be true in the interior but not at the water's edge where cattle could drink at the river without difficulty. It took about half the time to reach Ur as it did to land in Babylon.

The travelers were joyfully received at home. Emtelai felt greatly relieved for she feared for the safety of her son and had scolded Terach a number of times for permitting Avram to risk liberty, or health, or even life, on a journey which she considered unnecessary. The most joyful of all was little Sarai who had missed keenly the daily presence of her half-brother. She was happy over the removal of Zirru, whom she considered a rival. The eight-year-old girl had already chosen to marry Avram when she grew up.

Sabbattu welcomed his messengers but read the dispatch from the high-priest of Babylon with obvious disappointment. It made no mention of any alliance with Ur, the capstone of Sabbattu's statesmanship. The dispatch was vague and contained nothing of significance. He appeared shaken by the news of Ibi-Sin's capture and confinement in Hammurabi's palace. He questioned them closely and ordered them to maintain complete silence about the king of Ur's incarceration, since the information came from an unreliable source and could not be verified. Yet all the same he felt uneasy at this disquieting piece of news.

Something akin to gloom hung over the city. First and foremost the drought depressed the spirits of everyone. While there was no lack of grain, barley, or corn, yet vegetables and fruit, already exhausted, were growing scarcer each day. The local supply was replenished only by boats from northern climes. To avoid gouging or profiteering prices had to be fixed by law. The chief source of discomfort resulted from lack of water. Only the river supply was available and the high priest through his trumpeteers announced daily that everyone should boil the river water in the very hottest fire, then strain the mud through thin cloth, closely meshed fishing nets, or curtains, and let the grains of sand settle to the bottom of metal, clay, or wooden containers.

A sense of insecurity gripped the population. People wondered why the king did not appear. Rumors sprang up that he had been killed or captured or that he simply deserted his kingdom. Many wondered when the alliance with Hammurabi so glowingly painted by the high priest would materialize. The optimism stimulated by Hunate's high-flown oratory had by this time subsided to the vanishing point. Then disturbing rumors began to circulate about a demon entering their beautiful queen and tormenting her unmercifully.

In the temple proper the priests constantly harped on the theme of the gods being angry because enough sacrifices and offerings were not forthcoming. The climate in the temple was none too serene. The rift between Sabbattu and Hunate created a division in the priesthood. In the women's section a strong animosity had sprung up against Zur-na-na after her flogging of Keturah. While the bride of Nannar maintained a cautious silence, the priestess Tar-tu-khu did not. She disclosed the affair discreetly to her confidential friends. Even before the beating, Zur-na-na was cordially hated because of arrogance, hauteur, and the treatment of other priestesses as dirt under her feet. Now the women displayed quite openly their hostility together with a defiant disregard for her rank and royal descent. Not that Keturah was so beloved. But everyone agreed that this simple girl's airs and arrogant conduct were directed by the high priestess who dominated her completely. They also noted the new change in her. She became as natural and gracious as during her early arrival, due no doubt to the promptings of Tar-tu-khu.

Zur-na-na was well aware that the flogging incident had lowered her prestige. No one mentioned anything but the temple women were aloof and avoided speaking to her when possible. It was maddening to wait for their slow-in-coming answers even to her important questions. She could complain to the high priest but he would no doubt answer that she was mistaken or that she was unnecessarily sensitive. Besides, it was humiliating for one in her station to complain at all. The temple women seemed to act in concert and would all no doubt conspire against her should the occasion arise. Yet she could do nothing about it. For the first time in her life she felt a sense of helplessness.

Keturah also benefited by the experience. After the incident she realized how utterly alone she was. She had foolishly walked out on Sabbattu. Her conduct to Avram was stupid, vulgar, and altogether unpardonable. Never to her dying day would she say another word to Zur-na-na. Now she had no one. First of all it was necessary to make up with Sabbattu and that was easy enough. The priest was only too happy to take her into his arms again. Keturah realized that his protection gave her a feeling of security. Her confidante Tar-tu-khu would advise her sensibly how to get along with the temple women and build up a feeling of kinship and affection. It was far more pleasant to be liked than hated in her splendid isolation. She would, with the help of her confidante, invite groups of three or four into her room, listen to their gossip which was often amusing, diverting, and even entertaining. She granted Tar-tu-khu the pleasure of her body only on occasions and learned to maintain her dignified reserve. Never again would she become a plaything at the beck and call of any woman. She adopted Sabbattu's dictum: "Let everyone count but none for too much."

Zur-na-na no longer existed for her. Keturah always kept her door locked and opened only when she heard the name. Zur-na-na had knocked several times but when she failed to disclose her name, the door did not open. Keturah would pass without giving her a glance and would never acknowledge her greeting. On one occasion the high priestess met her in the corridor and tried to speak. In answer Keturah thrust her hand into a pocket folded in her clothes, drew out a small, short iron dagger, a weapon from Babylon and rare in Ur, and said, "I have nothing to say to you. If you every touch me again I shall use this and if necessary kill you."

Feeling alone and isolated Zur-na-na was wretched. She began to feel sorry for herself and faced the fact that she was really a failure. While the king's daughter in Larsa she attracted no suitor who might propose marriage. Therefore, she persuaded her father to obtain the post of high priestess of the Temple of Nannar at Ur. After serving the gods for more than 15 years she now had to confess that she was hated by the temple women and ignored by the priests. It was too bitter a pill to swallow that the fault lay in herself. Secretly she had to nurse her wounded pride, which longed for the recognition and honor due to her royal extraction. Her ego, therefore, received a spurt of elation when the high priest informed her that a request had come from the royal palace that she, Zur-na-na, visit the beautiful queen Shub-Ad.

# 10

# The Holocaust

CARRIED IN THE ROYAL SEDAN BY FOUR SLAVES ZUR-NA-NA arrived at the palace only to learn that the invitation was merely a demand for her services as priestess to minister to the sick queen. The temple doctor, a priest and an exorcist were also "invited." It took little time for the doctor to diagnose her ailment as melancholia caused by a demon that had entered her body. To drive the evil spirit out the doctor prescribed a diet of raw meat, wood shavings, snake flesh, crushed bones, fat and dirt, rotten food, all saturated with wine, oil and urine. He felt quite sure that the mere taste of this concoction would cause the demon to flee. The priest prayed to about six gods to effect her cure. The chief ceremony was conducted by the *ashipu* who put on a terrifying mask and a tiger skin. He began with incantations and closed with shouts, shaking of rattles, slapping his hands together, and raving for the *shed* to come out of the queen.

After the doctor, the priest, and the *ashipu* left Shub-Ad remained sitting on the divan, a pathetic figure of despair, no sparkle in her cherry-dark luminous eyes, neither pride nor spirit in her listless expression, her former queenly air now showing a haunted, frightened look. The palace chamberlain had explained to Zur-na-na that the queen's intellect was in no way impaired and that she saw and understood everything around her. Only her spirit seemed crushed, the work no doubt of a demon. Shub-Ad paid little attention to Zur-na-na as she sat at the extreme end of the chamber wondering what she could do and why she was there. At last the queen spoke without raising her eyes.

"Who are you and why did you come?"

Zur-na-na walked over to the sitting queen and remained standing. "I am high priestess in the Temple of Nannar and am here to help you."

"You can do nothing for me, nor can anyone else." Her voice was low and lifeless. "I am wretched and feel miserable."

"My queen, you are temporarily ill. You will recover and become your normal self, the most gracious and beautiful woman in the world."

For the first time the queen looked up and remarked, "I have seen you before and believe you are a princess."

"Yes, your majesty, my father was King Kudur-Mabug of Larsa."

She reached for Zur-na-na's hand and said, "Sit next to me You just can't imagine how unhappy I am. Everything terrifies me. I can't make the slightest decision about anything. I can't even select a dress to wear. My looks don't bother me any more. I find no joy in being beautiful. If my maid did not insist I would not use rouge or make-up. The effort of getting out of bed is frightening. When I go to sleep I hope and pray never to get up again."

"My queen, this will pass away. You have everything in the world to live for. Everyone knows how the king loves you, how proud he is of his wife, the most beautiful queen in the world."

"I shall never see the king again. I don't know whether he is alive. And I brought this misfortune upon our kingdom. The Lord Nannar told me that I will experience the wrath of a god." She looked at the princess and the ghost of a smile played on her lips. "I want to die and you can help me." She moved closer, her hand still retaining the right hand of Zur-na-na who put her left arm about the queen's waist and kissed her on the cheek.

"I would do anything in the world for Shub-Ad, except that."

The lady-in-waiting came in with three maids carrying wine and fresh fruit which they placed on several tripods in front of the queen. Zur-na-na got up and moved away.

"Your Majesty, here is the food prepared according to the prescription of the doctor. It will not be appetizing but the *ashipu* who supervised the preparation said it will swiftly drive the *shed* out of you."

"But I am not hungry and cannot eat," objected the queen.

"Please, my queen, eat it and you will quickly recover, something we are all so anxious to see," pleaded the lady-in-waiting. "May I suggest that you close your eyes and gulp a spoonful as fast as I put it in your mouth. Allow me to hold your nose. Please do, my royal lady."

No sooner did she swallow the heaped spoonful when she started to vomit and continued until she threw up everything in her stomach. When she recovered her breath, she pointed to the wine, then began hurriedly to eat the dates and figs in the plates on the tripod.

"Take that away. I would sooner die than swallow another mouthful. I shall order the chamberlain to send you home. How can anyone dare to feed me such garbage."

When they cleaned up the floor and removed the concoction the lady-in-waiting and the maids left. Shub-Ad motioned to Zur-na-na to sit with her. The priestess took the queen in her arms and fondled her like a child until she dropped off to sleep. After an hour she woke up. Zur-na-na gently disengaged her arms and got up to leave.

"Where are you going?" demanded Shub-Ad.

"I must return to the temple to perform my duties."

"No, you must stay here with me. You are the only person in this palace to whom I can talk."

"But, my queen, I came as I am. I haven't anything to change into, not even a sleeping gown."

"You can't go. You will wear my clothes. I will give you my gown to sleep in. You will stay right here. I will send a messenger to your high priest."

## II

A week passed since Zur-na-na had been installed in the palace as comforter and companion of the queen. One morning a contingent of about one hundred chariots pulled by asses dashed to the walls of Ur and stopped short before the large bronze covered wooden gates which were open. In each chariot stood two bearded soldiers wearing peaked helmets of leather, carrying bronze-covered shields and armed with bows, arrows, swords, and spears. At the head of the cavalcade rode the Babylonian Tartan, Nabunergal, on horseback. Almost simultaneously a number of boats came drifting down the Purattu and halted as anchors of rock attached to cables were thrown into the river. The large bronze-covered gates were quickly shut and the top of the wall was soon crowded with men and even a few women.

A soldier jumped out of each chariot and formed a

phalanx of one hundred behind the commander. An officer in charge of the walls called out, "Do you come in peace?" The Tartan shouted back, "Peace or war is your choice." The drivers also got out of their chariots, drove stakes into the ground, and tied the donkey bridles to the iron rods. Then they formed another cordon behind the Tartan. About 50 other soldiers left their boats and stood in formation near the others. By this time a more important military officer appeared on the wall and cried out, "If you wish to confer with our ruler, we will open the gates under a flag of truce and admit the commander with an armed guard of 12 men."

Trumpets sounded for silence and the Tartan shouted through a speaking-trumpet, "Hear ye, men of ancient Ur. First, I will speak to you, then I shall enter your city, if you so desire, and confer with your leaders. I, Tartan Nabunergal, come from my master, the great king of Babylon, the divine Hammurabi, who bade me to tell you that he has deep affection for the venerable city of Ur, to which the world owes so much. We in Babylon speak the language of Akkad, Assyria, and Amuru, yet in our temples we pray in the hallowed tongue of Sumer. Your gods are our gods, even if we call your Irnina our Ishtar, your Enlil our Nergal. Our great king's highest hope is the union of Akkad, Amuru, Assyria with all of Sumer. You probably know that the puissant Hammurabi is a great conqueror. But never was there a great, strong empire builder with so warm and soft a heart. Visit the cities which he has subdued; speak to the people of Kish, Agade, Ashur, Opis, Nineveh and ask whether they have any regrets about living in the empire of our divine king. They will tell you that they are better off than ever before. In 30 years he has united and solidified all his lands into a peaceful, happy, and prosperous empire.

"Now he wants all of Shinar between the two rivers to become a single united land strong enough to fight the whole world should the occasion arise. All of Sumer must be in that united empire. Without Ur his territories are not integrated; they are open to attack. Ur must become a part of Babylonia. So wills our divine leader. He wishes it and it will be to your best interest to come in peacefully and willingly. You will be most cordially welcomed. If you refuse then his army will use force to bring about this joint venture. Already your King Ibi-Sin is a guest in his palace. He eats at our king's table. Your king was captured while spying on our troop movements in our territory. But see with what kindness a captured king is treated. King Hammurabi is now besieging Larsa. This city will fall any day. Place no false hopes on Rim-Sin. He will soon be captured or killed. But he will never be treated with the gentle consideration shown to your king. After the fall of Larsa the august Hammurabi will come with his army to your walls. If you admit him peacefully and do his bidding, you will be happy and prosperous. If not, the sword will destroy you. Choose and choose wisely."

Shouts, screams, catcalls broke out. Some of the mobsters yelled, "Ur will never be the slave of Babylon." "We will never submit to Hammurabi." "Let's go down and kill these upstarts from Babylon." "Down with Nabunergal." "He talks better than he fights." But there were other cries. "Long live Hammurabi." "We want to be in Babylon's empire." Shoving and pushing started on the wall until a man fell off, but he was not hurt too badly. A trumpet on the wall sounded for silence. The trumpeteer announced that the sage and priest Khar-Sak wished to speak. When silence was finally restored, the priest called out, "Fellow countrymen, remember the life of an ambassador is sacred. Do not touch anyone from Babylon. If you do, the gods will destroy you. My Lord Tartan, our Adon Sabbattu, the high priest of Nannar, invites you to a conference in the temple. Come with your guard of 12 soldiers. We will protect you with our army. We promise you immunity on our priestly oath."

The bronze-covered gates opened. The Tartan rode on his horse followed by his guard of 12 armed men. The gate opened into the Temenos which surrounded the temple and bypassed the city. After Nabunergal dismounted Khar-Sak and two other priests conducted him to the apartment of Sabbattu, who was alone. He greeted the Tartan and a priestess served wine, fruits, and honied raisin bread. Sabbattu said, "My lord Tartan, your speech was relayed to me. I agree with you but as you see we suffer from dissension. I am head of the peace party, as you might call it. But the second high priest, Hunate, leads the war party and is fanatically bitter. I don't know what can be done."

"Easy enough," assured Nabunergal. "When King Hammurabi comes with his army he will besiege your city. If you want to save bloodshed, rape, murder, and destruction, see that the northeastern gate is opened on some dark night when there is no moonlight. Our army will enter and ancient Ur will be saved from complete destruction."

"I agree to do this, but what will become of me?"

"The king promised that he will take you to Babylon and give you a temple, or place you in his diplomatic service."

"Then we agree, noble Tartan."

## III

Consternation struck the city. The bold act of sending a small force of 250 soldiers to demand the surrender of so great a city as Ur struck terror in the hearts of the people. It was the kind of psychological warfare which four thousand years later was called a war of nerves. As soon as the Tartan Nabunergal left the temple, the priests assembled in Sabbattu's large reception chamber. The high priest gave his colleagues his own version of the conference with the Babylonian commander. He simply offered the king of Babylon the alliance which he had delineated on New Year's Day to the people assembled in the temple court. He stressed that unconditional surrender was out of the question. Ur would be willing to make a treaty of peace and friendship but only as an ally of Babylon. Meanwhile every preparation must be rushed for the defense of their city. All able-bodied men should be impressed and trained for military duty. All available men from the province might be drafted and brought to Ur. Even women should be enrolled for hospital duty, or to assemble medicines, or to prepare bandages for the wounded. A strong delegation headed by the assistant high priest Hunate must be sent to Elam for troop reinforcements, food, supplies, provisions, and matériel. Even the obstreperous Hunate could find no fault with this policy and procedure. He reluctantly consented, especially after the appointment to confer with the king of Elam.

A large crowd assembled on the ground floor of the temple, nervous and eager to know what was the plan of action. They were addressed by Sabbattu, Khar-Sak, and Hunate. The high priest repeated what he told the assembled priests. Khar-Sak assured the people that the entire priesthood was in complete accord with the policy enunciated by Adon Sabbattu; that everyone should have courage and not despair. "The gods will not forsake our holy city which has survived such great catastrophes, even the great flood itself. Ur, the eternal city, will triumph over all obstacles in war and in peace and will remain forever the crown of Sumer and Akkad." Hunate agreed with the alliance proposed by the high priest. "If this is acceptable to Hammurabi, well and good. We will then be allies equal in status to Babylon. If not, we will display courage and power that will astonish all nations from Egypt to India. We are arming and preparing for a conflict with Babylon. Remember our city is fortified with strong walls and manned by heroic defenders. I am heading a delegation to go immediately to the king of Elam for assistance. In a siege our city can defy Babylon and hold out indefinitely. We will never surrender. We are unconquerable."

The auditors were uplifted by the oratory and went away feeling encouraged by the thought that the capture of the king would not impede the efficient preparations for war. But the city was overcast with gloom and foreboding. Wasn't the drought in itself a sufficient plague without the additional affliction of a life and death struggle with the great power of Babylon? How could Ur stand a siege if water and food were not sufficient for peacetime consumption? Many people thought privately that a contest with Hammurabi would be as disastrous as it was futile. They hoped secretly that Ur would open its gates to the king of Babylon and avoid bloodshed, raping, if not complete destruction. Heartsickening fear began to grip the people while hope was rapidly vanishing.

## IV

At the palace the condition of Queen Shub-Ad continued unchanged. Zur-na-na became so necessary that the sick woman leaned on her entirely. She made all the decisions yet could not help her. When the speech of Nabunergal reached the palace she thought that the news about King Ibi-Sin would lift the queen's depression; but Shub-Ad listened apparently without the slightest reaction except to remain silent for several hours, seemingly engrossed in thought. Her condition continued to be a bewildering puzzle. Her thought process seemed unaffected. Her language was clear and rational, her understanding unimpaired. Yet a deep depression engulfed her spirit. She remained fearful, jittery, her will paralyzed, without capacity for any degree of enjoyment, every action a mountainous obstacle to scale, any decision a supreme effort impossible of achievement. She refused to see any doctor, priest, or *ashipu.*

Seeing Shub-Ad's desire to be alone, Zur-na-na felt free to take a vacation of several hours. She walked on the palace grounds, then bathed, washed her hair, changed clothes, and freshened up. She did not realize to what extent she had become a prisoner with the queen as her jailer. When she returned to the daily task, Shub-Ad motioned to her to sit alongside, holding her hand for moral support.

"I have something to tell you, Zur-na-na, and please don't laugh at me. I have finally come to a decision and feel better and stronger for it. I am determined to die." Her hand gripped Zur-na-na's more firmly than ever before. "My death will be more important than my life ever was or ever can be. I have decided to offer my life as a sacrifice to the gods. It will be an expiation for having offended the Lord Nannar. This, I know, has brought misfortune upon my people. My voluntary death for the glory of the gods will end the drought and bring copious rainfall. It will also prevent my kingdom from falling a prey to Babylon. The gods are extremely angry with my city and my people. Only my willing death will save and redeem them."

The priestess tried hard to convince the queen that she was ill yet would soon recover and reunite with her husband, but she found all such assurances useless. She felt a kind of strength enter and sustain Shub-Ad's will to death. All manner of argument she used was wasted. The queen had attributed her refusal to lie with Nannar as the cause that brought such tribulations upon Ur. To dissuade her, the priestess even expressed a serious doubt as to whether it was a god at all that desired her body. This only made the queen angry at the thought of anyone doubting her capacity to judge the evidence of her own senses. "Perhaps you consider me demented? Well, I am not," she asserted with conviction. The priestess felt all her efforts to dissuade the queen from dying would fail. She might not show the strength to determine anything else but she evidently did possess the will to die. Zur-na-na felt defeated.

"Don't think that I don't realize how weary you are of being with me day and night. You need a change. So go back to the temple and inform the priests of my decision. They should know. You don't have to return although I need you badly. My sedan will carry you."

"I shall go and come back tomorrow."

The queen kissed her on the cheek. "Is it possible that she might be on the road to recovery?" questioned the priestess. "Or is this death urge the only positive desire that she has? Evidently living has become too heavy a burden for her to bear. It appears to be her only release. But she has a noble soul. Only royal blood can come to so lofty a decision."

While being borne on the chair Zur-na-na's thoughts reverted to the temple. She felt no pleasure in coming back. The sanctuary had become distasteful. It occurred to her that she really had no home, not even the retreat for a rest. How satisfactory was her own life? She felt a kinship with Shub-Ad. After all she was also of royal blood. Yet was she capable of such a sacrifice? Then crept an insidious notion into her consciousness. Why not join the queen? Then her name would be forever linked with Shub-Ad. She really had nothing to live for. This joint sacrifice might induce the gods to relent towards Ur and the people of Sumer. The idea gripped her and would not let go.

She entered Sabbattu's residence but the *kadosh* informed her that the priest was very busy conferring with some military leaders. She ordered him to tell the high priest that she had an important communication. The *kadosh* brought back an invitation to eat the evening meal with Sabbattu. Going to her room she passed several priestess who nodded coldly and went on. The lower order of *kadashes* gave her the formal regulation curtsies. Not a word of welcome from anyone after an absence, although they doubtless knew that she came from the royal palace. She was hurt and felt despondent, especially at the thought of having antagonized these women unnecessarily. She washed, put some make-up on her face and eyes, and changed into a fresh dress. Sitting alone in her room waiting until eating time was too boring. She walked up the steps to the top of the terrace ziggurat and stood leaning against the side of the Nannar shrine which shaded her from the sun. She looked over the entire city, the old ziggurat, the other temples, the palace, the Temenos, the busy lanes crowded with traffickers, the waterfront, the surrounding country of parched soil without crops. Unbidden thoughts came to her mind. Was it the last time she would gaze at this panorama?

The high priest was disturbed to hear of Shub-Ad's decision. He questioned Zur-na-na closely about the soundness of the queen's mind. Did she talk irrationally? Did she reveal any other reason for wanting to die? Did she believe that her sacrifice would bring relief to the people? Did she reveal any signs of insanity?

"No more than I do. Can you detect anything wrong with my mind? Yet I want to join the queen and be her companion in Aralu. Of course, I know that I will need the priestly consent."

Astonishment registered in Sabbattu's countenance. Unable to make any kind of sacrifice himself, he could not understand such an intention in anyone else. He loved living and intended to cling to life regardless of the cost to his self-respect, honor, or reputation. He told her he would take the matter up with his colleagues who would come in later for a war conference. He would inform her of their decision on the following day. She left, went to her room, tossed most of the night in her bed unable to sleep.

Six priests of the highest echelon met in Sabbattu's reception hall to consider the war effort. Hunate with his delegation had already departed to ask help from the king of Elam. They discussed fully the queen's intention to die. They were but slightly affected by the pity, by the pathos of the queen's martyrdom in the flush of her youth and beauty. They dismissed the lamentable self-effacement with pious cant. What concerned them was the public reaction, the effect of the proposed sacrifice upon the war effort. They came to the conclusion that the incident could have a wholesome effect if skillfully utilized. Such a noble example would stimulate the people to patriotic fervor, to self denial, to higher personal sacrifice. But it must be carefully handled. And no one could manage this more deftly than the high priest assisted by the sagacious Khar-Sak. As for the proposal of the high priestess, such self immolation could only reflect high credit upon the temple, the priesthood, and the godhead.

At dawn Zur-na-na dozed off and slept until the serving priestess brought in her breakfast. She then bathed and as soon as she dressed a tap sounded on her door. The *kadosh* presented an apology from the high priest for his inability to see her; he was too occupied with war matters. The priests were deeply touched by the proposed voluntary martyrdom of the queen and the high priestess. They not only give their consent but would offer special prayers and dedicate a day in commemoration of the noble act that required the highest courage as well as devotion to the gods.

On her way out to see if the sedan chair was near the temple entrance, Zur-na-na walked through the corridor and passed Keturah's chamber. She suddenly had an impulse to see the girl. Her slight knock on the door brought the answer to come in. Keturah, still in her nightgown, was too surprised to say anything when Zur-na-na declared, "Now don't be disturbed, Keturah. I come only to bid you farewell. Queen Shub-Ad will offer her life to the gods and I will go along and do likewise."

"No—no—Zur-na-na," and Keturah was stumped for words, not knowing what to say.

"Why shouldn't I?" said Zur-na-na with bitterness. "No one will miss me. No one wants me. No one cares for me. It is better that I go with honor."

Keturah rushed up, kissed her on the forehead and with tears in her eyes blurted out, "You—you—mustn't—I–I will be your friend."

Zur-na-na gathered Keturah in her arms, kissed her on the mouth with deep feeling, sobbed a few incoherent words, said "Farewell," and rushed out of the room. She heard Keturah cry out, "Zur-na-na!"

## V

The decision of the queen and the priestess spread through the city with the rapidity of fire sweeping over the parched fields of the Sumerian countryside. The proposal to sacrifice for Ur and its people met with a universal approval that stimulated a strange phenomenon. The prevalent gloom, fear, anxiety, and frustration were to an extent modified and at the same time paradoxically intensified. A longing for consecrated martyrdom sprang up. Men and women of all classes expressed the wish to follow the example of the two women, the symbolic representatives of religion and government. The combined atmosphere of murk and awe produced a kind of mystical religious exaltation that yearned for mass suicide. People streamed into the temple offering their lives to the gods for the preservation of their ancient homeland. Such numbers came that Sabbattu was compelled to select several priests to interview and classify the willing sacrificants.

About 25 men and women from the upper and middle classes were selected. They came from the palace, the army, the temples, the wealthy merchants, the nobility. The rejected ones could participate in the death ritual by offering their jewels, clothes, finery, and ornaments for the female immolatees and spears, swords, gold daggers, armor, and robes for the men. Some brought artifacts of gold, silver, bronze, wood, and enameled clay for use in the nether region. Women cut off their tresses to be made into wigs fashionable among the wealthy to be worn at the funeral rites and buried together with the wearers. How much the agents and propagandists of Sabbattu contributed to this hysterical urge for mass suicide was difficult to assess. The eloquent assurances that the attendants and servitors of the queen would enjoy a special rank in a favored section of Aralu no doubt stimulated the volunteers for death or the donations of generous gifts. Confidence in the efficacy of human sacrifice as the dependable appeasement of an irate goldhead tended somewhat to brighten the tenebrous atmosphere of Ur.

The high priest was not slow in sensing the significance of human sacrifice that quickly reached to holocaust proportions. The annihilation of 27 human beings should not be passed over too lightly. It was an event fraught with, not only immediate but future, consequences. Out of such happenings arise myths that sometimes develop and expand into new religions. In any event Sabbattu lived in the immediate present and felt that the mass extermination should be carefully staged so that it would leave a lasting impression upon the witnessing generation and its descendants. It must be exploited to the fullest.

He, therefore, supervised the preparations that took on the character of a small-scale pageant. The women coiffured and bejeweled must be decked out in all their finery, the men properly garbed in their costumes—armor and uniforms. A service at the temple would glorify the voluntary martyrs in the presence of their families, friends, and the general populace. Nothing should be overlooked in pomp and ceremony to make it a spectacle never to be forgotten. As for a proper tomb, Khar-Sak consulted old tablets in the temple library and found the record of a large-scale massacre or blood letting of a religious nature that had taken place in Ur about 1000 years ago or even earlier in the days of King A-bar-gi and Shub-Ad, who was either a queen or a high priestess. She must have been a remarkable woman to have left a great name, which was adopted by the reigning queen of Ur at the time of her marriage to the unfortunate King Ibi-Sin now a prisoner in the palace of King Hammurabi.

In spite of his many activities in preparing for war and the grandiose funeral, Sabbattu found the time to send for Terach. Knowing that his sculptor had a son living in Harran, he asked whether he would leave Ur and settle there should the circumstances warrant a change. Then in the strictest confidence he disclosed his apprehensions about the fate of Ur when Hammurabi attacked. He was therefore planning to transport Terach and his family before the king of Babylon commenced the siege. Thus he would request Terach to take along some of his personal valuables for the priest did not know whether Hammurabi would take him along to Babylon or leave him in Ur. Should he be killed then Terach could keep the valuables, but should the high priest be taken to Babylon then he would send to Haran for his property. Then and there he delivered a tightly bound parcel after swearing the sculptor to the most bloodcurdling oath that he would honestly comply with the agreement.

Sabbattu then informed the image-maker about Shub-Ad and his wish to place her statue in the temple. Terach reminded him of the conversation about this statue which was never followed up. The priest doubted whether the queen would be in any mood to pose for an image of herself. He wrote a note on papyrus to Zur-na-na requesting her to help obtain the queen's consent if possible, but in any case to pose herself since the priests desired hers and Shub-Ad's statues in the temple. The next day Terach went to the palace and took Avram along to assist him. Shub-Ad refused to have her statue placed in the temple lest "the people point to it as the image of their demented queen." The priestess, however, did succeed in placing Terach behind a screen hiding the washroom door so that he could see and study the queen's face. She also permitted Avram to look at the pathetic figure.

All preparations were completed and the day for the lugubrious ceremony arrived. In the morning a huge crowd assembled at the temple. The prospective martyrs were brought in two large covered wagons, each drawn by three oxen, one carrying the men and the other the women. Shub-Ad and Zur-na-na did not attend but remained waiting in the palace. The ceremony lasted for two hours. The priests uttered their set prayers, the *kadoshim* and the *kadashes* sang hymns, the musicians played their instruments. The priests in charge did everything to prevent the ritual from sinking into a dismal lacrymal affair of despair or lamentation. The orators became lyrical on the theme of patriotic fervor, loyalty to the queen, and veneration for the gods. Families would hereafter be honored by the people and blessed by the gods for the noble and heroic sacrifices of their members or relatives, who would be venerated forever for saving their fatherland. The ritual closed with joint blessings upon the martyrs by all the priests.

The parade, actually a cortege, began on the Temenos at the gates of the temple. It opened with a file of the ba'iru for maintaining order. They were followed by the king's chariot drawn by two asses driven by two soldiers holding the reins and whips. The priests, chanting prayers and led by Sabbattu, followed. Three oxen drawing a covered wagon carrying the women ready for sacrifice moved slowly behind the priests. Behind the wagon marched a band of musicians playing solemn tunes on their instruments. A cordon of about 100 soldiers, fully armed with shields, spears, and swords, stepped in martial formation. *Kadoshim* and *kadashes* walked in eight lines singing hymns. Another covered wagon filled with men selected for the annihilation was slowly pulled by three oxen. Following the wagon walked the families, relatives, and friends of those about to die; they were old and young, men, women, and children, making up a nondescript group of several hundred. Behind them jogged along three open carts containing the artifacts, gifts, and personal effects of the sacrificants who needed these objects for their use or convenience in the regions underground. An additional band of musicians followed and the cortege closed with another cordon of troops.

The procession wended its way through the Temenos, the wider streets, then out of the city gates into a section that was old, run-down and inhabited only by the very poor. It stopped at what looked like a mound. This was known as the Royal Tombs which had not been used for many centuries. While the priests were considering a proper burial place for Shub-Ad and her new retainers they met difficulties in finding a pit large enough among the newer cemetery plots. They decided to examine the Royal Tombs. Perhaps they could find a suitable place that had been overlooked in the spacious life of the long-forgotten past.

The workmen cut a square opening in the wall, originally of mud blocks but now merged into a solid mound of earth in which the bricks were no longer recognizable. It was hollow and dark inside the wall, but the lighted torches disclosed a hollow pit 72 by 24 feet and about 6 feet below the earth level on the outside. The pit was empty; no objects of any kind were visible; occasionally the workmen stepped on skeleton fragments that cracked under their feet. At one extreme end they discovered a square tomb of limestone with a vaulted roof. In the tomb an empty clay coffin lay open. It appeared to the priests and the workmen that the large pit and the small tomb had been so completely rifled that not the vestige of an artifact, weapon, jewel, or garment, usually found in burial tombs, remained. This was not surprising, for in ancient Egypt or Mesopotamia the robbing of royal tombs or graves of the wealthy was a fine art practiced with such skill that it was surprising that anything remained for the modern excavator to unearth. A message was sent reporting the discovery to Sabbattu.

The high priest and Khar-Sak agreed with the others that the pit was no doubt the burial place of some king and his faithful servitors. Close investigation could not disclose his name. Sabbattu and the sage concluded that to use this vacant pit for Shub-Ad and her retinue would not be a desecration since no one knew who was being desecrated. An opening was cut in the wall large enough to permit a team of three oxen and a covered wagon to pass through. The height between the floor and the ground level above was filled with hardened mud and soil so that a ramp led from the opening to the end of the pit. Sand was sprinkled on the ground which was covered with reed matting. The tomb was whitewashed and the clay coffin painted; everything was ready for the ghastly mass burial.

Outside the priests began droning their prayers alternating with hymns sung by *kadoshim* and *kadashes.* The oxen hitched to the covered wagon carrying the women passed over the ramp and headed for the extreme west wall in the pit. The women were alighted and led to the opposite end near the tomb. The other wagon entered and the men were placed in various spots, some near the walls, others close to the wagons, the remainder in the center. The king's chariot also drove in with the two soldiers standing in the vehicle. All of the voluntary victims had been given that morning a dose of hashish sufficient to keep them in a cheerful mood throughout the trying temple service and the subsequent procession. Now the effect of the drug was wearing off and some of the women began to wimper, others to cry. The men also showed fright and several began to tremble, others to weep. Just at this time the royal coach drawn by four asses stopped at the entrance. Shub-Ad and Zur-na-na were assisted into the royal tomb by soldiers.

The priestesses carried closed vessels of strong opium mixed with poison and poured stiff doses into enameled containers held by nurses, who virtually forced the shivering women to swallow the large drams quickly. They likewise served the men and needed the help of soldiers to induce them to drink every drop. Shub-Ad and Zur-na-na were likewise fed but needed no urging. After several minutes some of the women buckled under and slumped to the matted floor. Soon all of the women were on the ground. The priestesses adjusted their complicated headgear, smoothed out their dresses, placed cushions under their heads. They were turned on their right side facing the direction of the queen, their knees slightly bent. Soon they were fast asleep never again to awaken.

The men took a longer time to fall asleep but reacted in a similar manner. They were stretched out in different places, their shields, spears, and swords lying alongside. Signors of the palace in splendid clothes were laid side by side in a row. Priests, skilled in the slaughter of cattle, cut the jugular veins of the oxen and asses. The animals, unable to breathe after the loss of blood, fell on the ground. Their drivers were left lying in the covered wagons. Both charioteers were placed in a sitting position within the vehicle. After swallowing the opium and poison the queen was stretched out on cushions in the coffin. Zur-na-na lay on a mattress with a small pillow under her head.

The prayers and chanting continued for more than an

hour while the families and friends of the sacrificed, directed by the soldiery, filed past casting a last look at relatives and intimates. Then many people, among them Terach and Avram, were allowed the same privilege of paying their respects to the martyrs. Armed men guarded the open entrance all night. The next day additional crowds came to inspect and respect the dead. On the day following, workmen closed the entrance with mud bricks, hardened in lime kilns. The pit was hermetically sealed and ultimately forgotten until 40 centuries later scientists, excavating the ruins of Ur, discovered this tomb by chance to the astonishment of a curious world.

# 11

# Smashing the Idols

TERACH WORKED FEVERISHLY TO GET THE IMAGES OF SHUB-Ad and Zur-na-na ready for the memorial planned by Sabbattu. The high priest hoped that the temple service might detract public attention from the drought that should end soon or life would become unbearable. Each day gained was important. But it was even more pressing to keep emotions on an even keel until Hammurabi would appear with his army. The holocaust of the 27 martyrs had the effect of diverting the minds of the people from the impending invasion. The memorial displaying the statues of the two women would, he hoped, delay any popular explosion seething against the leading figures of Ur who promised much and did nothing.

To Sabbattu's urging Terach replied that he could not possibly complete two life-size round statues in a few days. Then came an inspiration. He might finish the heads, which could be mounted on crude figures that might be draped with female clothes. The magnificent headgear of Shub-Ad including a large wig with the golden leaves and great earrings should conceal any deficiency in workmanship, provided the eyes and lips were painted and eyebrows penciled. The illusion should then be perfect. A suitable costume for the high priestess could no doubt be found in the temple. Sabbattu consented and ordered the memorial service to be held four days after the funeral-burial.

At no time did Avram pay the slightest attention to his father while modeling a clay image. Terach had attempted to teach him the craft but gave up in disgust. Now for the first time he stood watching the face of Shub-Ad taking form under his father's deft fingers. It was not a good likeness, for Terach had no model, living or pictorial, to work on. His drawing on papyrus hastily sketched before Shub-Ad could become aware of his presence behind the screen did little justice to the celebrated beauty of the queen, no longer alive. Yet her face, nose, and eyes could be recognized and the crude image fascinated Avram, who would watch his father work by the hour. For the first time he realized the importance of preserving a likeness of a human face that could go to oblivion so suddenly.

The image of Shub-Ad haunted him. He felt despondent and wandered about the city oppressed by a sense of guilt for having witnessed the entombment of 27 human beings without a word of protest. He could not stay away from the pit while it remained open. He got into the line of spectators and filed past several times to catch further glimpses of the bodies lying on the matted floor. To him Shub-Ad epitomized all the dead wantonly sacrificed to appease the gods.

From commiseration and self-reproach Avram entered the realm of appraising the moral implications of human sacrifice. What else was it but mass murder with the endorsement of the priests? But why should the gods delight in the sacrifice of men and women? The priests evidently believed they were carrying out the wishes of the gods by encouraging and even sanctifying the holocaust he witnessed. Wasn't there something abhorrent and even repellent about gods who apparently derived their pleasure in tormenting their suppliants? He envisioned the tragic face of Shub-Ad and the sad countenance of Zur-na-na as he saw them in the palace.

Criticism mounted to anger and anger stimulated the necessity for concrete expression of dissent, of disapproval, or even outright condemnation. Could it be that he alone sensed the obvious injustice, the callous cynicism that resided in the godhead? Surely others shared his disgust, his aversion for the ruthlessness of divine conduct. Why shouldn't a leader arise to voice the moral indignation that was no doubt seething in numerous hearts? The gods should become aware of the rebellion springing up in the human breast. Wouldn't anyone take the initiative?

What was his own responsibility in this matter? Was he too young, too inexperienced to influence public opinion? Khar-Sak once asserted that leadership must come from above, at least from the solid majority or from one who could express the unspoken intuitions of the masses. After all he, Avram, was but a foreigner even though his grandfather, Nahor, had settled in Ur at least a century ago. Yet Avram was still an Aramean, an alien. He could sense unspoken disapproval in the eyes of students in Khar-Sak's classroom. He saw one of them on the street and expressed sympathy for the loss of a relative who was among the sacrificed in the pit. The student drew himself up and declared he was proud of his kinsman who gave his life to the gods for the preservation of his city and his people. There was a rebuke in that boast, an intimation that an alien could never understand such lofty patriotism.

Not even Avram's family paid any attention to his denunciation of the inhuman sacrifices. Terach's only concern was the immediate success of the two statues and what the public reaction to them would be. Eleazer had neither appetite nor inclination for protest or rebellion. Avram's mother Emtelai saw only danger to her beloved son in his criticism of religion or government. Yet wasn't it his duty to register some kind of disapproval even if only for the good of his own soul? He could at least ignore the gods and not go near the temple for any ritual or service.

At the evening meal Avram begged his father's permission to stay away from the memorial set for the following day. It would disturb him to hear more about the martyrs. Besides everyone, even the servants and slaves, was anxious to attend if only to see Terach's two statues in full dress. He would stay home and mind the salesroom. Business on the memorial day would be quiet anyway since everyone who could would be in the temple. It would be virtually a public holiday. Terach consented.

## II

Few people were on the Street of the Ancients since almost everyone flocked to the memorial in the Temple of Nannar. Avram sat on a bench reading one of the tablets he had purchased in Babylon. He was in a mood to appreciate Gubarru's strictures of priests and the gods. Old Nosku came into the shop, a tiresome creature detested by everyone. Terach and Eleazer had ordered him out a number of times and told him to stay away, but he came back when they were not present. He always priced the images, haggled, and never bought. He placed his heavy, gnarled walking stick against the wall and examined the idols. He considered it a most important service he rendered in scratching off the fly specks with his finger nails. He tried to start a conversation but Avram, who did not like him, gave him little encouragement.

"What are you reading with such interest? Khe-khe-khe. About Ishtar in bed with Gilgamish? Tammuz? Or with the lion or the steed? Khe-khe-khe."

Garrulous, scrawny, toothless, his bony chin pointing upward and intensifying his comical aspect, Nosku had a maddening habit of inserting a questioning *yeh* in almost every sentence. But still more irritating was his laugh ending in a falsetto khe-khe-khe.

An old woman came in carrying a container of hot gruel, a wooden bowl, and a spoon. Stricken with arthritis, called rheumatism in the olden days, she walked bent over evidently in pain.

"The gods be good to you, young master. I brought a feast for the Lady Ningal. Everyone neglects her. They think they do enough when they give all their attention to her husband Nannar. Will you let me place the most delicious stew I ever cooked before the goddess? I shall come for the bowl and spoon tomorrow. I know the Lady Ningal will like it."

Avram nodded as she got on her knees with difficulty and prayed to her goddess. She left with a beatific smile denoting that she forgot her pain in the pleasure of serving Ningal.

Nosku walked over to the bowl, smelled the gruel, and observed:

"Now this is very foolish. As if a clay idol could eat. Khe-khe-khe. I will eat it for the goddess, yeh? When the old woman comes back tomorrow she will think Ningal has enjoyed her slop. Khe-khe-khe."

"Don't touch the bowl," commanded Avram. "You see how happy the old woman felt in serving her goddess."

"I am hungry. I need this soup more than the goddess. Khe-khe-khe. Shall I? Yeh?"

"No," asserted Avram, "and don't bother me."

"How much is this little one? It looks quite new. It is very small. Yeh?"

"Two measures of barley."

"That's too high. I think you should give it to me as a gift. Yeh?

"What will you do with it? Sell it?"

"What a stupid question. Khe-khe-khe. Worship it of course, you fool, yeh?"

"How old are you?"

"Seventy on the last new moon before the New Year. Yeh?"

"You are an objectionable old donkey. Yet you will worship this piece of clay that was finished only yesterday. One might just as soon worship you."

"Good. So get down on your knees before me. Yeh?"

"You are no doubt an old idiot; yet you have more sense than all these idols combined."

"Now this is blasphemy, yeh? You will now give me this little statuette if you don't want to be charged with desecrating the holy gods, or what's even worse, with atheism. Khe-khe-khe."

"Get your old carcass out of here, you slimey old blackmailer," and Avram rushed to pick up Nosku's gnarled walking staff leaning against the wall. Nosku ran out and barely missed the stick that Avram hurled at him. It hit the wall and bounced back. Avram was now in a blinding rage. He grabbed the staff and began pounding the clay idols with violent fury. Soon they were all in smithereens. When able to catch his breath he noticed the great statue of Nannar, which Sabbattu had ordered, standing in a corner. It was almost finished. Terach was working on the arm which stood stretched out but bent at the elbow. A ladder was standing near. A smile came to his lips; his rage was largely spent. Avram mounted the ladder and placed the staff resting on the open palm with the end leaning against the body of the statue. He began to laugh and all his fury vanished. Then for the first time he noticed the head of old Nosku in the doorway, his body evidently behind the house wall on the street. Suddenly he heard a loud khe-khe-khe and the head disappeared.

Several moments later he could hear familiar voices in the patio. The family, the servants, and slaves came in from the temple memorial service. He heard his father say, "Eleazer, please take this upstairs and put it in my bedroom. You can wash your feet when you come down. I want to talk with Avram." It was another tightly bound parcel from Sabbattu. Emtelai, Davarah, Lot, and Sarai went to wash their feet. Terach entered the side opening from the patio and stood transfixed. He managed to stammer, "By the belly of Nannar, what went on here?" Avram saw the bowl of gruel still steaming slightly and said with a straight face, "Well, you see, father, an old woman brought some broth for the goddess Ningal. As soon as she left the other gods claimed that it was for them. A fight broke out and Nannar in the corner got angry. He seized a staff and broke the little gods into small pieces."

Terach never quite understood his son. He could not discern the shadow of a smile playing on the youthful features. Was his son serious? Could it be that a miracle actually happened? But on second thought he came to the conclusion that Avram was not above shattering the idols with his own hands. There was no telling what his son might do.

"Now don't hand me that kind of yarn. You know that these clay images can neither walk nor talk. They neither see nor hear."

"Then why do you worship them?" smiled Avram for the first time.

There was no point entering into a discussion with his son. He knew from experience that it would get him nowhere. He began to feel uneasy and looked nervously at the street door. Then a sudden idea hit him. This crazy incident might be utilized. Could he induce Sabbattu to declare that a miracle happened? He knew of lesser occurrence that had inured to the benefit of the priests. A miracle could be quite profitable; it should promote the sale of images. It then occurred to him to ask whether anyone witnessed what had transpired.

"Yes, father; that old wretch Nosku. He made me very angry and I just lost all control of myself."

Everything went black for Terach. He tottered and almost fell.

"Why, Nosku is the worst scoundrel in Ur. He is treacherous, an awful liar and will utilize this business to his best advantage." Terach rushed forward to close the street door, then bolted it. He virtually ran into the patio and shouted for his two slaves to come down. He instructed the first who appeared:

"You know old Nosku. Run to the wine shop where he hangs out hoping to beg a drink. Tell him it is important that I see him immediately."

He ordered the other slave to bring in several barrels and fill them with the broken clay in the showrooms then to clean up every vestige of the destroyed images. Eleazer came into the showroom after washing his feet and drying them. He looked inquiringly at the barrels of broken clay and the empty counter. Avram took him aside and told him the whole story. By this time the slave returned and reported that Nosku was not in or near the wine shop. Terach asked whether he could find out where the old reprobate slept. The slave answered that he had been there but the wretched hovel was closed and Nosku was nowhere in sight. Terach led Avram and Eleazer out of the slave's hearing and into the patio.

"Eleazer, we are too disturbed to think. I fear Avram is in great danger and it might affect all of us. Tell us what is the best thing to do?" Eleazer always deferred to Terach as the master.

"Master," he advised. "I think you should go immediately to the high priest. He can best advise what should be done. If I were you, I would go at once. Delay might make it impossible even for him to help."

"Do you want to go with me?"

"No. I think I should be with Avram. We might think up a hiding place, at least for the moment, or until the matter clears up."

The day was ending and it was dangerous to walk on the dark streets of Ur at night unattended. Terach took along his two servants and one slave. They carried lanterns that burned oil.

Little Sarai came pattering down the steps and saw Avram with Eleazer in the patio. "Mother wants you both to come eat your supper. We are very hungry. Where is Father?" They went upstairs and Avram said to Emtelai, "Mother, let the children eat right away. We will wait for Father." He then signalled to Emtelai and Davarah to come into the next room. He did not want the children or the servants to hear.

"Father had to go on urgent matters to see the high priest. We must not remain. I am in trouble and must find a hiding place at once. But I don't know where."

"Why not my house?" suggested Davarah.

"We thought of that, but it would be the first place to look for me."

"But no one knows about the chapel underground where my Harran and Zirru's mother lie buried. No one will think of looking there."

Avram looked at Eleazer who nodded his approval.

"You must take it. You have no alternative. It's your only chance. But let's go quickly. I fear we are late already."

Avram received the key from Davarah. They both walked down the steps and opened the street door. In the darkness Avram heard Nosku's voice. "That's him! Grab him!" Temple guards held both until Nosku pointed Avram out. Two guards placed chains on his wrists. Then they fastened each hand to the wrists of the guards on each side of Avram as he walked to the temple prison surrounded by ten armed men.

## III

On being told that the high priest was engaged in an important conference Terach waited in the ante-chamber; a special concession from the *kadosh* who knew that the visitor came quite often and was always received. The image-maker feared that the delay might prove harmful to his son, yet felt confident that Sabbattu would somehow straighten things out. He did not quite understand the priest's protective interest but why ask questions if he always received the help for which he came. The matter of the parcels puzzled him and the priest did not make quite clear what he wanted. Terach seemed to fit in with Sabbattu's schemes which were no doubt very subtle. He had hinted something about a sudden change, or a journey, from Ur to Haran, but it all seemed quite nebulous, somewhere in the distance future. He had not yet started any preparations for traveling as he hoped that somehow such a drastic change would not be necessary. The priest did not always follow through with his words, which he sometimes seemed to forget. Weeks had gone by and the anxiety of an invasion faded not only in Terach but also from the minds of many people in Ur. One must be an optimist and hope that the gods would protect their favorite city.

At last Sabbattu came in and showed surprise on seeing his image-maker. Were the parcels lost or stolen? The account of Avram's escapade disturbed him visibly. He sent the *kadosh* to the temple prison and got back the information of Avram's incarceration on a warrant issued by Hunate. "Not so good," was the priestly comment. He dispatched a written note requesting the jailer to send the prisoner to him under an armed guard, who should wait in the anteroom of his reception chamber. To make it more official the priest stamped the papyrus with his seal.

Avram came in looking pale and tired. Terach was hungry and asked whether his son had eaten any supper. Avram had not had a mouthful since the forenoon meal. The priest offered him the fruit, wine, and raisin bread that remained on the tripods. Strengthened by the food Avram looked better.

"Why did you do it?" curtly asked the high priest.

"That awful Nosku made me angry and I was seized by an impulse to shatter the idols in the shop. I just could not control my feelings."

"That might make a good plea of insanity. Had I received the complaint I would have seized that fellow Nosku and had him thoroughly whipped, then ordered him to hold his tongue unless he wanted something worse. But it is too late for that. My foe, Hunate, a vindictive fanatic, saw the opportunity for a sensational trial, especially at this time of the disturbed mind of the people. I will try to get the case dismissed or at least postponed. But you, Avram, must cooperate fully."

"And what does that mean, your lordship?"

"Well, you must be ready to repudiate your hasty action as wrong, impious, and even criminal. You bear no hostility to the gods. You simply cannot account for this queer incident. You must be ready to make public penance and assure everyone of your devotion to the gods and your faithful service ever after. If you carry out such promises, I feel I can save you, although I believe that you are disqualified from the priesthood, at least for the present."

"I cannot meet your conditions, nor do I want to be a priest."

"Well in heaven's name, what's wrong with my conditions, as you phrase it? Incidentally, my sculptor, have you any men with you?" Terach nodded his head. "Then send them home, and I will order my personal guard to escort you." Terach left the room. "Now go on with your reply, Avram."

"Adoni, perhaps you fail to appreciate the significance of the holocaust several days ago. You and your priests approved it or it would not have happened. Your approval, I take it, reflects the wishes of the gods who were pleased with the sacrifice of 27 men and women. Do you think that this mass murder, and that is the proper name for what you call sacrifice, can go without the challenge or protest of thinking people, who perhaps are timid about denouncing so great a crime. If the gods are guilty of crimes then should they be worshipped?"

"Does this mean that you no longer serve the gods of our pantheon?"

"That is true," asserted Avram with conviction.

"So the long discussion, at your father's request, when I gave up part of the New Year festival for your enlightenment was wasted?"

"I thought I made my faith quite clear on that occasion," observed Avram.

"I considered your statements the argumentation of a young person who loves to hear the sound of his voice or wants to show how cleverly he can debate. But let's get down to practical matters. Do you want to save your life, which is in danger?"

"Yes, but not at the cost of my convictions, my principles, my soul, if that is the proper term."

"It strikes me that your smashing of the clay statuettes might be interpreted as your rejection of our religion, which is polytheism."

"That is correct," asserted Avram.

"Well then, there is nothing more to talk about. I can't help you. This means that you have pronounced your own doom."

"I have faith in the Most High God. He will help me," assured Avram.

"Who is he?" questioned Sabbattu, as if he did not know.

"El Elyon, the unseen God of justice and mercy, who created the heavens and the earth."

The high priest opened the door and called in the temple guards. They entered and conducted Avram back to prison.

"What are we to do now?" asked the downcast Terach in a weary voice that seemed to imply the end of all things.

"We have an old saying," commented the high priest. "The gods will help only those who are willing to help themselves. Is it possible that your son is world-weary and like Shub-Ad is seeking death? But he does not appear resigned. Or does he really believe that his God will come to his aid and save him? The only thing left for me to do is try to delay the trial. I am confident that with the coming of Hammurabi a great change will come."

"But when will he come?" questioned Terach in sepulchral tones.

"Quite soon, I believe," responded the priest. "Are my parcels safe? I shall have another for you tonight. Have you been preparing for the journey?" Terach shook his head negatively.

"Then prepare at once. Be ready to go on an hour's notice." Seeing the lack of interest in the crushed image-maker, he wondered whether he comprehended. "Do you understand my words?"

"Yes. But how do we travel? I have a family of five, that is counting Avram. Then there is Eleazer, the two slaves, and two servants who can be left behind."

"I shall have a boat ready. It can accommodate all including the servants who will come in handy especially for defense against robbers." The priest had his parcels in mind.

"But how can I leave Avram? It would seem like deserting him."

"Terach, I am placing in you the greatest trust I ever put in anyone." The image-maker looked up. He had never heard such earnest tones from him before. "I am in a position to know what will happen here. It will be a catastrophe. If Hammurabi meets with opposition he will destroy us. I am trying my best to prevent bloodshed, civil strife, and to save this old city, if possible. My intentions will be misinterpreted. Ur will suspect that I am with Babylon and Hammurabi will think that I am for Ur. I may be branded a traitor by both sides. I will get notice of

Hammurabi's approach. Then my personal guard, along with Avram and Zirru, will knock on your door after midnight. They will help to move your household to the boat. You and your family will be among the few who will escape. I may remain in Ur or Hammurabi might take me to Babylon. Then I will contact you. If you find yourself in deep distress, then open one of my parcels and take such gold or silver as you will need. If I am dead, keep the parcels as your own. Incidentally, Eleazer should be of great value. Put him in charge of your household immediately. In Haran I may invest with you and become a partner in some enterprise under the direction of Eleazer. So you see you have no reason to be discouraged."

He went into his bedchamber and brought out another parcel, then called his six guardsmen. As Terach was leaving, Sabbattu said, "If this is the last time we meet, farewell."

## IV

On a pallet of straw lay Avram looking up at the square opening high on the wall of the cell through which several stars were gleaming. He felt satisfied with his answers to the high priest; they relieved him of the guilt feeling that had oppressed him for not protesting the mass immolation before the concourse waiting to view the dead bodies. If enough people protested, the priests might adopt a different attitude and change the public approval of human sacrifice. It was really up to the priesthood to wean the people away from such cruel, malignant practices. If the priests would preach that the sacrifice of men and women was abhorrent to the godhead then such a scene which he witnessed would never again be seen.

"But what will happen to me now? Sabbattu was quite threatening. Nor did the priest display anger merely to frighten me into submission. How can one who believes in the Most High God agree to bow down before idols of clay. Didn't El Elyon say such gods were false? Does the Most High God know what I said to the high priest? What can I do to acquaint El Elyon with my rejection of these false gods? Can I speak in a voice loud enough to be heard in the high heavens?"

Avram became deeply absorbed in these thoughts while standing on flat ground without trees, grass, or any vegetation. It was night and only a thin crescent could be seen. Yet there was no lack of illumination. Plentiful light streamed from the stars; he had never seen so many before. They were larger than usual and looked like little round balls of silver that studded the sky and twinkled with bright little gleams of fire. It was as bright as if a full round moon lit up the heavens without the smallest cloud obscuring a single one of the countless stellar minusculae. The soft pellucid light felt radiant, warm, and cheering.

A strange silence prevailed from the arch of the sky and through the hemisphere that ended on the flat earth. It seemed as if the tiniest sound could travel from the ground and penetrate the highest heaven without the impediment of sighing breezes, the chirping of birds, the buzzing of flies or insects. The silence seemed a real presence that could be sensed or perceived yet not heard. Avram was neither lonely, isolated, nor frightened. The presence reaching from the firmament beyond the constellations to the lowly sod beneath his sandals seemed to cast a protective mantle which created a kinship with the earth and sky, the crescent, the stars, and the balmy atmosphere. He felt a part of an endless creative process that unified everything everywhere. The very silence seemingly a part thereof began to communicate in comforting, articulate terms:

"Avram, Avram."

Falling on his face, he cried out, "Here I am, Oh Lord God."

"Why are you downcast?"

"Evil men are bent on destroying me."

"They shall not. Look toward heaven and count the stars, if you can. So shall your offspring be."

"But, Most High God, the priests of the false gods are planning my death."

"Fear not, I am with you."

"I told them their gods are vain and thou, El Elyon, wilt protect me. Did I speak truly?"

No further answer came. Silence once more reigned supreme. The stars ceased twinkling. The dawn descended upon the earth like an exhalation. Avram opened his eyes and the sun was shining into them through the opening in the prison wall. He felt contentment and elation.

## V

At the morning temple service Sabbattu addressed Hunate:

"Tell me, adon priest, why the haste in rushing to arrest the son of our image-maker? Have you such strong proof of his guilt? Setting the power of the law upon a youth is a serious matter."

"I sent them to you, adon Sabbattu, but you were too busy. Those prosecutors and especially their leader were quite frantic. They made it appear as if the gods will be so outraged that they will bring new calamities upon our city. Judging from their demeanor the effect of the sacrifices by Queen Shub-Ad and her devoted band has been completely nullified. I never saw a more fanatical, malignant crowd. They intimated that if the priests won't act they would themselves. They boasted of a big mob behind them. I felt that I had to put Avram in protective custody."

"What is there so criminal," asked the high priest, "about the crazy act of a son smashing his father's idols in the workshop? Such an act, if deliberately done in a temple, is a different matter. But it would seem that the loss itself should be sufficient punishment. I have seen far worse offenses sloughed off, ignored, and forgotten!"

"You don't seem to gauge the public temper," warned Hunate. "The people have been jittery enough about the drought and the fear of invasion. The group sacrifice we thought would be an emolient. Now comes this image-breaking affair. I believe we cannot dare to play with the passions of a desperate mob by ignoring its demands."

"You wish, I take it, to throw the victim to the wolves."

"I didn't mean that. Let us assemble all the judges and consider this matter carefully. I shall send word immediately. They can assemble before sundown."

"Isn't that rushing matters?" questioned the high priest. "It shows we are panicky, frightened by an unwashed, unsandaled horde of hoodlums. I refused to be stampeded by a mob."

"I can't see any objection to the calm deliberation of our trained jurists. Such a discussion can only prove enlightening. I shall summon them with your permission."

# 12

# Condemned to Burn

WHILE SABBATTU WAS FINISHING HIS MORNING MEAL THE *kadosh* who attended him came in and said that Babaku was outside insisting that he had something urgent to communicate. Babaku was the bookkeeper who reported to the high priest the finances of the Terach establishment as well as all he heard and saw that might be of interest. The *kadosh* was ordered to admit him.

"My Lord, excuse this early interruption. I left my house and was on my way to work. When I arrived I saw the Terach house closed and a mob on the Street of the Ancients. They carried sticks and whips and shouted that they would beat up all the Arameans. Some yelled, 'Kill the foreigners who smash up our gods!' Then one of them, a vicious looking ruffian, got upon a pile of rubbish and screamed, 'We want to get our hands on Avram. He must be one of those Habiru. They are the worst people in the world. Will you permit those aliens, the race of Hammurabi, to insult our gods? No wonder they send us droughts and wars. This Avram must pay with his life. He cursed our gods and broke their images into pieces. Will you red-blooded people of Ur stand for this kind of treatment from foreigners who go about blaspheming our holy Nannar and Enlil and Irnina?' I could hear nothing more on account of the screaming. Some of the women were just as bad as the men. More and more were coming. I believe that the house of Terach and all its people are in great danger. I therefore rushed to tell you."

The high priest sent for the captain of the temple guards and ordered him to send ten armed men to protect the house of Terach, then to get in touch with the ba'iru and tell them to keep a steady watch until the excitement died down. He then told Babaku to be back in about an hour and take a parcel to Terach but not to stay until the danger was over.

No sooner did Babaku leave than Keturah rushed in breathless. "I hear that Avram is in prison. What did he do?" The priest informed her briefly of his offense. "I am sure my beloved man will save him," and she kissed him on the cheek. He told her of the difficulty in getting Avram to cooperate. She became more nervous and said, "I must see him. Please let me. I feel sure I can convince him." The priest replied, "I hope you will," as he wrote an order on papyrus and stamped it with his seal. He handed it to the *kadosh* and although quite busy, he waited for the prisoner.

"Avram, I hope you changed your mind since last night."

"Oh, I have no fear. My God will protect me."

Both the priest and Keturah were surprised at his assurance. They could not detect a shade of anxiety on his face. Sabbattu left the two alone and cautioned the guardsmen in the antechamber not to let anyone else in except the priest-teacher, Khar-Sak. Keturah threw her arms about Avram's neck, kissed and hugged him wildly.

"I hope you will do everything possible to get out of

this mess. Avram, why can't you follow the advice of Sabbattu? He is very wise and can save you, I am sure, if you will only let him."

"I am not worried. My God, El Elyon, will shield me."

"Avram, dear, I've learned a great deal since I saw you last. I acted very foolish then and I regret it deeply. I feel ashamed every time I think of it. The high priestess Zur-na-na, who was of royal blood, filled my head with a high sense of my importance. I am truly sorry about her early death. I learned that we cannot live alone. Sabbattu is fond of saying, 'those who live for themselves are left unto themselves.' All the priestesses began to detest me and I felt lonely and isolated until, contrary to Zur-na-na's teachings, I decided to be friendly with them all and to do just like the rest. Now this applies to you, too. Don't separate yourself from the world. Do as the rest do. If they serve the gods, then you do likewise. What is the sense in imposing your single opinion against the beliefs of everyone around you? You can only arouse hatred against yourself, and that is what got you into the trouble you are in now."

"I don't know whether you are mature enough to understand what I am saying, Zirru, but there is such a thing as the truth and some people must suffer for the truth, otherwise there would never be a change in human thinking."

"I understand you very well, Avram. I can only say that if this suffering were confined to yourself only, then you might have the privilege of choosing your own way of living or thinking. But unfortunately, your actions involve others who may suffer more than you. I don't suppose you realize that women bear grief far more than men. The position that you take brings sorrow upon your father and mother, upon my mother, Davarah, my brother, Lot, your half-sister, little Sarai, not to mention me. But I suppose

I don't count any more since I am out of your life. By what right, may I ask, do you bring suffering upon so many people? Isn't your manner of sacrificing for your God quite selfish and even heartless?"

"Zirru, these are truths you mention but they are petty truths. Isn't it far more important for the world to bring about the knowledge and worship of the true god of justice and compassion than to spare several people some suffering which they will soon get over anyway? Or should the search for truth cease until certain people leave this earth for Aralu?"

A knock on the door and Khar-Sak entered. Avram and Keturah rose to honor the sage. Keturah took her leave with the remark that the stubborn Avram was now in the presence of the wisest priest in all Akkad and Sumer.

"Sorry to see you incarcerated, my young friend. But an inexperienced, unselfish youth with a tender conscience will always get into difficulties. I have not seen you since that discussion on the New Year's feast. I was hoping that the visit to Babylon would make you more worldly. Evidently it did not."

"Thank you, adon teacher, for coming. It is always a joy to hear your wisdom." To Khar-Sak's surprise Avram seemed neither downcast nor perturbed.

"Adon Sabbattu," continued the teacher-priest, "has given me an idea of your situation. It simply boils down to this proposition: Should someone tell an untruth to save his life? This brings to mind a visit I had recently from a woman. Her husband, a merchant, takes long journeys in caravans or ships. While he was away she lapsed from virtue and did lie with another man. She does not think anyone knows about it. But should her husband ask if she remained true to him during his absence, what should she say? She has a truthful disposition and her husband takes her word without further question. If she tells him the truth, grave consequences will result. She was not thinking of herself although she might be thrown into the river for adultery. But what worries her is the effect of the scandal upon her family. She has children, some married and others single. Her husband has other offspring from concubines. Both she and her husband have numerous relatives who would no doubt feel disgraced. If she keeps quiet no one will be the wiser. If she tells the truth, everyone will suffer. What would you advise in my place, my youthful scholar?"

"This is a personal matter, adon Khar-Sak, and in no way applicable to me. In her case prudence would advise silence. In my case it is not merely a matter of holding my tongue. The court will demand something more affirmative."

"So you think, Avram, that you owe no duty to yourself or to your family in trying to save your life? We live only once and it is encumbent upon every one of us to prolong our lives to the fullest extent. Suppose you are required to pay homage to the gods worshipped by your father and grandfather. After all, the Lord Nannar is the patron and guardian of Ur, the city in which you were born. It is a matter of loyalty, of patriotism to honor him. Why can't you do what everyone in Ur does freely and gladly?"

"Because I cannot accept any god who permitted the sacrifice to himself of 27 martyrs, regardless whether they were willing or not. I serve El Elyon and will dedicate my life to further spread His worship."

"Avram, it is written in the *Epic of Gilgamesh* that Irnina-Ishtar was so enamored of the hero that to win him she stooped to conquer. If you are so anxious to spread the faith of your newly chosen God, why not do likewise? Pay the required adoration to the gods of Ur, then leave our city to pursue your dedicated aim to proselytise the belief in El Elyon."

"This is what is so repellent about your tolerant polytheism, which permits everything and forbids nothing. There should be a standard in morals and in conduct. What you suggest with the best of intentions to save my life is after all hypocrasy and lying. My stern, Most High God of Truth and Justice, loathes duplicity."

"May I suggest that you omit to mention your God at the trial?"

"That would be like rejecting Him!" exploded Avram. "I would rather die a thousand times than deny El Elyon, the God of my forefathers."

"I am afraid I will be unable to do anything for you. May your God protect you. Mine will not."

"I know El Elyon will," said Avram, his face registering deep faith.

## II

About two hours before sunset seven judges, of which five were priests and two laymen, assembled in the Temple of Nannar. The presiding judge, Su-bu-gab-ri, belonged to an old family of merchant princes, whose ships had sailed for a century to India, Egypt, and some of the East African ports. Su-bu-gab-ri had received the best education obtainable in Ur, a city with an old culture, and had traveled spending some time in India and Egypt, studying, carousing, and observing. His prestige, family connections and learning entitled him to the highest post in Ur's judiciary.

Su-bu-gab-ri opened the sitting by inquiring into the reason for the irregular procedure of calling the court together when not in its regular term. Hunate, who had issued the warrant, explained the nature of the case, the public pressure for immediate action, and the disturbed state of people's minds. "Public opinion is outraged by this wanton assault upon the gods in destroying their symbolic images. Everyone knows that the images of the gods are holy and their desecration is an offense against religion and a crime against the state. I fear the effect of this sacrilege upon the populace, which already is distracted by the drought, the imminence of invasion, and the recent death of the 27 martyrs."

A different interpretation was voiced by Sabbattu when he thought that there was no urgency in rushing this matter to the criminal court. "Everyone knows of far graver offenses than this petty incident being forgotten after the lapse of time. It is such a trial and its consequences that stir up public emotions to the cracking point. If there is excitement in the air, then let it calm down before we fan the fires of bigotry into hysteria. Let us give a rest to the nerves of a distracted people. It is far more important that we devote all our time and energy to the defense of our city, which may soon be invaded if we credit the words of Tartan Naburnergal. I would strongly urge the postponement of all hearings and trials to a more propitious time."

Another priest, a partisan of Hunate, commenting on the public's reaction towards the idol smashing, warned the court not to take the matter lightly. He gave a graphic account of the mob spirit. He was in the temple at the close of the memorial and saw people listening to a man named Nosku haranguing them about the desecration and profanation of the gods. The effect was volcanic. They were ready for riot, pillage, and even murder. The next morning a woman came to the temple and told him of the ugly temper displayed by the mobsters in front of Terach's house and workshop. They would probably have fired the house but for the timely arrival of the temple guards who scattered them. He could tell of other demonstrations on the waterfront and even in the open space in front of the royal palace but believed that a quick disposition of this case by the court would restore things to normalcy.

The presiding judge inquired of Hunate as to the number of witnesses who would testify and learned that there were none other than the accused in the temple prison and the prosecutor who was available. The judge then declared that there was no point in arguing as to whether or not the arrest should have been made when the culprit was already in confinement; that since the court was in session and both principals were ready, the trial should be over before sunset. The clerk declared the trial begun and Avram was brought in by the bailiff.

Nosku made a poor witness and created an unfavorable impression. The notoriety he gained gave him a puffed-up feeling of importance. The presiding judge instructed him to tell what he saw and heard in his own words. He began to orate and the solemnity of the trial began to deflate because of his comical mannerisms. The falsetto titter and the habitual *yeh* made the judges laugh at first, but they soon became tiresome, then obnoxious. The judge had to cut short his rambling speech and ordered him only to answer questions and omit the annoying cackle and the irksome *yehs*.

"You saw the prisoner, Avram, the son of Terach, break all the idols?"

"Yeh? I surely did, Judge."

"What weapon did he use?"

"No weapon at all, Judge. He used my walking stick, yeh? I never did get it back. I worked a long time . . ."

"Never mind the rest. What did he say when he was smashing them?"

"Judge, he was blaspheming horribly, khe-khe-khe. He was . . ."

"What words did he use?"

"I can't remember the words but they were shocking, yeh?"

"Were you in the workshop at the time?"

"I was out on the street, yeh? He grabbed my stick and wanted to hit me so I ran out. Khe-khe-khe. He threw . . ."

"How could you hear him talk on the street while he was breaking the images?"

"Oh yeh? He asked how old I was. I said I was seventy years old. Then he pointed to the little idol I wanted to buy and said, 'You were born 70 years ago and this idol was made yesterday, yeh? How can you worship it?' Khe-khe-khe. I said . . ."

"And that was said while you were on the street?"

"No. He asked that before, yeh?"

"And what did you answer to his question?"

"I told him I would report him for blaspheming and insulting the gods unless he gave me that little idol. Khe-khe-khe."

"Was that all he said?"

"No. He said I was an old donkey, yet had more sense than all the gods over there. Khe-khe-khe."

"Where was he pointing when he said 'over there'?"

"To the idols on the counter or shelf. I don't know the right name, yeh?"

The presiding judge asked whether any member of the court wanted to question the witness. Hearing none he curtly told Nosku, "You may go home."

"May I point out," ventured Sabbattu cautiously, "that a convincing case of blasphemy or derision or mockery has by no means been proven by the evidence. The prisoner was incensed by this despicable character, Nosku, and lost his temper. He acted like an enraged husband who breaks up the dishes to relieve his feelings. Now I would admit that such an act in our temple before an assembled concourse would serve to bring contempt or contumely upon the holy gods. I think the case should be dismissed at this point."

"But the accused did smash the statuettes of our gods," contended the presiding judge.

"May I be permitted to observe," begged Khar-Sak, "that I have been thinking about and studying the case and cannot find any law that holds it a capital crime to break images. I agree with the high priest that in the temple such an act would be reprehensible. But in the workshop it could be no offense. For instance, the sculptor might become dissatisfied and break up his handiwork to use the clay for another trial of his skill. I agree with Adon Sabbattu that the action against Avram, son of Terach, should be dismissed."

"We will consider these motions after we hear from the accused," declared the presiding justice with finality.

The deep voice of the clerk boomed: "Avram, son of Terach, step forward and face the Lord Nannar. Kneel, place your left hand on your heart, raise your right hand and repeat after me."

Avram stood up and declared, "Your honors, I cannot take this oath."

"Why not, prisoner?" demanded Su-bu-gab-ri, frowning.

"Because I no longer serve Nannar."

"Then swear him before another god," commanded the judge somewhat petulantly.

"I do not serve the gods of Ur," declared the accused.

"No? Yet you speak with the accent of one born in our city. Then what gods do you serve?"

"I worship El Elyon, Creator of heaven and earth, the God of my forefathers."

"Adon High Priest, I understand that the prisoner is the son of your image-maker. Is the father also a non-believer?"

"No. Terach is a pious worshiper of our gods. So was his father, Nahor. And so was Avram until recently."

"What caused the young man to reject our sacred pantheon?"

"I believe he was strongly affected by the recent holocaust. He expressed himself quite vehemently to the effect that the gods should neither permit nor accept human sacrifices, especially to themselves."

Su-bu-gab-ri reflected a while, then said quietly almost to himself: "He has convicted himself. There is really nothing further to ask him. Oh yes, do you admit smashing the idols of our gods in your father's house?"

"I do."

"Did you blaspheme, curse, mock, or revile the gods?"

"No, your honor."

"Then why did you do it?"

"I lost my temper. That creature Nosku irritated me."

"Does anyone wish to question the accused?"

Hearing no answer the chief justice ordered the guards to conduct the prisoner back to his cell.

"Now we can discuss our differences," continued Su-bu-gab-ri. "I think most of us believe in Avram's guilt. He confessed breaking images which are sacred. His rejection of our gods shows his feeling of contempt and opprobrium which really is tantamount to blasphemy. To me, he has violated our most important laws and should be punished. But we will entertain some discussions which may differ from our own conclusions."

"My Lord, chief justice," began Sabbattu, "I still maintain that there is no proof that Avram committed blasphemy, ridicule, mockery, or vilification of the gods. No matter how much we disagree with him we must be impressed with his honesty. Had he been guilty of blasphemy he would have confessed just as he admitted breaking the idols. As for the offense of smashing, our sage Khar-Sak, I believe, made it quite clear that breaking images is no crime in itself. I vote not guilty and that he be discharged."

"The most damaging confession," commented Khar-Sak, "in the eyes of our chief justice stems from Avram's rejection of our gods and his choice of another who is not in Ur's pantheon. Personally, I deplore this defection. But is this crime as great as it appears to some? To me, the outstanding merit and greatest virtue of our polytheistic faith is its inherent tolerance or liberalism. We believe in many deities and do not deny the existence of gods outside of our periphery. Nor do we resent the worship of other gods, even those we know not, by strangers or dwellers in our midst. We hold no grudge against those who serve Ammon-Ra of Egypt or the Brahma of India. We accord the right of free worship to others as we expect other nations to respect our beliefs. This is the most glorious feature in our religion.

"Why should we prevent anyone from leaving us, or from adopting another faith? Let's consider the case before us. A high-minded young man, earnest and moral, believes that another god has spoken to him. He is so convinced that he is willing to pay any price, even his life, for the right of serving this strange god. We may not respect his judgement but who can deny his honesty? You know it is much easier to conform. All he has to say is that he regrets his hasty temper in breaking the idols, something he would never do again. Then he could agree to bow down to Nannar and to serve him; hereafter he can do or believe as he wishes. Shall we punish a man for his integrity, for his sterling character? If you believe him too dangerous to have in our midst, then banish him. I vote for his acquittal.

"My fellow judges," admonished Hunate, "I fully disagree with my two colleagues and especially with the renowned sage, Khar-Sak, who is very learned and can make an absurd proposition sound like the wisdom of Ea. This vaunted liberalism is really false theory dressed up as a virtuous doctrine. Tolerance is the sign of a dying culture. When the will is lacking to oppose, it is then that tolerance makes a virtue of weakness or irresolution. What is liberalism but a mask for decadence. It never thrives in a healthy or virile society. It is degeneration taking on the guise of potency. What have we here but an alien Aramean who poses as a Sumerian yet is intent on undermining the lofty religion of a superior race. He can never be one of us, so he wants to destroy a faith, a way of life that he can never comprehend, much less assimilate or master. There is vindictive envy behind his protest of horror at our noble conception of voluntary death for the glory of our puissant gods. Only one who has the instincts of a savage would have the audacity to smash the gods of a sublime religion which took thousands of years for our valiant Sumerians to build up. He has the mentality of a simpleton to reject our Nannar, Enlil, Ningal, Ea, Irnina for an absurd god of whom no one has ever heard. Can he point to any nation or people other than his desert forebears that worship this El Elyon? And yet we are asked to tolerate this Bedouin with his desert god. I tell you, my colleagues, a mild death is too merciful for this Semitic Habiru. We should throw him into a fiery kiln and let his queer god come to save him."

"My colleagues of the bench," apologized Su-hu-gab-ri. "I cannot indulge in the fine-spun theorizing of the sage, Khar-Sak, nor of the second high priest, Hunate. My training was in law and commerce. I regard as the highest goal the protection of all forces that support and sustain our country, our society, our law and order. Religion is the mortar that cements society, that holds the state intact, that maintains orderly government. Contempt for the gods undermines our religion, weakens our institutions, and therefore must be eliminated with fire and sword, if necessary. Anyone who destroys the symbols of our gods incurs the hostility of the godhead. Anyone who rejects the gods weakens the foundation of our religion. I, therefore, consider Avram guilty and deserving of the death penalty."

The remaining four judges voted for conviction. The chief justice then pronounced Avram guilty by a vote of five to two. He then submitted the penalty for the court to decide. Sabbattu declared for banishment, Khar-Sak for exile. The rest of the court voted the death penalty.

"I cannot but applaud," declared Hunate, "the instincts of the plain people. Unconsciously they possess intuitive wisdom. They immediately sensed the guilt of this alien Semite as the potential destroyer of all things they hold dear. They became restive. They felt rightly that the gods would never forgive the affront of smashing their images until they were avenged. Immediately the common people called for his death. I think we should follow this intuition and not keep our people in suspense. I would suggest to use the furnace that bakes brick and is attached to the temple outer wall. The kiln should be red hot. At night the flames would be seen from a distance. The convicted criminal can be thrown in from the top of the temple wall. It will be a spectacle which the people will enjoy immensely. It will ease the tensions. It will immediately calm the raging excitement."

The suggestion of Hunate was put to a vote and carried five to two.

## IV

Nosku waited around until the trial was over. He learned the verdict from Hunate and felt that he had rendered a great service. He reached the wineshop in time and the sentence was received with such satisfaction that the owner decided to keep open longer than usual. Customers crowded the saloon and Nosku was treated so many times that he became tipsy. The drinking crowd sang, shouted, and decided to raid Terach's house but was turned back by the ba'iru on guard. They enjoined each other not to miss the pyrotechnic spectacle. They must enjoy seeing the desecrator of the gods burning in the temple furnace. The blustering roisterers brought home the news and the next day the entire city hailed the welcome verdict as just retribution for so vile a crime.

On the following day Sabbattu received a secret dispatch that Larsa had fallen, its King Rim-Sin had been killed, and Hammurabi was preparing to march on Ur. The priest sent another parcel to Terach and the messenger urged him to make haste and be ready for departure that very night but withheld the news of Avram's conviction. Under Eleazer's direction, Terach, Emtelai, the servants, and slaves wrapped up whatever they could in reed packets reinforced with hempen rope. They were able to work without interruption or disturbance in the locked and barred house. Davarah and Lot had been in the house since Avram's arrest. Together with the two slaves and Lot, Davarah managed to slip out and go to her house to take along clothes and woven cloth for the journey. By evening Terach's household was ready for the hasty, stealthy departure.

For several days the people of Ur had been watching the sky eagerly. For the first time in many months they could see thin patches of white clouds driven across the sky by breezes. They were certain that the end of drought was finally near. After they heard of the court's decision they felt certain that the gods were only waiting for the burning of the wicked culprit to send the much needed rain.

All day long workmen were getting the furnace ready for the burnt offering that would be pleasing to the gods. The furnace was a round kiln open on top. Blocks of mud mixed with straw or lime or clay were stacked near the furnace round wall which the workmen closed. The fire of bitumen would be lowered from above and fed until the exteme heat dried and then baked the mud blocks into hard bricks. The furnace was sanctuary property adjoining the temple wall and useful in burning up the accumulation of fat, skin, feathers, hoofs, and entrails—the remains of sacrifices which the altars could not consume. Besides keeping the temple grounds clean the garbage that remained from the offerings was combustible and economical for feeding the fire.

Towards sundown the temple courts were crowded with men and fewer women. More and more were coming until the ground floor was filled and people had to occupy the steps and all available spots where they could stand.

The overflow stood in the Temenos outside of the temple entrance. The priests and judges were on the Ziggurat terrace and on the parapet that surrounded the shrine of Nannar. Some priestesses watched from the open court where the *kedashes* were selected by men for intercourse. A minority refused to see a human being consumed in fire. A group was in Keturah's chambers trying to comfort her. She could not help sobbing although she felt hopeful that Sabbattu would somehow save her Avram.

It suddenly turned quite dark when a heavy cloud covered the setting sun. It was soon pitch black and neither the moon nor the stars was visible. The people were jubilant at the prospect of a quick end to the long, seemingly endless drought. The men on the temple wall threw into the burning furnace all the remaining fat, wood shavings, rancid butter, and broken reeds. The fire spluttered, crackled, and lit up the entire temple area with its brilliant flames. The tongues of red fire leaping upward could be seen from roofs of houses in a great portion of the city.

At a sign from Hunate, four men brought Avram from the cell. His hands were tied behind his back. They climbed the steps until they reached the top of the wall. They walked with Avram in the center and stopped about ten feet away from the furnace in which the fire was raging furiously. The four guards took hold of each arm and each foot and Avram lay in their hands, his face to the sky, and his feet toward the burning furnace. The guards started to move when suddenly a blinding streak of lightning and a deafening crash of thunder struck so close that the men let Avram fall on the parapet. Simultaneously, large raindrops fell thick and fast, increasing in velocity each moment until the downpour obscured everything, including the people from each other. The flaring fire in the furnace turned to smoke and was quickly extinguished. Darkness that was impenetrable covered the temple area as well as the city. The rain that became a freshet could be felt and heard but not seen.

Each one of the four guards could only think of his own safety. Each turned slowly and walked carefully on the wall unable to see his way. They finally felt the steps that led down into the temple court. Here they could hardly proceed on account of the press of people trying to reach some kind of shelter. Cries of hurt or pain were heard above the heavy rainfall. One pregnant woman shoved against the wall had a miscarriage. Some fell off the steps and were severely hurt. Many felt their way to the entrance and with the help of an occasional flash of lightning proceeded to their homes the best they could in the continuous downpour to which there seemed to be no letup.

The priests and the judges on the ziggarut slowly felt their way down the straight line of steps. Attendants covered with leather capes held closed lanterns that guided them into the corridor which led to the high priest's reception room. The priests managed to get to their own rooms. Sabbattu offered the judges dry clothes. When all felt dry, they sipped the wine offered by their host and ate such fruits and nuts that were on the tripods. Soon Khar-Sak and Hunate came into the room. A discussion arose with the chief justice's question as to the status of the convict. Was it proper to attempt his death again? The gods apparently did not approve of burning him. The high priest again voiced his opinion that Avram was not guilty and therefore the gods would not permit him to burn. Khar-Sak looked bewildered as he described Avram's expressed certainty that no harm could befall him since his God would surely protect him. Hunate scoffed at such nonsensical talk by learned men who ought to know that rain can fall at any time. Besides, who knew whether the Aramean was not struck by thunder sent by the god Enlil.

## V

Lying on his back, his eyes closed, Avram fancied himself dead. He could think only of the moment before he died. He had complete faith that the Most High God would protect him. Now he stood facing the fiery furnace. Was it possible that El Elyon would forsake him? He felt the guards grabbing his arms and feet. They were swinging him ready for the plunge. Now an extremely bright light flashed before his eyes; it no doubt was the fire of the furnace. The powerful noise was the sound of his body hitting the walls of the kiln. He was now in the darkness of Aralu and the God of his forefathers did forsake him. Bereft of all hope he must spend thousands of years, perhaps many more, in total darkness. He could never again pray to El Elyon who did not help him and perhaps could not even if he wanted to.

He became aware of a light shining through his closed eyes, then heard a clap of thunder. He opened his eyes and all was darkness but a heavy rain was pounding him. He tried to move and realized that he was lying on his back, his hands under him. He attempted to rise but couldn't. Able to turn over, he got on his knees and stood up with his hands tied behind his back. He could walk but could not see where. Never had he known such heavy rainfall. He was moving when suddenly a flash of lightning showed that he was on the wall dangerously near the edge. Another move and he could have fallen off. Cautiously, he walked down some steps until he felt soft muddy earth under his feet. Moving alongside the wall and feeling his way in the heavy rain he touched a round brick wall that was warm. This must be the furnace with its fire extinguished by the heavy rain, which at the same time saved his own life.

A warm feeling entered his heart, and not because his life was spared. The Most High God, the Creator of heaven and earth, had redeemed his promise. Kneeling on the wet, soggy earth he prayed: "Oh, God of my forefathers, I shall serve thee all the days of my life. My children and their descendants shall worship El Elyon forever."

The extremely heavy downpour continued but Avram found himself in a sheltered position between the temple wall and the kiln. The strong wind blowing from the north drove the slanting rain southward. The acute angle between the wall and the round brick oven almost kept the rain out. The downpour went on for almost two hours, giving Avram the opportunity to reflect about his situation. The court had evidently sentenced him to burn in the furnace. Would the judges mitigate the sentence because the timely rain extinguished the fire? They would probably set the burning for a future time. Therefore, he had no other course than flight.

The immediate problem was to free his hands which were tied with hempen cord behind his back. He became aware of pain in one knee. This was no doubt due to a cut received when he knelt to express thanksgiving to El Elyon. He recalled feeling something sharp cutting his knee. Kneeling, he felt the ground the best he could until finally he touched a sharp object, either flint or bronze, which some workman probably dropped. Able to pick it up with difficulty he finally cut the cord and released one hand. Now he could walk with ease. The rain was slackening although it did not stop completely. He decided to go to his father's house while it was still raining. The judges would hardly send out a searching party for him in such bad weather.

Walking as rapidly as possible over the soaked rubbish that cluttered the unpaved streets, he sometimes sank knee deep into puddles of water. When he reached Terach's dwelling he was surprised to see a large covered wagon drawn by two oxen in front of the door opening on the street. Avram went into the dark patio, then slipped upstairs and found everyone carrying bundles, packages, and small pieces of furniture in the uncertain light of the small clay lamps. They were loading the covered wagon until it was almost full. The women, Sarai, and Lot managed to crowd in among the bundles. The men had to walk with the six temple guards alongside the oxen and the wagon, thus forming a formidable defense group against robbers or marauders.

Everyone gave Avram a warm but rapid embrace for they were told not to tarry as it was urgent that they leave immediately. The amazement was mutual when he and Zirru-Keturah beheld each other. Neither knew how the other could get there. Terach's house had been closed with no outside communication since Avram's arrest. Consequently, no one knew about the court's sentence. Keturah knew but was told by Sabbattu to keep silent since the fate of Avram was in doubt. The priest had sent to the temple prison to ascertain his whereabouts and learned that the prisoner was not in his cell nor did anyone know what became of him. He felt confident that no harm could overtake Avram as long as his God could perform such unbelievable miracles.

# Haran

# 13

# The Caravan

ON THE VERY SAME DAY WHICH THE COURT HAD SET FOR THE burning, the high priest received a message delivered by Shadnego, the captain of the boat which had taken Avram and Eleazer to and from Babylon. Sabbattu began to use the Babylonian skipper after hearing good reports about him from the two passengers. The message stated that Larsa had fallen; that Rim-Sin was dead, and that Hammurabi was preparing in all haste to march south. The high priest wondered what would be the effect of Avram's burning on the populace. It might become difficult to prevent an inflamed mob from setting Terach's house on fire. He therefore asked Shadnego whether he could get the entire household of about 11 people on his boat that same night. He received an affirmative reply.

The skipper accompanied by the trustworthy *kadosh* informed Terach that a covered wagon would be at his door several hours after sundown to remove the entire family to the boat. The *kadosh* told him privately that Avram and Keturah would come in the same wagon. About three hours after sundown the covered wagon did reach the riverside. In the rain it would have been difficult to locate the boat among the other craft had not Shadnego posted several seamen on the wharf to direct the drivers where to stop. The Babylonian boat was tied to some wooden posts on the bank. Its deck was covered by a tarpaulin of sailcoth smeared with pitch that made it quite waterproof. The packets, the bedclothes, the small pieces of furniture were quickly stored on deck. Then the entire household found places, sitting or lying on the packages. Terach gave silver worth about six shekels to the captain for distribution among the temple guards.

Shadnego gave orders to pull up the stone anchors and drift down the river. He then called Terach, Avram, and Eleazer into his small cabin to decide on the course best to take. All the way from Babylon the Purattu had been so crowded with craft engaged in the war effort that Shadnego had difficulties in avoiding collisions. But apart from the perils of passing so many boats, it was next to impossible to steer upstream against a swift current swollen with heavy rainfall. There were two courses open. They could drift down the river to Eridu, then hope to join a caravan going north, possibly to Haran. West of the Purattu they would be away from war activities. Yet it was doubtful if any caravan was traveling because of the drought. The other course would be to drift down the rapid stream to the juncture of the Purattu and the Tigris. The boat could then sail for several weeks up the Tigris and reach Nineveh, a small city which no doubt had connections with Haran by caravan or otherwise. It was decided to stay on Shadnego's boat till Nineveh.

The family was of course interested in listening to the exciting events of the past few days. Keturah, holding Avram's hand, which was cold, became aware of his shivering and of his teeth chattering. All agreed that the malaria fever had returned because of his exposure during the past several hours. Drenched to the skin he had put on dry clothes only when he reached home. The course of travel was immediately changed. It was decided to stay in Eridu until Avram recovered. The servants and slaves were ordered to remain on board to watch the baggage, but Eleazer insisted that he stay with them. The baggage was too valuable to risk its loss. Of course, Sabbattu's parcels were carried to Eridu.

Two hours after sunrise the family arrived in Eridu, a very old city and quite important when a seaport. But sand and silt had extended its distance from the Persian Gulf. Now the city was on the decline. Seldom visited by caravans it became more and more dependent upon Ur. The owner of a big house gladly rented it to Terach for as long as he could stay. The atmosphere of the city had the charm of decadence. Manners and speech were cultivated. People boasted of their old families. Eridu felt proud in having Ea, the god of wisdom, as its patron. The inhabitants, apparently never too busy, loved to regale strangers with their myths and legends. Adapa, the great sage of Eridu, had been initiated in wisdom by the god himself; only Ea refused to impart the secret of eternal life. Another story related that the gods created man as a happy creature and gave him free will. But men did evil and were punished with the great flood. Only one man, Tagrug the weaver, survived and he could have lived on forever had he refused to eat fruit from the forbidden tree.

The attack of malaria was not as severe as on former occasions. Yet for three days fever and sweating followed shivering as regularly as night follows day. Avram never lost consciousness nor did he suffer brain fever as he did after being hit on the head following Zirru's selection as bride of Nannar. Yet malaria was sufficiently weakening to keep him in bed. Keturah nursed him day and night. She would not let anyone relieve her, yet managed to acquaint Davarah of her desire to marry Avram. Her "mother" tried to point out that Avram had become a fanatic since discovering his new God Who demanded sexual purity. From his point of view she had been defiled on becoming a temple priestess and no longer qualified to be the wife of a God-fearing man. At best, she could only hope to be his concubine. But Keturah insisted that she would not give up so easily.

On the fourth night Avram was sleeping soundly when Keturah crept into his bed. After midnight he happened to wake up, his face resting against firm nude breasts. There was enough lamplight to see who his bed companion was. Keturah began to kiss him. Her passionate embraces were undermining his will power. He soon succumbed. Never in his life had he imagined anyone could experience such a thrilling delight, such mad excitement. Exhausted, he quickly fell asleep. After sunrise he awoke and saw Keturah lying near him in all the beauty of her naked youth. He felt it was useless to fight his wild desire. This time he took the initiative and was soon enmeshed in a frenzied struggle to subdue and to conquer. Again he felt drained, weakened, and exhausted. After a restful sleep he got up refreshed and strong enough to leave the sick bed.

Following the midday meal Avram informed his father about his feelings for Keturah. Terach thought it unlawful to marry a temple priestess of the higher category. But he could see no reason why Avram should not take her as his concubine. When informed of his father's opinion, she readily consented. Immediately she went to the market place and purchased an olive carved out of jade which she wore as legal evidence of her concubinage. At the same time she brought home the news of Hammurabi's appearance before the walls of Ur. He had commanded the city to open its gates. Sabbattu stood on the wall and replied that Ur would gladly enter into an offensive and defensive alliance but would never surrender unconditionally. The king of Babylon was commencing the siege.

That same afternoon Shadnego and Eleazer brought additional news: A flotilla of Babylonian boats drifting down the river passed them. They could only surmise that Hammurabi was attempting the conquest of Elam west of the Tigris. Under the circumstances it would be unwise to pass the craft of Babylon and no doubt encounter a similar fleet and thus be caught between the two flotillas. It would be equally dangerous to retrace their course and attempt to sail up the Purattu and pass Ur and Babylon. On the other hand it was impractical to remain in Eridu which Hammurabi would take over as soon as he captured Ur. The Terach family was faced with an impasse.

Eleazer thought it expedient to fit up a caravan and proceed as far as Agade, which was north of Babylon. A city as important as Agade would possibly have a bridge that might span the Purattu. Then the caravan would get into safer country for the rest of the journey to Haran. If no bridge, then a ferry boat might carry them over. At the worse, the caravan could proceed along its course west of the Purattu and ford the river at some shallow point not far from Haran. This course might take several months and was not free from danger, yet less perilous than being caught between flotillas or armies. When captured by soldiers in wartime the danger of being robbed, then sold into slavery, was too great notwithstanding the fairness of Hammurabi's code of laws.

"Then where lies the wisdom of traveling at all in wartime?" questioned Terach.

"Master," answered Eleazer. "I always heard that it was safer to go by caravan during war. The robbers are more likely to join armies. Loot is more plentiful especially in the sack of a city. Those who do not enlist become camp followers and buy or win the captured from the soldiers. Some of the camp followers take their women along and profit by their prostitution among the soldiers. In other words the open country away from the war zone has far less robbers than during peacetime. Of course, there is always the hazard of attack."

"But isn't our group too small to make up a caravan?" further objected the image-maker.

"Yes, it is," admitted the man from Damascus. "But in my experience, once a caravan is organized it will be joined by people who for one reason or another wish to get away. They often have valuables and take along armed men for protection and that makes for greater safety for all. Of course passengers help to defray the expenses of the journey."

"Then should we spread the word that we are looking for people to take along?"

"That is exactly what we must avoid," cautioned Eleazer. "People generally want to make deals to their best advantage. If they suspect that they are needed they will pay nothing and brag about rendering us a great service. On the contrary, they must believe that they are enjoying a privilege in being accepted. We should even refuse some as a matter of strategy. By feeling anxious to go along they will pay more."

"What do you think, Shadnego?" asked Terach, to feel more certain that he was not making a mistake.

"I think Eleazer is right," assured the seaman from Babylon. "In fact, you have no other recourse unless you want to remain in Eridu and take your chances in the fortunes of war. But let me advise you to lose no time. If I know my countrymen, Ur will be taken very quickly. Our King Hammurabi is cautious. He takes no chances. He has been preparing for a long time. I believe he will take Ur on the first assault. Remember Eridu is only 15 miles away. I am willing to wager that he is waiting for the first pitch-black night. Then he will attack when everyone is asleep. He has done that before."

"What have you to say, my son?"

"I have only this to say. If El Elyon is with us it makes little difference whether we go to Haran or stay here. But if you have decided, I will go along."

"Since you agree," said Shadnego, "then you better start preparing for the long journey. I hope you have enough time. Are you coming with me, Eleazer?"

"No, Shadnego, I better start preparing. I will spend the night here."

"Shadnego, I will take the baggage off your boat tomorrow. Have you my account ready?" questioned Terach.

"I am afraid I shall have to charge you the cost of my return to Babylon. In this war disturbance I don't expect to carry back any return cargo nor passengers. I am sorry but I can't afford to take this loss. Will you pay with goods, eatables, or silver?"

"I suppose it will be silver. I really have nothing else. Let me know the amount."

"I will when you come for the baggage. Farewell," and Shadnego departed.

"Master, I didn't want to discuss business in his presence. But I must tell you the cost of fitting up a caravan runs quite high. I don't know whether your circumstances will permit such an outlay, although I am confident we will get back a part from passengers."

"Eleazer, I have silver with me. It is not mine, but I am

permitted to use it. So go ahead and do what you think best."

For the rest of the afternoon, the evening—minus the time for eating with the family—and late into the night, Eleazer sat with stylus and clay computing everything needed for a caravan from sandal latchets to a covered wagon drawn by two oxen. Next morning together with Terach and Avram he visited the market place to purchase some trifles but managed to extract from the tradesmen some valuable information about the static condition of business in Eridu. "How can one help becoming panicky," complained a trader, "with Hammurabi besieging Ur which is only 15 miles from here?" A small merchant, struggling to make ends meet, lamented, "Things are at a standstill. You can buy at your own price. Why hold on to merchandise? For the Babylonian soldiers? Why I know a man who has a large wagon with two big-horned oxen. I believe he would take half of the market price for the whole outfit."

"What is the market price?" questioned Eleazer.

"At least 20 shekels in silver, if not more," replied the merchant.

"And he would sell the team and wagon for 10 shekels?" asked Eleazer.

"He would grab it."

"Take us to him. I believe the adon here would be interested."

The merchant looked sharply at Terach then at Eleazer, evidently regretting his hasty talk. If these are legitimate buyers then he spoke too loosely.

"Well, now you understand," said the merchant apologetically. "He never gave me that price. It is only my guess. I probably spoke too quickly."

"I understand," acknowledged Eleazer. "He won't give

you any commission at that price. Take us to him. If my friend will buy the team and wagon, he will pay you one tenth of the purchase price."

"Agreed," assented the merchant.

The owner of the wagon and two oxen wanted 30 shekels in silver and scoffed at the offer of ten. Sulmatu appeared to be in comfortable circumstances and said that while not forced to sell, he would consider 25 shekels. After much haggling, the merchant raised the bid to 12 shekels with the assurance that he expected no commission. Both parties finally agreed and went to a scribe in the market place who drew up a clay tablet in proper form and duly witnessed. Terach had to open one of Sabbattu's parcels and weighed in silver the sum of 12 shekels. Sulmatu then offered some finely carved alabaster vessels for which Eridu was famous. Eleazer showed but slight interest so the Eriduan kept lowering the price. Finally it looked so cheap that Eleazer told Terach that they could be sold farther north at a handsome profit. When the purchase was made, Sulmatu complained that the prices were truly ridiculous but why leave them for the soldiers of Babylon to steal. He wondered why anyone would buy anything at all in view of the pending invasion.

Terach informed him of their departure and asked if he could get someone to drive the wagon to the waterfront. Sulmatu offered to drive it himself since he had nothing better to do. Terach ordered his servants and slaves to move the baggage from the boat and load it on the wagon while he argued with Shadnego who wanted 50 shekels for the passage from Ur to Eridu and the empty return to Babylon. Terach considered the price exorbitant and complained that he did not even have enough silver to purchase equipment and food much less pay for a boat which he would not use. After much haggling they agreed upon 20 shekels. This haggling did not affect their friendly relations, for bargaining had been the normal practice in the East from time immemorial. No deal could be enjoyable without the voluble argumentation that displayed the keenness and mentality of both sides.

For the rest of the day Eleazer, Avram, and the merchant were purchasing supplies for the journey. The merchant was helpful, to say the least. He knew the weakness of other merchants and their pressing need to sell. The 10 per cent commission made him feel quite prosperous. They acquired three other wagons, somewhat smaller, and drawn by two asses each. One wagon they stored with large, clay water barrels covered by tops made of platted reeds soaked in pitch. The second was reserved exclusively for barley, grain, lentils, corn, wheat, dried figs, and dates together with green fruit that would ripen during the journey. The third wagon was partly filled with straw, the sleeping quarters for those who could not find room on top of the bundles in the ox-drawn cart.

In the evening Sulmatu came with three other men. They wished to join the caravan. They had their own wagon and would bring along food, water, a blacksmith, and carpenter should repairs to their wagon become necessary. Terach referred them to Eleazer. The four Eriduans were surprised to hear that the charge would be ten shekels per head to travel as far as Agade. Their two workmen could come along gratis if they agreed to repair the other wagons or join in the defense should robbers attack. Sulmatu questioned the reason for such unjust charges and Eleazer replied:

"I know this sounds strange to people without experience in traveling, but for four years I worked on caravans and know that these are the usual charges. It seems simple enough for the stay-at-home people to say 'I furnish everything and only want to follow without imposing any duty or responsibility upon you.' But experience shows that it does not work out that simply. If you run short of water, what will we do? Let you die of thirst? If you have no food left, shall we let you starve? Then you say, 'but we will pay for the food and water we use.' I know you will and can pay but in the desert water and food can become priceless. One of you may become ill. Then we must detour the entire caravan to the nearest city or town for a doctor. Once we admit you into our caravan, we become responsible for you and responsibility leads to inconvenience, services, or delay."

The usual wrangling followed and a compromise was reached. Each would pay five shekels to go as far as Agade. Should anyone decide to reach Haran, then he would pay five more. They said goodnight with the understanding that their silver would be weighed and delivered to Terach on the following morning.

The night before retiring and after sunrise Eleazer kept adding to his list of necessary articles such items as needles, thread, bronze nails, tools, bread, freshly baked, flint with bitumen for making fire, wooden bowls and spoons, knives of flint or bronze, cloth for repairing clothes, and the numerous articles that seem unimportant at home but become highly essential when needed. He and Avram met their mentor, the merchant, and proceeded with their purchases. By this time practically all of Eridu knew about the caravan that was forming and prices began to stiffen. Many were talking about going along but no one acted. Terach stayed at the house waiting for Salmatu and the three men to pay down the silver as agreed the night before but they did not appear. Everyone seemed to think that there was plenty of time and that the caravan would not pull out so soon.

Shortly after the midday meal rumors began to circulate that Hammurabi had captured Ur. Rumors expanded into alarming reports of a horrible massacre that had taken place; that the soldiers of Babylon had decimated the city's population. Panic reigned in Eridu. Salmatu, together with the three men, hastily brought the silver which Terach weighed to the sum of 20 shekels. Other people came to inquire about going along. In the market place the panicky merchants were cutting prices, eager to turn goods into silver. One man offered a wagon with two asses for five shekels which Eleazer readily paid. Soon Eleazer filled the wagon with his purchases at bargain prices and consulted Avram about the advisability of a quick departure. Avram questioned the truth of the alarming news and Eleazer admitted the possibility of exaggeration yet declared that they had no right to risk capture in Eridu or on the road. They decided to advise Terach to depart that same night and as soon as possible after the evening meal.

Near sundown a group representing 20 men and women came to the house and offered to pay 50 shekels to join Terach as far as Agade. They had among them six armed men who could help to drive and do repair work. Terach accepted feeling that it was too much silver to turn down. Besides, they had three wagons with water and provisions and the men would be useful. It was agreed to start out three hours after sundown. Sitting at the evening meal with the family of which Eleazer had virtually become a part, Avram observed:

"I do not understand the anxiety of these people to flee Eridu. This fear of the Babylonian soldiers is, I believe, without reason. When we were in Babylon we heard that Hammurabi is a just ruler who doesn't practice cruelty unnecessarily. If Eridu surrenders without a struggle to a

Tartan, there would be no need for massacres or killings. The king of Babylon has won the affections of the cities he conquered by his mild treatment. If I were an old-established resident of Eridu, I would remain without fear."

"Wouldn't that apply equally to Ur?" asked Terach.

"It would if Ur had opened her gates without fighting. And that is exactly what the Tartan Nabunergal had warned them about when he stood before the crowded walls. If I had not gotten into trouble, I would not have left the city especially with a protector like the high priest." No one of the household except Terach knew of Sabbattu's orders to leave Ur for Haran.

## II

It was midnight before all the passengers, their wagons and followers, assembled at the house Terach was occupying. The nine wagons drawn by asses and oxen made quite a brave show. With a half moon shining the light sufficed for driving in the open country. The territory west of the Purattu was outside of Babylon's jurisdiction and therefore beyond the highways maintained and guarded by the king's soldiers. Fortunately, one of the men in the last group of 20 knew the direction northward consisting mainly of narrow goat paths, sometimes straight and more often winding. He was told to stay as far west of the Purattu as possible for Terach had no desire to run into any company of Hammurabi's soldiers who might be leaving Ur to take over the territory partly desert and seldom fertile, hence unsettled.

The pace was approximately two miles per hour. About every two hours Eleazer ordered a halt, to water and sometimes to feed the animals. The people went out for a drink, a stretch, or simply to break the monotony. Night travel was much cooler and therefore preferable to riding or walking under a scorching sun. The caravan rested midday for about six hours. Everyone, including the cattle, ate, drank, and rested. Those who could slept in the shade cast by the wagons. After the heavy afternoon meal travel resumed for about four hours. From 10 to 11 at night they stopped for water or food or relaxation, then the journey resumed until daybreak. On the first morning a breakfast of fresh fish was prepared, which Eleazer had brought in a container of water, a rare delicacy on such a trip. It had to be eaten before it spoiled in the water which the sun would soon warm up. Riding resumed until about ten o'clock in the morning. This regimen was followed rather rigidly. The men walked as a rule along both sides of the wagons for protection but mainly to lighten the weight pulled by the animals.

On the fourth night out, one of the wheels went into a hole and instead of stopping immediately and waiting until sunrise, the driver whipped the asses to pull the wagon and thereby broke the axle. There was nothing to do but wait until daylight. Everyone had gotten out of the wagons to inspect the damage, then went back to finish his night's sleep. Keturah remained, took Avram's hand and led him along the goat road under the numerous stars and the quarter moon. They reached a grassy plot, sat down under a tree, and listened to the unfamiliar sounds coming from distant farmhouses and to the birds that were commencing to chirp. During the hectic period of escape from Ur, the malaria attack and the preparations for the journey, Avram had scarcely spoken to her although she walked with him alongside the moving wagons.

Fascinated, he sat watching the stars without number. The moon no longer held for him its former enrapture, due perhaps to her close association with Nannar, the false god. The words of El Elyon came into his consciousness: "Look toward heaven and count the stars if you can. So shall your offsprings be." This promise will be fulfilled as was the Most High God's assurance that no harm would befall him while in the power of those evil men who sought to destroy him. A warm feeling flooded his heart. El Elyon had selected him to fulfil a great destiny. He had already experienced the power of his God, who could wrest him from the flames of the fiery furnace. He was chosen by the Most High who demonstrated his superiority over all other gods. Never again would he fancy that El Elyon had forsaken him as he thought when he sensed himself dead. He now felt ecstasy and exaltation through complete faith.

Keturah watched the uplifted expression of his countenance and would have been thrilled if she could believe that his sublimation arose out of the love she lavished upon him. But she was too well acquainted with his moods that could vary from dejection to elation.

"My beloved, I feel that you are happy. I am glad to see that you are not depressed by the monotony of this long journey. Tell me, Avram, what are you thinking about?"

"I am feeling deep gratitude to my God for saving me from the flaming kiln. It was indeed a miracle which only El Elyon has the power to perform. As for the journey, I do not find it tiresome at all. In fact, I like the open spaces far better than the crowded city. Out here I feel nearer to the Creator of heaven and earth. The stars at night and the sun by day constantly remind me of his watchful presence in the sky above."

"Have you any feeling of anxiety about the future?" questioned Keturah. "After all, you are going into a new, far away country. You may not like Haran after coming out of Ur which I believe is the finest city in the world.

There Father Terach has no such connection and protector like Sabbattu, who is responsible for my being with you."

"Keturah, since you like that name better than the accustomed Zirru, the Most High God can bring on the same prosperity in Haran as is found in Ur, if not more. He will not forsake us. He will watch over us as a shepherd over his flock. As for Sabbattu, yes, he has been helpful for which I am thankful. Yet I always feel that whatever he does is for his benefit and not to help us. I can't feel a deep confidence in him."

"Oh Avram, I love you so and am happy to go with you anywhere in the world. I feel deeply grateful to Sabbattu and to El Elyon for restoring my beloved to me."

One by one the stars were returning to their abode in the heavens. Soon only the morning star twinkled with its accustomed brilliance. The sky in the east was getting gray while in the west darkness still prevailed. Keturah's arms tightened about Avram while kissing him in her loving embrace. Her tempestuous passion quickly obliterated darkness and dawn. He lay in her arms in delicious exhaustion. After a while he disengaged himself and said, "Let's turn around to see the sunrise. I love that sight."

## III

It was daylight when Avram and Keturah returned. There they saw a rather dull-witted shepherd standing with a small herd of goats and sheep watching the caravan and the men crawling or jumping out of the wagons. Eleazer had been questioning the slow-minded herdsman but could get no information as to whether Hammurabi had taken Ur. In fact, he did not seem to know that a war was on. Perhaps he did not understand Eleazer's Sumerian which was not very articulate. Avram asked about the roads going north and the heavy rains but before the dull shepherd could get on with his answers, two of the six armed men in the last wagon took a lamb each and were about to walk off when Eleazer asked them sharply what were they doing. They answered in surly tones that the sheep would make several good dinners. Eleazer ordered them to put down the lambs but they did not comply. Eleazer blew his whistle and Terach's two slaves and two servants came running up. Terach got out of the wagon and Sulmatu came up quickly with his two armed retainers. The two sheep dogs began to growl and the shepherd was about to sick them on the men when they put down the lambs and walked away.

Eleazer confided to Terach and Avram that he had been uneasy about the six whose appearance and demeanor he did not like. They were, no doubt, testing out their strength in trying to take the lambs. If successful, they would attempt to take over the caravan. He had heard of such things happening. Terach imparted Eleazer's suspicions to Sulmatu, who ordered his two men to wear their bronze daggers and keep the spears handy while he and his three associates did likewise. By this time two of the men who had negotiated for the 20 in the three last wagons came up to inquire. Terach told them of the lamb incident and of his suspicions. The two men assured him not to be uneasy for they would disarm three of the men. The other three were trustworthy. They felt confident that there would be no more trouble.

A middle-aged man with a nine-year-old boy stood watching all that transpired. He came up and asked whether he could be of assistance since he was a builder and knew about repairing wagons. Terach's four men and Sulmatu's retainers were examining the wheel that had been caught in the water hole. The builder looked under the wagon and found the axle broken. He informed Terach that a new axle or crossbar connecting the two opposite wheels was necessary for the wagon to function. There was a small village about five miles north but off the goat road to the east where an axle might be obtained. If not, it might be necessary to trade his wagon for another in better condition and pay something additional. He would advise that everything be taken out of the wagon, and that the broken axle be tied with rope. The asses could then pull the wagon with very little load on the broken, tied-up axle.

Terach thanked him and asked what was he, an intelligent man, doing in this wasteland inhabited by such primitives as the stupid shepherd. He replied that his name was Nasu-Rimmon, a Sumerian builder, long established in Erech. Three years ago he had built a home for a prominent merchant. At the time he warned the householder and his architect, also a man of influence, that the soil was soggy which indicated that there was water not far beneath the proposed structure. It was hazardous to build there. But the merchant and the architect asserted that there was no danger since the earth was solid enough to support the structure, and water itself holds up land. In addition, both were influential enough to silence all objectors. The house, partly of burned brick and wood, was built about three years ago. Everything went well until . . .

"As you know, adon," declared the builder, "the drought was very bad. The water under the house was fed by a canal which dried up completely. The dry canal in drawing out all the sub-soil water created a vacuum. One day shortly before the heavy rainfall, the house caved in and killed the merchant's boy of ten years. Our city had been taken by the king of Babylon and the Code of Hammurabi became the law of Erech. That code decrees that if a house falls due to an error in construction and kills a child, then the child of the builder or the architect must die. It was in vain that I reminded the merchant of my warning. He became bitter and demanded a life for a life —my boy for his. The case was called and I pleaded the true facts. When I saw the faces of the judges prior to the verdict, I left the court, took my boy and fled across the Purattu into this land outside of Babylon's jurisdiction. Here is the boy criminal."

While talking, Nasu-Rimmon kept his eye on the men tying up the broken axle working under Eleazer's direction. The job was proceeding satisfactorily, yet he suggested that while raising the wheel they should fill the water hole with dirt. Then the wheel would move on solid ground and not slip back should anything go wrong when the donkeys start pulling. The wagon started moving and bid fair to reach the village, barring further mishap.

Terach expressed sympathy to the father for the plight of his son and asked whether he could assist him in any way. Nasu-Rimmon suggested going along so they could talk in the wagon until the village would be reached. He said he was in touch with his sons who were carrying on the building business. In fact, he had seen one of his sons the day before and learned that the court had turned down his appeal. Nothing further could be done. He couldn't return to Erech if he wanted to save his boy. He had been considering Eridu but his son said that it was taken over by Hammurabi and was now Babylonian territory.

"Was there loss of life or pillage in the taking of Eridu?" asked Terach, remembering Avram's predictions that no atrocities would take place.

"My son said no. Everything was as peaceful as before.

The Babylonians are not cruel if a city surrenders without resistance. There is only a change in government and higher taxes."

"Do you know what happened in Ur?" questioned Terach, unable to conceal his avid curiosity.

"I understand that the gates of Ur were opened secretly at night and from the inside. There was some killing, mainly of soldiers who resisted. But now everything is as peaceful as before."

"Do you know who opened the gates?"

"The rumor is that suspicion points to the high priest of Nannar."

After three hours of slow travel the caravan reached the village, which was Nasu-Rimmon's hideout. He knew practically everyone there and was able to locate a blacksmith who also repaired wagons. The blacksmith had a broken wagon but the axle reinforced by a bronze bar was in good condition. Eleazer struck a bargain with him to sell the axle and place it on Terach's wagon. While waiting for the completion of the job, Terach asked the builder, "What are your plans? Do you expect to remain here?"

"No. Sooner or later someone will inform on me to get a reward from the merchant. Then the ba'iru will swoop down and take us both illegally. Who can fight the power of Babylon? I have very little silver for traveling. My son tells me that building is at a standstill. The war has driven prices sky high. People are waiting for costs to come down. I really don't know what to do."

Terach had been thinking over his own situation. "What will I do in Haran? My household has become quite large. Avram is now married or what amounts to marriage. Soon children will come. My house and furniture and stock of images in Ur will probably be confiscated."

Suddenly a notion struck him. Why not take Nasu-Rimmon along to Haran? It might be profitable to go into building. Eleazer together with Nasu-Rimmon might develop a thriving business. He could use Sabbattu's silver and pay him back—that is, if he ever comes to Haran. It is difficult to speculate what will happen to the high priest. Perhaps he is no longer in the Temple of Nannar. It is possible that I may succeed to the priest's gold, silver, and valuables. After ruminating for a while, Terach said, "Nasu-Rimmon, why not come along with us to Haran. That city is clearly out of Babylon's jurisdiction. You and your son would certainly be safe there. Your knowledge of building should be quite useful. I might even go into business with you."

"On the wagon all the way to this village I was thinking of the same thing. I could not suggest it since I have no silver to pay for the cost of food or transportation. I am very happy to accept your invitation."

At the village everyone went out for a stretch. The well in the center was fed by a spring of fairly clear water, and the head of the place permitted the caravan to fill their barrels and buckets for half a shekel. The sole shopkeeper sold out his entire stock of provisions to the strangers, who mingled freely with the villagers and listened to gossip about the war. The occupants of the last wagon, consisting of four men and two women, decided to turn back when they learned that Eridu escaped maltreatment and was now peacefully occupied by the soldiers of Babylon. The two men who attempted to take the lambs from the herdsman and a companion were not to be seen anywhere. Eleazer surmised that the three shifty characters decided to turn highwaymen after seeing with what ease they could have robbed the shepherd had there been no caravan present. After sunset the caravan continued its course to encounter more breakdown, incidents, and delays, until a month later it reached the Purattu River opposite Agade, the former capital of Sargon's Akkadian empire.

# 14

# On the Puratu

AGADE ON THE PURATTU ABOUT 50 MILES NORTH OF Babylon was for centuries a small undistinguished city in Akkad. Suddenly it rose to dizzy heights as the capital of the first great empire in history. Its prominence and power were due to a single person, one Sargon whose father no one ever knew. His mother was a priestess charged with the pious duty of serving any man who came to offer the temple a small supply of silver or a measure of grain for the pleasure of lying with her.

Sargon became "King of Universal Dominion" and great enough to inspire the legend that his mother secretly placed him in a basket boat of rushes rendered waterproof with pitch and set afloat on the Puratttu. The reason for such caution has never been disclosed. A workman found and brought the baby home. Somehow he became cup bearer to the king of Agade and subsequently displaced him. He was able to capture many cities, kill many men, and take much plunder. One of his conquests evidently stemmed from sentiment. A king had taken Lagash and violated her goddess. Sargon avenged her by carrying Lugal-Zaggin, a chained prisoner, to Nippur. Sargon went on with his deeds until he conquered Elam, governed all of Akkad and Sumer between the two rivers, fanned out as far as the Mediterranean, and ruled a goodly portion of western Asia.

Towards the close of Sargon's 55 years of reign, the myth makers in the temples were ready to deify the first of the great Semitic conquerors. But a revolt started that ultimately pulverized the far-flung Akkad and Sumer empires. When Terach's family visited the former Akkadian capital three centuries later, it had become again a provinçial town with hardly a fragment of its former splendor. About 1200 years later the Assyrian Empire arose on the ruins of Hammurabi's kingdom. But under Ashurbanipal the magnificent capital was no longer Agade but Nineveh.

## II

After the tiring journey the hearts of the weary travelers were gladdened to behold Agade on the opposite bank of the Purattu. They were eager to walk on city streets again but no bridge spanned the river. There had been a fair-sized flat bottom boat of Egyptian make to ferry passengers across the river but, confiscated for the Babylonian flotilla, it was now far south, perhaps moving soldiers and chariots into Elamite territory. Yet necessity stimulated inventiveness. Lying idly were several large rafts which their owners tied together and rendered fit for transporting separately the oxen, the asses, the wagons, the travelers, and all their baggage and freight.

The travel-worn caravaneers were happy to find beds in the several inns that could accommodate them. After a rest of several days they regained perspective. All the passengers desired to return to Eridu but had to seek the method of transportation. They had no stomach for jogging along in wagons pulled by slow-paced donkeys. To their joyful surprise they learned that prices were high, that the war had created a shortage in commodities and in all manner of equipment from oxen to sandals. Inquiry showed that they could realize good prices for everything they brought along. Sailing down the river in the rapid current would bring them in no time to Ur and Eridu. But few boats were visible. Yet when their wants became known, seamen somehow appeared and bargaining began. All the passengers disposed of their properties and arranged for passage from Agade to Eridu.

The solution did not come as easily in the Terach household. Eleazer argued that if the caravan remained intact it could be utilized in business journeys to Nineveh in the east and as far as Carchemish or beyond to the west. Avram who did not mind traveling in the open country agreed with him. But the women insisted vehemently on selling the equipment and sailing for Haran, which was on the Belikh, a tributary of the Purattu. The memory of the many hardships of caravan travel was too recent. They recalled the heavy rains that made the soggy road impassible for two days and the donkey breaking a leg making it necessary for three men to pull one of the wagon shafts to the next village some six miles away. The women won over the aging Terach who suffered from the inconveniences of sleeping in a wagon. The oxen, asses, wagons, and the foods, which the chartered boat could not carry, were sold at a good profit and the household moved into the boat.

Sailing against the current from Agade to Haran took more than three weeks; it was much easier and far more pleasant than traveling by caravan despite the inconvenience of sleeping on deck even if a tarpaulin shaded against sunshine or kept off the rain. Avram spent most of the time, particularly at night, meditating. What was his duty towards El Elyon? Was it sufficient simply to express his gratitude in thanksgiving prayer? The recent events in Ur, including the attempt to throw him into the flaming furnace, were sufficient proof of the iniquity inherent in the false gods. But was his personal rejection of paganism enough? The world, no doubt, needed a more righteous faith to live by. A purer system of ethical conduct could only be attained by the rejection of gods who were cruel, licentious, and malevolent.

"Why did the Most High God," mused Avram, "speak twice to me? He certainly performed a miracle at the burning oven. Was it all merely for my personal benefit? Am I, or any other individual, of such importance? Surely El Elyon expects something in return. Is my personal belief in Him sufficient? How can I serve Him with more than mere words? He mentioned that my descendants would become as numerous as the stars above. It will certainly be my duty to teach my children to serve, to worship, to adore El Elyon. But is that enough? Shouldn't I begin by telling everyone I meet about the Most High? How He is better, greater, and more righteous than all the other gods? But is knowing about Him enough? Isn't it necessary to do that which is pleasing in His eyes? To live according to His precepts? To walk in His ways? But what are His precepts? His ways? What does he require of us? I don't know. I can only guess."

Terach happened to walk by the tied bundle of clothes upon which Avram sat. A thought came to Avram's mind:

"Father, do you know how your forefathers served El Elyon? What did they do besides believe in Him?"

"I really don't know. I never saw my grandfather Serug who was in a position to know."

"But your father Nahor did know. Didn't he tell you?"

"He talked a great deal but I paid little attention to such matters."

"But wasn't it of interest to know the beliefs, the ways, and customs of a bygone age?"

"My son, it is difficult to explain the state of mind that prevailed in a different generation. When Father Nahor came to Ur it had recently been taken over by the king of Elam. The Sumerians, proud of their history and achievements, were humiliated and bitter. They let out their hatred against all foreigners. They resented hearing any other language except their own. They looked down on anyone who spoke with an accent. Everyone had to be completely Sumerian and nothing else. In that kind of an atmosphere children resented belonging to any alien group. We pretended not to understand Aramaic. Nor did we want any identification with any alien minority. Thus the Aramaic or the broken Sumerian of your grandfather Nahor, his foreign manners and especially his poverty, were embarrassing to his children. Secretly we wanted to forget rather than remember the traditions, the legends of our forefathers who probably stemmed from the desert."

"But, Father, can't you recall such things as they were forbidden to do? It must have slipped out unconsciously in Grandfather's talk."

"I see. You mean such prohibitions as murder, robbery, adultery, which all codes proscribe? Let me think and see whether some of Father's talk will come back to me. I will let you know later."

Davarah and Keturah were standing at the deck's railing watching a scene on land. Keturah cried out, "I hope he does not catch the animal." Avram walked over and saw a man chasing a calf which was trying to elude him. When it could get no farther on account of the river bank it was caught. The man pulled the dagger attached to his belt and began amputating the calf's leg. He finally succeeded and started devouring the meat of the severed member, its blood all over his face. Avram shouted, "You are a beast," but the boat was too far away and the man evidently too famished to care about what he said.

"Now, that is something for the law to prevent," exploded Avram with exasperation. Seeing the builder from Erech, he continued: "The Code of Hammurabi should prohibit such cruelty instead of convicting an innocent boy on account of the death of another child."

"I don't see any reason for such resentment," observed the builder. "A man is desperately hungry. He sees a stray calf and decides on having a meal. Eating calf meat is something all of us do. The difference is in the method of reaching the meat. Had he cut the calf's throat there would be no criticism. Cutting off the leg which also brings on death is something you condemn. I can't see why one method is less humane than another."

"This demonstrates," rejoined Avram, "the crying need for a more compassionate religion. You are merciful enough when it comes to your own. You are ready to give up home, family, and city to save the life of your boy, which is very commendable. But you do not conceive that another live creature also desires to go on living. At least it is anxious to escape suffering. Slitting the throat is probably not painless. Perhaps it might be wrong to slaughter an animal for our enjoyment. I don't know. But cutting its throat is the simplest, the least painful way of ending a life. Yet cutting off its leg does not necessarily end its existence. The wound can even heal. But what kind of life would a cow lead walking on three legs? Isn't it far better to slit the throat and put an end to suffering?"

Terach came back and beckoned to his son. "I now

recall some of my father's words. His forefathers did have some kind of code which they called something like 'Noah's Seven Commandments.' What they were I do not know nor can recall. You know, boys pay little attention to such dry subjects as law."

"I know one of them," and he told his father of the calf incident and the builder's reaction. "I will be compelled to get up a code for the worship of El Elyon, and the prohibition against cutting off any part of a living animal to eat will be included."

## III

The boat reached Mari, an old kingdom that possessed many things of interest to travelers. Its art in some respects was more original than one could see in all other cities of Sumer and Akkad. Some ot its statues, particularly the lion guarding the gate of the palace, seemed almost alive. A large painting on the wall of a temple was very striking with its trees, religious scenes, and human figures wearing fringed shawls, felt caps of another land, probably of north Syria. But the amazing sight was the great palace on six acres containing 250 rooms, no longer occupied by the last king of the long reigning dynasty. King Hammurabi, when he captured the city, appointed his own patesi who ruled over Mari in the place and stead of the king.

Ruminating that evening on the deck, Avram could not but marvel at the age of many cities he saw in Shinar between the two rivers. There was no telling how old they were. The temples, palaces, houses, walls, canals, and statuary showed that for thousands of years men had been building, planning, organizing, creating, and thinking. Yet their religion was in many respects naive and even childish. When would men learn to make laws and establish customs that might render life more secure, decent, attractive, and civilized? Certainly the gods were neither encouraging nor initiating a better life for the people. Then it was up to men to change outworn modes of thought or conduct. But who would begin the reforms that might revolutionize religion and society and bring on a superior morality? Avram questioned himself quietly: "Was I selected to begin calling on the people to renounce the gods and worship El Elyon who will inaugurate a new order in which men will live cleanly, justly, morally, and humanely?"

"What are you saying to yourself, my son?" asked Emtelai.

"I was thinking, Mother, why did the Most High save me from the burning furnace? Surely He expects something of me. What is it?"

"How do you know the Most High God intended to save you?" questioned Terach. "After all, wasn't it a downpour of rain that fell upon thousands of people, men and women, good and bad, at the same moment?"

"I knew He would save me, for two nights earlier He said He would protect me from enemies who were planning my destruction."

"But that was only a dream, something that comes to many people," insisted Terach. "That doesn't signify it was a miracle."

"If it was a dream, then El Elyon chose to appear to me in that manner."

"As for a miracle," ventured Keturah, "I can tell you it was. I shall never forget that day as long as I live. We knew that morning that my Avram was condemned to burn. You did not know it at home, for mother says that the house was locked and you did not know what went on outside. You just can't imagine how I felt. The priestesses tried to console me. My only hope was the high priest. He, only, I believed, could save Avram. As the time for burning neared, I became more and more panicky. We were in a room and could see flames of the kiln go higher and higher. Darkness came quickly, almost suddenly. The furnace fire lit up everything, the sky and the temple. The guards were leading Avram and stood ready to throw him in. All hope in me was gone. Suddenly, a streak of lightning, the brightest I ever saw, and a clap of thunder, the loudest I ever did hear, came at the same moment. I thought the entire temple was destroyed. Everything went black like pitch. All we could hear was the rain, the thickest I ever heard. All the priestesses cried, 'A miracle; the gods do not want Avram burned.' When I saw the high priest he was shaken and said, 'Avram's God saved him. I know Nannar wouldn't.' "

"May I inquire," ventured the skipper evidently impressed, "how I can get an image of this God? I would place Him on board for good luck."

"Captain," answered Avram, "He has no body, no face, no form. He is a spirit and governs the world without the help of anyone. He has neither father nor mother, nor wife, nor son, nor daughter."

"What do you call him?" asked the skipper, reverence written on his countenance.

"El Elyon, the Most High God, who created heaven and earth and all things therein."

"You say your God appeared to you?" questioned Nasu-Rimmon, the builder from Erech. "How did you recognize Him if He has neither face, nor body, nor form?"

"By his voice. One who hears that voice can never doubt who is speaking. Those words become engraved in the heart. I shall never forget them no matter how long I live."

"How can I become one of his followers?" inquired Hankas the skipper.

"By believing in El Elyon, by observing His precepts and rejecting all other gods," asserted Avram.

"I would also worship Him," declared Nasu-Rimmon, "but why reject the gods of my ancestors, of my people, and of my city?"

"Because El Elyon is the true God. The others are false," responded Avram.

When the passengers were asleep on deck Avram stood near the railing, gazing in the lambent moonlight at the calm river, the passing landscape, the trees, the occasional farmhouses. The tranquil beauty of the night induced a feeling of gratitude to the Most High who governed the universe with His power and wisdom. Evidently He looked on the foibles of men with patient tolerance. He no doubt had laws and rules of conduct for the orderly processes of mankind. But what were they? Without realizing it he was saying, "Most High God, enlighten me. How can men best serve thee? What are the statutes and ordinances which they must obey? If people ask me I know not the answer."

He did not know how long he stood or when he reclined on his couch of bundles. He became aware of a scene in the far distant past. Two white bearded patriarchs in garments long discarded and forgotten were ministering at an altar on which the sacrifice of a young goat was being offered before a group of men standing and sitting on the grass.

"Oh men of old, men of renown," asked a young man, "how can we best serve our God? What can we do to please Him?"

"Peleg," answered Eber the son of Shelah, "abstain from transgressions. Do not commit murder, or adultery, or incest, or robbery. Do not blaspheme. Do not cut off and eat the flesh of a living animal."

"You must only worship El Shaddai," added Shem the son of Noah. "The Almighty God requires of you to be righteous and to commit no act of injustice to your fellow man."

"Isn't His name El Elyon?" asked the youth Reu.

"El Shaddai, the Almighty Power has many names," answered Eber. "He is the same as El Elyon, the Most High."

"Since no man has ever seen the Most High God," continued Reu, "how do we know He exists?"

"We must believe. We must have faith," asserted Eber, the devout worshipper of the Most High All Powerful God.

"It is true that we never saw El Shaddai," admitted Shem, "yet how can we doubt His existence? When our father Noah said that a flood would destroy all flesh everyone laughed. He began to build the ship. People shook their heads, tapped their foreheads as he passed and said he was demented. Finally it was completed and stood there 300 cubits long, 50 cubits wide and 30 cubits high, with three floors. We gathered animals in pairs and people mocked us when we forced them with difficulty into the ark. Father said the flood would begin in seven days. He could only induce mother, his three sons and their wives to enter the ship. The rest of our kin jeered and refused to come.

"Clouds began to gather and hid the sun. On the seventh day thick black clouds made the day almost seem like night. We were in the ark and through the open door could see the rain begin to fall. Father closed the door and everything was dark. We could only see each other by the dim light of a small clay lamp that burned olive oil. People began to knock on the door and the sides crying to let them in. The rain beat against the sides and top of our ship with increasing violence. There were times when it sounded like rolling thunder. After what seemed like several days we felt the ark sinking, then falling, as if earth underneath was giving way. The water was swirling around us. We could feel it beating against the third story. Then it steadied and by the motion we knew it was sailing on top of the ever rising flood.

"It rained 40 days. We could tell a new day only by the crowing of the cock, the chirping birds, the cries of animals begging for food. The force of waves hitting our ark was getting stronger. At the end of 40 days a mighty stormwind struck. Our ark creaked as if falling apart. At one time it leaned on one side and seemed about to turn over, capsize as seamen say. We thought the end had come. Then the rains stopped, the winds diminished, the waves subsided. For 150 days longer we floated on the waters without wind or any wave moving.

"I speak to you about this not to tell you a story which everyone knows. I wish only to acquaint you with the power of El Shaddai. This ark was not built so well as to withstand such strong winds or waves. Our father knew little about building boats. A far stronger ship could not have withstood such buffeting. We were saved only by the Almighty God. We did not see Him. But we heard His voice in the stormwind. We felt His might in the waves. Our belief in Him shall go on forever."

Avram woke with Keturah bending over him. "You must have been dreaming, Avram. I could hear you talk but could not make out what you were saying."

## IV

There was something vaguely regal about little Sarai now eight and soon to be nine. Tall for her age she carried herself with a graceful pride that bordered on arrogance.

Hauteur might well have compensated for her imagined deficiency in pedigree. She found it difficult to swallow the unpalatable truth that her mother had been Terach's concubine. Her grandfather, a well-to-do Aramean merchant, went down in his own ship during a storm while heading for Egypt and left his family impoverished. Terach would gladly have made her his wife, especially since Emtelai lost her figure and beauty after Avram's birth. But he could not overcome the opposition of his wife who threatened divorce. Terach could not afford to lose the dowry she brought him with her marriage. Not having come as yet under Sabbattu's patronage, he was struggling to keep up appearances. Thus, Sarai's mother had no better alternative than to accept inferior status in the Terach menage. She died when giving birth to her child.

Emtelai reared the child and proved to be a good mother. A pretty girl, bright and winning, Sarai was petted, generally liked, and everyone playfully called her "the princess." Zirru was seven years older and hostility burgeoned into hate when the obvious affection between Avram and Zirru ripened into love. Sarai had but slight fondness or even respect for her father. He was aging and several generations separated him from his daughter, who naturally looked up to her half-brother as sole mentor and protector. Being precocious she had strong affections, and the notion soon developed into conviction that she would marry him when she grew up. Both law and custom permitted marriage between half-brother and sister, provided they were not of the same mother. She thus looked upon Zirru as the intruder bent on stealing her future husband. Her animosity reached out to Davarah and Lot since they occupied the place of mother and brother to the waif, born out of wedlock, who had wormed herself into the affections of her own beloved Avram.

It is needless to comment on her changed attitude when

Zirru was selected by the temple. Proudly she boasted to acquaintances of the high honor accorded to her "beautiful cousin" on being chosen the bride of Nannar. She simulated a fondness for Davarah and again became the playmate of her cousin Lot. The joy of being rid of her hated rival helped sustain Sarai during the absence of Avram in Babylon. Thus when he held her in his arms on his return and kissed her, she was thrilled beyond words and felt confident that he would love her passionately several years hence when she would grow up into an irresistible beauty.

But her world caved in when Zirru, now Keturah, returned so unexpectedly. In the preoccupation of packing, moving, and sojourning in Eridu, Sarai could avoid the embarrassment of welcoming her adversary. She happened to overhear Davarah telling "her daughter" that Avram would never marry any girl who had been defiled as a temple priestess. These words sounded like music and she began to feel secure again in the thought that she alone would after all marry Avram. But a cold fury clutched her when Keturah flaunted her love quite openly. Sarai offered to relieve her in nursing Avram at Eridu and felt rebuffed when her services were refused.

The world turned black when Keturah became a "wife" to Avram. To Sarai the distinction between wife and concubine was not quite clear, and even after Emtelai tried to explain she was no wiser. Psychologically, she was unable to accord inferior status to the position that her own mother had occupied. If a concubine was merely a mistress, then her mother was a kept woman, a situation hardly above that of a slave. Then she herself would be no more than Terach's offspring by a harlot, a status which Sarai could never bring herself to accept. She must forego the pleasure of denigrating Keturah's standing because of concubinage. She must not let her feelings run away. She had to recognize Keturah as a legitimate wife notwithstanding her personal aversion to such an elevation for a temple prostitute. Of course, Sarai hardly knew the distinction between the bride of Nannar and an ordinary *kedashe.* She must even assume and maintain a friendliness towards Davarah and accept Lot for a playmate.

When Nasu-Rimmon joined the caravan, Sarai exhibited fondness for his nine-year-old son; she made it quite obvious that she preferred him to her cousin Lot. Yet the boys became comrades. Not possessing the guile nor the social awareness of girls, they neglected her unconsciously. She felt ignored but pride would not permit her to be snubbed. With veiled subtlety she began to undermine their comraderie. She implanted in each a suspicion of the other. Lot began to think that Etana felt more clever, hence superior to him, while the boy from Erech became certain that Lot looked upon him as a mere country boy. She played up to each and acted as if she could love him who would ignore the other boy. Bad blood was beginning to simmer between them.

The skipper Hankas made it a practice to stop whenever he spied a village or town on the riverbank. The passengers got off to stretch. Hankas looked for spring water to fill the tanks and buy fresh fruit, vegetables, or such provisions as were obtainable. Terach strolled with Nasu-Rimmon exploring the prospects of a building enterprise in Haran. Avram and Eleazer discussed the possibilites and hazards of a caravan as a business; Emtelai, Davarah, and Keturah visited the two stores to see what they had for sale.

Lot, Etana, and Sarai, walking together, passed an apple cart standing not far from a house. The fruit looked tasty and luscious. Sarai remarked, "I would love to eat one of those red apples but I haven't any silver with me." She never did carry silver but liked to pretend that she did. Etana scanned the house and concluded that the apple seller was bargaining inside with his customers. He grabbed two apples and gave one to Sarai. Just then the cart owner appeared in the doorway and shouted, "Put back those apples, you little thief!" He ran to the cart and grabbed a green switch. Etana and Sarai threw the apples back into the cart but the apple dealer, a brutal-looking peasant, cut Etana on the legs with the switch. The three began to run and the rustic threw the switch and hit Lot. They were soon out of range with Lot holding the switch.

"Are you hurt, Etana my pet?" asked Sarai when they stopped running. "It was all my fault. I'm sorry I ever mentioned apples." She kissed him on the cheek. "There, you'll be all right now." Glancing at Lot she whispered sweetly, "I know you did it for me."

Lot took her words as a rebuke, a kind of reflection on his courage, or at least on his initiative. If she sought to arouse his anger, she succeeded. Losing his temper he blurted out, "I don't think it was at all smart. I was taught never to steal."

"Do you mean to call me a thief?" exploded Etana forgetting the sting on his legs.

"What would you call it if not stealing?" cross-questioned Lot.

Etana rushed at him to get the switch out of his hand. Each was tugging at the green birch. They were soon rolling on the ground hitting each other. Keturah rushed over to them. She had left the two women and was looking for Avram. She tried to wrench the switch out of Lot's grasp.

"Give me that birch rod, Lot. Now stop this fighting."

They stood up glaring at each other. "What is all this about?" she asked of Sarai.

"You never saw boys fighting before?" answered Sarai with an irritating smile and a haughty toss of her head.

"You seem to be enjoying this. I wouldn't be surprised if you put them up to it. It would be just like you to instigate a quarrel," asserted Keturah with exasperation.

"What you think or say makes little difference to me," countered Sarai slowly and with studied insolence.

"Now I don't like your tone nor your words; you seem to forget I am older than you. You don't seem to know who I am."

"Yes, I know; a *kedashe* expelled from the temple."

Holding the switch in her right hand, Keturah grabbed Sarai, turned her around and began lashing her on the backside and on her legs. Lot exclaimed, "Don't do that, Zirru. She is a little girl," and held her right hand. By this time Emtelai and Davarah came up and inquired, "What's all this going on?" Emtelai led Sarai away crying. Keturah buried her face in Davarah's bosom. The group proceeded to the river and when they reached the boat Sarai cried out to Keturah, "You will regret this all your life!"

When the time came to eat, Keturah refused all food. Davarah asked, "My dear, what is the matter?"

"I feel sick. That little brat upset me."

"Oh come now and forget this. This is the best meal we have had on this boat. The fresh fish was baked on the stove near the river. I know you will enjoy the hot soup, the newly baked bread, the apples and pomegranates."

"I just can't eat. It must be seasickness."

"What's wrong, my child?"

"I feel nauseated. I want to vomit. I think I'm going to die."

Davarah smiled, motioned to Emtelai to come over and said, "Emtelai, my child is dying. She feels nauseated and wants to vomit."

Both women began to laugh. Keturah showed impatience and with a touch of anger said, "What's funny about me dying? You seem to be happy."

"We are, my dear. You are pregnant."

## V

Hankas the skipper invited Avram into his tiny cabin and said, "I believe in your Most High God. But what must I do to serve Him?"

"Never kill anyone," replied Avram. "Do not rob. Never commit adultery or incest. Never do an act of injustice to your fellow man. Do not cut any meat from a living animal to eat and leave it to die. Do not worship false gods. These are the laws which my forefathers obeyed."

"I am willing to follow all these commandments," agreed Hankas. "But now I want to put up on this boat some kind of testimonial to show that I am a worshiper of El Elyon. I have here some soft clay and a stylus but I am not good at inscribing. How will this look on a tablet after it becomes hard? THIS BOAT IS UNDER THE PROTECTION OF EL ELYON, THE MOST HIGH GOD."

"I think it is excellent," assured Avram.

The skipper took a tablet of soft clay from a shelf and handed a stylus to Avram.

"Would you mind inditing these words?"

After Avram completed the words in cuneiform wedges Hankas thanked him and declared, "This tablet will remain on this shelf as long as I sail the boat. When I sell it I shall remove the tablet and keep it in my sleeping chamber. I know that no harm can befall any place where it stands. At the last village we stopped I bought a ram and it is on board. Tomorrow we pass a spot which I always liked. It contains an altar on which I can sacrifice the ram to the Most High God. This offering will celebrate my conversion to the belief in El Elyon."

The next day the boat stopped at a place on the west side of the river. All the passengers, Hankas, and several of the crew alighted. The spot was filled with weeping willows which created a melancholy atmosphere. The trees shielded the ground from the fierce rays of the sun and reduced the excessive heat so that the temperature was cool and delightful. One felt tempted to lie down and rest on the grassy sod. The group followed Avram and Hankas to the altar under a tall tree of hanging moss. A seaman led the ram by a rope tied to his large horns. Avram stood with Hankas at the altar.

Two seamen began shearing off the thick wool which covered the animal. It was too valuable to burn or throw away. The ram, placed on the altar, was held by the men. Avram cut his throat and he soon expired. The seamen hacked off the large horns which Hankas desired as a frame to support his tablet. They next skinned the ram and cut away the good tasting meat, which was roasted on fire in the altar. The roasted meat they distributed among the people who smelled its sweet savor and enjoyed the delicious taste. Wine was served to wash down the delectable tidbit. Meanwhile the remainder of the sacrifice was thrown on the burning altar. While the intestines, the bones, the stomach, heart, lungs were consumed, Avram declared, "This day we dedicate to El Elyon, and in His honor shall celebrate the several events for which we are thankful. In bringing this offering our captain declares his acceptance of El Elyon as the Most High God, Whom he will hereafter worship. Personally, I wish to express thanksgiving for my recent escape from the flaming furnace. Only the miracle wrought by El Elyon saved my life in Ur. We must further express our gratitude to Him for helping us escape the perils and dangers, known and unknown, in traveling by caravan and boat during the past months. May I also add my thanks for the pregnancy of my wife and pray that she give birth to a son.

"All who desire to join us in prayer and thanksgiving to El Elyon and El Shaddai, the Most High and Almighty God, who are both one and the same, kneel before this altar and say, so be it."

Everyone including the children, except Terach and Sanu-Rimmon, fell on their knees and said, "Thanks to El Elyon and El Shaddai, so be it."

About 1500 years later, captives out of the Land of Judah rested on this self same spot. Their feelings were recorded by a poet of their midst in a dirge that subsequently became celebrated throughout the world. The poem began:

By the rivers of Babylon,
There we sat down, yea, we wept
When we remembered Zion.
Upon the willows in the midst thereof
We hanged up our harps.
For there they that led us captive asked of us mirth:
'Sing us one of the songs of Zion.'
How shall we sing the Lord's song in a foreign land?
If I forget thee, O Jerusalem
Let my right hand forget her cunning.

# 15

# Nahor ben Terach

AFTER SPENDING A MONTH ON THE BOAT THE TERACH FAMILY, servants, and retainers landed in Haran, situated on a tributary of the upper Purattu. Haran might have been called the crossroads of southwestern Asia. Its very name derived from the Assyrian *Khurranu,* meaning roads, implied a center through which caravans passed going east, west, north, and south. Here goods of all kinds were sold, bought, and bartered. It was inhabited by people of various stocks, races, beliefs, and customs, from polished Sumerians to half-barbaric Habiru, from conquering Amorites to primitive Hittites, from merchants of Phoenicia to Aramean shepherds.

Sentimental and even romantic episodes stem from Haran as recorded in Genesis. Here Eleazer seeking a bride for Avram's son found in Rebecca the suitable wife for Isaac. In Haran, Jacob fell in love with Rachel and served seven years to obtain her. His 12 sons, founders of the future tribes in Israel, were born in this city which two millennia later figured in Roman history under the Latin name Carrhae. The Roman millionaire Crassus, friend of Julius Caesar and a member of his Triumvirate, was defeated and killed at Carrhae and later the Roman Emperor Caracalla was also defeated at Carrhae and murdered not too far away at Edessa. Haran with its long past has disappeared so completely that archaeologists are unable to unearth it.

The Terach household, including retainers, servants, and slaves, numbered 14 souls. It was not easy to find accomodations in the busy city. They had to be content temporarily with a caravansary that accommodated travelers. Difficulty was encountered in finding a permanent house that would be large enough. Finally they located two separate places that were for rent. One house was sufficient for Avram, Keturah, Lot, Davarah, her slave, and Eleazer. The larger dwelling could maintain Terach, Emtelai, Sarai, Sanu-Rimmon and son, the two servants and both slaves. The houses were a short distance from each other.

The next step was to locate Nahor, the second son of Terach, who had lived in Haran for 13 years. Born of a different mother he was older than Avram by 15 years. Nahor had married Milcah, the daughter of Davarah and Harran, the oldest of Terach's three sons. In the Terach household little was ever said of Nahor and consequently Avram knew nothing of him. When he realized that he would soon meet his brother, Avram wanted to know something about him and the reason for his settling in Haran, so great a distance from his birthplace, Ur. Terach and Emtelai were reluctant to talk but Avram learned the full story from Davarah.

Harran, the first born, was industrious, sensitive, honest, and considerate, the very opposite of Nahor, who neither wanted to attend school nor help his father in the shop. He frequented low company, hung around the waterfront and the ba'iru and often stayed away all night. Friends with the son of a skipper, Nahor decided to run away from home when he reached fifteen. He worked on the skipper's boat which stopped in all the cities, towns, and villages on the Purattu as far north as Haran, where he remained for a year doing various chores to keep himself alive. Then he began to feel homesick and took service on a boat which after many stops finally reached Ur.

At seventeen, Nahor was toughened by his roaming and various experiences. He felt confident that he knew the ways of the world and wanted the good things of life without the ambition to get them through hard work. Having had many affairs with females, he knew he was attractive to women and therefore counted on a profitable marriage that would provide him with all his wants, and even enable him to live the life of the privileged. On his return he was welcomed as a prodigal son. While he never said farewell on leaving, he did have the consideration to send word of his flight by his friend, Kagina, the skipper's son.

At home he found considerable changes and even some improvements. Harran, always rather frail, was ailing. Davarah carried on the weaving business and did quite well. Through the influence of the priest Sabbattu, she could sell her woven material to the temple of Nannar. She even bought a female slave and at times could afford to employ a servant. They were handy in helping to tend the pregnant girl whom the priest had placed in her charge. When the girl, Anunu, died, the priest continued his interest because Davarah was raising the baby Zirru. Through Sabbattu's patronage, Father Terach had become the image-maker for the temple and he had the exclusive right to sell his idols there. All in all, the family was on its way, if not to affluence, at least toward financial security. Terach now hoped that Nahor would settle down and take a hand in his business.

The home of Terach was bustling with activity. He had acquired two slaves and two servants. The house was short of sleeping space. On the other hand Davarah had a vacant room since Anunu's death. There was no man to defend the home for Harran was too frail and too sick to be of much use should robbers break in. Davarah therefore invited Nahor to sleep in the unoccupied chamber. He usually came in late and slept late. Either the slave, the servant, or even Davarah herself would serve him breakfast, the only meal he ate in the house.

One morning Nahor got up later than usual. It was already past noon. Davarah accompanied by her slave and servant went to deliver some finished cloth to the temple. Lot was playing at a neighboring house. Harran had been out that morning and came home tired and went to his chamber for a midday sleep. Only Milcah was at home to serve Nahor some food. Milcah had just turned fifteen and was becoming conscious of being pretty and well formed. An affection sprang up for her kinsman the moment he arrived. Nahor had that indifferent look of one who had knocked about in the world and knew how to impress with his arrogant air, his bold eyes, his proud carriage. Milcah began to pay attention to her looks, her clothes, her posture, her walk. She knew she would be alone with Nahor that morning and rouged her lips, used make-up on her face and eyes. Her young breasts with their pointed nipples seemed almost to hold up the thin shift without an undergown. All morning she had been practicing a coquettish motion of her head in the mirror of polished copper. When she heard her kinsman coming into the eating hall she touched her shift with a whiff of musk and walked out of her chamber slightly swaying her hips.

She served him the most palatable food in the kitchen together with a goblet of wine. When through eating, he looked up and noticed her for the first time.

"What a pretty girl you are. Where have you been keeping yourself? How is it I never saw you before?"

"Because you never looked at me," she pouted, with the toss of the head that she practiced all morning.

He got up from the divan and stood close to her. She did not move away but tried to look into his eyes with her chin up and as much challenge as she could muster. He took her in his arms and pressed a warm, slow kiss on her lips. She breathed hard and with effort broke away and hurried into her room. He took a deep breath and left the house. For several days he did not see her. He would leave early and return late, even after midnight. Late one evening he walked into the livingroom. Everyone was asleep and he saw her sitting on the divan sewing or fixing a dress by the light of a clay lamp. He stood close to the tripod that held the lamp and said, "Working so late? You must be anxious to finish your dress for a party."

"I am going tomorrow to the temple with a group to celebrate some kind of festival."

"Well, you must be careful. Some young priest will grab you and consecrate you in his room," laughed Nahor.

"Let him. I know you won't." Again she tossed her head and this time gave him a side glance that was challenging and at the same time inviting.

He sat next to her, took her in his arms and gave her a long kiss while pressing her down with her back resting on the divan. He felt a response in her lips and kissed her again. This time her arm hugged him while the other hand encircled his neck, then stroked his hair gently. He got up and pulled her up. With his arm around her waist he walked her slowly towards his room. In front of the door she whispered, "Please don't." He opened the door and gently forced her into the sleeping chamber with slight resistance on her part. He crushed her in his arms, kissed her with unrestrained passion, and felt the hot breath in her responding mouth. He pulled the shift over her head, removed her sandals, laid her nude body on the bed and deflowered her. When about to shriek with pain, he smothered her mouth with his overpowering kiss.

A week later he came in late one night, his breath smelling of wine. He walked directly into Milcah's room. For a time he kept coming into her room at night, then stopped. She then fell into the habit of coming into his room. This she kept up for several months until one night, while lying in his arms, she whispered in his ear, "Do you know, dearest, that I missed my period this month?"

"Oh, sometimes it comes late. Don't worry," he answered drowsily.

"But this morning I felt nauseous and vomited."

He maintained an ominous silence.

"What am I to do?" Her voice had a troubled timbre that denoted anxiety.

"I don't know," he answered somewhat gruffly.

"Is that all you have to say?"

"Yes," was the reply.

She got out of the bed and put on her sleeping gown.

"I can't keep it a secret. Soon everybody will see me with a big belly. There is nothing else for me to do but to tell Mother."

"Let me think it over and I will tell you in the morning."

"You better think carefully whether you want your child, when he grows up and asks who his father was, to be told that it was his granduncle, Nahor ben Terach, who seduced his niece in his own brother's home." All her love was turning to bitterness.

After a sleepless night Milcah got up early and went to his room. It was empty and all his belongings gone. She decided not to speak to anyone immediately but wait for Nahor to tell his intentions. She went back to bed and slept rather late. Her mother was already out attending to business.

In the early dawn Nahor carrying his packet of belongings walked to the waterfront. His first impulse was to get a job on a boat but he found that all the boat owners he knew had sailed away. There were other boats in the harbor but Nahor knew of the dangers in taking service with a rascally captain. He had heard of crewmen being sold into slavery in far away countries. The familiar wine shop had not as yet opened so Nahor decided to visit his friend Kagina, the skipper's son and ask his advice. It was still early when he knocked on the front door. Kagina's mother opened the door and recognizing Nahor invited him in. While her son was asleep she served his friend a light breakfast with some hot fruit juice. Finally, Kagina got up and asked with surprise what brought him. Was he in some trouble? Nahor told him the whole story. Kagina, older than Nahor, was surprisingly logical and cerebral. He asked, "Well, what do you want of me?"

"Kagina, what shall I do?"

"Marry the girl, you fool. Don't you know a good thing when you see it?"

"But I'm too young to marry. I just don't feel like it."

"It's not what you want; it's what you have to do. There are laws in Ur. It's a criminal offense to seduce a girl, plant a baby in her, then run away. Nahor, you're a no account bum."

"Oh, I'm not running away, Kagina. I don't even know where to go. Besides, your father's boat is not in the river. I can't go even if I wanted to."

"Listen, you idiot. Do you want to go back to Haran? You wasted two years and what did you accomplish? In Haran you were an outright hobo. Here in Ur you can be somebody. You come of a good family; your father has good connections in Nannar's temple. She is a fine, pretty girl and a wonderful lay, as you tell me. Your brother is ailing and as you say is not expected to live long. You will then be the oldest and inherit your father's estate. Do you want to kick all this into the fire by running away? Then you become a fugitive from justice. Your father has to say the word to the priest Sabbattu and you will be clamped in the temple prison."

"Well, I'll think it over. I can't decide now, this minute."

"Nahor, have you silver with you, any barley in your scrip?"

"No, I haven't."

"Then how will you live? Walking the streets won't feed you. Listen to me and stop being an ass. Go back to the girl immediately. Make up with her. Tell her you were frightened at the sudden thought of marriage, its responsibility, and that sort of thing. Girls are sensitive and it is not difficult to lose their love. If you must marry her, and you have no other recourse, then it is better to maintain her love than earn her hatred. Let me repeat what a very wise man said recently: 'If you are going to do something, then do it like a prince and not like a beggar.' "

Still Nahor could not bring himself to take the plunge. The real truth was that he preferred single life with many affairs than being tied down to one woman. He slept several nights at the hovel of an old woman and gave her some of his belongings in payment. All day he wandered about the more obscure streets and swapped his wearing things for food. He imagined his affair had become public news and avoided the people he knew. He felt lonely, miserable, a vagabond and sorry for himself.

One morning, after washing in the river, his feet wandered towards the Harran house. Before he knew it he walked in and found the house quiet. He opened Milcah's door and there she lay in bed asleep. He took her in his arms and kissed her. She wept softly, nestling her head against his chest. Lamely he explained his nervousness about marrying and settling down. He had to have time to think it over all by himself. He had been very unhappy. Now he really knew he loved and wanted to marry her. Between her sobs, Milcah was able to say, "After you disappeared without a word I had to tell mother. Of course, she spoke to Grandfather and Emtelai. I need not say how upset they were. They will be very happy now. You did not eat, did you? Let me prepare breakfast for both of us. Mother and Father will join us about noon. They will be glad to see you."

Harran and Davarah came in time for lunch. After eating, the four sat on the divan and discussed the marriage. Harran had set aside about 50 shekels in silver as a dowry for his daughter. Father Terach would no doubt contribute a similar sum for Nahor's marriage portion. As to what Nahor would do to support his wife, that would be discussed later. Meanwhile he and Davarah should go and tell the news to Father Terach. Though pressed financially Terach thought each should give 100 shekels. The final sum agreed upon was 150 shekels from both.

The wedding was held at the home of the bride. Besides the family, both sides invited their friends. Kagina, the skipper's son, stood as a sort of best man for the bridegroom. The priest Sabbattu received a donation for the Temple of Nannar and invoked the blessings of Irnina to promote love, passion, and fertility to the couple. All the guests sang the ancient traditional wedding song of Sumer:

Bridegroom, dear to my heart
You have captivated me.
Let me stand before you
I would be taken by you to the bedchamber.

My bride, let me caress you
Let me enjoy your goodly beauty
Your caress is more goodly than honey
Give me more of your caresses.

Bridegroom, sleep in our house until dawn
You have taken your pleasure of me.
My mother will give you delicacies
My lion, father will give you gifts.

My bride, because you love me
Give me more of your caresses
I know where to cheer your spirit
I know how to gladden your heart.

For several weeks after the wedding, Nahor did nothing. Then he began to consider the future. He could join his mother-in-law in her weaving enterprise; or he might go into idol making with his father. But neither business was especially appealing. Then he began to sense that neither his father nor Milcah's mother were very pressing in their suggestions to join them. He also began to notice the cool greetings he received from people he knew. Evidently the story of his conduct that led to the marriage got around. Suddenly he conceived a distaste for his birthplace. Ur was too conservative, too backward, too old-fashioned. Haran began to beckon. With 150 shekels in silver he could really do something there. Haran was a progressive place, full of new people who attempted things, who didn't mind taking risks, who didn't waste their lives talking about their noble ancestors.

Neither Terach nor Davarah approved of his design. But by opposing him they might bolster his determination and make up his mind for him. They were aware of a stubborn unreasoning streak in his make-up. Besides, too strong an opposition might cause him to desert his wife and run away as he did before. They kept silent and he read the silence as their assent. When he learned that Kagina's father was preparing a journey up the Purattu as far as Haran, he paid for a passage for himself and Milcah who, eager to see the world, regarded the trip as a lark. She told her mother to expect them back. But they remained in Haran.

## II

Eleazer and Avram went looking for Nahor. After inquiring of several merchants in the market place, they spoke to a trader, an Aramean, who sometimes bought woven material from Nahor's wife. While talking he pointed out a lad of about fourteen, who just passed, as the son of the man they were seeking. Avram overtook the boy whose name was Uz, the first-born of Nahor. Avram brought him to Terach and they ate the afternoon meal all together. Uz was the oldest of five brothers. His father operated a farm several miles outside of the city walls and had shepherds who grazed his goats and sheep out in the open country wherever they could find good pastures. His mother had several servants who spun and wove flax and wool, then dyed the finished cloth.

Terach hired a wagon drawn by two asses and took

along Avram, Keturah, Emtelai, Davarah, Lot, and Sarai. The farm, scarcely more than 15 acres, grew corn, lentils, barley, peas, and had some fruit trees chiefly of citrons and pomegranates. The one-story house of brick and wood was a rambling hacienda with a number of rooms, to which Nahor had added from time to time. Somewhat removed from the house were a number of tents occupied by Habiru shepherds who preferred this desert habitation to the more civilized dwelling of the cities.

Nahor was a disappointing sight. Gone were the days of the slim, handsome, dapper youth. Scarcely past 30 he looked middle-aged, gross and overfed. His sunburnt features, though shaven after the Sumerian fashion, took on a coarseness that seemed sensual and almost brutal. Nor did the years improve Milcah. Her five sons had evidently exacted a heavy toll. Heavy and plump she was decidedly on the fat side. Her expression disclosed neither happiness nor serenity. A habitual frown seemed to indicate a constant watchfulness, a close attention to her workers lest they shirk their duties or perform their tasks slovenly.

Milcah naturally welcomed her relatives. When she last saw Avram he was between two and three years old and Keturah less than one year. Milcah could not but marvel how closely she resembled her mother; she had a similar smile. And now they were married. How rapidly the time went by. She wanted to know all that had happened in the interim, but Davarah thought it better to wait for Nahor who had to leave and attend something urgent.

The story of Milcah was neither long nor inspiring. After the lengthy boat ride with many delays and few adventures, they reached Haran. She was lonely and felt homesick; it took time to become adjusted. Nahor tried to get started but lost with each venture until the silver of his marriage portion was gone. Milcah would not let him use her dowry. After her son Uz was born, she decided to imitate her mother and start weaving. It took time to learn, then to teach others. Her progress was slow and her success quite moderate. They lived frugally in a small house in the city.

"How did my brother manage to become a farmer?" questioned Avram, his interest aroused.

"One evening Nahor came home all excited. He had done a good stroke of business without investment. He had known an attractive young woman named Reumah when he first visited Haran and had seen her several times since our coming. She was married to a farmer who inherited this farm. For some reason he had to go by boat to Babylon. He never returned. One day a young woman and her brothers came to the farm and asked for him. Reumah did not know what they wanted and told them she did not know why her husband left or what had become of him. Reumah could not manage the farm herself nor could she sell it without his signature. So she proposed to Nahor to take it over and give her one-half of the profits.

"I didn't quite like this deal. First of all, I never was on a farm. Then I suspected an intimacy between them and I didn't want to live under the same roof with her. But Nahor overcame my objections. I had to admit the advantages of living rent free in a large house where I could expand my weaving. We both felt insecure and I always heard that a farmer never starves. He can always raise sufficient food. And strange to say, I did not find Reumah objectionable. In fact, she would help me with the weaving when I gave birth or if I had a large order to fill. After a time Nahor took her as his concubine. I was rather relieved because I became tired of bearing his boys one after the other. It was a relief to sleep alone. Reumah was thus able to bear him four children."

"Is she still here?" asked Davarah.

"No, Mother. About three years ago, suddenly out of a clear sky, her husband turned up. He had been living in Babylon and was quite successful, so he said. He was vague about his business. Nahor thought it was something unlawful. He really came to sell the farm although he pretended being anxious to see Reumah. Nahor bought the farm rather cheaply but had to raise some silver from a usurer at high interest. Strange to say he offered to take Reumah back and stranger still she consented. She left me two of her boys and took the girls with her. I believe that by this time she had enough of Nahor and was glad to leave him."

Nahor returned and said to Terach, "Father, why don't you pay off the wagon man and let him go. Stay with us overnight and I shall return all of you tomorrow."

While Terach was carrying out the chore, Avram said, "Nahor, we heard about your life here in Haran. Before we go into our story, I would like to know how you became what I understand the Egyptians call a *shepherd king*."

"One evening," reminisced Nahor, "six vagabonds, that is four men and two women, came here asking for something to eat. They are called Habiru, a bunch of dirty beggars, all ragged and without sandals. True to my upbringing, I fed them and let them sleep on the grass. Overnight I thought I might make use of them. But they knew nothing of farming; they were only shepherds. I wanted to send them away but Milcah thought she might use the two women to help around the house and for her weaving. The men asked to be employed as shepherds but I had neither sheep nor goats and nothing to feed animals except corn husks and not enough of that. They wanted to stay since they were Habiru and we Arameans and could understand each other. The cheek of such scum to compare themselves with us! I told them to be off. Now you tell the rest, Milcah."

"I told Nahor to run along and attend to his own affairs while I talked to the women. They were not beggars at all. They were proud and self-respecting. The two women, recently married, were slim and would be quite attractive with nice clothes. They were graceful, especially when they walked to the well with a pitcher on the head. They wished to stay with us because they felt they might soon become pregnant and wanted a permanent home. I told them we had no place as our house was all filled up. We have built on more rooms since. They said they were accustomed to living in tents and knew how to put them up at little expense. As for weaving, they could catch on quickly and would do housework.

"Then I spoke to the men. They explained that pasturing sheep and goats could be profitable provided there was no cost in feeding. These animals breed rapidly and wool has a steady market. I asked how they fed them without cost. They answered that they take a herd and go into the country looking for grazing land. Shepherd dogs are a necessary protection against robbers. The flock stays away from 10 to 20 days. 'Suppose you find no free pasture land,' I asked, 'what then?' They answered, 'As long as we stay away from desert or rocky or wasteland there is always pasture especially in a settled country. An experienced shepherd keeps his eyes open and when he passes a farm that has been harvested the owner usually welcomes a flock that can nibble away the grass and make his land clean as a bone.' They required to begin with no wages just to prove that sheep raising could be profitable.

"I served them a hearty breakfast," continued Milcah, "and let them wash up in the pool which following the heavy rain was overflowing. Then I gave them some of our clothes. I was much slimmer then so my old dresses made the women quite happy, especially after they saw themselves in my polished bronze mirror. The men now looked like ordinary dwellers of Haran. I had to insist on Nahor giving them a tryout and even offered to pay the expenses out of my weaving business. I forced Nahor to take them to the city's market. They found three old tents at bargain prices. They also bought from different farmers some young sheep, a ram, several goats, and ewes. So we went into raising sheep and goats. Now we have several nice herds and this side of our business sometimes pays much better than the farm, particularly when the price of corn and barley is down."

"Oh, for the love of Ishtar, or Irnina, as you say in Ur," growled Nahor, not pleased with his letdown by Milcah. "Can't we talk about something other than those dirty, miserable Habiru? I am waiting to hear what happened in Ur since I left."

"May I go out and see the farm?" begged Avram, irritated by Nahor's churlishness. "I can't add anything to what Father, Mother and Davarah will have to say. Come Keturah."

The couple wandered over the enclosed farm examining the growing corn, barley, lentils, fruit trees, the well, the pools that caught and conserved rain water. A belt of grass surrounding the house was utilized during the heat of the day while that part remained in the shade. They watched the children, who now included Lot and Sarai, playing a kind of game that might be called Hide and Seek. In one corner of the field a flock of goats and sheep stood nibbling grass, corn shucks, leaves, or lying down peacefully chewing the cud, or drinking out of the trough that held rain water collected in the pools and carried by terra cotta pipes. Near the farm flowed a narrow stream which became useful when rain water was unavailable.

On another corner stood about nine tents, gray and black, of heavy sailcloth or goat skins stitched together. In the open, women were cooking barley or lentil soup, corn in goats' milk, or baking bread. Near one tent a sheep was roasting. It had broken a leg while grazing and carried for miles by the shepherd. Custom decreed that in such a case the animal became the herdsman's property. If cured, it remained his; if not, he alone could dispose of it or use it for food, the greatest of delicacies to shepherds. The tents were occupied by single families and when the children grew up they slept elsewhere to preserve the strict moral code that prevailed. Some of the men were absent, grazing the flocks. When one herd returned, then the remaining one of the farm immediately vacated and went out seeking pasture. All differences that arose were settled either by the acknowledged leader or by the owner of the herds. A complete system of rules and regulations had evolved during untold centuries of sheep herding.

Sending Keturah to the women, Avram introduced himself as the brother of Nahor to several men sitting on the ground in a tent. They returned his saluatation but without enthusiasm. He then asked if he could come in and talk with them. They nodded, their expression denoting suspicion if not hostility. Avram quickly perceived that they bore resentment to Nahor and naturally identified him with his brother. He sat down on the ground and informed them of his group leaving Ur Kasdim to escape the destruction that threatened the city. He had never before seen his brother who left Ur during his infancy.

"May I ask who you are and of what land you come?" inquired Avram.

"We are called Habiru," answered a middle-aged man, dark, muscular, bearded, and dignified. "Why, we don't know. I am of the third generation of my family who left the desert in search of water, food, and the chances of survival."

"Who gave you that name and what does it signify?"

"I don't know. From Egypt to Babylon we are known as Habiru or Hapiru. Some say it means 'foreigners'; others hold that because we come from beyond the river; still others maintain that because we are descended from a man named Eber."

"Why have you come this far? Why didn't you remain in Canaan or in Aram?"

"On leaving the desert we tried to settle on the seacoast in Philistia. But the Philistines, not long in the land themselves, would not permit us. We applied to such cities as Jericho, Hebron, Beersheba, or Shechem, and they required of us to serve Baal and Ashtoreth. But when we saw them casting live children into the burning bellies of Chemosh or Moloch, we would having nothing of them. Sodom and Gomorrah would permit us but when we witnessed their wickedness we would not live among them."

"Tell me, pray, what gods do you serve?"

"We worship only one God. Some call him El, others know him as Yah."

"Where does he reside?"

"In the desert on a mountain."

"Are all of you shepherds?"

"Some of our people are soldiers. They are mercenaries

to the different city kings in Canaan. Many have distinguished themselves in warfare. Some even serve Hammurabi, king of Babylon. Then many of us are mechanics good at repairing things. They go from place to place seeking work. Some are traders who became rich merchants in many places from Dameshek to Babylon. The rest who have no other occupation remain shepherds."

"This may sound strange to you," declared Avram. "But do you know that I am descended from the patriarch Eber and serve the God of my forefathers, El Elyon? Others call him El Shaddai. He dwells in the heavens above."

"A troupe of boys rushed up shouting, "Uncle Avram and Aunt Keturah. Come to the evening meal. Father is waiting for you."

Going to the house Avram said to Keturah, "I like these Habiru. They must be good people if my brother Nahor dislikes them."

"Now don't go and tell him that, my beloved," she cautioned.

Milcah did herself proud with the feast she prepared. Two lambs were roasted. Soup was served with various delicacies. Wine was passed around in generous sized goblets. Those who refused wine received fruit juice or cow's milk. For dessert apples, pomegranates, citrons, and pears alternated with nuts, dates, raisins, and figs. It was truly the eventful celebration of a united family.

Nahor had been partaking of wine immoderately. His humor was heavy and coarse. One of the boys whispered in his ear. "Father, you don't let us play with the Habiru boys, but Uncle Avram sat in the tent and talked nice to them."

"Your Uncle Avram likes to break the laws," grunted Nahor. "That's why the whole family had to flee from Ur."

It was sleeping time for the children and Milcah felt uneasy as to what Nahor might say or do in his besotted condition. She sent all the children to bed. Nahor kept on rambling:

"I can't see why anyone should want to smash up the gods. No wonder they decided to burn you in the furnace. Breaking up the gods is criminal and deserves punishment."

"But not as criminal as seducing one's niece in the home of his own brother," retorted Avram.

"I am going to cut his heart out," snorted Nahor as he rose, staggered, fell, and passed out.

"Come, let's go to bed," pleaded Keturah.

# 16

# In Haran

IT TOOK MONTHS FOR OLDER MEMBERS OF THE TERACH CLAN to adjust themselves to the new life. Everything seemed strange. Language, clothes, customs, houses, temples, manner of speaking, variety of people, methods of trading were all quite different from the place whence they came. A kind of nostalgia settled over them. Everything about Ur seemed perfect while the ways of Haran were raw, backward, and vulgar. Surely they would never get used to the hurry, the bustle and could only regard the place a busy crossroad rather than a city. On the other hand, the children were entranced with the novelty, the rapid pace, the energy of Haran.

The overriding problem was what to do; how to make a living. Terach became enchanted with the thought of building. Tired of idol making, he considered building of homes, structures of any kind from dwellings to palaces, a superior creativity to sculpting. Together with Sanu-Rimmon he looked at the various dwellings and the man from Erech was especially impressed with the number of habitations springing up. They stopped to look at a house in the course of completion that had unusual features. Instead of the perennial flat roof, it was slanted and formed a gable which served as a kind of canopy over the door. He had never seen anything of a similar design and guessed it to be the work of some foreigner reproducing the style of his native land. This type of roof suited a country that had plenty of wood. Such construction in Erech or Ur would be prohibitive on account of the scarcity of forests. Besides Haran was higher, cooler, and the flat roof not as indispensable as in the hot, low, table lands of south Sumer, where after sundown it was a repose for the family.

While inspecting the almost completed structure a man came up and asked in mixed Babylonian and Aramaic what they thought of the house. He was short, stocky, barrel-shaped and had a large protruding hooked nose, obviously a Hittite. Terach answered in Aramaic that it was interesting and unusual. After inviting them in the Hittite informed them that it was a new style out of his native city, Hattusas. Sanu-Rimmon pointed to the liberal use of rock, plentiful around Haran, but not to be found in Erech, Ur, or throughout Sumeria. The oven-baked brick made out of a reddish clay-like soil was strengthened with straw. What interested him most were the hinges that joined the doors to the jambs. The Hittite called this material *iron* and said it was harder and far more durable than copper or that mixture of tin and copper called bronze. He showed them nails, bars, and bolts made in his country of the same metal, unaware that it was destined to revolutionize not only building and warfare but the entire life of man.

The Hittite Dulashish showed interest on hearing that Sanu-Rimmon was a builder from Erech who had fled to save his boy's life. Dulashish scanned him closely then invited him to come the next day and bring the boy to play with his own grandson of the same age. The mother of the boy would be able to translate what he said into Hittite. He himself would gladly answer all questions and give him whatever advice he could.

On the way home Terach thought it a good thing to become friendly with a fellow builder in a new and strange place. Sanu-Rimmon confessed that he had qualms about going into building in a city where the techniques were probably different from his own Erech. While it should not take long to catch on yet someone had to instruct him. In fact, he would be willing to work for Dulashish without pay until he knew enough of local usage or custom to start building on his own. At the Terach house Avram, Keturah, Davarah, Eleazer, and Lot were visiting. The women became suspicious of any friendly gesture from a stranger in so self-seeking and conniving a place as Haran. Eleazer immediately showed interest in the new metal mined and smelted in the Hittite country. It seemed to him that there was a ready market for processed iron not only in Haran but in all of Shinar between the two rivers.

The next morning Sanu-Rimmon went with his son to see Dulashish. The boys became chummy while their elders were engaged in shop talk. The Hittite's daughter did the translating with more or less facility. The problems of the trade were essentially the same as in Sumer. It might be better for the builder to put up the house himself and then sell it, provided there was a ready market for homes. In building for a fixed sum there would always be a hazard of loss. It was more satisfactory to make a contract that set the fee to the proportionate over-all cost of the entire construction, what in later times came to be known as the cost-plus method. But owners seldom agreed to such an arrangement.

The Hittite invited Sanu-Rimmon to the midday meal at his home. Dulashish seemed in comfortable circumstances yet lived rather frugally. The daughter was a widow in her early thirties. Her late husband had been in partnership with her father. One day it started to rain and he ran out to pick up a long iron bar. They knew that water rusted iron. A sudden bolt of lightning struck and killed him. Such incidents sometimes happened in Hattusas and people said that the storm god Teshub was displeased when men took iron ore out of the earth; he therefore struck them with a lightning while they held the metal.

After eating, Dulashish went back to work leaving the guest and his daughter talking. Each told the other about their native homes. When the Hittite returned they were still talking while the old mother prepared additional food for the visitors. Dulashish complained about the work getting too much for him; he really needed an assistant to take the place of his dead son-in-law. Yet after the evening meal he, in spite of being tired, insisted on taking Sanu-Rimmon to the Terach home accompanied by his two armed workmen. On the way he proposed that the stranger from Erech and his boy move in with them. He could then learn faster about local building and acquire the language quicker, since at Terach's he would continue to speak Sumerian only. It became quite obvious that the Hittite wanted him for a son-in-law.

That night Sanu-Rimmon lay in his bed thinking. Wasn't there some logic in the old man's scheme? He needed an assistant to assume the burdens as well as take over the active management of the business. The time may not be far off for the old man to retire. He couldn't know the extent of the Hittite's resources but they must be quite substantial considering that he could build on his own. Now as for himself, just where did he stand? Without means in a strange land he could only become at best a foreman but more likely a common laborer. As for Terach's ambition the matter was not so simple. He might supply the capital but nothing more. His son Avram did not look like a man of business nor could he be useful in construction. Furthermore, wasn't there a hazard about venturing in a new city without experience of local conditions? As for himself, this opening was made to order. A wife for himself, a mother to the boy, a going business to receive him, and a home for the homeless. Then he thought of his family in Erech. Why not bring them all to Haran? His sons could expand the partnership into large proportions. His wife would not relish the position of second place and inferior to a younger woman. But one simply can't have everything he kept repeating until he fell asleep.

The next morning he moved out after explaining everything and getting the consent of Terach. Five days later Sanu-Rimmon proposed marriage and a week later the wedding was held in the newly completed house since the old home was entirely too small. The participants were largely Hittites with a few Arameans and Amorites. Of course, the entire Terach household, including the servants and slaves who were on the boat, as well as Nahor's entire family were honored guests. The bridegroom took Terach aside and expressed appreciation and gratitude for the splendid hospitality accorded him when he was in dire distress. He added that if Terach would consent he would be happy to defray all the costs of the journey. But the former idol maker answered that he valued friendship far above silver. But Terach was far from pleased.

## II

As month followed month without any tidings about or from Sabbattu, Terach began to feel that perhaps he would never hear from him. Probably such thinking might be mere wish-fulfillment. Subconsciously or perhaps secretely, he did not wish to receive any such tidings. Unconsciously he began to take on the attitude or even the manner of a rich man. If the priest was in prison or no longer living then he, Terach, would inherit a tidy sum, perhaps real wealth. He really did not know. The parcels were all sealed except the one he opened when the necessity arose in Eridu.

With a growing sense of affluence, he began to entertain high hopes with Sanu-Rimmon in the center; through him he might reach a distinguished place as a builder. He even began to plan the first structure. It should be a pretentious home that would harbor his entire household including retainers, servants and slaves. For with Avram, Keturah, Davarah, Lot, and Eleazer living elsewhere he began to feel lonely. Actually outside of his wife he had no adult in the house with whom he could exchange a word. With Sanu-Rommon leaving, or as he felt, deserting, his world tumbled, so to speak. He could no longer act the role of the patriarch presiding over his clan. His disappointment was keen.

Eleazer and Avram had unconsciously absorbed Terach's grandiose dream of building dwellings, warehouses, country manors, and even palaces or temples. In a project of such proportions everyone would find a place. They did not know to what extent Terach could finance such scheming. They had been lifted into the clouds, as it were, by his enthusiasm which was contagious. Now with the puncture of the fanciful afflatus they landed back on terra firma.

While Terach could find consolation over his disappointment in reveling over his newly found wealth, Avram felt the pinch of necessity reaching him. Head of a household and expecting a child, he had to find the wherewithal to earn a living. Being supported by his father was as undesirable as it was embarrassing. He turned to Eleazer for suggestions. But Eleazer could only draw upon his own experience, which was limited to operating a caravan. He regarded Haran as the central point through which caravans were constantly converging from all directions. Thus to begin with it might be simpler to join a caravan rather than operate one. He ascertained that a passenger could rent space for himself and baggage to and from Nineveh on the Tigris, or other places as far as Hattusas, the Hittite capital.

Avram and Eleazer decided first of all to try Nineveh, a small inconsequential city under the sway of Babylon but 1200 years later to become world famous when Sennacherib would make it the capital of the Assyrian Empire. If the two caravaneers would be successful in a small way then their next enterprise could be expanded. Davarah and Eleazer drove down to Nahor's farm and selected woven material out of Milcah's warehouse. The travelers took along other articles and wares for barter or sale and reached Nineveh by slow stages.

The Assyrians, tough traders and extremely unpleasant, preferred the superior, famous cloth made in Babylon, though far more expensive. Each Assyrian seemed to carry himself with a chip on his shoulder. Though under Babylon's heel the people displayed insolence, venom, hate and disdain towards foreigners, possibly as an outlet of their secret inner resentment against Babylonian conquerors. Avram decided to have no truck with such arrogant boors. Thus when Assyrians attained power centuries later their cruelty, barbarities and ruthless ferocities earned them such bitter resentment that after a single defeat they disappeared from the historic scene as if reluctant to show their stony faces to the world.

The caravan did not linger at Nineveh. The other traders felt about the same as Avram. The manager for a consideration made stops at various towns and certain villages for his passengers to display their wares. Eleazer proved a skillful bargainer. Little by little he disposed of the entire stock at better prices than obtainable at Nineveh. But Avram conceived a dislike for trafficking and looked back to the day spent on Nahor's farm with a lingering regret.

## III

On coming back home a surprise awaited the travelers. During their absence a flotilla of boats crowded with troops had sailed up from Babylon and stopped at Haran. Of all people Sabbattu showed up. After paying the respects of Hammurabi to Nimur-Hadad, king of Haran, and visiting the high priest of the moon god, called Szin, in Semitic lands, Sabbattu accompanied by a cordon of Babylonian soldiers came to see Terach. Getting over the first shock of keen disappointment on hearing the news of the priest's arrival Terach, after the lapse of several days, was able to conceal his chagrin. He welcomed his patron with profusions of cordial respect.

Emtelai served the former high priest some wine, nuts, cookies, and fruit while Terach related the happenings since fleeing Ur, not omitting the pressing necessity of opening one of the parcels to use the silver. Sensing the priest's anxiety over the packets Terach led him through a hidden underground passage into the subterranean rocky vault underneath the house. By lamplight Sabbattu counted the packages and examined their unbroken seals. His face registered relief while expressing satisfaction with Terach's careful management.

The burden that bore down on Sabbattu suddenly lifted; his care-laden features brightened. He had been worrying about the safety of the parcels. Should they even be located the problem faced him of storing them in Haran until he could return from his assignment. He could not very well ask the king to hold valuables that were neither Hammurabi's nor government property. He could of course place them in the Temple of Szin but knew from experience that priests were skilled in tampering with seals and often examined sealed packages left with them for safekeeping. Now the problem was solved and the parcels were safe in Terach's hidden vault.

When Emtelai brought in more wine he was sufficiently relaxed to inquire about her health and adjustment to the new environment. He asked about the members of her family and when he learned that Davarah happened to be in the house he expressed the wish to see her.

"How is my daughter?" was the first question. "I would like to see her."

"Keturah is in the eighth month, all distended and as big as this room," laughed Davarah. "She would not be seen as much as she wants to see my lord for she is very fond of him."

"Who was the father?" Would it be possible for the child to be his? He began to count on his fingers the last time he slept with her.

"It is my son Avram," answered Emtelai and seeing his surprised look, she continued, "They were married in Eridu. It must be at least ten months ago."

The priest searched the folds of his garment and brought out a gold ring, earrings of gold with ruby pendants, a carnelian necklace, a belt of lapis lazuli connected with silver clasps, leather sandals dyed red and banded with silver, a small purse of gold, a handful of silver, and a container of various kinds and colors of make-up.

"Please give this with my love to my and your child. She always referred to you as her mother. Tell her I shall pray to Irnina to give her an easy birth, to Nannar and Ningal to grant her good health, and to Enlil to keep away all evil spirits. Thank you both."

"Would Adoni care to have the midday meal with us? It would be a great honor," ventured Emtelai.

"I would like to but the soldiers are outside. I must take them back to the barracks before they start rioting for food," answered the priest more gracious than his usual habit. As the women were leaving he suddenly held up his hand addressing Emtelai, "Incidentally, I suppose you know all about the attempt to throw your son into the burning furnace. I shall never forget that scene. The sage Khar-Sak and I did everything possible to save him. On the court we voted against the death penalty but nothing could help him. I felt he was gone when suddenly a clap of thunder and flash of lightning seemed to stun everyone. This was no accident for our gods of Ur were wrathful with him. Only the God of Avram saved him. This I firmly believe."

After the women left the room, Sabbattu sat sipping the wine, thinking in silence. He finally said, "Terach, I know you are wondering about me. What am I doing here?

What happened in Ur? How did I escape? Where am I going? Terach, I trust you and have given you more of my confidence than any other person, dead or alive. But I cannot tell you everything. These are state secrets known only to Hammurabi and me. I told you far in advance what would happen in Ur. I knew that Ur could not oppose Hammurabi, nor could any other city or kingdom for that matter. Even Egypt would fall like a ripe plum should my king undertake its conquest.

"Ur surrendered and I am blamed. They say that I betrayed the city. But see what happened. Not a person was killed except the few soldiers who tried to resist. No woman or girl was violated. Not a house or ship was plundered. Hammurabi entered and announced from my temple that everyone should go about his business as if nothing had happened. No one would be injured or disturbed. Trade must go on as usual. The ba'iru policed the city as before and everything went on as the king promised. Ur is now more secure; life is safer and prosperity is on the increase. Yet I am the traitor responsible for these great benefits. For such blessings a memorial should be erected in my honor. Instead public rage became so pronounced that Hammurabi, who is my friend, had to remove me and install Khar-Sak as high priest.

"Then Hammurabi invaded Elam and proceeded to invest the capital city, Susa. He took me along as adviser since I am of Elamite descent. Susa was faced with the same prospect of bloodshed, pillage, rape, and destruction. I managed to see Kudur-Lagamar (in the Hebrew scriptures, Chedorlaomer) and proved that his course was ruinous. It would be best for him and the kingdom to enter into Hammurabi's federation of lands as an ally rather than as a conquered province. Suppose he did pay his share of the costs to maintain the peace and security of an empire? Wouldn't it benefit Elam to be a friend of Hammurabi rather than his enemy? Kudur-Lagamar saw the light and opened the gates of Susa. Again I saved a kingdom the unspeakable horrors of bloodshed, conquest, and destruction.

"Immediately I suggested to Hammurabi a plan to extend his empire to the Mediterranean without war or conquest. He should invite all city kingdoms, large or small, west of the Purattu to enter peacefully into a league of nations under the leadership of Babylon. Each kingdom would remain independent under its own rulers and pay a proportionate tax to uphold the alliance. This arrangement would stop the perpetual wars between the different cities. The constant warfare between the city kingdoms in Shinar destroyed the power, prestige, and independence of Sumer. With peace maintained by might then robbery and piracy could be eliminated; law and order would prevail everywhere; safety of travel would promote trade and bring about a flourishing prosperity shared by all. Hammurabi approved my idea.

"Then I proposed a novel scheme. A force of about 500 troops directed by five different kings but all under the command of Kudur-Lagamar should be sent to Canaan, Phoenicia, Damascus, and Philistia. These countries are divided into any number of city kingdoms often at odds with each other. Because of no unity among them Egypt is trying to get a foothold. My idea is for the leaders of this small army to approach each city and propose for their own defense a peaceful alliance with the nations that comprise the empire of Babylon. The object is twofold: The Mediterranean people will see that with such a small force Hammurabi has no intention to conquer them. If the league is formed, then the Babylonian empire will reach from Elam to the great sea in the west as far as Egypt.

When the conquered people see Kudur-Lagamar heading an expedition with the king of Babylon under his command they will be convinced that they are the allies of Hammurabi and not his slaves. This strong alliance will keep Egypt out of Asia."

"How does Adoni fit into this expedition?" asked Terach, curious to know the ultimate fate of the valuable parcels.

"Hammurabi decided on four instead of five kings and selected Kudur-Lagamar as commander. He chose his own son Amraphel to represent Babylon. Eriaku (Arioch in Genesis), king of Larsa and Tudgula (Tidal in the Bible), the leader of volunteers out of many nations will be confederates. The kings themselves are not appearing in person. I am the adviser and negotiator. I have already conferred with Nimur-Hadad, king of Haran, and believe he will join us.

"This is a distinguished assignment," conceded Terach, "but isn't it also a post of danger? Some of the city kings may not understand and seize the leaders as hostages."

"True," assented Sabbattu. "They may even attack us. But I believe they will fear reprisals by Hammurabi. While on the subject, let me mention again. If you are convinced that I am no longer alive you keep the parcels. Otherwise, you must return them when I get back. By the way, where is the favorite of El Elyon? I would like to see Avram."

"He and Eleazer are on a caravan to sell and buy in Nineveh. They should be back soon. Avram will want to be present when the baby is born."

Sabbattu rose and said, "If I remain much longer I shall come to see you again; otherwise, farewell."

The story that Sabbattu told Terach caused Eleazer to remark: "Saving a great city like Ur and preventing murder, rapine, and pillage is a worthy act even if the method displeased such a patriotic fanatic as Hunate. The results, I think, excuse the questionable procedure."

"I believe," admitted Avram, "that the results might sometimes justify the means. But somehow it is detestable to open the gates surreptitiously at night to admit the enemy. It so happens that Hammurabi is a just ruler and permits no excesses. Yet an Assyrian commander might have acted differently. I distrust Sabbattu and don't believe that he cared about saving Ur or protecting the lives or property of its people. This step seemed the most beneficial to him, the best strategy to save himself from the perils lurking in a conquest, especially since he became the most important figure in the city and actually the ruler."

## IV

Keturah was nearing the time to give birth and Avram detected uneasiness that betokened fear. When he asked whether anything was ailing her outside of the ordinary discomforts of child bearing she admitted her fear of the *shaidim* that lurked near the bedside waiting to pounce upon the newborn child.

"Do not be frightened, my Keturah. No harm shall befall you. My God will protect you from evil spirits."

"How do you know, Avram? You might be his favorite as Sabbattu told your father recently. But he has never spoken to me."

"El Elyon said to me, 'Look toward heaven and count the stars if you can. So shall your offspring be.' Keturah, you are bearing my child. The promise of the Most High applies to him."

"Avram, I believe in El Elyon, but what harm is there for the Temple of Szin to send the *ashipu* here to exorcize away the evil spirits? The Most High God cannot concern himself with everything. Surely he would not be angry if the exorciser should perform his function."

Avram maintained silence. Wouldn't the *ashipu* invoke the false gods? And that would be compromising with the forces of evil. Yet, is it right not to mitigate the suffering of a young girl who believes the *shaidim* might injure her or the baby or both? Her mother when giving birth probably died of fear. Caught in the dilemma and not knowing what to do he said and did nothing.

While waiting for the baby to come Avram was agreeably surprised to receive a visitor, the captain of the boat Hankas, who had become a believer in El Elyon. After landing the Terach household at Haran, the boatman from Agade had occasion to go down as far as Ur where by chance he met on the waterfront Kagina, the friend of Nahor. Kagina had inherited his father's boat and shipping business and became interested when Hankas asked whether he knew Avram, the son of Terach an image-maker for the Temple of Nannar. Hankas went on to relate:

"Kagina, who is a very smart man, was stirred as he told me how you broke the idols in your father's workshop and how you were sentenced to burn in the furnace. Then he told me of a strange occurence, a thing that would not leave his mind. It had been bothering him since that awful night when the soldiers were about to cast you into the fiery kiln. A sudden thunderbolt knocked you out of their hands. No one knows what happened after that. Neither your body nor your clothes or belongings could ever be found. To make the matter still more mysterious, your father and his entire household disappeared on that terrible night when no one could go out on the streets on account of the heaviest downpour that anyone could ever remember. For days not a soul could talk of anything else. People stopped talking about you only when they were panic-stricken at the sight of Hammurabi's army before the city walls."

"How did the priests explain this miracle to the people? Did Kagina say?"

"The priests let rumors out that the demons grabbed you and your father's family and rushed all of you to the lowest pit in Aralu."

"Did you hear perchance as to what happened to my father's house? It is a good sized structure of 14 rooms with a court and patio."

"Yes, Kagina showed it to me. I believe it is on the Street of the Ancients. It was all locked and boarded up. I told Kagina that I would like to know its legal status since I expected to see the family one of these days. He advised me to ask the new high priest who has a reputation for honesty and fairness. The high priest was surprised to hear that all of you were alive. As for the house, he said that no one has claimed it. Nor did the new rulers confiscate it."

Eleazer walked into the house for the midday meal. He and Hankas greeted each other warmly. Avram excused himself to see how Keturah was getting on. While answering each other's questions, Hankas suddenly asked, "Are the builder from Erech and his boy here? I looked up the family when I docked near the city gate and would like to deliver a tablet from his son."

Eleazer told what happened to Sanu-Rimmon. When Avram returned, the meal was served with Hankas delivering the prayer: "May El Elyon bless all of us at this table and in this house." He told how Sanu-Rimmon's family received him and described how thrilled his wife was to hear that her husband and son were alive and safe in Haran. His sons seemed downhearted and said no one had yet commenced to build. Prices were too high. People were waiting for the high costs to come down. Eleazer agreed to take Hankas to see Sanu-Rimmon the next morning but the skipper stressed that unless Avram went along no one could read the clay tablet.

That afternoon Emtelai called to see Keturah and became aware of her nervous tensions. Together with Davarah she urged Avram to abandon his stubborn, senseless objections to permit the temple exorciser to declaim his incantations that would rout the demons or at least hinder them from harming Keturah or the baby the moment it entered the world. He listened to their cogent arguments that articulated the birth pains as more than sufficient without the additional terror of the evil spirits swarming about the suffering mother. He promised to consider the matter but after pondering late into the night he was still puzzled and could no longer reach any decision.

After midnight Avram went to bed but tossed about restlessly. Finally he fell into a profound slumber. Again he was in Ur wandering about in the Temple of Nannar until he stopped at the stall that sold animals and birds. He purchased a heifer, a ram, a she-goat, each not older than three years, then a turtledove and a young pigeon. He knew the priest in charge and borrowed a long bronze sacrificial knife and a cleaver. The temple slaves led the animals and followed Avram beyond the south wall near the kiln which was still smoking, though the workers were all gone. The slaves tied the four feet of each animal and both feet of each bird and departed. Avram slit the throat of the heifer, the ram, the she-goat; soon they lay dead on the ground. He then raised the cleaver and divided each in halves; he placed each half opposite the other at a distance of about ten feet apart. Then he slaughtered the birds and laid the turtledove alongside one group of halves and the pigeon on the other side.

The sun was setting and Avram felt tired, perhaps from the task he had performed. He sat down on the grass, his back resting against the temple wall. Over him crept a drowsiness that soon descended into a heavy slumber. Everything turned pitch black as impenetrable as the darkness of that memorable night when he miraculously escaped the flames of the nearby kiln. Dread seized him and he felt frightened as if this time he would not escape the burning oven. Then the door of the kiln opened and the furnace within began to move. It was all aflame, the sides red and smoking through the open top. The furnace passed between the halves of the animals and the birds on each side. A short distance behind, a flaming torch followed the furnace in the same direction. Behind the torch Avram could see himself walking through the same path formed by the slaughtered animals and birds. A familiar voice resounded:

"Avram! Avram!

"This is my covenant with you. My spirit is now upon you. My words shall not depart out of your mouth, nor out of the mouths of your children, nor out of the mouths of your children's children, sayeth I, your God, from henceforth and forever."

When Avram awoke in the morning he looked up at the heavens above, then fell on his knees, bowed down until his head touched the ground. He then prayed:

"My God and the God of my forefathers. The covenant established between Thee and me shall be everlasting. I hereby swear that this covenant shall be kept by me and I hope and pray that it will be maintained by my descendants throughout the generations for evermore."

He then went over to Keturah's bed, kissed her and exclaimed joyously, "Have no more fears, my Keturah.

Nothing will happen to you nor to our child. The Most High has spoken to me again. I am not concerned with the *shaidim.* They are powerless if my God forbids them to harm you."

"If they are harmless," she argued, "then why not let the *ashipu* perform his incantations? Who will be hurt thereby?"

"That would be an acknowledgment that the gods who order the demons are potent. It would also show a lack of faith in El Elyon. We can only serve the Most High by ignoring the false gods, their power and their pretensions."

After breakfast Hankas arrived and went with Avram and Eleazer to Terach's house. The skipper repeated the result of his investigations in Ur. Terach told Emtelai that all four were going to see Sanu-Rimmon at the home of Dulashish. She could skip the midday meal since in all probability Sanu-Rimmon would invite them to eat with him. As soon as the men left, Emtelai rushed over to Avram's house and assured Davarah that now was an excellent opportunity to take Keturah to the Temple of Szin. She could not walk that distance so the women hired a chair carried by four men.

In the temple Keturah ordered a pigeon to be sacrificed and left an offering for the temple. The priest prayed to the gods and the *ashipu* exorcised the demons from causing any injury either to Keturah or the unborn child. When they returned home Keturah's eyes were bright, shining, and glad. She admitted that no harm could now befall her. She had the protection of Avram's powerful God as well as the favor of Szin, Ishtar, Irnina, Ningal, and Enlil.

Four days later Keturah gave birth to a boy. Her delivery was neither over-extended nor too laborious. At the family feast Avram named his firstborn Zimran.

# 17

# Carchemish

WHILE THE SKIPPER HANKAS WAS TALKING ABOUT SANU-Rimmon's family in Erech, Eleazer noticed that Dulashish did not listen. It occurred to him that the Hittite probably did not understand Sumerian. He therefore drew him aside and asked in Aramaic where in the land of the Hittites could articles of iron be obtained.

"What kind of articles have you in mind? Why do you want such information?" cross-questioned the Hittite suspiciously.

Eleazer explained that he and Avram had recently returned from Nineveh on a selling-buying trip and now were contemplating a caravan journey to the west or north. He thought that tools made of iron should have a good sale in Haran. He had been informed that only the Hittites could mine and smelt iron ore. They were the only people who could fashion such hard metal into daggers, knives, hatchets, or rims for wheels.

"I really don't know who makes or sells iron objects," replied Dulashish. "My brother in Hattusas picks up such tools or articles wherever he can find them. Then he sends them by caravan or boat. I am afraid I cannot give you any such information."

"Don't you know in what place the iron wares are made?"

"No, I don't."

Eleazer sensed that Dulashish was unwilling to impart the information which unquestionably he knew. He could not assign any reason for such reticence. He mentioned to Terach and Avram the Hittite's strange secretiveness, which he did not understersttand.

"What is there so difficult to understand?" questioned Terach, who knew the tricks of trade practiced by competitors. "When Sanu-Rimmon and I first met Dulashish he pointed with pride to the iron hinges and declared that no building in Haran has them. But wait, I will get this information from Sanu-Rimmon."

II

The Terach family was now obsessed with the problem of making a living. Terach had slipped into a comfortable state of mind; he didn't need to work any more. But that notion was dispelled by Sabbattu's visit. And since he abandoned the idea of becoming a master builder, he must perforce fall back on image-making. Yet that craft was no sure means of supporting a large household. While the idols he saw in Haran were in no way superior to his own workmanship, it was not so easy to market statuettes in a place where he was unknown. He recalled his early struggles in Ur before Sabbattu became his patron. The hope of Sabbattu not returning would come to the fore to be immediately thrust into the subconscious.

Anxiety also pervaded the household of Avram. He was constantly discussing his problem with Eleazer. Without consulting anyone, Davarah decided to reenter the weaving industry. The slave she brought along from Ur would be most helpful. If Davarah had been successful in Ur then why not attempt the same project in Haran? With plenty of experience in weaving she was far more skilled than her daughter Milcah, and even she was moderately successful. As for capital she managed to bring along the silver she had; but her stock of woven cloth both in the temple stall and in her home in Ur had no doubt been stolen or confiscated. In any case, she could not retrieve that loss.

Eleazer could only think of caravans. While the venture to Nineveh was no shining success yet it was no loss either. The costs and expenses of the trip were covered by the profits. After all the scale of the enterprise was rather small. A larger venture might have paid off quite well. The prospect of bringing iron to Haran appealed quite strongly. The question arose whether to form their own caravan and seek passengers or join one as they did before. But a venture of any size needed a sizeable investment. Would Terach join the enterprise? If not, would he advance the funds and get back his loan with the liquidation of the venture?

It happened that Terach was in a receptive mood. If some kind of business could sustain his household then he would not be compelled to go back to idol making. The time was opportune. He had the wealth of Sabbattu in his hands and could utilize part of it for some legitimate enterprise. If the undertaking proved successful the borrowed silver would be replaced. Should it end in a fiasco the loss would not be due to dishonesty. And who knows, perhaps the ex-priest, now a political or military adviser, might never return to Haran.

Sanu-Rimmon was not much help in giving information about where to buy iron wares in the Hittite country. Either Dulashish did not know or else he convinced his son-in-law that it was to their best interests not to disclose such knowledge. Terach agreed to finance the venture for half the profits. They decided to go first to Carchemish, which as a caravan and trading center was equal to Haran. It was not yet the important city that it became later as capital of the subsequent Hittite Empire. Hattusas, the capital, was near the Black Sea, hence too far from Haran.

When the skipper Hankas heard about the proposed journey he offered to take Avram and Eleazer in his boat if they would pay only the wages and food of the crew. Questioning in the market place disclosed that caravans went fairly often from Carchemish to Haran; nor would it be difficult to get passage and space for freight. Again the partners took along all the woven cloth that Milcah had. On being told that commodities were always useful for barter they took from Nahor on credit all his excess grain, corn, lentils, and barley. They also brought along a stock of women's finery including the perfumes, paints, musk, and jewelry for which Babylon was famous.

## III

Hankas sailed his boat down the Belikh tributary into the Purattu, then upstream to Carchemish. The journey took several weeks. Avram spent much of the time in discussions with Hankas, who had a strong interest in religion. The skipper had made numerous attempts to turn heathens toward the belief in El Elyon. His success was moderate but by no means disappointing. He told Avram:

"It is difficult to win over a person who in early life has come under the influence of the temple with its many gods. The first thing he asks is to see the image of the new God. He simply cannot conceive of a God without face or form, who never comes down to earth to mingle with men and women. Then he wants to see the temple with the priests who preside over sacrifices and rituals, who march gorgeously attired in long ceremonial processions. Finally, he asks about the priestesses with whom he might lie."

"With which class of people have you been most successful?" inquired Avram.

"The Habiru," replied Hankas. "Some of them were mustered out of Hammurabi's army and remained in Agade. They seemed to understand me without much difficulty."

"Who are easier to convert, men or women?"

"A certain type of woman responds very well," explained Hankas. "If she is naturally modest and chaste she will be disgusted with those temple priestesses called *kedashes.* She will say these holy women as nothing but harlots. Such a convert is also attracted by the Seven Commandments of Noah."

"What about the men?"

"The most responsive are those who complain about the greed of the priests. They say that offerings to the temples are for the benefit of the priests who live off the fat of the land and are neither moral, nor good, nor holy."

"What do you do after they agree to serve the Most High?"

"I find that gathering them together in a group keeps them interested. In fact, they seem to gain strength and enthusiasm from each other. At first, I would invite them to my home. Then they objected to my paying for the food and drink. So each contributes his share of food, drink, and fruit which the women prepare and cook. They look forward to these gatherings."

"What kind of a service do you hold?"

"Well, if I am present I tell them about you and how El Elyon saved you from the burning furnace. Sometimes I speak of the Noahide commands. At other times I tell them about the garden and the great flood, and your ancestor Noah. I find that sacrificing a dove, or a goat, or a lamb on the altar provokes strong feeling."

## IV

Carchemish was in many respects another Haran. The fertility of the Purattu Valley could maintain a steady, limited economy yet not sufficient to promote prosperity for an expanding city. Growth and development could only result from bartering and trading, the commerce of an emerging economy before coined metal could become the convenient medium of exchange. Caravans meeting and crossing each other gradually established a central place for the exchange of wares. Caravansaries sprang up offering rest, comfort, and even amusement to the weary traveler. More and more wanderers, nomads, escaped slaves, and former malefactors found permanent residence in the growing metropolis that assumed an outer respectability which concealed secret duplicity.

Not that all the immigrants were disreputable or questionable. A Semitic nomad might be an austere spearman, or a repairer of metalware who still possessed the rude virtues or faults of the desert. People of all the Near East lands from Egypt to Elam, from the Caspian to the Red Sea, could be found in Carchemish. But the majority were Hittites, that people of mixed origin who gradually infiltrated as immigrants and who subsequently outnumbered the indigenous groups. Who were these Hittites? Like all the ancient peoples, their origin is unknown, lost in the *Volkerwanderungen* of the prehistoric past.

The Hittites have disappeared. As a racial, national, or religious entity they were so completely forgotten that for several millennia virtually the only reference to them could be found in the Bible. But modern archaeologists excavating in the soil of Asia Minor have unearthed the remains, the languages, the history, the laws, the art, and the culture of a powerful Hittite Empire, having its early capital in Hattusas and later in Carchemish, that rivaled Egypt and Babylonia. They differed from most ethnic or national groups in that they seemed to be free from that complex which frowned upon intermingling with or marrying into foreign stocks. Their original strain appears to have gone astray among nations. According to some anthropologists the "Hittite nose" is still visible among some Jews and Armenians.

For a week or more Avram, Eleazer, and Hankas circulated about the city observing and questioning. They gathered the impressions they thought necessary before transacting business. The owner of the caravansary was especially helpful in clearing up matters strange or vague even to Eleazer. As for iron ore it was neither mined nor smelted nor cast at or near Carchemish. But some ironware came in by caravan, and while it could be bought cheaper up north in Anatolia the expense of travel pretty much equalized the difference. Iron objects were used as media of exchange. Such staple articles as nails, hinges, knives, hatchets, daggers had a set price used in the market among merchants in the barter for food or merchandise. Later the landlord informed Eleazer, "Profits are much larger when selling to individuals. Women especially are ready buyers of things for their personal adornment. Their only drawback is lack of silver. But somehow they manage to get things for barter and exchange either from their husbands or from other men. Operating a caravansary teaches many things unknown to the average person."

"How can I know which man or woman is a prospective

purchaser?" questioned Eleazer. "I have no open shop for customers to walk in and ask for things."

"But I know," answered the owner. "I have a ready list and can send word to a number of potential buyers. I know how women love the secrecy of the attractive room I have here with wine on the table. They would buy your entire stock of cloth, jewels, or cosmetics, if they could. Of course I receive a commission on the purchases."

"But they can buy nice things in the shops," protested Eleazer. "I, myself, saw many fine articles of women's wear in the market place."

"First of all they believe they buy much cheaper from the caravans. Then they may want to keep their purchases a secret. You can imagine their reasons."

"Well, I would only take payment in gold, silver, or certain things of iron. I doubt whether we can afford the time for petty transactions even if the profits are greater," opined Eleazer.

"You'll be surprised how an accumulation of small deals adds up. But suppose you try it for one day. You can then judge for yourself."

"While on the subject," reflected Eleazer out loud, "I am wondering how I can locate merchants or wholesale buyers."

"I know them all. Why don't you appoint me your agent? I know I can be very helpful. I assure you I will earn my commission and you will be well satisfied. You probably don't know that most business is done in these caravansaries. We are equipped for it. I have a large warehouse here with many compartments. Your grain or merchandise is locked up and you alone possess the key. You can show your goods and when they bring iron you can inspect the same leisurely, then store it after you complete the deal. I even have a scribe on hand to draw contracts on clay tablets."

"Let me talk things over with my associate and I will let you know."

Eleazer felt quite relieved to find someone to help him in a strange city with matters which he could not do alone. He recalled the valuable service rendered by the merchant in Eridu. It was the sale of cloth and other items to individual buyers that saved the Nineveh trip from being a complete fiasco. He talked the matter over and Avram readily consented. Knowing how he disliked bargaining and haggling Eleazer suggested that Avram and Hankas inspect the city, visit the temples, and study their gods while the trafficking and trading went on.

## V

While standing on the Hankas boat sailing up the Purattu Avram beheld the sawtoothed walls of Carchemish, and felt a sense of disappointment. The city before him seemed squat, flat, and square having a practical unimaginative aspect. Different were the ancient cities of Sumer dominated by high-terraced ziggurats resembling pyramids flattened out on top and supporting shrines that glittered in the sunlight. Wandering about the city he felt the same disappointment about the royal palace and the temples. They somehow resembled fortresses. The architecture also displayed but slight imagination. While not expecting another Babylon yet he did want a city to look more inspiring than a walled camp. By contrast, the antique past seemed to cling to Ur like a garment, its walls browned by centuries of sunrays turned to a vermilion purple. In Eridu the majestic temple, its square columns resting on a stone-faced platform, commanded a view for miles outside the city. Entering Erech one sensed an antediluvian atmosphere and expected to meet Gilgamesh and the half-human Enkidu treading the narrow triangular lanes.

The statuary revealed an artistry in no way superior to the architecture. While by no means a connoisseur of art Avram did manage to learn from his father some elementary notions as to line, expression, grace, design, and craftsmanship. The ornaments on public buildings were in bas-relief. On a stone wall the two fully armed soldiers seemed provincial imitations of Babylonian sculpture. A large statue of some king or god seated on a square throne seemed a rectangular, upright block of stone, stiff and rigid, without expression, dignity, or form. At his feet crouched two lions displaying more life and expression than the god himself. It was in animals that the Hittites showed a degree of originality. They stood out half revealed and partly submerged in the wall.

The Hittites might have been deficient in art and architecture but in some respects were tolerant, humane, and more progressive than other empire builders. Some of their laws were milder than the code of Hammurabi which exacted an eye for an eye. They resembled the Sumerians in requiring damages as compensation for personal injuries rather than punishment for wrongs inflicted upon individuals. They also subdued weaker neighbors but at least regarded them as confederates instead of conquered subjects. They never uprooted defeated nations to transport and settle them in distant lands, as practiced by the ruthless Assyrians, who anticipated the Nazis in the theory and practice of *Schrecklichkeit.*

An imaginative quality is apparent in their literature. Hymns reveal a sense of guilt and the healing power of confession. Their treaties disclosed a sense of historic cause and effect as well as a concept of international law based on fixed principles among the great powers and toward minor states. These treaties in a literary genre contain a preamble, a citation of aims and precedents, references to past agreements, and the invocation to the gods to punish for the violation of pacts. Public proclamations are phrased in poetic prose. The judicial decrees disclose a sense of justice and a tendency toward the humane rather than insistence on the strict letter of the law.

The civilization of the Hittites impressed Avram sufficiently to converse with a learned priest in the Temple of Teshub, who was the counterpart of the storm god Enlil of the Sumerian pantheon. He inquired, "Why do you worship such a multiplicity of gods? Aren't a thousand too many to remember?"

"My son, it is not necessary to worship all the gods. Just serve as many or as few as you can or wish."

"How is it you have so many?"

"We are a tolerant people. We respect the god worshipped by any nation, even those who differ from us."

"But such a large number of gods cannot all be true. How about the false ones? What do you do about them?"

"There are no false gods, my son. If a people elects to serve a god there must be truth in him. At any rate, to them he appears strong and real. When we conquer a nation we do not destroy or degrade their gods. We permit them to continue their worship and even include such a god or goddess in our pantheon. We do not require all the people to serve all the gods. Even we, the priests, do not know them all."

"Doesn't the inclusion of foreign gods coincide with the policy of your king to make a conquered nation more content to live under his rule?"

The priest looked intently at Avram and replied after a

pause. "Religion is more than mere belief in the gods. We regard religion a way of life designed to enhance happiness and banish wretchedness. If the admission of a god into our temples will mitigate the sorrows of a defeated people, we accomplish something truly worthwhile."

"Alleviating misery," commented Avram, "is always meritorious. But what have good works to do with the acceptance or rejection of a god? Shouldn't we seek above all things a god of truth and justice?"

"Truth is a word on everyone's tongue. But how do we determine truth? Incidentally, which god do you serve?"

"El Elyon, the sole creator of heaven and earth."

"I never heard of him," declared the priest with a patronizing smile.

"But your descendants will," assured Avram. "He will be worshipped when your thousand gods will be forgotten."

## VI

While Avram and Hankas were delving into the laws, customs, and religion of the Hittites, Eleazer was matching wits with the shrewd traders coming to and going from Carchemish. The caravansary's owner turned out to be as helpful as he promised. Women bought most of the cosmetics, and to a lesser extent jewels or cloth. They paid with gold objects, silver, or iron utensils which included their husbands' daggers or swords.

Eight days were consumed in bartering and trading. Eleazer wanted iron chiefly and no one had a large stock of the hard metal. Every trader had a limited accumulation that came into the city in small quantities. The flow from Anatolia was steady but the weight too heavy for wagons to haul in sizeable loads. Eleazer therefore had to deal with a number of traders in exchanging his wares for their bars, bolts, nails, hinges, axles, rims of wheels, hatchets, battle axes, spear points, and household utensils. The entire storeroom was soon filled and more space was needed.

The problem of transportation arose. Hankas could take on only a small supply of iron lest the weight sink his boat. Wagoners refused to carry iron altogether. Either the vehicles were not strong enough or the load would be too much for the asses to pull. One wagoner agreed to hitch up two additional donkeys to each wagon but his cost was prohibitive. Finally the caravansary owner came to Eleazer's assistance. He was able to obtain three wagons with sufficient donkey power at a reasonable price. Eleazer cautioned about the hazards of robbery, especially after many of Hammurabi's soldiers had been demobilized. He thought that Hankas should take along all their gold, silver, things of value and some ironware. As for the iron transported in the caravans there would be small danger of robbery on account of their weight and bulk.

The following morning the caravans pulled out. The 15 wagons in the procession were guarded by eight armed mercenaries, usually sufficient for the comparatively short distance between Carchemish and Haran. The caravan had gone about 30 miles and was proceeding on the second day along a narrow path parallel to a low mountain range. The sun was nearing the horizon when suddenly the travelers beheld an unusual sight: six men on horses galloping toward them. Avram had never seen such "large asses" but Eleazer heard that the Hittites had been domesticating wild horses to use them in warfare. Some said that these large, powerful animals pulling chariots made of iron would be invincible in battle. The riders sat on bags of canvas containing moss of the willow tree.

At a sign from one of the horsemen the caravan halted. The director jumped out and walked over to their chief. Both spoke for several minutes and the manager blew his whistle, the signal for everyone to come over to him. Twenty men, six women, and the eight armed mercenaries assembled around the director; he explained that it was a holdup. The chieftain, the notorious outlaw Karanoshish, who had a reputation of robbing the rich and helping the poor, informed him that if no one resisted everyone would be free from harm, violence, or capture. All he wanted was their gold, silver, commodities, and merchandise. If they would act peacefully and surrender their belongings he would leave sufficient food, wagons, and asses to take them back to Carchemish.

The passengers were considering whether to surrender without a struggle. Each of the six horsemen was, to be sure, armed with a sword and dagger, besides a bow slung over his shoulder and a quiver of arrows suspended from his neck. The travelers on the caravan looked at their own eight mercenaries and were about to voice a protest when they beheld other outlaws riding donkeys coming to reinforce their leader. About half a mile away they also saw men running toward them leading large hounds. Virtually all the travelers came to the conclusion that discretion would be wiser than heroism.

The passengers together with the mercenaries were lined alongside the wagons and searched for gold, silver, precious stones, or concealed weapons. The outlaws took whatever they found. One of them, a diminutive, officious oaf was especially objectionable. He spoke roughly to a tall, strong driver and received a sullen answer denying that he had anything of value on his person. The diminutive robber drew his dagger and slashed him across the face. Another outlaw took umbrage at the remark of a passenger and sicked a vicious hound on him. The dog sunk his teeth in the man's genitals. Avram gave up several pieces of silver and the highwayman took the dates, figs, and nuts out of Eleazer's scrip. Both had some silver concealed in their clothes which escaped the rifling hand of the robber.

After all the passengers and the mercenaries were disarmed the outlaws inspected the wagons. They removed the contents from the lesser filled vehicles and packed the booty more closely in the remaining ones. Three wagons were left empty to transport the caravaneers back to Carchemish. The outlaws replaced the drivers with their own men but ordered the three who drove the iron-filled wagons to stay and continue driving for their captors. Avram and Eleazer could only wonder at this exception.

The highwaymen pulled the wagons away and were soon out of sight. The caravaneers felt nervous about remaining on the spot of their holdup and began pressing the director to return, although it was getting dark. The three wagons began trudging back slowly but yet faster than their pace in coming from Carchemish. The men walked alongside the wagons to lighten the load for the asses. Once out of danger the passengers began to criticize and find fault with the director for giving up without even the token of resistence. Walking with Avram alongside the shrunken caravan Eleazer observed quietly, "Do you know I am beginning to think there was something suspicious about this holdup. If you recall we met with difficulties in hiring wagons to carry the iron. Some didn't want to move it at any price. Then our landlord gets someone with three wagons at a very moderate price. Wasn't there possibly some understanding with the chief bandit? I wouldn't be surprised if the caravansary is also implicated."

"As far as we are concerned," declared Avram, "it makes little difference whether the robbery came as the deliberate act of the outlaw himself or planned with associates in Carchemish. To us it spells ruin. Father Terach borrowed our investment from the silver left in his keeping. The question is how will Father replace this large sum when the priest calls for it. He should soon return from Canaan."

"Oh, he will allow your father plenty of time to repay the debt. I wouldn't worry about it. After all, he does owe your father something for saving his hoard. In fact, he should even wipe off the amount that was lost as compensation for the great service your father rendered him."

"Well, I have small faith in Sabbattu. In fact, I harbor suspicions that I don't care to mention."

"But you can't deny," rejoined Eleazer, "that he was helpful at a most critical time."

"That's true. Yet when you consider it carefully everything he did somehow redounded to his benefit ultimately. But even should he cancel the debt, how will we live? Now we have two households and nothing to start with. Frankly, I am worried."

"Oh, we will get along. I feel optimistic. Perhaps the priest will advance a sufficient sum with which to make a fresh start."

"I doubt it," answered Avram dejectedly.

## VII

Anger swept over Carchemish. Merchants and traders were agitated to learn that a caravan could be robbed so close to the city. As in Haran the economy of Carchemish was largely dependent on the caravan traffic. If the route to Haran was not safe how could they remain in business? The disturbed state of the people's mind reached into the palace. The king ordered an investigation and sent out a cohort to capture the robbers. Hearings proceeded until all the participants, including drivers and the mercenaries, were heard. The king announced that he would send soldiers with each caravan of more than ten wagons.

Avram and Eleazer had to wait a fortnight to get passage on a caravan to Haran. Eleazer gave the royal scribe a complete report and obtained a tablet in cuneiform with the king's seal confirming the extent of the loss as well as the nature of the wares in transit. Before leaving Eleazer made a confidential statement of his suspicions which included the caravansary proprietor as well as the owner of the three wagons.

To Eleazer the dejection of Avram seemed a natural reaction to the robbery and its consequent effect upon earning a living in a new, unfamiliar environment. But he could hardly penetrate into the more profound agitation that perplexed Avram and that was his inability to fathom the enigmatic ways of El Elyon. If Eleazer had listened he might have comprehended the musings of Avram.

"Have I offended the Most High? Perhaps He thinks that I should forego the labor of earning a livelihood in order to devote all my energies to His service? The robbery of my future substance could have been prevented by El Elyon, who saved me from the burning furnace. Yet He refused to intervene. I wonder why? Surely He has some purpose in subjecting me to this misfortune. But He did reveal himself to me. Later He ordered me not to fear the priests in Ur. Yet He did enter into a covenant that will be binding upon my progeny forever. Does He want me to leave all business activities to Eleazer and devote myself completely to His service? The conversion of Hankas demonstrates that the heathen could be brought to worship El Elyon. Yet the duty of begetting offspring and rearing them in the faith of the Most High God clearly devolves upon me. Which course shall I pursue?"

On the return journey Avram had plenty of leisure time in which to continue his cogitations. Was the Most High disappointed in him? Is it possible that El Shaddai has regretted his choice?

"But why be so certain I have been selected? I may have been called but not chosen. Can it be that He has rejected me for someone more fit to carry His message to all mankind? And yet El Elyon did enter into the covenant with me." Then came before him the scene of the fiery furnace passing through the divided animals. "Avram! Avram! This is my covenant with you. My spirit is now upon you. My words shall not depart out of your mouth, nor out of the mouths of your children, nor out of the mouths of your children's children, from henceforth and forever."

"No, it can't be that God is subject to the change of moods. God is not a man that He should break his promise. No doubt He has a purpose in afflicting me. After all I have received only benefits from Him. Is He satisfied that I am able to stand adversity without questioning or denying Him? Have I ever been tried and tested?"

The word *tested* struck him suddenly with the force of a thunderclap. Wasn't the Most High God putting him now to the test? What has really happened? He was robbed of his substance only. His life and his freedom have remained unimpaired. He then recalled Eleazer's words: "This bandit has acted with surprising forbearance. He could easily have taken everything and killed us to eliminate the evidence against him. Or he could have taken us captive and sold us all into slavery for a sum far more than he could realize for the wares and merchandise in his possession. Is it possible that your God has again performed a miracle? In saving you, He has saved all of us."

The mist enveloping his spirit evaporated gradually. How foolish to expect the Most High God to act the part of a fond mother to her only child. The God of his forefathers did come to his aid in times of great peril when his life was in jeopardy. Did he want Him to be like a nursemaid guarding against every mishap that might befall her charge? Adversity comes to every person so why should he be excepted? He must never again question the actions of El Elyon. Whatever He does is just. The robbery was a test of his fitness to be the messenger of His God to the nations. Again Avram faced the future with serenity. He has been chosen for the greatest task ever imposed upon a human being. He must never waver nor show weakness.

# 18

# Sabbattu's Duplicity

THE FAMILY WAS DEPRESSED BY THE ROBBERY. AS IF anticipating difficulties ahead, Davarah had already begun her weaving and waited for Eleazer to come and help in disposing of her finished product. The only person who showed equanimity, surprisingly enough, was Terach. He dismissed the loss sustained as incidental to the hazardous operation of caravans. Then Hankas came with the cargo intact. Eleazer advised against selling the iron in bulk to dealers. Instead he hired a stall in the market place and with the help of Terach's slaves disposed of the ironware at good profits. Then he took in Davarah's and Milcah's woven cloth and sold them much slower and at far smaller profits. When Terach saw how readily the iron sold he favored forming a caravan and taking on passengers and freight. He recalled how well Eleazer managed the journey from Eridu to Agade. In fact Terach became insistent for quick action when his enthusiasm was hastily curbed. News came of Sabbattu's return.

One morning Sabbattu came to Terach's home again accompanied by a cordon of soldiers. In contrast to his former arrival the ex-priest bore a triumphant air and carried himself with an arrogance that was objectionable. Brusquely he demanded his parcels and called in soldiers to move them out of the underground vault. Each soldier carried a package and went away leaving the remainder of the cordon stationed in front of Terach's house. He sat down with the air of a monarch who commanded everything he surveyed, sipped wine and chewed the burnt almonds that Emtelai brought in.

"Terach," he commenced proudly, "you see not only a high priest but a conqueror. I expect to receive a high post in Hammurabi's empire."

"I am eager to hear about your exploits, Adoni," ventured Terach, but more interested as to what he would say about the robbery near Carchemish.

"Well we left Haran, stopped at all the cities in our path, and were received everywhere respectfully and dismissed honorably. The kings listened to my suggestion about joining Hammurabi's empire as allies and promised careful consideration. Then we entered Canaan and proceeded south along the Jordan River. We stopped at a mountain city called Urusalem. The king seemed especially receptive and expressed anxiety over Egypt's intention to invade Canaan. Incidentally, we passed Salem on Mount Moriah, a small place, and the politician priest, Melchizedek, came out with his retinue, offered us bread and wine and blessed us. I believe your son has a high regard for him since he also worships El Elyon.

"We passed through the strongly fortified city of Jericho. The king and the people welcomed us joyfully. We expected a similar reception as we went down into a low plain which contains five cities. It was midday and everyone rested. The troops laid aside their arms and relaxed in the excessive heat. Suddenly without any warning we were attacked on all sides. Fortunately our troops are hardened and well trained in warfare. Immediately our men formed a phalanx. Our scouts quickly handed the regulars their swords, spears, shields, and helmets. They were soon armed and had little difficulty in warding off the attack. Our opponents were poor soldiers and gave way rather quickly then fled. The few captives informed us that five cities—Sodom, Gomorrah, Admah, Zeboiim, and Zoar—had formed a league to destroy us.

"We held a war council and decided to attack the five cities or lose prestige throughout Canaan. Our captives, all from Sodom, the largest of the five cities, were terror stricken and expected to be tortured or executed. I informed them how they could save their lives and their city from destruction if they carried out my instructions. I told them to go back to their city and say they escaped from us. We would then appear before Sodom, demand surrender and start the siege. After midnight they should wave a white banner, overcome the guard, and open the gates. They carried out my orders. We entered the city and met with little or no resistance. When the other four cities saw Sodom taken, they quickly capitulated. These places are now subject nominally to each of the four kings commanding our little army. Actually, they are under Hammurabi's control. So through my advice and guidance Babylon has added a piece of Canaan to her empire. It will take no time before the whole territory, including Philistia and Phoenicia, will be ours."

"Adoni, to conquer without the loss of a soldier is an act of true statesmanship," flattered Terach, as he began to wonder what the priest intended to do regarding the spent silver. He felt uneasy the moment he detected the change in his manner.

"I shall soon know the gratitude of kings. By the way, Terach, how is my daughter? Has she given birth yet? Is it a boy or a girl?"

"It is a sturdy, bouncing boy. And she is more beautiful than ever."

"Is Keturah the wife of Avram? I think I know his prejudice toward a temple priestess."

"No, my lord. But they are very happy with each other."

"My daughter should not be a concubine. It is not fitting and I don't like it." He seemed absorbed for a while then said as if he had overlooked something, "By the way, you are still holding one of my parcels. Why didn't you return it with the rest?"

"Because I am unable to raise the silver," Terach replied and related the fate of that parcel from first opening it at Eridu until the robbery near Carchemish. "But I expect to repay you though not immediately."

"How can you repay me if you lost everything?"

"If you will advance me enough to make a fresh start, I am sure we will make enough to repay both the old debt and the new one."

"How will you earn so large a sum? You owe me now more than 1000 shekels in silver. This is a large sum for me to lose. How can I risk lending you more?"

"Eleazer sees great possibilities in importing ironware from the Hittites and selling the utensils in Haran. He assures me that we can't miss, judging from the profits he earned from the limited supply brought in by our boat."

"Terach, I have a proposition that will solve your problems. Here is a chance to get out of debt and build up a tidy competence besides. You know I am getting older and feel quite solitary living in the great city of Babylon where I am a stranger. The only person I have in all the world is my daughter. I want her with me. If your son will release her, I will cancel the debt and advance you several hundred shekels in silver with which to make a new beginning."

"But Avram and Keturah love each other. How can I propose it to them?"

"Terach, you are not a realist. Don't you understand that you are bankrupt? I can get a judgment against you for 1000 shekels and send you to the debtors' prison. Besides, I have a criminal charge for the conversion of my silver to your own use. Soon your entire family will have neither shelter nor food. You say Avram and Keturah love each other. Can they live on love? Should I look on idly and see my daughter a concubine to a beggar and a religious fanatic as well? In Babylon I can marry her to a man of substance and standing, perhaps to a member of the nobility. Your son will have no difficulty in getting other concubines if he has the wherewithal to feed them. Now if you have an ounce of sense left, you can only accept my proposition. You have no other alternative."

"I shall speak to my son," said Terach deeply depressed.

"Do so. I would like to greet my own daughter. I shall be free the day after tomorrow. Send her with Davarah to the Temple of Szin, the name here of our great Nannar. Let her ask for me. I am staying there. Do not fail."

## II

Terach called Avram, Emtelai, Davarah, and Eleazer to a family council and repeated the talk with Sabbattu. Avram sat silently thinking that the Most High was putting him to another test, perhaps more severe than the robbery. The women obtained slight relief in castigating Sabbattu as an even greater scoundrel than hitherto realized. Davarah said, "How can he put on such a virtuous air? All of us know that he is not the father of Zirru. Oh, I can't stand the new name but she insists on being called Keturah. I suppose it reminds her of the power and prestige she enjoyed in the temple."

"That beast wants this beautiful girl for himself," added Emtelai. "He has no intention of marrying her to anyone. He sees the opportunity to put the squeeze on us. But I admit that we are in desperate circumstances. What do you say, Eleazer?

"I admit your situation is bad but not hopeless," answered Eleazer addressing Terach. "I can't help believing that if the priest thought he could recover his silver he would not make this offer at all. He threatened you with a judgment but in a court of law you have a counter-claim. The judges must take into consideration the risks and difficulties we all endured in saving his entire hoard. You are certainly entitled to some compensation for rendering so great a service. My guess is that he won't sue at all."

"But, Eleazer, what about the criminal charge of converting his property to my personal use?" questioned the dejected Terach.

"This is merely a threat to frighten you, Father Terach," responded the Damascene. "In the first place, you had his permission to use the silver should the need arise. Without opening the parcel you could never have left Eridu and have saved his entire hoard from capture or confiscation by the soldiers of Babylon. I wouldn't be frightened by his threats if I were you."

"But you don't understand," continued Terach somewhat heartened. "The judges are mostly priests and they will believe him and not listen to me."

"There is truth in what you say," admitted Eleazer. "But could he risk having the entire story come to light?

Obvious questions will arise. Why was it necessary for him to remove his wealth surreptitiously? This was prior to the coming of Hammurabi to take Ur. I would venture a guess that the priests, at least those in the Temple of Szin, know about his betrayal and his secret opening of the wall gates at night. Sabbattu wants people to forget rather than remember all of this. There is a popular saying in my birthplace, Damashek: 'Do not stir sleeping dogs; they bite.' "

"Then there is nothing to worry about. We can even ignore Sabbattu," remarked Terach feeling a load lifted off his heart.

"There is still the need of obtaining silver or merchandise for trading," suggested Eleazer. "There is no sense in quarreling with him. You may still persuade him to grant you a loan. You might remind him of his obligation to you. I take it you know things he would not want to become public knowledge."

"Why so silent, Avram?" questioned Emtelai. "Have you nothing to say?"

"As far as I am concerned, Mother, I would ignore Sabbattu and his demands," responded Avram as if his trend of thought had suddenly snapped. "Personally, I would sooner see him make a quick journey to Aralu before I ever hand over my Keturah. I am not afraid that we will all starve unless we get help from the former priest. I rely upon my God. I know He will come to our assistance. But ought we decide anything without consulting Keturah? We should know her wishes in this matter. After all she is the one most vitally concerned."

That morning Avram brought little Sarai a string of pearls which he had purchased in Carchemish at a place cynically called *The Thieves' Market*. He happened to wander into that spot without knowing its name or reputation. A boy approached and offered to sell him the pearls. Avram showed no interest. Then the boy lowered the price until it looked like a give-away. Avram had no idea of its value and considered it a cheap trinket until afterwards Eleazer told him it was costly and no doubt stolen. Avram thought his little half-sister might be pleased with the gift. Sarai was so thrilled that she climbed on his lap, put her arms about his neck, kissed him and said, "We were worried when you sailed for Carchemish. Keturah was so worried that she went every few days to the Temple of Szin to offer a sacrifice and get the priest to pray for you." Avram asked, "When did Keturah begin this temple going?" Sarai answered, "I don't know. But she did go with Mother and Davarah before she had the child. She was so afraid that she sacrificed a dove and gave an offering to chase away the demons from her bedside." "How do you know this?" he asked. "Did you go along?" "No, but mother and Davarah said so."

Avram wondered whether any man really knew what went on in the mind of the wife of his bosom. Should he decide, refuse, or give his consent, Keturah might be hurt and perhaps become too embittered to forgive him. Who knows, perhaps she might be attracted by the lure of the greatest city in the world. She might want to live in wealth and luxury in Babylon. She should, by all means, be consulted first.

"Then why not tell her?" questioned Terach.

"I think it best for Davarah to talk to Keturah about the whole matter with all its implications," suggested Avram. "There are some things a woman, especially a mother, could handle far better than a husband."

"It seems to me that she should know your attitude about the whole thing. She might think by your silence that you want her to leave. A woman needs constant reassurance. She might be influenced by Sabbattu's glowing promises," cautioned Emtelai."

"I think Avram is right," said Davarah. "You can leave it to me. I am to take her to Sabbattu anyhow. It would be best for Zirru to tell him her own feelings in this matter. Who knows, she might persuade him to advance us some silver. I think she can influence him better than any of us."

Everyone agreed to let the decision rest with Keturah, who alone should tell her intentions to the former priest. When the family council seemed over, Eleazer declared, "Ever since Hankas brought the news that the house in Ur had neither been seized nor confiscated I have been thinking that Father Terach should go down by boat and try to dispose of his property. The legal title remains in him and he alone can sell it."

"I have been thinking likewise," agreed Terach. "Now I am forced to sell it. I will go down to Ur if you go along with me, Eleazer. Avram can't show his face in Ur without getting into trouble. The court might carry out its sentence if he is caught. But as far as I am concerned I don't expect any difficulty. The excitement has by this time died down."

"I am willing to sail down the river with you, master."

## III

That night while Keturah lay curled in Avram's arms she told him of the long talk with Mother Davarah and what had transpired at the family council that day. She then asked, "Why couldn't you tell me all this yourself, dear?"

"Because, my Keturah, I did not want to influence your decision."

"Why is it that men understand so little about women?

A girl does not want to make such a decision all by herself. She wants the man to take her in his arms and threaten to break every bone in her body should she ever think of leaving him."

"But would that be fair to you, my sweetheart? I believe you know that our entire family, except Nahor of course, is broke, completely. We don't know whether we can ever get a new start. Here comes a powerful person, rich, influential and on the way to becoming one of the most important men in the empire of Babylon. He considers you his daughter and offers to give you every luxury besides a high place in the society of the world's greatest city. He talks of marrying you into the nobility. This is a great temptation, I assume. On the other hand, with me you may suffer bitter poverty for the rest of your life. Is it just or fair to force you to give up such a wonderful opportunity?"

"Oh you foolish boy. Don't you know I love you? You are the father of my child. Do you think I would give you up to become even the favorite wife and queen of Hammurabi himself?"

"It's wonderful to hear you say this."

"And don't think I won't say these very words to that priest right to his face when I go to see him.

"I wouldn't get him angry if I were you. Try to be diplomatic. He can be helpful to all of us if he is so inclined."

## IV

When Davarah and Keturah came to the Temple of Szin they were told to wait in the foyer into which a number of priestly chambers opened. After ten minutes a door opened and Sabbattu dismissed a visitor, evidently a royal councilor, with marked courtesy. He invited both women in but Davarah excused herself stating that she had business to attend to in the market place and would return in not less than an hour. As soon as he closed the door he folded Keturah in his arms and kissed her a number of times with such passionate gusto that she protested.

"These are not fatherly kisses. They are much too passionate. Please let go. Don't forget that I am a wife and a mother."

"Ah, how beautiful you are. You never looked as well in your life. I can't keep my eyes nor my hands off you."

"Please restrain yourself. I came because you sent for me. Please remember you are no longer my lover. So don't take such privileges. I shouldn't have let Mother go."

"Why so coy? I held you in my arms before. I came for you and you are going with me."

"Who says so? You are mistaken, sir priest. I stay here with my husband and my child."

"You are not a wife. I shall take care of your child and give him the education and training that he can't get anywhere."

"If I am not a wife, it is because you made me a *kedashe*. Avram is too decent a man to marry a harlot."

"Don't be a country girl. I thought Zur-na-na had made you into a woman of the world."

"She tried to make a *tribade* out of me. When I repulsed her she decided to die with Queen Shub-Ad. Among the temple women there were whispers that you had some hand in the queen's death. Did you?"

"Now don't stoop to muck raking. I made you the bride of Nannar and I will make you one of the great ladies of Babylon. You will attend the king's great banquets and sit with royalty. You belong to me body and soul."

"You know, Sabbattu, you might be a clever priest but

not smart enough to cover your dishonesty. Do you think I put any faith in your promises? You told me the god Nannar wanted me. It turned out you were the god Nannar. You pretend to have gaudy plans for me. All you want is to sleep with me. You say I am beautiful? But beauty fades rapidly in women. And there are plenty of beautiful girls in Babylon who are purchasable for prices you can well afford. After several years in Babylon you will place your daughter in a temple, this time as a common *kedashe.* Or I may even be compelled to become a street prostitute. No, thank you. I love Avram and prefer to remain his concubine and bear his children."

"But how will you live? The family will soon be in dire need."

"If necessary, I will join Mother Davarah in her weaving business. But I won't worry while Eleazer is around. He has great business ability everyone says."

"Eleazer will no doubt leave. What else can he do? Starve with the rest of the family?"

"He will never leave us. Your trouble is that you can't appreciate the value of honorable, high-minded people. You entrusted your whole fortune to Terach. Did you get it back? How many people would have returned it? I know what we went through in the journey from Eridu to Haran. This was all at your instigation in order to save your parcels which I suppose is temple property. Terach had to use up some silver to fit up the caravan. How else could he get away? Everyone said the soldiers would take everything they could lay their hands on. And after going through all these trials and dangers on the caravan and boat, he delivered your fortune safely. Now you have the gall to threaten him with a prison sentence. How can I have any faith in you? All I can say is that you should feel ashamed of yourself. All your acts show that you have no character."

"Now my little Zirru, don't get so wrought up. I never intended to use the law against Terach. It was simply a ruse, a trick to get you. They say everything is fair in love and war. You don't seem to understand how much I love you. I would do anything, even commit a crime, to get you. I suppose it is foolish to be so madly in love, but I just can't help it."

"You don't know what love is with all your wisdom. Your idea of love is to fondle a girl in bed. When you satisfy your lust you are ready to kick her out. You say you love me? Do you show any feeling for the people I love? You know how good this family has been to me. I am not related yet they treat me as one of their own. Yet you are ready to crush them all, to make life miserable for them. Love teaches sacrifice. I would do anything in the world for them. I would give my life to help them. That's love."

"Oh I intend to help them. But first, I want to make sure I possess you. This talk with Terach is what in warfare is called a feint, a sham attack to attain an objective. As soon as you consent to go with me, you will see what I shall do for them. They will never be in want for the rest of their lives."

"And if I don't go with you?"

"Oh, I'll do something for your sake but nothing like if you would."

"Will you do it now?"

"If you give me some love."

She looked at him and saw lust burning in his eyes. Now was the time to act. To deny him would antagonize him still more. She sat on his lap, put her arm about his neck and said, "Irnina knows that I don't want to give myself to you. But if I am ready to lay down my life for this family, why not make this sacrifice." She gave him one of those maddening kisses taught her in the temple, then asked, "Will you cancel the debt immediately?"

"If you take off your dress."

"Will you help them get started again?"

He pushed her off his lap and removed her clothes. He laid her down on the couch. When his sensuality was appeased he said, "My love. Let Eleazer come to see me this time tomorrow. I will arrange the details with him. He is the only man of sense in the family."

When Keturah left the room Davarah was waiting for her. The "mother" noticed Keturah's flushed face and somewhat disheveled hair.

"I think I accomplished something," Keturah remarked trying to talk casually. "He said he would strike off the debt and promised to do more besides."

"When? You know he can break his word."

"He wants to see Eleazer tomorrow and arrange the details with him."

"How did you accomplish this, my dear?"

"I paid a woman's price."

## V

Sabbattu welcomed Eleazer and served wine with fruit. He put on the friendly demeanor that he could assume when the occasion arose. Eleazer tactfully congratulated him for his splendid victory and without loss of life. King Hammurabi would certainly appreciate such statesmanship and no doubt elevate him to one of the highest posts in the empire.

"Yes, I expect an important promotion," agreed the ex-priest. "It is for that reason I sent for you. My duties will multiply to an extent that I will have little or no leisure for my personal affairs. I need a competent manager to look after my household, one who understands trade and can transact business, someone to take all burdens off my hands. I therefore want you to be my steward."

The features of Eleazer registered surprise. What were the priest's intentions? To detach him from Terach's family? How good was Sabbattu's word for anything? But it would be well to hear what he has to say.

"I am taken by surprise, Adoni, and am highly flattered. I doubt whether I can qualify. But in any event I am devoted to Terach and Avram and would not want to leave them at this time when their fortunes are rather low."

"I am also devoted to Terach and his family. I have been his patron for years. With my help he has done quite well. I had their interests in mind in choosing you. Of course, you understand, that in you I am not seeking a housekeeper. I believe you have business acumen. I expect to turn over all my silver and gold for you to operate business on a large scale. Babylon, as you know, is the world's center. We will need agents and representatives in many places. Terach and Avram will handle all our affairs in Haran, an important trade center as everyone can see."

"I would like a little time to consider your generous offer. It's only fair to consult Terach and Avram. They have been very good to me. I am really a member of the family. I look up to Terach as a father and to Emtelai as a mother. Avram is a brother to me and Keturah a sister. I know they will do nothing to impede my success in life. You do not desire my answer immediately, do you, Adoni?"

"Yes, I want to take you with me to Babylon."

"I can't go right now. I promised to accompany Terach to Ur. We are looking for a boat to carry us."

"To Ur?" This time Sabbattu registered astonishment. "Does Terach intend to go back to Ur? This is incredible after all that has happened."

"As your lordship knows, Terach has a house there with furniture, besides images in the temple stall. Davarah has also her stock of woven cloth in the temple. He wishes to dispose of his house. At this time he is badly in need of silver. If he cannot sell the furniture, images, and Davarah's cloth, he intends to ship these things by boat to Haran."

"What makes him think that his and her property have escaped pillage during a conquest? Soldiers have a way of grabbing everything that is not nailed down. His house has no doubt been confiscated for lack of an owner. Isn't he going on a fool's errand?"

"The boatman who carried us from Agade to Haran has become a great friend of Avram. In fact, he worships El Elyon with equal fervor. He has recently visited Ur and brought back the news that Terach's house is standing all barred and bolted. The new high priest Khar-Sak told him that the house has not been confiscated. The temple owns the ground but has not yet taken action. Terach feels that now is the time to sell it. He alone holds the legal title."

Sabbattu became abstracted and seemed unaware of anyone's presence. As was his habit he gesticulated his thinking as if carrying on a conversation. The news of Terach's intended journey disturbed him exceedingly. He had assumed that the image-maker would never return; that he would relinquish the house left behind. Terach's journey, he sensed, portended danger. Hunate and other enemies would no doubt elicit some damaging information. They might ask why did Terach flee with his entire family? Who instigated and later assisted the flight? Terach had little reason to conceal the action of the high priest who entrusted him with the valuables to take along. The question as to the whereabouts of the gold, silver, and jewels which belonged to the temple treasury arose while Sabbattu remained in Ur under Hammurabi's protection. He was aware at the time that suspicions pointed to him. Now Terach could confirm and even prove this accusation to the hilt. But how to prevent the idol-maker's visit? Of course a Babylonian soldier might easily dispatch him. But that would arouse more suspicions and ultimately bring the entire matter under investigation. Terach's family was now aware of everything, no doubt. There was but one thing to do. He must buy the house and pay whatever sum Terach might ask.

"Eleazer, I've been thinking about this journey to Ur. It is fraught with danger. Public opinion is strong against Terach. He is suspected of whisking Avram out of the city on the night when the great rainfall prevented the burning. But what drove the people to distraction was the disappearance of my daughter who was then the bride of Nannar. They accused Terach of abducting his granddaughter so that his son Avram could marry her. As the image-maker, they said, he could come and go as he pleased."

"The skipper Hankas," disputed Eleazer, "informed us specifically that all feeling about smashing the idols has died down. People seldom mention it."

"Feeling has no doubt subsided," rejoined Sabbattu, "but Terach's reappearance would again rekindle public passions, I fear. In any case he cannot afford to take the chance."

"We talked it over," declared Eleazer, "and decided that Terach would be disguised. It will be up to me to ascertain the possibility of danger. That is why he wants me along, I suppose."

"Listen to me, my young friend. I am truly concerned about Terach's safety. I am a real friend even if the family doubts it after my talk with him the other day. I was and still am anxious to have Keturah come with me to Babylon. It is galling for me to know that my beautiful daughter is a concubine. In my anxiety to get her released I probably drew the reins too tight. But it was only strategy that was probably unwise. I would never do Terach any harm despite some words I might have said too hastily. I want to help him and I shall. By stopping him from going to Ur I am rendering him a great service. While mulling before the thought crossed me that I have some kin in Ur and should do something for them. Then it occurred to me why not buy the old house as a home for my poor relatives. What value does Terach put on the antiquated homestead that is quite rundown?"

"I don't know what he would take for it, but I don't agree that it is dilapidated and rundown. While it is no palace it is a 14-room two-floored house in excellent condition. I think he said it should be worth about 5000 shekels in silver. It is well located on a good street and not too far from the Temple of Nannar."

"Five thousand shekels?" and the ex-priest whistled in amazement. "I don't want five houses, I just want one. I believe the old fool is becoming senile. I'll tell you what I am willing to do and I think it quite generous. I will give him 1000 shekels for the hovel. This sum is to be set off against the debt he owes me. Then I will advance 500 shekels in silver for him and Avram to start making a living."

"Your lordship, I am not authorized to make any deal for Terach. But I know he won't take that. He and the family feel that you owe him some compensation for saving your valuables and carrying them from Ur to Haran."

"This has become a family obsession," snorted Sabbattu with assumed anger. "My daughter has already made a strong plea for this so-called compensation. But they seem to forget that a large household lived more than a year at my expense. The flight from Ur saved the life of Avram who on discovery would have been executed. But it is useless to reason with people who are swayed by emotions only. I will raise my bid to 2000 shekels of which half will go for the cancellation of the debt. This is not trading, it is philanthropy."

"I can only submit your offer," reminded Eleazer whose expression did not seem too encouraging.

"You don't show much enthusiasm," asserted the priest. "I look to you for assistance. I know they will be guided by your opinion. This is not encouraging from one who will be entrusted with all my wealth."

"I didn't say I will accept your proposition, Adoni. My first loyalty goes to Terach and Avram. The entire family has been very kind to me." The former priest could see that Eleazer would not swallow his bait.

"Well, I am disposed to drop the whole thing. This is not a trade; it is charity. I can't remain here haggling indefinitely. Important matters of state are awaiting me in Babylon. Here is my final concession. I will give Terach 3000 shekels for the house, furniture, statues, and Davarah's cloth. Of course, 1000 shekels will be deducted to pay the obligation. This is the last offer and I have nothing further to say."

"I shall submit this deal and bring you the answer, my lord."

"I have no doubt about his acceptance," assured Sabbattu. "I am doing this for my daughter. I do admit that they treated her well. I suppose I am becoming a softhearted, sentimental fool. But I must get away. Bring

Terach and Davarah here tomorrow. I shall have the scribe here with stylus and clay. Let Terach bring along his evidence of ownership. The copy of the tablet filed in the Temple of Nannar would be best. Otherwise I won't get a proper description of the property. I want the high priest here to seal the contract. As for you, consider my proposition carefully. I will make of you a man of business of very high importance. Farewell."

## VI

The proposal of Sabbattu was greeted by the family with joyful transports. Emtelai went over and kissed Eleazer.

"How did you do it?" inquired Terach. "I don't think I could even get 1000 shekels for that house. It is now damp and moldly after being boarded up for more than a year in that humid climate, so unlike the dry atmosphere of this hilly city."

"I said nothing," responded Eleazer. "I let him do the talking as soon as I felt that he didn't want you to visit Ur. You know too much for his peace of mind."

"Did he give you any reason?" asked Emtelai.

"He intimated that he was generous for the sake of his daughter. He admitted that the entire family treated her very well."

"The old hypocrite!" asserted Emtelai. "What a villain!"

The next day Terach, Davarah, Eleazer, and Keturah went to the temple and met Sabbattu in his chamber. Terach's slaves took along the scale to weigh gold and silver, also the clay tablet, the original of which had been filed in the Temple of Nannar at Ur.

Sabbattu ordered the scribe to indite in cuneiform clay tablets the deed for the house from Terach; separate bills of sale from Terach and Davarah conveying their furniture, furnishings, spindles, tools, equipment, as well as all statues and images in their home or in their stalls at the Temple of Nannar; a satisfaction and cancellation by Sabbattu of all debts owed by Terach. The grantees were three kinsmen of the priest in Ur. Since it would take at least two hours to complete the tablets with the help of Terach and Davarah for detailed information Sabbattu invited Keturah to go out and inspect the interior of the Temple of Szin not open to the general public. Walking on the temple grounds he said, "I hope you are satisfied with what I did for the family. You see, I carried out my promise to you."

"Oh yes," she answered. "I think you were sweet. I shall give you a kiss when we are alone."

"Only a kiss?"

"Well, we shall see."

"My darling, you saw but a small sample of what I can do. Why don't you realize what's in store for you if you come with me to Babylon. I want you so badly."

"I believe I am pregnant again although I am not certain. Surely you don't want a big-bellied girl with you in that great city."

"I'll accept you in any way you are and take good care of you afterward. I know you will come to me sooner or later."

"Why do you think so?"

"Because one of these days Avram will take a real wife, perhaps rich, ugly, and demanding. I know you will resent walking behind her and carrying her chair to the temple, as is required of concubines. Then you will come to Babylon."

"Suppose I get to be fat and ugly?"

"I will take you in whatever shape you are, because I truly love you."

The tablets were completed and bore the seals of Terach and Davarah impressed alongside their names in cuneiform. Sabbattu signed his name with the stylus, then impressed his seal. The witnesses were the scribe, Eleazer, Sabbattu, and Keturah. The priest opened two parcels and said to Terach, "You may weigh the silver and several gold pieces on your scale. I'll take your word for it." He did not disclose that he had already weighed the metal. "Meanwhile lend me your slaves to carry the tablets to the high priest. I want his personal authentication. Come with me Keturah and I will introduce you. Perhaps you may sometime need his priestly influence."

The deal was completed with the delivery of the tablets and precious metal changing hands. Sabbattu remarked to Eleazer, "Come to Babylon within 60 days if you desire to become my steward." He then bade Terach and Davarah farewell and said, "Keturah, come have the midday meal with me. I am leaving tomorrow and don't know when I shall see you again."

# 19

# The Farm

SABBATTU'S SILVER COULD BE LIKENED TO A SPRING FOUND unexpectedly in the desert by parched nomads ready to perish for lack of water. Terach was slowly drifting toward senility. Backed by a treasure trove safely stowed away he recovered his illusion of well-being. The incident confirmed Avram's trust in the Most High, Who might subject him to trials, yet in the end would never forsake him.

Again Terach turned to Eleazer who had demonstrated that ironware from the Hittites could be sold advantageously at Haran. Eleazer learned of a large, well-armed caravan making round trips to Carchemish at regular intervals. The manager agreed to take Eleazer along with the assurance that he had the facilities to haul the iron. Avram and Eleazer went to Nahor's farm. It was high time to pay the debt to Milcah for her woven cloth and the amount due his brother for the commodities which they had taken along to Carchemish. Keturah wanted a change in her daily routine and rode along with the baby in her arms.

Nahor received the silver gladly for he had despaired of payment since learning of the robbery. But his pleasure was marred when he heard that Terach's house in Ur had been sold. As the oldest son, he and not Avram would have inherited the property. Yet, since he received payment from his brother he offered his remaining barley, corn, lentils, and grain on credit but insisted on charging the account only to his father. Milcah was pleased to turn over her entire stock for the venture but Avram could not take it all since he had already arranged to use Davarah's complete output.

At the midday meal Milcah happened to remark that about eight miles away a temple with its farm was for sale. The temple dedicated to Hebat, a goddess of Hurrian, had fallen into decay together with the decline of her worship. There were no serfs to work the land and all worship had ceased due largely to the hostility of the god Szin and the goddess Ishtar, whose priests had carried on an unremitting persecution for a number of years. The temple and farm consisted of about 30 acres 11 miles from the walls of Haran. Bounded by a tributary of the Naar Belikh the land was also on a canal, which had been purposely neglected because of the machinations of Szin's high priest. Milcah recalled the well-stocked, efficiently managed farm of 15 years earlier when she and Nahor first settled on land. It could be brought back to its former flourishing state under proper management. The diners were surprised when Avram declared that he would like to see the property.

"Why do you wish to see it?" questioned Nahor. "Don't tell me you are thinking of becoming a farmer."

"Perhaps," replied Avram.

"With all your learning? Why this is a comedown," jeered his brother. "Perhaps you wish to step into the priest's sandals since he is now in his dotage? He did not succeed because Ishtar wouldn't let his crops grow. But your newly discovered God might be a good farmer."

"Avram," intervened Milcah, not caring to see a flare-up between the brothers, "if you wish to see the farm why not go now. I shall be glad to go along. We can easily return before dark."

She called one of the Habiru shepherds who drove quite well and knew the way. He hitched two asses to the farm wagon which carried Avram, Eleazer, and Milcah. The farm, overgrown with weeds, had lain fallow a number of years. The canal badly in need of dredging was not functioning. In the center of the land stood the small temple surrounded by oak trees. Nearby a rambling hacienda contained a number of chambers formerly the residence of the priests, the *kedashes,* and several of the temple functionaries. Two smaller houses had been occupied by the workers who attended the shrine, or who took care of the farm. The entire property had a rundown, ragged and disheveled appearance. "The abomination of desolation," remarked Avram to his companions.

Two old women greeted them and stated that only they and the priest lived on the premises. The priest was too old and infirm to receive them. They had been living in the same house since young girls when they entered the service of the goddess.

"Why did the temple fall into this state?" asked Avram.

"Because of the persecution we suffered from the Temple of Szin backed by the king of Haran. As you see the canal has not been drained for years. Instead of assistance we received maltreatment."

"Why were you oppressed? I understand that Haran permits the worship of many gods."

"Sir, we had a thriving temple and drew many offerings and sacrifices from the immediate neighborhood. The high priest of Szin offered to buy the land including the temple. Our priests refused to sell. Then the harassment began."

"Of what land is your goddess?"

"Hebat is worshipped in Hurrian."

"We were told that this place is for sale. What do they ask for it?"

"I really don't know. But a priest was sent from Nuzu to dispose of the entire property. He is now in Haran and will gladly speak to you."

The former priestess gave his name and the caravansary in which he was staying. The three inspected the buildings and Eleazer thought it could be rendered habitable but the cost might be somewhat high. When they got back to Nahor's farm the sun was setting. They ate the night meal with the family and Avram together with Eleazer departed the next morning.

## II

For several days Avram mulled over the feasibility of acquiring the farm. Strange that of the entire family he alone should have such leanings. Nahor of course operated a farm but it was neither his choice nor preference. Adverse circumstances and dire necessity forced him into this vocation. The family knew that its successful management was due to Milcah, whose tact and friendliness kept the Habiru from deserting. And without these shepherds the entire operation would deteriorate and even collapse.

Avram's father decided all transactions. But Terach had the city man's contempt for the rustic. Success and accumulation were his guiding principles. The approval and respect of his fellow men above a certain stratum counted most. He would have preferred being a merchant but a superficial facility in fashioning idols together with early training forced him into the craft. He had neither the urge nor the creativity of a sculptor. He might be called a competent technician who could execute without the inspiration or passion of an artist. A strong acquisitive instinct led to the traffic rather than to the creation of statuettes. Feeling no joy in creativity his interest centered in quantity rather than quality. The large distribution in the temple stall encouraged him to acquire the output of unsuccessful competitors. Unhampered in selling he might have become rich but his patron, really a partner, drained off the profits beyond the amount essential for the support of his household.

Terach could only look askance at the notion of his gifted son going into farming, a calling looked down upon by the middle and upper classes, except for the nobility who operated their large estates through overseers or foremen. But planting was no occupation for Avram, who, according to Sabbattu, had the learning to become a priest and ultimately even a high priest. Yet farming might deter him from meddling with the gods, an avocation that had led him to the burning furnace. But arguing with his headstrong son would be useless; it might even strengthen the absurd intention that might, if left alone, weaken and even evaporate. Then together with Eleazer his son could operate a caravan and develop into a merchant prince. But let the negotiations commence. The price and terms might be a deterrent. He therefore suggested that Avram take Eleazer along and see what the priest had to offer.

The priest interrogated Avram closely. Did he represent anyone? Was he the agent of any temple? What was his object in buying the property? Who were his associates? Which god did he serve? After admitting that he had never heard of El Elyon the priest offered to sell the 30 acres with everything thereon for 5000 shekels in silver.

Eleazer showed no interest and he reduced the sum to 4000. When Eleazer shook his head negatively the priest wanted to hear his offer. The answer was 1000. "This is absurd," remarked the priest in apparent disgust, yet he did not break off negotiations. Such was the manner of trading in the Orient from time immemorial. After bargaining back and forth the amount settled to 2000. Eleazer felt that the rockbottom figure had been reached.

Then began a new tug of war. The seller wanted all cash. The buyer pointed out, as if the priest did not know, the rundown condition of the property and the large sum necessary to render it fit for occupation and planting. The seller relented to half cash, the balance within a year. Eleazer answered that this was the equivalent to all cash for a year which would run by before the repairs and the clearing could be completed. The terms were then reduced to one-forth cash and the balance in three annual payments. After much haggling Eleazer offered on a take-it-or-leave-it basis 100 shekels in cash, the balance in 19 annual installments.

Another argument arose as to interest on the mortgage. In view of the greatly reduced price the priest held that the interest should be one-sixth, which in modern terms would be equivalent to 10 per cent. It must be remembered that to the Sumerians 60 represented what 100 is today. For that reason they divided the hour into 60 minutes and the minutes into 60 seconds, the modern heritage from ancient Sumer. This rate was too high for Eleazer, who argued that the cost of repairs and clearing should offset the interest charge. After much debate the parties agreed on 1/20th, which in our reckoning would be about 4 per cent interest. Eleazer then asked, "What about the old priest and the two women? Are you taking them along with you?"

"No," replied the priest. "They lived here all their lives. They must remain. They have no place to go."

"Who will take care of them?" questioned Eleazer.

"They look after themselves and each other."

"But they are getting quite old," pointed out Eleazer quite obviously. "The priest is now helpless and without the women he couldn't live another day. In the near future the women will also become helpless. Wouldn't it be best for you to take them along to Nuzu so they could spend their last days among their own?"

"I have no authority to move them," replied the priest. "They must die where they live. Here they can serve their goddess to the very end."

"Let them remain," whispered Avram in Sumerian so that the priest could not understand. "I won't turn anyone out of his home." But the practical Eleazer saw the opportunity to benefit by this situation and addressed the priest:

"After you go back to Nuzu, you will have no further contact with them. The responsibility of feeding and looking after them will fall on us and we won't let them starve. But this responsibility is truly yours. I would therefore propose that the interest on the mortgage be abated during their lifetime. When the last of the three dies then the interest payments will commence."

After more argumentation the priest finally consented to Eleazer's proposal. Both parties agreed to meet the next day, provided Avram's father consented to the deal, for without him they could not act.

## III

When Avram reached home Milcah was waiting to tell him that the Habiru on her farm were in a state of excitement. The driver had told them that Avram intended to purchase the temple farm. The entire group was ready to quit Nahor and go to work for him. Milcah came with the same driver and wanted Avram to inform him that if he bought the farm he could only employ those whom Nahor would release. Actually only the men wanted the change. The women were content to remain with Milcah for whom they had a high regard. Her farm was their home; their children were born there; she settled their quarrels and adjusted the problems that often arose between man and wife.

The incident somehow cheered Avram and even helped to decide the perplexing matter of buying the farm. It was no easy decision to undertake a project about which he knew nothing. He had gotten accustomed to lean on Eleazer in all practical matters. But Terach made it clear that he wanted Eleazer either to operate a caravan or make trips to and from Carchemish to obtain ironware and sell it in Haran. Nor did Eleazer display a keen desire to operate a farm or supervise shepherds. But the readiness of the Habiru to render him faithful service soothed Avram's anxiety.

The obvious reason for acquiring the farm was to earn a living. Of course, engaging in the caravan trade would no doubt be more profitable. But the real cause of hankering for a farm lay deeper than Avram's dislike for bargaining and haggling. The unexpected sale of the house at Ur for a price byond its normal worth seemed nothing less than a miracle. Personally he could assign no valid reason for the priest's action. Eleazer's explanation of Sabbattu's concern for the opinion of the people in Ur did not convince him. Under Hammurabi's protection what did the former priest care about the people's opinion, especially after the bloodless victory in Canaan? Too many knew that he opened the city gates to admit the enemy. What could be worse? Stealing the temple silver was not comparable in the degree of infamy to high treason. His reputation could really sink no lower.

For this vile person to act with surprising generosity to a family sunk in the mire of despondency seemed nothing short of the miraculous. Did Sabbattu do this of his own accord? Or was he carrying out the behest of a supernatural power? The faith that had begun to crystallize in Avram during the past year had settled deeply into a conscious conviction. Subconsciously he began to believe that his actions were directed by the Most High. Recent happenings apparently unconnected seemed to form into a set pattern that determined his future conduct. Were the series of consecutive events—the purchase of Terach's house by Sabbattu, the chance visit to Nahor's farm, the coming of the priest from Nuzu, the liberal terms unprecedented in Haran—simply coincidental? Avram preferred to see the divine hand guiding his destiny. Clearly it was the wish of the Almighty that he acquire the farm. The future would disclose the purpose of El Shaddai.

Terach displayed a mounting enthusiasm at the thought of owning a caravan. He would furnish the silver and Avram together with Eleazer could operate the enterprise. He could therefore hardly contain his disappointment on hearing of Avram's determination to buy the farm. His feelings were somewhat mollified when Eleazer disclosed the easy terms and more important still that it was a good buy, in fact a real bargain. He almost recovered his lost enthusiasm on learning that in Eleazer's opinion there would be a considerable profit in a resale after the land was cleared and the buildings repaired. Perhaps Avram might make a business man after all, something he had never expected. So when the son came requesting a loan the father, to everyone's surprise, did not demur. He actually exhibited a cheerful countenance.

Thus the deal was consummated and the farm changed

hands. Avram bought a wagon with two donkeys and brought Sanu-Rimmon to give an estimate as to the cost of rehabilitating the buildings. A neighboring farmer suggested burning the weeds and thistles as the easiest way of clearing the overgrowth. Ordinarily such a fire might be hazardous to the neighbors but the river and the canal bordering two sides of the farm reduced the danger of the flames spreading. Yet the burning should be done in sections to prevent a general conflagration. The Habiru driver brought over four herdsmen who were especially eager to leave Nahor and work for Avram. They pointed out that the grass between the weeds could nourish their flocks for weeks, especially since the goats and sheep would drink the river water.

The next important step was to dredge the canal and repair the bank. Remembering that Sabbattu had introduced Keturah to Zaradan, the high priest of Szin, Terach and Avram proceeded to the temple and took Keturah along. They gained ready admittance when the *kadosh* reported to his chief that the daughter of Sabbattu was with the two men who wanted an audience. Admiration was written on the countenance of the priest when he greeted her.

"Why did you come to me?" asked Zaradan. "I have no jurisdiction over canals. That is the responsibility of the king's supervisor of rivers and canals."

Terach explained that they were strangers from Ur and knew no one to direct them. He had been the image-maker for the Temple of Nannar and a fervent follower of the moon god. He brought an offering of ten shekels to the Temple of Szin, whose suppliant and worshipper he would ever be. He had just purchased a farm which was necessary for the support of his household. He would follow his craft of image-making if he, a stranger, could market his statuettes in Haran.

"Where is this farm you purchased?"

Terach looked at Avram who answered, "It is called the Temple of Hebat, a goddess of Hurrian, situated about 11 miles from the city gate."

"Are there any worshippers left in this so-called temple?"

"None, your lordship," answered Avram, "except the old priest in his dotage and two old women, former priestesses who look after him."

"A fitting end for those infidels who serve false gods," gloated Zaradan, whose smug expression, in sharp contrast with his covetous eyes, registered the satisfaction of triumph over a crushed adversary. "I warned them not to lure away our worshippers and even offered to buy the ground that contains their temple. But they refused and with such insolence as if they were native born Amorites." He struck the bronze gong and the *kadosh* appeared. "Is there anyone waiting?"

"The Hittite priest, Adoni."

"Take these two men to Kinabu, the supervisor of rivers and canals. Here take my seal with you. Tell him I would appreciate anything he can do for them." Turning to Keturah he went on, "Would you mind waiting in the anteroom until I get rid of this caller? I want to talk about your father for whom I have a high admiration."

The conference with the Hittite was one of many discussions about setting up a temple to Szin at Carchemish. After half an hour Zaradan dismissed the priest and invited Keturah back into his chambers.

"I wonder whether you appreciate the fact that your father is a great man. He will soon be very important in Babylon. He is anxious for our king to become a friend and ally of King Hammurabi. I favor the idea. It is for his daughter that I am helping the men who came with you."

"I thank you, my lord."

"Oh I would do this and much more even if you were

not Sabbattu's child. You are very beautiful. I could refuse you nothing." He filled two goblets with wine and offered her some salted fish, a delicacy for which Haran was noted. "Are you married to the young man?" Keturah moved a fold in her dress and revealed the olive-shaped jade denoting her marital status.

"Daughter of a high priest and the concubine of a farmer?"

"I was the bride of Nannar and fled with my husband's family prior to Hammurabi's taking of Ur. Father consented. He thought the Babylonians might destroy or pillage Ur. When soldiers capture a city they have as little respect for a priestess as for a slave girl. I could not become a legal wife so I took the next best."

"My dear, I could do a great deal for your husband. He could hold an important post under our king. Your father-in-law might even become the sculptor for my temple. It is really up to you."

"My lord, I am the mother of a boy and expect another child by the end of this year. I love my husband and am satisfied to remain the concubine of a farmer. I thank you for your interest all the same."

Terach and Avram returned. Their quest was successful. The supervisor promised to dredge and repair the canal. Terach left the ten shekels of silver with Zaradan and thanked him for his assistance.

## IV

It took months to rehabilitate the farm. Water was the first problem. The old priestesses drew their water from one well which functioned rather poorly. The other two wells had to be re-dug and cleaned out to allow the underground springs to flow freely. The workmen of Sanu-Rimmon began with the roofs which had to be patched and covered with pitch to prevent the rain from flooding the rooms. But the rain had to be conserved by building wooden gutters under the eaves to catch and empty the water into terra cotta down-spouts leading to cisterns, which also had to be cleaned and partly stored with lime to absorb impurities. The animals did not relish the river water which was muddy. Wooden troughs near the river had to be filled with water to allow the mud to settle and sink to the bottom. The large pond was cleared of sand and debris to enable the cattle and the herds of sheep and goats to drink the water accumulated from the clouds or drawn from the canal through terra cotta pipes.

Nahor's shepherds brought their flocks to nibble the grass between the weeds and thistles. The herdsmen had nothing else to do except watch and keep the goats and sheep from straying. Avram therefore hired them as day laborers to burn the weeds and young tree trunks as soon as the flocks nibbled away the foliage. The shepherds watched the weather and when feeling little or no wind they set fire to half an acre at a time and took care to prevent it from spreading. As more shepherds or day laborers appeared they began to clear away the stubble for the soil to be broken with the plow. The progress was slow but steady.

No architectural changes were attempted yet the alterations made the houses more habitable. Paint and whitewash helped greatly to cheer and brighten the inner and outer aspects of the dwellings. The little temple with the square posterior containing two chambers and the round anterior snuggled among oak trees which cast a comforting shade during the midday heat. The front semi-circular atrium contained a stone altar in the center; a number of idols leaning against the rounded wall were overshadowed and rendered somewhat insignificant by the large alabaster statue of the goddess, Hebat, standing in the back center. The roof was partly open to emit the smoke of burning sacrifices. The wide front entrance without a door seemed to invite everyone passing by.

For days Avram pondered what to do with this fane of idols. He had no use for the structure yet it seemed a pity to destroy it. The little brick building nestling among the majestic oaks did have a certain charm. Then came an inspiration that made his heart pound wildly. Why not convert it into a shrine to the Most High, a sanctuary dedicated to the worship of El Elyon?

He mulled over the proper changes necessary to make it a fit place for worshiping his God. The idols must be evicted. The most fitting spot for an altar was in the open, under the heavens. The present altar should be enlarged and placed on a pedestal of rock. The semi-circular stateroom which could easily accommodate 50 people might become an assembly hall, useful on occasions to feast a group of loyal worshippers. The interior should be painted white and several large chairs for visiting guests might face the wide opening which could be closed with a double door. For such purposes the roof ought to be extended and made rainproof. But the sudden entrance without vestibule or portico somehow lacked dignity. A more elevating façade must do honor to the Almighty God. The introduction to the sanctuary should be heralded by two square columns holding up a rectangular pediment supporting a stele in large cuneiform script: EL ELYON, SOLE CREATOR OF HEAVEN AND EARTH.

Most of the Habiru were from Nahor's farm but some came who had seen service in Hammurabi's army. All of Nahor's workers would have left him but Avram accepted only those whom his brother had released. They became strongly attached to him and worked diligently to rehabilitate the farm. Avram endeared himself by acting naturally and treating them as human beings. He would sit with them and eat what they ate. After each meal they joined him in thanking and blessing El Elyon for the food.

As soon as water became plentiful and several rooms were completed the Habiru brought their wives and children from Nahor's farm. All workers could now eat hot food cooked by the women and a liveliness permeated the group. Yet they were not comfortable in houses of brick and complained of feeling closed in by the solid walls. Avram took several in his wagon and visited the market place. They selected old tents of heavy tarpaulin cloth or some made of goat skins. With poles and rope they strung up their tents near the river and could thus breathe fresh air and bathe every day. More nomads applied than Avram could use since the restoration would soon be completed. But the newcomers stayed on and were fed with the rest. The Habiru came to regard Avram as their chieftain and called him their sheikh.

The effects of rehabilitation were becoming more visible every day. The neighboring farmers had come to regard the temple farm as a kind of wasteland rapidly degenerating into a swamp especially when flooded by the canal water after heavy rainfall. They were amazed at the renovation effected by a young city man without knowledge of agriculture. They asked each other why they did not think of buying the farm in its dilapidated state. One day the adjoining neighbor came to inspect and offered to buy it. Avram showed surprise and asked what would he pay for the reconditioned property.

"Three thousand shekels," answered the farmer without hesitation.

"That is about what it will stand me with all improvements completed. The mortgage to the priests runs to 1900 shekels."

"How is that payable?"

"One hundred shekels each year."

"Then I will pay you 2000 shekels and assume the mortgage."

"Tell me why do you want so much land? You have a large farm now."

"I will use ten acres, sell ten to a farmer I know, and hold the rest."

"What would you do with all the houses?"

"A religious group would take them over."

"What god do they serve, may I ask?"

"I don't know the god. They are Hittites and you know how they are spreading in every direction."

"Well, let me think it over," declared Avram who had no intention of selling. Yet the offer was encouraging especially when Avram had to see his father, who put on a wry face whenever his son came to borrow silver. He needed about 500 shekels more to pay all debts and have sufficient capital to start planting, buying cattle, goats, sheep and keep going until the first crop would be gathered. He now planned to drive to town the next morning and see his father.

While supervising the conversion of the pagan sanctuary into a shrine for the Most High he wondered what to do with the idols stacked outside along the wall. The two old women had no space for them and accepted only the statue of Hebat for which they found a place in the old priest's chamber. The smashing of idols had proved a dangerous affair which Avram had little desire to repeat. Could they be sold? Then came the idea of presenting them to his father, who, finding time heavy on his hands, had begun to make images. These idols could be displayed among Terach's statuettes.

The next day Avran accompanied by two Habiru brought the idols to his father. He was surprised and delighted to see Eleazer who had just returned with the caravan from Carchemish. The journey was a success. Eleazer brought back a good load of ironware which he intended to sell in the stall at the market place. He related a surprising and welcome bit of news. The king's troops had tracked down the outlaws with the information extracted from their confederates, among whom was the caravansary's proprietor and the owner of the three wagons. They together with the outlaws were tried and convicted. Some were executed and others, less guilty, imprisoned. The soldiers had recovered less than half of the iron that had been robbed from Avram on the former journey. Terach was jubilant.

Eleazer was curious to hear about the farm. Avram went into detail about clearing the land; rehabilitating by Sanu-Rimmon; the repair and clearing the canal; cleaning of the wells, the pond and the pool; transforming the temple into a shrine to the Most High; tents for the Habiru; installing roads out of broken rock to reach the wells, the pond, the tents without sinking in mud during rainy weather. Terach had gone out to inspect the idols and was pleased with some that showed good craftsmanship, especially for the two out of black diorite. He came back in time to hear about the offer of the farmer to purchase the property.

"That's what I call an excellent deal," exclaimed Terach enthusiastically. "You can invest the profit with me for half interest in the caravan business. We can grow rich and you will become a big merchant one of these days."

"Father, I am not happy in a caravan. Only Eleazer can

operate it successfully. I am content to work the farm, increase the flocks of goats, cattle, sheep, and worship my God at the altar I shall dedicate to Him. You can help me greatly by advancing sufficient silver to pay off all my obligations."

Terach expressed his disappointment but felt too elated to refuse his son's request. The neighbor might increase his offer and Avram may be a better trader than anyone suspected. His indifference was probably put on to make the purchaser more eager. He certainly would not refuse if offered 5000 shekels. Terach weighed the silver and handed it over to his son. Later he felt consoled over the disappointment in watching Eleazer dispose of the ironware at good prices. He even rented additional space and put up his idols for sale alongside of Milcah's and Davarah's cloth.

After several weeks the farm was cleared, plowed, and planted. The houses had been repaired, whitewashed, and painted until they presented a shining, inviting appearance. About eight Habiru families occupied the tents. The shepherds among them were buying from neighboring farmers rams and goats, lambs and ewes. Several cows furnished milk. Asses were harnessed to the plows and the wagons. The Habiru did the rough work under the direction of a Hittite, a skilled manager with knowledge of farming. At first Keturah and Davarah felt strange and isolated. But they soon began to realize that the spacious open air was healthier than the ill-smelling city lanes filled with garbage that was never moved and rendered foul from the slops unceremoniously dumped from the houses into the narrow streets. Lot made friends with the Habiru boys and Keturah's growing child showed better color and ate more heartily. In fact, the farm was livelier than the cooped-up existence in Haran.

The women considered the occasion worthy of a celebration. Avram paid scant attention until Terach agreed with them. He had not enjoyed a feast for a long time and looked back wistfully to those gatherings in Ur with himself presiding as patriarch over his clan. He even offered to pay the cost. The day was set on the festival of the New Moon when everyone abstained from work. The entire family, including Eleazer, came in a holiday mood. The Dulashish family, Sanu-Rimmon and son, were present to honor the Terach line. When the Habiru on Nahor's farm heard of the affair they insisted on joining their fellow Bedouins to rejoice with "their sheikh Avram." This incensed Nahor who never concealed his disdain for "those nomads" yet resented their eagerness to leave his service or their deference for his younger brother. He therefore refused to appear. Avram thought it proper to invite six of his neighboring farmers and their families.

The feast began with a religious service. The family, the guests, including the Habiru, the servants, and slaves, gathered near the altar facing the newly transformed sanctuary. For a sacrifice Avram offered a goat upon the altar. He thanked the Most High God for the many favors bestowed upon the family wandering on that long perilous journey by caravan and boat from Ur to Haran. He knelt and prayed to El Elyon to bless everyone present with health, shelter, food, long life and safety from war and pestilence. Excepting Terach, the entire family, the Habiru, the servants, and the slaves fell on their knees and responded with "So be it."

The servants and slaves of Terach and Davarah together with several of the Habiru women served the guests with wine, bread and honey, pomegranates, apples, small pears, dates, nuts, and the juices of fruit. The main courses were baked fish caught in the canal and the river, also the roasted meat of goats and sheep, prepared deliciously by the wives of the Habiru. When they had finished eating, the neighbors went over the farm on a tour of inspection. They entered the shrine and Repake, the next door neighbor, wondered what had become of the images. He asked Eleazer who was surveying on his own.

"The owner presented all the idols to his father, the former maker of images at the temple of the moon god at Ur," answered Eleazer.

"Where does he keep the statue of the god to whom he prayed? We would like to see it."

"There are no images of El Elyon. He has neither features nor limbs. He is the great spirit who resides in the heavens above."

"But surely he worships Ishtar." When Eleazer shook his head in the negative, the farmer went on: "How will he raise a crop without the help of the goddess of fertility?"

"Avram relies solely upon his God, the Most High, who blesses the soil to bring forth a rich harvest."

"I don't like this," declared Repake to his neighboring farmer after Eleazer went his way. "Our great goddess will be angry and may withhold her blessing from us also. We probably should not plant this coming season. I am certain that Avram will fare no better than Hebat, the goddess from Hurrian. Ishtar refused to let anything grow for her."

"It might be just as well," remarked the neighbor. "When the new owner will run into the anger of Ishtar and reap no harvest, he will become discouraged and let this land go for our price."

"I will report this matter to Zaradan, the high priest. He will advise us whether or not to plant," concluded Repake.

# 20

# Creeping Hostilities

TO ELEAZER THE OPERATION OF A FARM LACKED THE stimulus of managing a caravan or trading in the market place, but to Avram it offered the repose and inspiration necessary for contemplation. Always in the open he felt nearer to the Most High, Who no doubt watched his actions from above. Yet he could not help from discerning that for the men laboring at the same tasks day after day without cessation except for an occasional holiday it was dull and stagnating, especially for nomads accustomed to roam from place and scene. What could be done to make their lot less monotonous?

Contemplating under a quarter moon his thoughts drifted back to Babylon, the most stimulating place he had ever seen. He recalled the lively crowds on the avenues, dressed in their best, going to various temples or wandering in the market place and shopping areas. Some ambled on donkeys or drove their carts out in the open country. Others rowed small boats on the canals or traveled as vacationers on large ferry boats sailing the Naar Purattu. The pace was leisurely because it was a *Shabbattum,* the day of rest. A thought flashed into his mind and stimulated his heart to beat wildly, a usual occurence whenever he became gripped by a new idea. If in Babylon a day could be set aside for the cessation of labor then why not in Haran?

He could not recall how often the *Shabbattum* occurred. Was it on a day before or after the full moon? But what did it matter how or when the Babylonians observed their day of rest? And since the shops in the market place or on the city streets were open for business the *Shabbattum* was not observed by everyone. Would it be possible to set aside four days out of each month for periods of rest: the new moon festival, the two half-moons, and the full orb? Who would stop him? The farm was his private domain. He had full right to inaugurate as many days of rest for his workers as he saw fit.

Mulling further Avram questioned why not dedicate the rest day to the Most High? He could assemble his family, followers, and servants, offer a sacrifice, utter prayers, tell them about El Elyon and the life they should lead. He set the next full-moon day as the time to rest for everyone, including the cattle and the asses. All were instructed to bathe and wear clean clothes. Avram sacrificed a pigeon for a burnt offering, then asked everyone to kneel and repeat the prayer with him. He then preached to the congregants about their duty to live according to the Seven Commands of Noah and illustrated their importance by dilating upon the sin of incest. It was highly displeasing to the Most High God for a father to sleep with his daughter, a mother with her son, or a brother with a sister. For such a crime the sinner would surely suffer the wrath of El Elyon. The sermon was followed by the midday meal. Food was served to all present and they joined Avram in thanking El Shaddai for His gifts.

When Avram saw the joyful faces of men, women, and

children and the pleasure they derived from this holiday, he announced then and there that every seventh day would be called the *Shabbat,* a term to denote rest from all labor. During the week he sensed the eager anticipation for the coming *Shabbat* and began to wonder if he could forge a community based on faith and observance out of diverse elements, out of people as removed from each other as his own sophisticated family and the lowly Habiru, the primitive nomads from the Arabian desert. It then dawned on him that the children born or raised on his farm and taught to serve El Elyon only would as they grew up know and worship no other god.

Immersed in the problem of forging a community out of people dedicated to the service of El Shaddai he was unaware that his sermon struck close to home. The Habiru women had been noticing the condition of the Hittite supervisor's unmarried daughter. They did not dare to mention anything scandalous about Avram's agricultural expert, the foreman in charge of plowing, seeding, and harvesting. But their chieftain's earnest discourse emboldened them to inform Davarah that the young girl was pregnant. They also said that the Hittite's wife had even complained of her husband's neglect because he preferred sleeping with his own daughter. Davarah felt it her duty to tell Avram.

Honest people have no conception of criminal guile. Nor can the innocent fathom the quirks imbedded in the psyche of the depraved. Avram just couldn't understand how the soft-speaking Hittite who operated the farm efficiently could be guilty of incest, the most revolting sin of the moral code.

"I feel sorry for him," mused Avram. "Yet what else can I do but send him away. To keep him on might indicate that I approve of what he does. This would set a bad example to the people here. I want to weld them all into a god-fearing community which will serve El Elyon and follow his commandments." Yet he could not dismiss the matter that easily. He sat up late thinking: "Dismissing him is but a form of punishment. But who am I to judge people? If he broke the divine law El Shaddai will punish him. Just what purpose will be served in dismissing him? He will continue his sinful life in another group and spread the evil. Wouldn't it be better to teach him to repent and cease his sinful doings? Surely the Most High God of compassion, of justice, of righteousness does not delight in cruelty or in punishment. I will try to carry out what my God desires. I will speak to the man and if he confesses and humbles himself publicly before El Shaddai and promises never to commit the sin again, I will instruct the people to forget his offense and treat him with the same respect as before. The girl will have to be removed until she gives birth; then I must find her a husband."

With this resolution in mind Avram went to bed. In the morning he sought the Hittite but could not find him. His wife had not seen him since the night before and assumed that he was sleeping with his daughter. It became quite obvious that he disappeared and deserted his wife and children.

## II

Nor was Avram aware of the mounting hostility in the immediate neighborhood. It had started when his neighbor Repake offered to buy the land. Avram's refusal to sell angered him, yet he accepted the invitation to be a guest at the house warming. Repake regarded him an intruder who had no business in agriculture, the occupation for a respectable native. The prayers to the unknown god proved a further irritant. Ignoring Szin or Ishtar for the worship of a questionable deity was surely an insult sufficient to anger the moon god or the fertility goddess. Quite sure that Ishtar would afflict the land with sterility Repake and another farmer decided to consult the high priest of Szin as to whether they should plant for the following season.

"We can never understand the ways of the gods," responded Zaradan. "Sometimes they favor the unworthy and even smile on the wicked. It is impossible to foretell their actions. If I were you I would plant. Even should our great goddess deny a crop to your infidel neighbor it does not follow that your land will be touched by her curse."

Yet Repake withheld from plowing and sowing. But when he saw Avram's crop growing he grew more angry. Avram no doubt worshipped a demon and employed magic to make his soil fertile. All self-blame he heaped upon Avram with mounting bitterness. It also galled him that his neighbors did not go along with him. They planted and were now raising bumper crops. As the harvest time drew near it became quite obvious that Avram's farm had produced the largest crop of all. When the neighbors asked how was it that he, untrained in farming, could in his first undertaking raise a bigger crop than any of the experienced planters, he answered, "It is very simple. My land has been lying fallow for a number of years. It has absorbed much rain and moisture. It has been fertilized by years of vegetation and self-growth. After a long rest it has yielded more than if planted every year."

Interest in the God of Avram asserted itself. Curiosity seekers began to come on the *Shabbat* mainly to watch the service. They would listen to Avram's preaching then ask questions. The poorer farmers were particularly impressed. In Avram's shrine they were never required to make offerings. If they brought along an animal or bird he would sacrifice it for them but only to his God. Why should the priests who never work live on the fat of the land, they questioned? The women approved the absence of *kedashes,* and asked, "Why should we who work hard on the land and lose our looks and figures in child-bearing be compelled to compete with those temple harlots whose only task is to look pretty so that they can drain our men of their silver?"

For a time the larger planters ignored Avram and his new God. What did it matter as long as their harvest was big and prices good? They scoffed at Repake for refusing to plant. When they heard that Keturah would give birth to her second child they concluded that either the fertility goddess was indifferent or Ishtar might be unable to bring on sterility to a follower of the new God.

Yet as time went on a change came about when they became aware of the disaffection growing among their laborers. Even the serfs and slaves grumbled at the hardness of their lot and pointed to the workers on Avram's farm enjoying days of complete rest four times during every month. Some of their laborers stole away to see what transpired on the rest day. They came back and reported the enthusiasm prevailing on Avram's farm. Not only were the workers jubilant for the cessation of work but experienced a joyful veneration for the God who commanded a day of rest not only for people but even for animals. Several of the larger planters went to see Avram and asked why he should deliberately lose so many valuable work days, especially during the plowing, planting, and harvesting seasons.

"Do you see any signs of neglect on this farm?" cross-questioned Avram. Seeing their negative head shakes he continued. "It's difficult for comfortable land owners to understand the plight of laborers, free or slave. What have they to look forward to? Toil without end, day after day, except on some holiday or because of bad weather. Giving periods of rest raises their spirits and makes them work more diligently on the other days. Instead of a loss I find it a gain."

"Is this your personal idea or the command of your God?" asked another farmer whose expression denoted sympathy.

"My God did not tell me in so many words to set apart rest days not only for workers but for ourselves and even for the animals. I am confident however that El Elyon approves of it."

"How do you know it?" questioned the sympathetic planter.

"I firmly believe that He sends me certain thoughts that are beneficial. But why don't all of you come on our *Shabbat* to see for yourselves the state of mind of our workers? It will open your eyes."

## III

The advanced pregnancy of Keturah was raising two-sided comments in the farming vicinity. The friendly visitors to the *Shabbat* celebrations saw Avram's God blessing the fruit of Keturah's womb with offspring. The opponents, chagrined as when Avram harvested the biggest crop in the neighborhood, declared with malice: "Wait, the child is not yet born. It may well be a monster cursed by Szin and Ishtar. Nor is the mother free from danger. The *shaidim* will no doubt afflict her and the brat she will bring forth."

These rumors were reported by the friendly workers who came to the weekly feasts. The Habiru women relayed the gossip to Davarah, and Keturah heard it from her "brother" Lot. She became agitated and begged her "mother" to take her to the temple of Szin for the *ashipu* to exorcise the demons as he did before the birth of Zimran. Both women knew that Avram would become angry and forbid their going to the pagan sanctuary. They bided their time until Avram happened to mention that he would be away most of the next day for he wished to take a load of barley to the king's tax collector. Davarah suggested that Eleazer go along since he knew how to argue with the king's official who always assessed a larger sum knowing that the tax payer would haggle for a reduction. The women wanted him to take them to Emtelai. Keturah wished to get away for a change. Besides, this was a good opportunity to visit the market place and purchase some necessary things for the lying-in.

The three women walked a short distance but had to take a chair carried by four men for Keturah to reach the temple. They told the priest of Keturah's father and of her friendship with Zaradan, the high priest. But when she gave the liberal offering of five shekels in silver the priest stated that she would get the strongest incantation which the temple had to offer. He led her into a closed room, lit up dingily by a clay lamp. The *ashipu* then came in and struck a bell that rang sweet, silvery, sonorous sounds. The priest started the invocation:

"Ye seven baleful master spirits!
Ye seven fearsome Undugs!
Come out of darkness,
Come out of your tombs,
Come out of the caverns in mountains,
Come out of the arid deserts,
Ye wicked *shaidim* who wander nefariously over the face of the earth,
Ye who bring destruction to man in cities or in solitude,

Ye who smite the aged and helpless,
Ye who have no couch among gods or men,
Ye who are not male or female,
Ye who have neither wife nor son,
Ye who heed neither prayers nor supplications.

As a priest of Szin's temple I now invoke Szin, Ishtar, Nergal, Ea, Marduk, Ningal, and Baal to command ye to obey my instructions:

Behind me ye are not to howl,
Behind me ye are not to shout,
Ye shall not cause a wicked Undug to seize me,
By the heavens be ye exorcised, ye vicious, unsatiable demons,
By the earth be ye exorcised, fearful, relentless spirits."

Keturah then noticed the stone images of seven black demons of the most horrifying aspects. She became frozen with terror on seeing their eyes light up revealing the most horrendous visages imaginable. The seven differed from each other in face, form, wings, hands, and feet. Then baleful eyes glinted with cruel malevolence with the most ruthless, malicious ferocity. She then realized what the evil eye meant. A smell of sulphur and brimstone filled the room. The priest noticed Keturah swaying and caused her to sit down on a small couch lest she faint from fear or the stupifying odor. Then the *aspiru* sounded a gong that sent forth a harsh, crashing, metallic clangor and began a long incantation that ended:

"Where Keturah, daughter of Sabbattu, high priest of Nannar goes
Ye are not to go.
Where she enters ye must not enter
Ye are not to put your foot
In the imprint of her foot,
Ye must not come near her body,

Where she sits ye are not to sit,
Ye must not enter her house,
Her roof ye shall not haunt,
Ye must not walk before her,
To follow her footsteps ye shall not,
Near the body of Keturah, daughter of Sabbattu, high priest of Nannar
Ye must not come,
Nor shall ye touch the offspring of her body."

The *aspiru* continued to strike the gong that emitted the deafening clang which struck more dread into the nervous woman with the child in her womb. Gradually the evil glint in the eyes of the fiends waned, and the sickening odor subsided. The priest and the *aspiru* led the trembling Keturah out into the open for a breath of fresh air. The priest enjoined her never to disclose to anyone what she saw or heard lest the seven demons come for her.

When the three returned to Terach's house Keturah felt badly shaken. She would take only some hot milk which Emtelai prepared; then she retired to the chamber that had been empty since Sanu-Rimmon left to get married. She did not get up for the evening meal and Avram decided to remain overnight. Riding about 12 miles in the darkness would be fatiguing as well as hazardous.

At the meal the discussion ranged from business to farming. The tax collector reduced the assessment but not by much. He inspected the quality of the barley, accepted the wagon load, and gave his receipt on a clay tablet. Obviously he did not want the additional bother of reassessing. Eleazer reported that the sale of iron was not as brisk as in the foregoing year. The reason pointed to competition. Another merchant had brought a stock of ironware from the Hittite country and started price cutting. This necessitated price reduction. Should other merchants follow suit then the importation of iron might cease to be profitable. In fact Eleazer wondered whether it would be worthwhile in the future to go through all the difficulties of importing the heavy metal.

Avram analyzed the ups and downs of farming. It so happened that he raised a bumper crop and the prices were high. But a crop depended on rainfall; too much or too little could be ruinous. Then the scourge of pests or worms was always present. A swarm of locust might consume a growing crop in its entirety. Fortunately he had the Habiru who could eliminate the thorns, thistles, brambles, weeds, or nettles quite well. The *khamsin* winds from the desert together with excessive heat could prove harmful. Even birds might peck the fruits off the trees. After bypassing all these evils large crops could lower prices and render the output useful for the animals only.

"How are you going with the herds?" asked Eleazer.

"So far, rather encouraging. In the beginning they multiply slowly. But here again we run into problems. The high cost of feeding makes it necessary to send the herdsmen out to find free pasturage. Here they run into the hazards of robbers, of not finding grazing land, lack of water, carrying along food for themselves and the sheep dogs, picking up diseases. I sometimes think it might be better to keep the flocks on the farm and raise the feed ourselves. At present the goats and sheep are nibbling the leftover produce of friendly neighbors. Our shepherds are the Habiru and how we can manage without them I can't guess. They are faithful and work for small wages. Fortunately I hit upon the idea of the *Shabbat*. Remember this day of rest in Babylon? The workers are grateful to desist from labor every seventh day."

"That runs to more than 50 days a year," observed the practical Eleazer. "Wouldn't that be losing too many work days?"

The snoring of Terach, who fell asleep at the table, interrupted further discussion. Emtelai woke him and led him to his bedroom. She gave the two young men a sad look which signified that he was aging. She reminded Sarai that it was past the usual bedtime. But the young girl begged off and said she enjoyed listening. Eleazer, then Davarah stated that each had to get up early for a good day's work and retired.

Sarai remained alone with her half-brother. The growing girl looked excessively thin and angular. Her features were regular, her dark gray eyes clear and sparkling, her mouth pretty; yet the young girl might grow up either plain looking or beautiful. She sat on his lap and said, "Avram, we see you so seldom. I do love to hear you talk. Why are you so occupied? How is Keturah feeling?"

"She complained," replied Avram, "that this day was too much for her. She was tired and wanted some rest."

"Did the temple tire her out?"

"What temple?" questioned Avram rather sharply. "Did she go to a temple?"

"The Temple of Szin. She was frightened by the priest exorcising the demons from her bedside when she gives birth."

"How do you know this? Did you go along?"

"No. But I heard Mother Emtelai tell it to Father."

Avram became silent and concentrated in thought. Sarai kissed him on the cheek, slipped off his lap, said good night, and ran off. This information disturbed him. It seemed that the Most High God made but slight impact upon the immediate family, which included his father, mother, Davarah, and Keturah. Evidently they were too deeply attached to the gods of their childhood. Yet if Keturah stood in mortal fear of giving birth without exorcising the *shaidim,* just what could he do about it? Wasn't it unjust to let her undergo deathly terror at such a critical time? Talking would only lead to a quarrel which might affect her badly. She seemed far too nervous already. It might be wiser for the time being to say nothing.

For about a week Keturah felt depressed and wanted someone to be with her all the time. She begged Avram to pray to the Mighty El Elyon to shield her and the unborn child from the evil spirits. Avram assured that no harm would befall her or the child. Didn't the Most High protect the family from all harm since He first appeared to him in Ur?

"I am afraid I offended the Most High God. I know you will be angry and never forgive me because I went to the Temple of Szin."

"I know about that," declared Avram. "Did the priest help you to meet the ordeal of giving birth?"

"He made me feel much worse. He frightened the life out of me. I will never go to him again. Never. Never. But will you pray for me? Your El Elyon will do anything you ask."

"Yes, I will pray for you. Yet I feel certain that no evil will befall you."

Feeling the first twinge of pain she grasped his hand and when he attempted to draw away gently, she gasped, "Please do not leave me."

"I simply want to call Davarah. I will be back. You will soon give birth."

Davarah assembled her slave, the deserted wife of the Hittite, and several of the Habiru women, of whom one acted as a midwife. Keturah had labored in pain for two hours when she heard a baby cry. Davarah washed the newly born and held it up. It let out a lusty yell and Keturah saw it was a boy. She smiled to Avram and said, "Kiss me, dear," and went to sleep.

## IV

Heavy spring rains and the long celebration of the New Year in the first month of Nissan caused Avram to postpone for about six weeks the feast celebrating the birth of his second son, whom he named Yokshan. On a day of rest a crowd assembled numbering more than a hundred comprising all his family, his workers, the Nahor household, and a larger group than usual of the neighboring farmers.

The ceremony which was becoming a ritual began with the sacrifice of a young ram. The only variant was a thanksgiving to the Most High for the birth of the child and the safety of its mother. Prayers for the welfare of both, uttered by the father, were joined in by all who served El Elyon. They knelt, repeated the prayer, and closed with "So be it." The ceremony was followed by a discourse, which had become a feature of the *Shabbat* service.

"I am thankful to this large assembly for the honor of your presence. I wish to take this opportunity to explain some phases of our belief, which I know have been puzzling many of you. You may wonder how it was that I had a full crop without the blessings of the fertility goddess. The same friends are no doubt curious to see the mother and the child, which came without any invocation to Ishtar. But perhaps the greatest marvel is that neither mother nor child was stricken by the demons who no doubt had open access without interference from the gods or goddesses.

"There is no intention here to belittle or disparage any god whom anyone here worships. But I do want to make it clear that I believe our God is more powerful, more just, more righteous than any other god. He is unseeable, unknowable. I do not even know his name. We call him El Elyon, which simply means the Most High, or El Shaddai, the Almighty. He will cause our crops to grow regardless of the hostility of any other god. Our children are born without the help or hindrance of any fertility goddess. We do not fear the *shaidim;* they have no power over the worshippers of El Elyon. Before the recent birth my Keturah became very much agitated, something quite usual among pregnant women. Without my knowledge she went to one of the temples in order to have the demons exorcised. But she came back more frightened than ever. I assured her that she had nothing to fear since the Most High would protect her and the child. Have either of them been plagued or molested by evil spirits? See for yourselves.

"Our God is just, righteous, and merciful. He punishes those who murder or steal, who commit incest or adultery. He abhors those who cut a piece to eat out of a living animal. He admonishes us to speak the truth only and never allow falsehood to escape our lips; to behave in a kindly spirit towards our fellow men, even to those who transgress or injure us; to speak evil of no one; not to curse any living being no matter how angry we might become. We must have compassion and be merciful to everyone. He approves of giving a day of rest twice every fortnight to all who work and even to animals. May our God, El Elyon, bless all of you."

The reactions to Avram's missionizing were not quite apparent on the surface. On the whole, the invited guests displayed a correct attitude, perhaps not too friendly yet pleasant. A few showed warmth; the majority concealed their feelings under a courteous mask. But later the

Habiru women told Davarah that workers on the larger farms reported the hostile attitude of their masters who voiced resentment at Avram's disparagement of their gods. Yet the workers felt that the real cause of hostility was due to the days of rest which Avram instituted. It was setting a bad example that might encourage the laborers, free or slave, to demand regular rest days. Davarah related the gossip to Keturah who remarked, "It might be well to visit the temple and thank the gods for the easy birth of my second child. I believe I should show my appreciation with a sacrifice."

"I can take you along the next time I go to the market place to deliver some cloth to Eleazer."

"That's good, Mother. When you are through you can come for me at the altar for the sacrifice of birds. Incidentally, do you think a pigeon would be sufficient? I hate to ask Avram for a silver offering. You know how he feels about the gods, although I was surprised how calmly he took my temple visit to exorcise the *shaidim*."

"He said nothing when he saw how agitated you were. But don't let him know about any future visits. He is kind enough but can become quite ruthless where it concerns his God. This is something you and I can't understand. The pigeon will be all right. But I will give you some nice material with a beautiful design to present with the bird. I am sure the priest will like it."

"Mother, if I am not at the altar then come to the high priest's antechamber. I may stop in to greet him. He says he is a great admirer of Sabbattu. When I went with Terach and Avram about the canal, he helped because I was the daughter of his friend. So he said. I want to ask whether he heard anything from Father."

The priest recognized Keturah, congratulated her on her successful delivery, and was pleased with the cloth offering. After the sacrifice Keturah went to the high priest. Zaradan was in conference with the priestess Habliya. He introduced Keturah as a former bride of Nannar and daughter of a high priest. He had received a message from Sabbattu and expected to see him in Haran; when Sabbattu would come he did not know. Zaradan was in a hurry to keep an appointment and told Keturah to come in the day after the full moon. Visiting him at the moment was a delegation of farmers who would no doubt complain about the proselytizing activities of her husband. It was important for her to come. He had to run off but suggested that the women remain and chat.

The priestess, Habliya, daughter of an Amorite chieftain, expressed interest in the unusual occurrences of Keturah's young life. Habliya invited her to her chamber whenever she found herself in the temple. The *kadosh* informed Keturah that a woman was waiting for her in the antechamber. Keturah told Davarah what the high priest had said. Both concentrated on the method of reaching the temple without Avram's knowledge. Fortunately, Keturah was not compelled to nurse her baby. The Hittite's daughter gave birth to a stillborn child, at least such was the information that mother and daughter gave out. She therefore had the milk to suckle Avram's son.

Davarah asked for the wagon. She had to deliver more cloth to Eleazer and buy some dyes in the market place. Keturah went along and was let off at the temple entrance. Zaradan received her literally with open arms and kissed her before she could resist. He got quickly down to business:

"My lovely one, those farmers brought grave accusations against your husband. They charge him with violating extremely serious laws. According to them he has disparaged our gods and is guilty of blasphemy. He virtually denies the existence of all the gods in our pantheon. Yet he claims to worship a god who has neither hands nor feet, neither face nor body, neither eyes nor ears, who is neither male nor female. No one has ever seen him nor can he be seen. It is quite obvious that his god is no god at all. He evidently does not believe in any god and is thus guilty of atheism. The penalty for these two offenses, blasphemy and atheism, is death and not only by the laws of Haran but even in the liberal and humane code of Hammurabi. What have you to say about these accusations, my beauty?"

"My lord," gasped Keturah thoroughly frightened, "I know nothing about the laws or the gods. Avram is my husband and I love him."

"Do you or the rest of the family believe as he does?"

"Adoni, all of us except Avram serve the gods of Ur. Before giving birth I came to this temple and was frightened out of my wits by the exorcising I heard and saw. After birth I brought an offering here and a sacrifice. Our father Terach was always a believer and made images for the Temple of Nannar. Can't you help us? I know you could."

She sat on his lap, embraced him and gave him one of those kisses that could melt any man not made of stone.

"Suppose I would, what then?"

"I will do anything you want."

"I am willing but will your husband cooperate in refuting these charges?"

"He will never give up his God, not even if you burn him alive."

"My Keturah, the best thing I can do for him is to do nothing. Let him believe as he wishes but not spread his poison among our followers. If he will agree then I can save him."

He embraced and kissed her. She knew that he was her man. She could dominate him through his sensuality. His lust would never be completely assuaged. He would always long for her. There was no need of exacting any promises in advance. He would certainly come back for more. She therefore permitted him to have his way. When he could breathe more easily he murmured, "I love you. I love you." Lying in his arms she said, "Zaradan, I believe you really do love me. Now, if you want to retain and enjoy me, do one thing. Keep my Avram here in Haran. If he should die then my father will come for me. He says he could marry me to some high noble of Babylon. Then I would sit with royalty at the king's banquets. If you make it difficult for Avram, he will leave just as he left Ur, a greater and far more attractive city than Haran. Now do this: Send for Avram. I can't deliver any message. He must never know I go to the temple or ever see you. Make the best arrangement with him possible. Oh, he can dispute about the gods better than you. My father could never get the best of him in argument. Remember, if you want to enjoy me, it's up to you to keep my husband here in contentment. Now let me dress. My mother is coming for me. She might be waiting in the antechamber now."

# 21

# And Terach Died in Haran

FOLLOWING THE SUGGESTION OF KETURAH THE HIGH priest sent for Avram and repeated in fuller detail the charges he had outlined to her.

"As for blaspheming the gods," argued Avram, "I believe Adoni has been misinformed by people who are hostile to me. I have at no time disparaged publicly the gods worshipped here or in Ur or in Babylon. I consider the Most High Whom I serve greater and more powerful than all the other gods. I was raised in an atmosphere where I listened constantly to the comparison of the many gods in the pantheon of Ur. My father was the image-maker for the Temple of Nannar. In his display room people would come to buy but spent most of the time talking. There were many discussions as to whether Nannar was more powerful than the sun god Utu. Some would argue as to the superior merits of Irnina, whom you call Ishtar, over Ningal, the wife of Nannar. The fact that some considered one god more potent than another is not disparagement much less blasphemy."

"But when you reject the gods of your birthplace as unworthy of worship," questioned Zaradan, "what is that other than contempt? And what is contempt if not blasphemy?"

"Contempt is an inner feeling," explained Avram, "an attitude, whereas blasphemy is abuse, slander, a spoken insult calculated to bring a god into scorn, disrepute, or contumely. Contempt may or may not be silent, but blasphemy must always be spoken. I have never spoken contemptuously of the gods, regardless of how I felt. I don't believe any court could convict me of blasphemy."

"But why should anyone think contemptuously of the gods?" again questioned Zaradan. "They are the forces of nature. Whether they are separate beings or connected in some way with nature I do not know. And that accounts for their multiplicity. Thus there are gods of light and darkness, of love and fertility, of the earth and sky, of thunder and lightning, of fire and water, of wind and rain. We believe that rivers, mountains, springs, and forests have their own gods. They represent or are part of all life and creation. I cannot understand why a serious-minded person cannot accept the gods just as he accepts death and destruction, love and hatred, war and peace."

"Here is the great difference that divides us," declared Avram. "I believe El Elyon is the sole creator of heaven and earth and of all life. He is not a part of nature Who must obey its physical laws blindly. He is above and superior to nature. He can change or control the storm winds, the actions of men, even the course of the stars. He can prevent or stop wars. He can restrain lightning and thunder."

"If your God is as great and as powerful as you say He is then why can't we include Him in our pantheon? I will speak to my colleagues and see whether we can make a place for Him in our temple among our gods."

"The Most High stands alone," asserted Avram. "He

will not share his worship with any other god. We who serve Him must discard the other gods."

"Where is the land over which He has jurisdiction? What people or nation serves Him exclusively?"

"El Elyon is God of the whole world. He rules out of the heavens. He is not bound to any limited territory or mountain or water."

"You evidently stand alone in this worship. Your father told me in your presence that he serves our moon god. Your wife, I understand, came to us before giving birth to exorcise the demons. What I don't understand is how you came to this belief."

"The Almighty revealed Himself to me. He informed me that my forebears worshiped Him even before the great flood, but my father and grandfather forsook Him for the gods of Ur. I simply reverted to the faith of my ancestors."

"Before giving up the gods of your father did you learn anything about the religion in which you were born?"

"I studied for the priesthood under Khar-Sak who is perhaps the greatest mind and the most learned scholar in all of Sumer. He succeeded Sabbattu as high priest of Nannar."

"Then surely you must know that you are violating the tenets of our faith. They must have told you that the gods have divine supremacy over the territories they rule. You as a private individual cannot come into a new country and introduce there your own familiar God. You are an interloper if you seek to establish your God in a place where a god already holds sway. The only wise thing for you to do is to transfer your worship to the gods of the new land in which you desire to make your home."

"Nothing in the world will induce me to forsake my God. He means more to me than father, mother, wife, or child. But even if my faith were not so strong, how could I serve the innumerable gods included in the term *polytheism* recently coined by the intellectuals of Babylon?"

"But why can't you serve our gods who, under different names, are worshipped by all the people on earth?"

"Because they are neither just nor righteous nor compassionate. Let me illustrate. Last year in Carchemish I heard of the goddess Anath, the beloved of Baal, who is the highest god in Canaan and Phoenicia. She admired and coveted the bow made by some one for the virtuous young prince, Aquat. The goddess asked for the bow and the prince refused. Even her offer of immortality could not change his refusal. Anath became wrathful and extracted permission from her father, who is also father of the other gods, to slay Aquat. The goddess thus acquired the bow she coveted. Far from condemning such unnecessary murder the gods actually applauded killing a young innocent prince, the future king of the country. The religion of polytheism thus permits anyone to covet, even to kill, in order to obtain his heart's desire. Such a deed is abhorrent to my God of justice and mercy, Whose conduct furnishes an example for all men to imitate."

"There is no limit in discussing the gods," observed Zaradan. Let's get down to the reason for your coming here. Certain farmers in your vicinity are charging you with blasphemy and atheism. They fear that our gods will in their anger blast the entire section and prevent crops from growing. They want some action taken against you. I sent for you on account of my friendship for your father-in-law. But we are getting nowhere. What suggestions have you to offer?"

"In the first place," countered Avram, "I deny their charges. Secondly, they are not worried about the anger of the gods. What irks them is my setting aside every seventh day for everyone to cease work. They are fearful lest their laborers or slaves grow restive and also demand a *Shabbat.*"

"Did your God institute this innovation?"

"He did not. But I know my God approves of it. I witnessed the *Shabbattum* observed in Babylon and thought it might prove a beneficial institution."

"But you use this day for prayer, feasting, preaching, and converting our people. It is a device, they say, to lure the followers of Szin and Ishtar to serve a strange God."

"I do not lure anyone," exploded Avram. "The farm is open and if the neighbors, whosoever they are, wish to come they are welcome. My ancestors have always observed the rules of hospitality."

"Yet you do use this approach to build up a cult. They say you have quite a following. How large is your converted group?"

"I don't know what you mean by cult or following or converted group. I simply utter a prayer of thanksgiving to the Most High. Some kneel with me and respond with a 'so-be-it.' I have no ceremony, no initiation. No one is asked to give up his gods. No one is asked to pray or say 'so-be-it' or listen to my discourse. I speak of my God's commands to lead a clean, decent life and avoid sin. I don't know which ones serve El Elyon except some of my Habiru workers. I have not even converted my family."

"Suppose the king orders you to quit observing a day of rest. Suppose he commands you to forego all sacrifices, prayers, discourses, and feasts. What will you do?"

"I will leave Haran just as I left Ur. I can then go to a land that will permit me to serve my God in my own fashion."

"You do not seem concerned with the grave charges overhanging you. Suppose you are arrested and tried for blasphemy or atheism. These are religious violations which carry the death penalty. Your judges will be priests who will surely convict you. What do you hope for then?"

"I rely on El Shaddai for protection. The Almighty God will save me."

## II

For about a month Keturah waited to see what would happen. Avram did not mention his discussions with Zaradan and continued observing the seventh day of rest and the feasts as before. She could, however, notice a falling off in attendance. The laborers or slaves of the antagonistic farmers stopped coming altogether. The friendly farmers and their workers were present but in ever decreasing numbers. Keturah was curious to know what the high priest was doing and what he intended to do. She waited for the time when Davarah would visit the city and the opportunity came.

When Keturah came to the high priest's antechamber several men were waiting to see him. The *kadosh* took her through a side entrance leading to a private room and informed Zaradan. After a short wait the priest came in, hugged and kissed her, and said, "You came at a bad time for me. I do want to see you but this happens to be a busy day for me."

"I can come only when the opportunity offers. You know I must keep these meetings secret."

"Did your husband tell you about our conversations?"

"No, he did not."

"Well, then I will be brief. We had a long discussion which ended just where we began. He does not fear a conviction and not even the death penalty. If it were not for you he would have been tried and no doubt sentenced. After my conversation with him I decided that the best service I can render both of you is to do nothing."

"Did the neighbors forget all about their complaints?"

"No. They came and asked what I was doing. I informed them that after a close investigation I concluded that they had no proof of his guilt. He is a very fervent believer in his God and they had no evidence of his blasphemy. But I enjoined them to cease going to his Sabbath celebration; also to keep their laborers away from his farm. I hope the matter will die down. I told them to go on planting and disregard the infidel in their midst. If they complain to the king I will tell him the same. Now I must go. Kiss me and come to see me as soon as you can."

Davarah had promised to come for her in about two hours. To while away the time Keturah thought she might stroll about the temple compound and see the things for sale. As she was leaving the section inhabited by the priests, Habliya, the priestess, came up and exclaimed, "What a surprise to see you!"

"I came to consult the high priest but he was too busy to talk more than several minutes."

"Waiting to see him later?"

"No. He can't see me at all today."

"Going home?"

"Yes, when mother comes for me. I thought I would wander about the shops for an hour or so."

"Oh, that's too tiresome in the heat of the day. Suppose you come to my room and tell me more about your very interesting life."

Keturah was not too keen about visiting the priestess, who appeared to be about ten years her senior. She sensed a cool hardness within, the honeyed manner notwithstanding. Her smile seemed forced, her laugh brittle. She could hardly detect a single quality that was winning or that could draw anyone. Yet her face was rather attractive and her figure not bad. Talking to her was better than wandering about alone. Habliya asked numerous questions about the famed Ur Temple of Nannar, the most celebrated of all sanctuaries dedicated to the moon god. She even wanted to know the temple's instructions in the nuances of love making about which she heard so much.

"Do you miss the honors paid to you in the Ur temple?"

"No. I can't say I do. While there were some pleasant features in the life there, I prefer the love of my husband and my two little boys, even if the older one is growing into quite an urchin."

"Yet you do grow tired of the same domestic humdrum all the time?"

"I have servants for the housework. Of course, the children do keep me tied down. But I love them even if at times they wear me out."

"A wife and mother needs some recreation. What do you do for amusement?"

"Oh, I come to the city and go shopping with my mother. Then we must return. Our farm is about 11 miles from Haran."

"We have some small intimate parties every now and then," confided the priestess. "You would fit in very well and enjoy them greatly."

"Are you short of girls in this temple?"

"Yes and no. The priestesses are mostly elderly women. Of course, we don't want to mix with the common *kedashes* who sometimes come direct from the embraces of dirty riffraff."

"What is your high priestess like?"

"Oh, she is no longer young. In addition, she is ailing. Frankly, I would like to succeed her. You could be very helpful."

"Who me?" What can I do for you, an authorized priestess?"

"A great deal. A word from you would go far with our high priest."

"Why I scarcely know the man."

"Judging from the way he looks at you, I might guess that he would refuse you nothing. He is in love with you and I have no doubt about that."

"He is a friend of my father. The day I met you I came to inquire if he knew when my father was coming to Haran."

"But after giving you the information he told you to come and see him when he had more leisure. A friend of the father can love the daughter. It even helps sometimes, if I know men. And you do, too."

"You know him better than I do. Why don't you ask him yourself?"

"Yes, I know him and have even slept with him on occasions. I asked him for the position at the very time that you came. That is what I was there for. His answer to me was evasive, but not to you. In fact, I should be jealous of you."

There was a knock on the door and the *kadosh* came in with Davarah. Habliya bit her lip in chagrin and said, "Keturah, I would like to see you when you come in again. Don't stay away too long."

III

Davarah brought a bit of surprising news:

"The boatman, Hankas, came to town and brought along a new wife. The first one died of some plague. His two sons left him. The elder joined Hammurabi's army and the younger went to Babylon and entered a business house. The poor man became lonely I guess and married again."

"What is she like?" asked Keturah.

"Rather good-looking and still young, that is much younger than Hankas. Sipara seems quite gay and not fat. I know Avram will be glad to see him so I invited them both to come with us and spend some time on the farm. We are to pick them up at Terach's house."

"Oh, I hate to run into that sneaky little Sarai. I haven't seen her for some time, not even at the feast after my Yokshan was born. I suppose she avoids me, too."

"She is growing up. For a time she seemed plain, but now Sarai is blossoming out into a pretty girl, though a little too thin."

"Just like the snake, which she is."

"Oh come now, Zirru, she is not a snake. She simply wants your husband. She would like to be in your sandals."

"Well, she will never get him."

"Don't say never. We all get older; beauty fades and men have roving eyes. They like the young ones the older they get."

"I will then utilize all the knowledge I acquired at Nannar's temple and will make Avram love me more than ever."

"Talking of love, do you know who is smitten with her? Amihud, the son of Sanu-Rimmon. He goes to the school in the temple we just left. He sees Sarai every day and reads to her the lessons on his clay tablets. Sometimes he asks Father Terach or Eleazer, when he is around, to explain things he does not understand."

"If she should marry him she will make his life miserable ever after."

"Amihud is not the only one to fall under her spell. My grandson, Bethuel, the only one of the boys who does not take after Nahor, is tongue-tied in her presence. He seizes every opportunity to drive the wagon, no matter how difficult the task might be, just to see her."

The wagon stopped in front of Terach's house. Keturah greeted Hankas and welcomed Sipara. She seconded

Davarah's invitation to the newlyweds to be guests on the farm. She also asked Eleazer to come along but he declined because the drive took too long and the return would disturb his entire working day. While Keturah and Terach were chatting with the married couple, Emtelai drew Davarah and Eleazer into another chamber and said in confidence, "For the first time in a great while Nahor came to visit his old father. He urged Terach to go into a separate chamber so that they might talk confidentially. I would not have known what they said had Sarai not slipped in and hid in the clothes press. You know Sarai has a talent for eavesdropping.

"Nahor did the talking. The sum and substance was that the aging Terach should put his house in order. Rather than make a will that would enable his heirs to fight among themselves, it would be better for Terach to convey the estate during his lifetime. There was no need to provide for Avram. He has a larger farm than Nahor; it works laborers and would soon have more cattle than Nahor. Besides, Avram's harvests were bigger than his brother's. Terach should turn everything over to Nahor, who is not only the oldest living son but the husband of Milcah, daughter of Harran, the first born. Lot would no doubt inherit his mother Davarah's estate. When I become a widow I should live with my son Avram. As for Sarai, now growing up, she could marry Uz, the oldest son of Nahor.

"Eleazer, I thought you should know about this. I know that Terach will consult you. Not that I am trying to influence you for I feel sure that you will advise my husband honestly and to the best interests of all. Nor do I think that you should be left out. I will tell Terach myself when the occasion arises."

The heart of Avram overflowed on beholding Hankas and he was overjoyed to hear that his friend contemplated changing residence from Agade to Haran. Avram immediately offered the boatman a partnership in the farm and in the herds. But Hankas thought agriculture might be too passive for one used to constant movement on the water. Besides, he feared that his wife would find rustic life monotonous. She had always lived in the city and would probably be bored with the country. But he would join Eleazer in trading on the Purattu and touch the various cities or towns from Babylon, or even Ur, then proceed up the river as far as Carchemish and even beyond. Avram favored the idea and felt certain that his father would approve.

Avram then informed his friend about everything that happened since seeing him last. The subject most important to both was the spreading of the faith of El Elyon. But Avram harbored doubts about the future. Should he risk the displeasure of the high priest by adopting more vigorous measures to convert the idol worshipers? The warning from the high priest was quite definite that such a course would be fraught with peril.

For a while Avram sat thinking, then made the observation: "Hankas, one does not forsake the city of his birth without some good reason. Did you perchance suffer persecution for abandoning the gods to serve El Elyon?"

"While I was not banished," replied Hankas, "I did begin to feel some hostilities which, at first, I ignored. You see, my first wife was a homebody and mixed very little with people. Then some kind of sickness visited our city. A number of people, including my wife, died. A rumor began to circulate that the gods sent an epidemic because I brought some unknown deity, perhaps a demon, into the city. Both of my sons left me and went to Babylon. I attributed this to the natural longing of youth for the big city. I married again and was surprised that some good friends did not come to the wedding feast. Then my wife said that she was snubbed by people she thought were old friends. One man informed me that many resented my forsaking the gods. I became disgusted, sold my house, turned my property into silver, and decided to join you."

Hankas relished the spirit prevailing on the farm, and was especially intrigued by the *Shabbat*, the service, the sacrifice, the discourse, and the feast. While the visitors were not as numerous as during the preceding year, he was nevertheless delighted when a Habiru pointed to those who came from other farms in disregard of the orders by their employers to stay away. To Hankas the day of rest took on a sanctified atmosphere which everyone seemed to feel and appreciate. He felt happy and gave thanks to El Elyon for enabling him to come to His sanctuary.

## IV

At his home Terach sat conferring with Avram, Eleazer, and Hankas as to the feasibility of a partnership in the trading business which Eleazer was operating. The skipper had 300 shekels in silver to invest but his chief asset was the new and larger boat he acquired before leaving Agade. Eleazer agreed that transporting merchandise, commodities, or even metal by boat was easier, pleasanter, and more economical than by caravan. All the parties consented that Hankas should own a half interest for his silver investment but the boat would remain his personal property. Of course, the business would defray the cost of its operation. Avram was able to inscribe the agreement on clay tablets in triplicate, one to file in the

Temple of Szin and the other two for Terach and Hankas. It also was decided that for greater convenience Hankas and Sipara should live at the Terach house. But the skipper insisted on observing the day of rest on Avram's farm.

While the men discussed their business affairs Keturah and Sipara drove off sightseeing. The wagon passed the temples, the royal palace, and went through the wider streets where the wealthy and the fashionable resided. To Sipara the city compared favorably with the much older Agade but fell woefully short of the splendors of Babylon, which she called the most wonderful place in the world. She fairly glowed at the very recollection of the great city:

"I won't mention the great buildings, the tall, enormous temples, the wide avenues lined with beautiful trees. To appreciate these wonders you must see them yourself. What I like best is the life there. No people enjoy themselves as much. Their parties are the gayest anywhere. The women know how to flirt yet stay within the bounds of good taste. The men with their oiled hair and platted beards pay compliments gracefully and without too much exaggeration. They hint at subtly what they are really after. On the street a man will come up to an unattended woman and start talking love to her yet without giving offense. I might walk with my husband and a pretty woman would stop and invite him to her house and say to me courteously that I could remain in a comfortable place while he is enjoying himself. Oh I just love Babylon."

"Didn't you have gay parties in Agade?" questioned Keturah.

"Oh yes, until I married Hankas. Then all the good times stopped."

"Why?"

"Well, you see Hankas's idea of pleasure is to talk about

his strange God to someone, anybody, no matter who he may be. And his God does not want people to get a thrill out of life."

"Why did you marry him if his ways are not like yours?"

"My dear, a widow without means hasn't much choice. When my husband was killed in Hammurabi's war he left me nothing at all. I had to go back to my family. They are poor and can hardly feed themselves. I became too much of a burden. I grabbed the first man who asked me."

"What kind of man was your first husband?"

"He was a petty officer in a Babylonian company stationed in Agade. His family was well-to-do and sent him silver with every boat. We lived up to everything he received and the extras he could squeeze out of the townsmen for favors or for letting them get by with some infringement. We had a great time together and belonged to what they call in Babylon "the smart set." Sometimes we would revel all night. Everyone drank heavily. The next morning I would find myself in some man's bed and my husband would open his eyes in some woman's home. But this was too good to last. When war broke out he was called to join his regiment in Babylon. I understand he fell in the attack on Larsa."

"I am surprised you tell me all this. Suppose I go and tell?"

"You won't. But if you do I can always deny it and say you are jealous and afraid that I will take your husband away. You probably don't know how easily men can be fooled."

"It strikes me how funny the gods shift things about," observed Keturah. "Here you would give anything to be in Babylon yet I have the opportunity to live there and refuse to go."

She told Sipara all about her "father" and how he resented his daughter being only a concubine and how he offered to take her to Babylon. There she could marry some nobleman and become a great lady. But she preferred remaining on the farm in Haran.

"All I can say is that I would love to be in your place," Sipara assured her. "But remember, should you ever decide to go, I shall go along."

"Sipara, don't tell me you would leave your husband?"

"I would exchange Babylon for Haran any time."

## V

Weeks passed before Keturah could get to the Temple of Szin. Again Zaradan was occupied and while waiting in the anteroom the *kadosh* informed her that Habliya wished to see her. Keturah had decided to ignore the priestess whose ambitions were no concern of hers. Disturbed by this persistence Keturah made up her mind to cut off all relations with an evil person whose mere acquaintance was a liability.

"So you are avoiding me," greeted Habliya without the artificial smile or sweet manner she assumed before.

"Your affairs are none of my business," asserted Keturah, impatiently.

"This is very much your affair if you know what is good for you."

"I don't care to get mixed up in a temple intrigue. I came here merely to know whether the high priest heard from my father."

"And nothing else? Are you sure?" The priestess dragged her words slowly and her jeering tone made them even more insulting.

"I don't have to sit here and put up with your insinuations," responded Keturah with as much dignity as she could summon, and rose to go.

"No? Of course the erstwhile *kedashe* of Ur and present concubine would not mind if her husband knew that she wiggles her tail while in Zaradan's arms. But that might be old stuff to him."

When Keturah entered the priest's chamber she burst into tears. He took her into his arms and tried to soothe her. Finally, she calmed down and told him all about Habliya's demands and insults. He assured her that he would take care of the priestess, who would be reduced in rank should she do anything disturbing to her. To raise Keturah's spirits and make her responsive to his embraces he informed her that he had quieted down the farmers; that they would cause no further trouble about her husband's worship of his strange God.

After Keturah's departure Zaradan sent for the priestess and pretended to be in high dudgeon.

"I thought you had sense but am disappointed to find you merely a venom-tongued vixen. If you think this girl can sway temple policy then you are simply a village scold. Don't you know that temple positions are used as pawns in the diplomatic chess game? The power of appointment does not rest solely with me. The king also has something to say. Virtually every family has a girl to spare; one too homely to marry; another whose virtue had suffered a lapse; a third with a child showing up before marriage. This might be true in a palace as in a peasant's hut. The post of high priestess in a prominent temple is often a safe retreat for a king's daughter. So if you wreck your spleen on this girl you will be degraded, I promise, to the rank of a common *kedashe,* the paramour of the contemptible rabble."

"You forget that I am the daughter of an Amorite chieftain."

"And please remember that her father, the former high

priest in Ur, is high up in the counsels of King Hammurabi."

Riding in the wagon towards the farm Keturah sat silent and distracted. Davarah finally asked, "My dear little Zirru, is anything troubling you? Tell mother what is wrong."

Keturah opened her heart and relieved herself of the burden that was oppressing her and concluded, "Now, what I have been doing with each of these priests is wrong, I know. Avram will never forgive me if he ever finds out. But I will have the inner satisfaction of knowing that what I did was necessary and even essential to the welfare and happiness of two families and the people depending on them."

Davarah kissed her "daughter" and said, "Men never know what women go through for the ones they love. Their sacrifices often count for nothing and remain unappreciated where a man's pride is hurt."

When the two women arrived at the farm they were told that Nahor had come for Avram because Terach was very sick. Having no wagon handy Avram went reluctantly along with his brother. When they reached Terach's house their father had already expired. Following the custom the entire family present sat up all night, probably to watch the dead lest the *shaidim* carry off the body. Eleazer and Hankas joined the family in the night vigil. An issue arose as to the place of burial. Each son wanted the father to lie in his land. Nahor argued that as the older son he had prior right. Furthermore, there was a vault under his house in keeping with the custom prevailing in Ur. In the chapel under the home the dead remained a member of the household; he could consume the food left for him and not be compelled to eat the dust in Aralu. Terach had believed in such rites and did at no time worship the God which Avram discovered. Both Emtelai and Eleazer had to agree with Nahor's contention.

On the following day Terach was interred in the chapel underneath Nahor's house in the presence of his entire family, the servants, the dependents, and the laborers of all three households. A simple epitaph can be read in the Book of Genesis: AND TERACH DIED IN HARAN.

# 22

# The Transgressor

THE PASSING OF TERACH WROUGHT LITTLE CHANGE IN THE daily life of his clan. Emtelai, though aging, managed the household as before. The presence of Eleazer lent a comforting sense of security. The servants and slaves continued their performance of the household duties without neglecting their care of the stall in the market place. The prodding of Hankas forced Sipara, Emtelai and Sarai, to spend every seventh day on the farm. Milcah, finding Avram's house lively on the rest day, brought along her younger boys. Her Bethuel needed little urging when he knew that Sarai would be there, although none too happy when she brought along Amihud, son of Sanu-Rimmon. Lot felt isolated because of the feud between Keturah and Sarai. But when he sensed that Bethuel resented Amihud he became fast friends with his cousin.

Nahor's urging of his father to provide for his heirs, meaning himself, resulted in the cancellation of Avram's debt in the sum of 800 shekels in silver secured by a second mortgage on the farm and the livestock. This made Avram free of debt, except for the long term purchase money mortgage to the priests of Hebat at Nuzu.

The rest of the estate remained intact except for the allowance that supported Emtelai and Sarai, besides the necessary expense of maintaining the home, the servants, and slaves. Terach had directed Emtelai to set aside a dowry for Sarai. She also, at her discretion, could provide for Eleazer and Lot such sums as she deemed reasonable. Terach had appointed Eleazer the executor and Nahor became infuriated when told of the will.

Hankas got along very well with Eleazer and learned from him everything he could about trading. The stall in the market place continued to be the outlet for the goods, wares, and commodities they bought and sold. A merchant approached Eleazer and showed him a large shipment of iron ware that had just arrived. It was more than he himself could handle conveniently. Eleazer agreed to take part of the iron at the original cost inscribed in the bill of sale on the clay tablets that was signed and witnessed. Eleazer and Hankas decided to carry the iron by boat to Babylon and bring back in exchange women's finery, jewelry, perfumes, and such artifacts as could be sold in Haran. When Sipara heard the name Babylon she pricked up her ears and insisted on going along. Whenever Eleazer went on a caravan Terach had done the overseeing at the stall. Now Emtelai, Davarah, Milcah, and even Sarai took their turns in watching the customers, the servants and slaves, the weights and measures, the barters and exchanges.

## II

It took little time for the boat to course down the Belikh and the Purattu to reach Babylon. Both Eleazer and Hankas had but a superficial acquaintance with the great city. Nor did they know any of the merchants and consequently had no inkling of what transpired behind the magnificent façade. They were surprised by the lack of interest displayed at the mention of iron. The shrewd traders exhibited little appreciation for the possibilities in the new metal. When Hankas demonstrated the superior hardness of his iron dagger over bronze a successful trader declared, "What you say may be true but I am here to increase my silver and not to educate people. Why waste breath in demonstrating the merits of a new metal when we can sell the bronze or flint articles with no trouble at all?"

Eleazer went to a leading merchant and demonstrated the relative strength and hardness of both metals. He then asked why the military leaders did not discard the bronze armor for the superior resistance of iron. The merchant answered, "The smelters know about iron but are ignoring the new metal deliberately. The reason is simple. They have their plants and know how to mix copper with tin to produce bronze. These smelters are skilled in making armor out of bronze to fit large numbers of soldiers without the necessity of alterations. To manufacture armor out of iron will necessitate a complete overhauling of their apparatus. They are doing well so why disturb the present state of things?"

"Don't the army chiefs know that with a superior weapon in their hands the defeat of an enemy is inevitable?"

"The military heads are hopelessly conservative. They do not believe in change. Besides, they point to their own success in conquering an empire for the king. Success is their best argument."

"Who can bring about the necessary change?"

"Only King Hammurabi himself and he is getting too old for new ideas."

"But as a leading subject of your king and a prominent

merchant, haven't you a responsibility in such an important matter? The Hittites have iron weapons, armored chariots, and big strong animals they call horses. Soon they will become invincible. Isn't it your duty to start an agitation about changing over to superior weapons if for no other reason then to insure your own safety?"

"He who first attempts any change for the public good will get into trouble. I am without any ambition to become a martyr. But there is a far simpler reason. The army is my best customer. If I antagonize the powerful military chieftains, I will surely lose my business. No, I will leave it to the king's advisers and the wise Chaldeans."

"Getting down to practical things, what shall I do with my iron? Please advise me."

"Take it back and sell it in Haran."

"It is unbelievable that Babylon the great should be far behind the times," complained Eleazer. "It is jeopardizing the safety of the empire and its people."

"But it is the best place in the world to live and it will remain so," declared the merchant, his confidence unshaken.

Eleazer spoke more wisely than he knew. More than a century later the Hittites swooped down on Babylon. They conquered and all but demolished the city that Hammurabi had made great.

At the evening meal the three sat discussing the new dilemma. To return with the entire boat load intact would be a confession of failure, without counting the cost of traveling back and forth. Hankas thought of consulting his son who was in the midst of the business world. Sipara came up with a suggestion that somehow had escaped the men. Why not consult Sabbattu whom everyone considered wise? Eleazer wondered what the ex-priest's feelings would be toward him. Surely not friendly after the refusal to become the steward of so notable a personage. Sipara said she would go alone and convey the regards of his daughter. She could then ascertain his attitude towards everyone. But seeking anyone in the large city would be like sifting the well-known haystack. Hankas said he would ask his son who was in a position to find out. Meanwhile Eleazer and Sipara would inquire at the various administration buildings where the business of ruling an empire was conducted.

On the following morning they first tried the large building near the royal palace situated on the grand canal with the main entrance on the wide avenue lined with trees. It proved to be the right place and the captain of the guard ordered one of his men to conduct Sipara to a spacious room facing the canal. Sabbattu was clad in the raiment usually worn by the select group of Chaldeans, the wise men of the East, who had the distinction of advising King Hammurabi. The room was elegantly furnished. Tapestries hung on the walls and thick rugs lay strewn on the floor of burnt brick. Sipara introduced herself as a close friend of Keturah. The former priest received her cordially and inquired about his daughter, the state of her health, the number of her children.

"She is truly beautiful, Adoni, and sends you her love. She is eager to see her father and wonders when my lord will visit Haran."

"We who serve the king have no time for ourselves. I can leave only when his majesty sends me on a mission."

She informed him of Terach's death, about Avram's farm, and of her husband, the friend of Avram and fellow worshipper of El Elyon. He asked whether his daughter ever expected to come and live with her father. She answered, "I am doing everything possible to induce Keturah to go to Babylon. I am willing to come along with her.

My husband is a religious fanatic like his friend Avram. He does not care to enjoy this life. But I do, and Babylon is the place for me. I am sure he would release me."

A slave announced that someone was waiting to be received. Sabbattu invited her to return and take the midday meal with him in his house. Was there anyone waiting for her? She answered that Eleazer was outside.

"Bring him along. I wish to see him."

## III

The boat rowed by two oarsmen sped along on the grand canal. Sabbattu pointed out the various temples, palatial dwellings, and public buildings. The boat stopped at a dock that led to an imposing mansion. The ex-priest conducted his guests into his home which was furnished with the best of furniture, curtains, carpets, gold, and silverware obtainable in Babylon. Statues of the higher gods made of bronze, alabaster, and diorite graced the hall, the living room, and the walks in the garden. A young woman entered and Sabbattu introduced her as coming originally from Susa, the capital of Elam. She was of middle height, rather dark, olive-complexioned with flashing brown eyes and black hair curled up into a knot, liberally rouged, and fairly reeking of perfume and musk. She eyed Sipara suspiciously and appeared to be wondering if the visitor had come to replace her as mistress to the lord of the mansion.

Two female slaves served wine with salted burnt almonds as a fillip for more wine. The four entered the dining hall and the slaves brought in barley soup, fresh fish from the river fried in olive oil, bread, fruit, and dried figs cooked in honey. The small talk centered about the great cities and their peculiarities. The enormous palace in Mari exceeded in size and room count any building anywhere not excepting Babylon itself. Eleazer was not sure whether it was larger than the vast palace in Knossos. Of course, Babylon surpassed in size and splendor every other city, yet Eleazer thought that the great cities of Egypt had more charm and possibly more glamor. Carchemish like Haran was up and coming but more crude than even Dameshek or Tyre. Antiquity perpetuated a peculiar atmosphere since no place could compare in rare quaintness with such old Sumerian cities as Ur, Erech, Nippur, Larsa or Eridu.

The former priest ordered his Elamite mistress rather peremptorily to show Sipara the house and grounds while he and the visitor talked of business matters which the women would no doubt find dull and perhaps boring. Sabbattu questioned Eleazer closely about the affairs of each member of the Terach clan. He wanted to know how Terach's estate descended to his heirs, who was Sipara's husband and his connection with the family. Appearing satisfied with the frank answers, he then asked their purpose in coming to Babylon. Eleazer informed him of the iron and his surprise in being unable to dispose of the hard metal. He repeated the conversation with the most prominent merchant in Babylon about the myopia of the military heads in failing to perceive the superiority of iron over bronze for the armed forces.

"Was the merchant's name Zab-Ahiramu?" interrupted Sabbattu.

"Yes, Adoni," answered Eleazer.

"Did he refuse to take your iron in exchange for merchandise or jewels?"

"He did, my lord."

"Have you any other comments? I find them interesting."

"The trouble is, if I may express an opinion, the Babylonians are blinded by their victories. They consider themselves invincible and like the Egyptians look down with contempt upon all other nations. They regard the Hittites as savages hardly above the level of beasts. They disregard people who have learned how to take a certain rocky ore out of the ground and smelt it into the hardest known substance. Out of the smelted iron they cast swords, spears, shields, and armor. They have tamed the horse, which is almost twice as large and five times as strong as the donkey. They hitch these splendid, powerful animals to their chariots. With superior weapons and better transportation they are becoming a formidable military power. But the army chiefs of Babylon choose to regard iron as inferior to the much softer bronze. I wonder whether a great king such as Hammurabi understands that the Hittites are becoming a force among the great powers and chiefly because they have and know how to utilize iron and horses."

The former high priest listened attentively to Eleazer's words and sat musing: "What a splendid argument this would make before the learned Chaldeans. Strange no one speaks of Hittites or of iron. Yet who can gainsay the truth in the remarks of this young man who has the intellect for an advisor to a king? What a pity he did not become my steward. But why not take the boat load of iron off his hands? I can always bully-rag the tartan Nabunergal into buying it for the army. All I have to say is that out of friendship I am letting him get the credit for testing out new and superior weapons. If he is not interested, then I will speak to Hammurabi myself. That will make him jump. I'll see that Zab-Ahiramu gets a good price for the metal. This young man may be useful even in Haran. I believe he and Avram are completely honest."

"Eleazer, I want to talk with the same candor that I

spoke to Terach. He never disappointed me nor did he ever betray my confidence. In spite of what some may think I was very helpful to the family, as you well know. Now keep all this in the strictest confidence. Do you promise?"

"I do," replied Eleazer.

"You wonder whether Hammurabi understands what goes on in the world. I also doubt it. He is no longer as aware as he used to be. After all he has reigned a long time. Now he is getting old. He may show wisdom in not expanding the empire at this stage of his life. For that reason I am not angry although deeply disappointed."

"I don't know whether you are aware of it but I was very helpful to the king. Without my assistance he would never have taken over Ur, or southern Sumer, or all of Elam with hardly the loss of a soldier. My acts, beneficial to him and to those lands and their people, have lowered my reputation in the world. I know it. But did Hammurabi appreciate it? Well, I suppose he showed the usual gratitude of kings. Oh, he gave me plenty of honor. I am reckoned among his select Chaldean advisers. I stand near him on all public celebrations. People think I have great power but it is all empty and without substance. I expected to be appointed a *patesi* of some province or at least of some city. But nothing happened. Then I began to plan for a worthwhile post in some land outside the empire. I schemed up an alliance of nations, tribes, kingdoms, and cities under the hegemony of Babylon. Hammurabi approved of it. As you know, I set out for Canaan with a troop of 500. This venture resulted in the conquest of five city kingdoms in the plain. We returned without the loss of a single life. These cities are now paying tribute to Hammurabi. I thought I demonstrated how easily he could take all of Canaan, with Philistia and Phoenicia thrown in. But our king did nothing and lost the golden opportunity. I expected to be rewarded with some governorship. All I got was the nice office you saw and there I sit like a faithful dog watching the tribute come in from Sodom, Gomorrah, Admah, Zeboiim, and Zoar."

The unpleasant recital seemed to depress Sabbattu, who reached for a goblet of wine to banish the ill humor that was gripping him. He pointed to a filled goblet but Eleazer declined while wondering why the ex-priest should reveal such intimate matters to not only a stranger but a social inferior. In fact, it seemed surprising that one so prominent should have a commoner at his table. There was some proposition forthcoming and it was necessary to have a clear head to match wits with so shrewd a character who could be quite unscrupulous. After draining the wine cup Sabbattu continued:

"But expensive living turned out to be my biggest mistake. In Babylon I was immediately surrounded by flatterers, by toadies who took me in tow and showed me how to conduct myself in the world's capital. They constantly talked of my high prospects and the necessity of identifying myself with the aristocracy. I must live among them to be one of them. I should entertain lavishly to build up contacts with the great and the influential who alone could bring about my promotion to high office. They picked this house and selected the most expensive furniture. I did not know until later that these sycophants collected commissions on everything I purchased. Under their direction I entertained the nobility profusely but found they did not reciprocate. I lived among them but did not become one of them. They accepted my lavish entertainment but did nothing for me in return.

"Soon I began to realize that I was living beyond my means and that my wealth was diminishing. No appointment as governor or *patesi* was forthcoming. If I went on at this rate I would soon be in poverty. The king gave me a small allowance as one of his Chaldeans. I had to put a stop to this extravagance with everything going out and nothing coming in. I dismissed these toadies and ceased the high living. I took stock and found that my resources had shrunk to an alarming extent. It was necessary to make up the sums I had spent. I was told that lending out gold and silver on interest was profitable. Merchants paid interest anywhere from 20 to 50 per cent. I obtained the services of an agent reputed to be an expert in making loans.

"Again I had to learn something to my cost. I had no idea of the dishonesty and corruption that prevailed in the business world of Babylon. Living beyond means, I find, is an accepted practice. Merchants put on a big front to conceal the emptiness behind the façade. Competition is too keen to enable them to be prosperous. Most of them are in debt and looking for someone to bail them out. So when my agent offered to lend them gold or silver, they grabbed the opportunity to obtain more than they needed. How much my agent secretly got for himself I shall never know. So after receiving several instalments all payments stopped. All I could do was to foreclose my chattel mortgages and take over stocks of merchandise that I did not want. You spoke of the prominent merchant Zab-Ahiramu. I made him a loan which he could not pay back. Now I find myself a partner with more than half a share in his business. But I don't want to be a merchant.

"Now why am I telling you all of this? Simply to let you know the difference between the Terach family and the sharpers of this big city. I do appreciate the honesty of Terach in his dealings with me. I also have confidence in you. It is regrettable that you did not become my steward.

You would have done very well for yourself. But I wish to do business with your group. In fact, I am ready to transfer my holdings from Babylon to Haran. We can start immediately. I shall instruct my partner, Zab-Ahiramu, to take all your iron in exchange for such wares as you can use. Be careful about prices. Zab-Ahiramu is very tricky. As for the iron we will sell it to the army. The tartan Nabunergal is very friendly to me. At least he says so. Now as for the rest, you can fill up your boat with all the merchandise you can use out of the stocks that I foreclosed. You may take it all on credit and pay when you can. I know you will find these deals profitable. In fact, I am considering a partnership with your group. Our combination could become the biggest business house in Haran."

Eleazer became highly elated at this unexpected stroke of luck, a veritable windfall. The problem of iron suddenly evaporated, and to their obvious advantage. But what was behind all this? The priest was no philanthropist even if at one time he bragged that he was. Eleazer remembered how ruthlessly he could act when thinking that Terach was in his power. One must be very careful with so unscrupulous a person. Yet why did Sabbattu bare his innermost feelings with such candor? He sounded truthful enough.

But what Eleazer did not know were the anxieties which the priest did not disclose. Trouble threatened to build up against him in Ur. His relatives had sent a message that a priest of Nannar accompanied by several guards had come to their home and asked many questions: Why did they acquire the house? Who purchased it for them and from whom? Were they related to the former high priest Sabbattu? Where was he now? What did they pay for the building? What did they do for a living?

Where did they get the silver with which to make the purchase? Did they also buy the woven cloth from Davarah and the images from Terach? The relatives said that they answered every question truthfully as far as they knew. Did they do right?

This message was disturbing. Did it mean that the temple authorities were seeking the treasure that had disappeared? His memory reverted to the hectic days when Ur was taken over. The king's demeanor was gracious to the high priest toward whom everyone in the temple acted with marked obsequiousness. Then he accompanied Hammurabi to Elam. The quick capitulation of Kudur-Lagamur appeared to enhance his power and prestige. The royal entourage returned to Ur and immediately the king's manner seemed to have undergone a change. It was courteous and correct but no longer warm or friendly. The high priesthood went to Khar-Sak and Sabbattu accompanied the king of Babylon. He waited in vain for an appointment to a post. It only occurred to him after receiving the message from Ur that the priests must have complained to Hammurabi and charged him with rifling the temple treasury. They might have started an investigation and probably ascertained that he sent out not only packages but also a large wagon with guards who removed Terach, his family, and Keturah on that fearful night in the heavy rainfall.

Was it possible that the temple authorities were determined to locate the missing gold and silver? Some of the priests might come to Babylon to investigate the source of his wealth. He might be called upon to explain how he was able to purchase a sumptuous mansion and live in the style of a rich nobleman. His involvement in trading was generally known, at least to many merchants. How shortsighted to expose himself to suspicions and invite an investigation into his affairs. On hearing of Terach's death he felt momentarily relieved. But soon the misgivings returned. Terach's family also knew about the parcels and although secondary witnesses their testimony was by no means worthless. Obviously he must divest himself of all visible holdings; he could not start too soon. The presence of Eleazer was truly providential. He must take a chance with some honest people. At any rate, it was his only course. Eleazer noting Sabbattu's preoccupation waited and finally ventured, "Adoni, I do appreciate your generous offer. I know that Avram and the rest of the family will be grateful. But we would not care to over-extend our resources or our credit. I do not want to buy more than we can pay for. Credit is only a temporary accommodation. The time comes when the obligations must either be met or insolvency stares one in the face. We will take whatever goods or wares we can use but only on consignment. We will pay for what we sell and reserve the privilege of returning all unsold articles. Of course, we want the prices low enough to meet competition."

On the following day Eleazer and Hankas went to the storehouse of Zab-Ahiramu. Yes, he knew about the iron but wished to examine the wares before hauling so heavy a load to his warehouse. All three went to the boat and Eleazer produced two shields, one of bronze and the other of iron. He handed the merchant an iron-tipped spear at the same time inviting him to strike each shield with all his might. His blow made a sharp dent in the bronze but left hardly a visible mark on the iron buckler. "Yes," admitted the merchant, "iron is much tougher than bronze. I see how much advantage the ironclad soldier would have over bronze armor. But will the military heads see it? That's the question."

In exchange for the iron Zab-Ahiramu filled the Hankas

boat with merchandise and a wooden box packed with jewelry, semi-precious stones, perfumes, musk, dyes, and paints for face and hair. Sabbattu hired an additional boat and ordered his agent at the storehouse to store it with such goods and wares as Eleazer might select. The bills on consignment were inscribed on clay tablets.

## III

Several years slipped by while Avram farmed with moderate success; his herdsmen steadily increased the number of goats, sheep, cattle, and asses. Emtelai aged and Davarah's energies began to wane. She had to give up weaving and sold her business to her daughter Milcah. Keturah gave birth to another son and named him Medan.

Eleazer and Hankas carried on their trading by boat and sometimes by caravans but maintained their headquarters in the stall at Haran's market place. They managed to dispose of a goodly portion of the goods and wares sent by Sabbattu, who at times accepted payment in iron, which began to sell in Babylon. Quite a sum accumulated that was owing to the priest but he instructed Eleazer either to lend it out on interest or place it in a metal casket properly sealed and store it in the Temple of Szin under Avram's name. Yet he preferred that they use his silver in their trading but with the proviso that half of the net profit go to him. He did not require the cash. All he wanted was a strict accounting of each transaction for his personal records.

The anxieties of the former high priest were by no means groundless. After Eleazer and Hankas left he immediately determined to dispose of the mansion with its furniture for whatever sum he could realize. Finally, he succeeded in selling the property for half the amount he paid. He then moved into a poor but respectable neighborhood occupied largely by his fellow Chaldeans and lived modestly. Just then two priests arrived from Ur and laid their complaints before the king. Hammurabi listened and had his scribe take down their charges on a tablet. The king sent for the former high priest of Nannar and ordered him to refute the accusations.

"I trust your majesty appreciates that my name became tarnished with the capture of Ur. But my conscience is quite clear. I feel that I rendered my countrymen a great service in saving the city and its inhabitants from destruction by fire and sword. I knew that Ur could never withstand your majesty's onslaught. But the people of Ur think differently. To them I am the traitor who delivered the ancient city to the enemy."

"What about that house in Ur which you purchased after leaving the city?"

"Your sacred majesty, the owner of this house was the sculptor of my temple. He made images of the gods and had them sold at one of our temple stalls. He was my protégé. In fact my daughter was raised in his family. I helped him in every way I could. But these artists are impractical. He would fall into debt and I had to lend him silver. Over the years the amounts accumulated until he owed me a considerable sum. Prior to your majesty's conquest he, together with his family, left Ur and took my daughter along. They settled in Haran. When your majesty's force of 500 armed men journeyed to Canaan we sailed up the river as far as Haran. There I saw my daughter at the home of the sculptor, Terach. He insisted that I take his house for the debt he owed me. The conveyance was inscribed at the Temple of Szin in Haran."

"But you acquired an expensive mansion here in Babylon, didn't you?"

"Oh king, live forever! This mansion was never mine. I

simply acted for someone who deemed it necessary for reasons of his own to conceal his identity. I do not enjoy living in such magnificence. My parents were poor and I lived quite simply at the Temple of Nannar. The mansion was sold sometime ago and I now live in a modest house among the Chaldean sages. I don't care to live pretentiously."

"How do you support yourself? Do you receive any subsidy from my government?" questioned the king.

"Your majesty, I do get a small allowance as a Chaldean sage. But it is quite petty and far from sufficient even for my modest needs. I came to Babylon with some silver I had accumulated through the years mostly from gifts or family bequests. On the advice of friends I loaned out this silver on interest. My agent proved unskillful. I had to foreclose my mortgages, to use legal terminology, and thus became the owner of several stalls in the market place. It is the incomes from these shops that support me."

"Have you any silver or valuables stored for safekeeping in any temple here or elsewhere?"

"None, your majesty."

The king dismissed Sabbattu then turned to his vizier:

"This scoundrel thinks he has covered his trail but he has left some tracks open. We could ask him embarrassing questions but let them hang over his head. While we have little doubt of his guilt we must not forget that he did render important service in Ur and Elam. Let him keep his loot. This temple is no doubt receiving other and perhaps more valuable offerings. It is unfortunate that religion should have such leadership, yet these priests can be useful. They can help us govern better than more virtuous men. When the Ur priests come to you just advise them to go home. We are investigating the charges and will notify them of our decision."

## IV

Sarai had developed into a beautiful girl and many young men looked hungrily at her. But Amihud, the son of Sanu-Rimmon, admired her most; in fact he was truly in love with her. He would see her at least once a day if only to read the clay tablet he had inscribed that morning in the class at the Temple of Szin. He would also tell her of the things studied or discussed. Amihud was no scholar; one might even call him an indifferent student. He would gladly quit the classroom to go into building with his father. But Sanu-Rimmon nursed the ambition to see his son become a priest and therefore insisted that he attend the temple school.

One morning the teacher was indisposed and his classes were suspended. Amihud left the priest's division and walked to the temple compound to get a fruit drink. It was hot and the student felt a burning thirst. He opened his scrip and found no barley or anything with which to barter for some fruit juice. While leaning against the burnt-brick wall that shaded the pathway from the sun, a priestess walked by going to her quarters. Habliya knew the youth and had smiled her greetings before to him. For the first time she spoke and asked whether anything was ailing him.

"I am only thirsty. I would enjoy some fruit juice but have nothing in my scrip."

"Oh, you poor boy. I have some citrus mixed with honeyed water. Follow me to my room but don't let any man see you. I don't mind the women' they do far worse."

At her invitation he sat on her couch and enjoyed the refreshing drink. She asked many questions. What city was his original home? His father's occupation? Why did he leave Erech for Haran? Then she asked what was always interesting to women. Did he have a sweetheart? He told of his love for Sarai, her exquisite beauty, her subtle mind, but alas she did not love him.

"What? A handsome boy like you? What's the matter with her? Didn't you take her in your arms, kiss her passionately, take off her dress, and make her love you?"

"She belongs to a family which believes that when a girl comes to her bridegroom's bed she should be a virgin."

"What kind of people are they?"

"Arameans. They guard their women closely and permit no love making with their girls and more especially with their married women."

"Your Sarai must be a cold fish. Doesn't she love someone?"

"Yes, she loves her half-brother. Both are from one father but different mothers."

"Then she can marry him legally."

"But he is already married. At least Keturah is his concubine."

"Keturah did you say? Is she young and pretty?"

"She is very pretty."

"Is she the daughter of a high priest and the concubine of a farmer living about 10 or 12 miles out of the city?"

"Yes. How do you know her?"

"Are the two young women good friends?"

"No. They hate each other. There is some kind of jealousy there, I suppose. Sarai is very proud and never mentions her."

"Do you want to please your Sarai? Then let me see her. I know something that will interest her very much. She will love you for it. Bring her to the temple on the next new moon festival, say about midday and to this room.

Now since you had no instruction today I will give you a lesson and a very important one. I will teach you how to make a girl love you."

Habliya took him in her arms, kissed him, and removed his kilt.

A fortnight later Amihud brought Sarai to the temple of Szin. She had little difficulty in getting away. Emtelai was hardly aware of what transpired about her, although she had her lucid moments. Habliya acquainted Sarai with the secret amour that went on between Keturah and Zaradan. Sarai listened and declared icily, "I don't know why you told me all of this. I am not interested in the least."

# 23

# Get Thee Out

HANKAS AND SIPARA WERE DRESSING AND GETTING READY TO depart for the farm to celebrate the day of rest. Eleazer and Sarai had decided to remain with Emtelai. While the servants and the slaves could look after her it seemed to Eleazer that someone more close to her should at all times remain in the house. His anxiety was justified only too soon. Walking about the house Emtelai fell down several steps leading to the basement and broke her hip bone. She was immediately lifted and placed in her bed. Hankas and Sipara drove off to the farm and notified Avram. Eleazer went to the Temple of Szin for a doctor and refused the proffered exorcisor or priest. The physician could do very little other than bind her hips so that the broken bone might mend.

Avram left the *Shabbat* service and feast to the direction of Hankas and rushed in his wagon to be with his mother. He took along Davarah and the Hittite woman whose husband had deserted her. He found Emtelai in temperature and in pain. During a short period of clarity she wanted to speak with her son. When everyone left the room she said, "My Avram. I don't know how long I shall live. But remember Sarai will soon be alone. She is beautiful and has a good head. She would make a good wife for you. She has no equal anywhere except Ningal and Irnina, Marduk, Ningal"; she trailed off into incoherence. She never recovered lucidity and died three days later. Again the matter of burial came up. Avram wanted his mother to lie on his farm near the shrine of El Elyon. But he had to agree that it was more fitting for his mother to lie next to her husband, Avram's father.

After the burial Avram and Davarah remained at the Terach home until Sarai protested that such attention to her was unnecessary. With Eleazer, Hankas, and Sipara in the house she was neither lonely nor isolated. Avram returned to the farm with Davarah but made it his business to see Sarai at least once a fortnight. This was besides every *Shabbat* when Eleazer, Hankas, and Sipara insisted on bringing her to the farm.

Avram found himself thinking about Sarai quite often. She was no doubt beautiful but some strange attraction about her, some elusive charm, drew him. Yet there was a subtle, distant quality in her that made him feel he could never penetrate the innermost recesses of her mind, her heart, her soul. She was affectionate enough and always appeared happy to see him, yet somehow he felt a distance that in some vague way seemed unbridgeable.

About half a year or so later Eleazer received a message from Zab-Ahiramu that he was short of ironware, the use of which had taken hold in Babylon. He could use a boatload of not only weapons but of such articles as hatchets, hammers, bolts, nails, bars, and whatever other household utensils the Hittites made. He would even accept an additional boatload and pay the freight from Carchemish to Babylon. Thus their connection with Babylon was growing more and more profitable. The use of Sabbattu's silver enabled Eleazer and Hankas to purchase at bargain prices the goods and wares of merchants who were in distress. Hankas hesitated about making the journey alone. He lacked the self-confidence to handle so extensive an assignment all by himself and therefore insisted that Eleazer accompany him. Sipara of course expressed her desire to go along.

While the three were preparing for the journey Avram visited Sarai and invited her to live on the farm, at least during the absence of her in-dwellers. She refused for the reason that she was not lonely. Avram showed impatience.

"But you cannot live alone in this big house. You seem to forget that the servants and slaves are not young and are no longer vigorous enough to protect you from robbers or malefactors. I suppose you know that beautiful girls are often stolen and sold in foreign lands to a king or a chieftain or even to common brigands overloaded with gold or silver."

"Oh, but I am not that beautiful." She laughed teasingly and seemed to enjoy his annoyance. To plague him further she continued smiling roguishly while saying, "Why, I have a whole group of young men to protect me. They swear that they love me and would save me from such naughty evildoers. They now call me Sarah (princess) instead of Sarai."

"Sarai, or Sarah if you prefer, please talk seriously. I am concerned about your safety. As your brother I am responsible for you. Why can't you come with me? Call it a short visit for about a month or two, if you wish. I am actually begging you. Is it fair to refuse?" When she shook her head negatively, he asked, "Tell me why you refuse? You must have some good reason."

"If you must know the truth, Avram, I cannot be under the same roof with Keturah."

"Sarai, you are now an adult. Everyone says you are extremely bright. I thought you had outgrown childish nonsense. Suppose you did have a quarrel with her years ago. Can't you forgive and forget? I am sure Keturah would welcome you as a sister and a friend."

"I am not so sure. But my feelings against her are too deep. I can never forgive her. Nor can I become her friend. And the cause is not in what she did to me personally."

"Now you are getting me curious. If she did nothing to you personally, then what could she do to merit such hatred? I must know. Please tell me."

"Now don't press me, Avram. You will be sorry you asked. You will feel very much hurt."

"Sarai, don't keep me in such suspense. Say it no matter how I might feel. Come. Speak. Please do."

"Avram, Keturah has been unfaithful to you."

"She could not help herself," exploded Avram, yet seemed relieved. "She was forced to become the bride of Nannar in the temple at Ur."

"I am not speaking of Ur. I mean she has been false to you right here in Haran."

These words struck with the force of a club hitting him on the head. For a while he sat dazed as if in a stupor. Then he got up and paced the room in deep agitation. Finally he collected his senses sufficiently to stand over Sarai sitting on the divan and asked, "How do you know this? Are you not repeating idle gossip? This is a very serious matter. You should not speak of it unless you are certain of the truth."

She told Avram of the apparent intimacy between Amihud, son of Sanu-Rimmon, and the priestess and repeated Habliya's statements as fully as she could recall them. For a time Avram sat listening as if transfixed then got up and said, "When Eleazer and Hankas leave for Carchemish I shall send two or three of my strong Habiru to guard this house until they return."

Without another word Avram left. He got into the wagon, rode off sitting next to his Habiru driver brooding and trying to think the matter through. But his thoughts were halting and jerky. He felt a bitter anger towards Keturah and kept repeating inwardly: We were lovers since childhood. How could she do such a thing? This line kept revolving in his brain with the regularity of a refrain. Did her conduct grow out of a need to satisfy her lust? Strange she always displayed such tender regard toward him, even during those burning moments when locked in her passionate embrace. He could not coordinate his thoughts, which kept reverberating around the same theme until the wagon reached the farm.

The evening meal had been completed and Keturah was in the bedchamber with her youngest born. Davarah explained that they did not wait for him since he usually dined at the Terach home whenever he visited the city. She offered to serve him some food but he brusquely declared that he would not eat though he did want to talk to her. He repeated all that Sarai had said and wished to find out whether she knew how true the statements were.

Unfortunately they were true, corroborated Davarah. But Keturah was no mere wanton even if she did appear to act like a harlot. Davarah went fully into the reason for Keturah's conduct and ended, "This poor girl is determined to sacrifice herself for the good of you, me, and the entire family. It was an act of unselfish devotion. She feared you were in great peril and would suffer this time that which you so narrowly escaped in Ur. When I asked what if her conduct with the priest should come to light, she answered that if necessary she would give up her life for all of us so why not make this sacrifice?"

Throughout the night Avram wandered over his farm. No one disturbed him since the watchmen were fast asleep on their posts feeling certain that they would awaken the moment the cattle or sheep should start moving in mass. His first impulse had been painful anger toward Keturah. Yet after hearing from Davarah he gradually relented and slowly began to drift toward compassion. Basically he felt that Keturah was a gentle, kind soul and not inclined toward immoral or unchaste conduct. She had been frightened and felt the only way out was to submit her body to the high priest. Yet what she did was sinful in the sight of El Elyon. Even under the humane code of Hammurabi adultery was punishable by death.

Walking near the river reminded Avram of a scene that made him shudder whenever it reappeared in his memory. In Ur a woman was suspected of adultery. She pleaded her innocence and had to submit to the required water test. Among a large concourse Avram stood on the banks of the Purattu and saw the woman thrown into the river. If she could save herself she would be proclaimed innocent. If she drowned, then surely she was guilty. A surge of pity gripped him as he watched the struggling woman beating the water frantically, helplessly and then go under. A strong sense of injustice assailed him. "Was this a fair judgment of her guilt?" He inquired of his father and Terach answered, "The gods will never let the innocent drown." "But," protested Avram, "if she could only swim, then the judges would surely have declared her innocent."

He kept on walking in the darkness, thinking: Could he ever stand by and let his Keturah be thrown into the river? Wouldn't it be his duty to prevent such a miscarriage of justice? Again he felt anger surging within him, this time not toward Keturah but against such unfair, savage, unreasonable laws. In his agitation he could not think rationally. If Keturah was guilty, which clearly she was, then how could there be a miscarriage of justice? Suddenly it occurred to him that she was not liable to such punishment. She was not his lawful wife regardless of how he felt toward her. Legally she was a concubine and could not be guilty of adultery. But could the matter rest there?

He walked on cogitating. Should he send her away? He had the legal and moral right to do so. But wouldn't that be cruel? Who would take care of the children? He could not separate her from them. And what would become of her? She might in her desperation become a *kedashe* in the temple. He wouldn't care to see that. Wouldn't the boys then be raised in the temple and castrated to become *kedoshim*? He then recalled Sabbattu's offer to take her with him to Babylon. The ex-priest said something about marrying her to a nobleman and giving the boys the best education that the world capital had to offer. When they grew up these boys would no doubt get high posts in the government.

Strange he should feel such little affection for them. He had even spoken to Hankas about training them in the service of El Elyon. But the two older boys showed no interest. Actually they asked Hankas why they could not celebrate festivals at the Temple of Szin, or Ishtar, or Shamash, or Nergal, just like the other boys of the neighboring farms. But then Avram reasoned that the boys were reflecting Keturah's loyalty to her gods. A sudden suspicion crossed him. Were they his sons? Looking back he recalled that Zimran was born not long after leaving Ur, but he could no longer remember the time that intervened between her leaving the Temple of Nannar and his birth. As for the other boys they were born in Haran.

What should he do about Keturah? He could not go on cohabiting with her. Obviously there was but one course to follow and that path led to compassion. She must remain on the farm, raise her children, and live outwardly in the same manner as before. No one need even know about any change in their relations. Only he would sleep in a separate chamber and have no sexual relationship with her. By the time Avram reached this decision the chirping birds were announcing the dawn of a new day.

## II

Conditions favored Avram. Hammurabi's empire brought peace throughout Mesopotamia and even beyond. Egypt, temporarily in a decline and in no mood for expansion, posed no threat to her neighbors. The Phoenician cities of Tyre and Sidon were at the beginning of their trading careers and had not as yet accumulated sufficient wealth to tempt their covetous neighbors. The Hittites were gathering strength, power, and wealth with which to start an empire and a civilization. Thus the peaceful state of the Fertile Crescent enabled Avram to accumulate cattle and sheep, gold and silver.

Riches attract followers and multiply servants or slaves. The Habiru increased on the farm to several hundred. Hearing of the gracious generosity of the Sheikh Avram groups would come uninvited and remain without being told to leave. Some fitted in as shepherds or servants. But those who were not needed remained as voluntary slaves. This custom arose out of a stringent economy when the homeless or the dispossessed found mere existence a desperate struggle. In order to survive men sold themselves for a period of years as indentured servants; they practically were slaves. They and/or their families had at least food or shelter until better times would come. Curiously this custom was immortalized in the twenty-first chapter of Exodus beginning: "If thou acquire a Hebrew servant, six years he shall serve; and in the seventh he shall go out free without pay."

The aggressive missionizing of Hankas began to increase the crowds that assembled for the *Shabbat* feast. The boatman proselytized quite openly, both in Haran at the Terach house as well as on the farm. These activities influenced Avram as he began to lose the caution induced by the high priest Zaradan. People talked openly of their belief in El Shaddai and of His Almighty power. The group on the farm celebrating the day of rest seemed to take on the potency of an organized force. Avram became more and more aware that out of this nucleus a religious community might be fashioned.

The trading of Eleazer and Hankas was bringing in good profits. The use of Sabbattu's silver and the wares, merchandise, jewels, and women's finery which his agents sent from Babylon, increased their business substantially. The partners found it profitable to visit Babylon as often as possible. They always brought back a cargo that was salable. Sabbattu informed them that on their next journey he might return with them to Haran. Not only did he wish to visit his daughter but he had an important diplomatic matter to take up with the king.

Their journey lasted longer than usual. First, they had to sail down the Belikh and the Purattu to Babylon and pick up cargo to barter for iron at Carchemish. The upstream sail was slow and tedious. Selecting iron and bartering their cargoes took twice as long as their former visit to the Hittite metropolis. The heavy freight slowed the sailing downstream. In Babylon they also remained longer than they formerly had. More than five months had elapsed since leaving Haran. By this time Sabbattu was ready to sail with them back to Haran.

In the interim changes were slowly building up in Haran. Avram saw to it that Sarai was neither neglected nor left alone too often. He seized every possible occasion to drive his wagon to the city and stop to see and eat with her. On the eve of each rest day he offered to have her brought to the farm but Sarai objected to spending the night there. She preferred starting out early in the morning with the Habiru guardians in order to be present at the service and partake of the feast. When her turn came to watch at the market stall Avram offered to take her place but in any case to mind the shop with her.

It became quite obvious that Avram was courting his half-sister. No one expressed surprise; in fact everyone considered it quite normal for him to take a real wife. They knew that Keturah was only his concubine even if she neglected to wear the olive-shaped jade. Whenever the Habiru, stationed to protect Sarai, came to the farm they informed their wives or friends about Avram's constant and steady visits. One even said that he saw the Sheikh Avram kiss his future wife. One eavesdropper confided in friends that he heard the chieftain propose marriage but the beautiful girl answered that she would not be his wife as long as Keturah remained in his house.

The rumors circulating around the farm could not but reach Keturah. Some were reported by Davarah; other news items were brought by Lot, and even her first-born, Zimran, repeated some of the gossip. Their effect was naturally depressing. She had been hoping that Avram would get over his anger and resume conjugal relations. He had always treated her gently, tenderly, respectfully, and considerately to a degree that she felt she was his wife. Of course, she had gone through some devastating heartaches since the night when Davarah came into her bedroom to tell her that Avram had discovered her infidelity.

She could not sleep. During that harrowing night each moment seemed an hour while waiting for him to come and reproach her. Yet she felt that after a time he would forgive her. He was not the kind of man to chase after women. He would surely come back. How could he stay away remembering the passionate love she showered upon him? Should he even stray or be snared by some other woman she felt confident that he would return to her.

When the sun rose he had come into the bedroom and did reproach her, but he was more hurt and sorrow-laden than angry. He told her that Davarah had informed him of the reason for her unfaithful conduct. But why did she take it upon herself to solve such a serious problem? The least she could do was to consult him. Her sacrifice was totally unnecessary. He would never live with her again as man and wife but she could remain on the farm, occupy the same room and raise her children. Yet she continued to hope that he would relent and take her back. Could any man forget her endearing caress, her torrid embrace? He had too much kindness in him to be cruel. Surely he would get over his hurt and anger and everything between them should become as before.

"And now," she ruminated, "there is gossip that Avram is actually choosing Sarai as my successor. A successor?

But not a concubine. They are saying that he proposes to make her his lawful wife. Incredible! How can he select that miserable hypocrite, the sneaky Sarai? Why Emtelai herself called her an eavesdropper."

The latest item of gossip reached her: Sarai had refused to marry Avram as long as Keturah remained on the farm. This filled her with rage and fury. What impudence! What gall! Could Sarai dare to impose conditions? Why was she so confident? What made her so positive about Avram's feelings toward her? But what could she do about it now? Remain the discarded concubine? Or leave obligingly so that the snake Sarai could become the lawful wife of her own Avram? She just could not reconcile herself to the situation in which she found herself. She felt a strong need to unburden her feelings to someone near her own age. But Sipara was in Babylon. She had only her foster mother to fall back on. Davarah, no longer young, would no doubt give cautious advice, typical of the aging who no longer remember the problems, the heartaches, the temptations of youth. Davarah listened closely then observed:

"My little Zirru. I really don't know what to tell you. In my years of experience I've learned that life does not offer a solution to every problem. Time itself has a way of adjusting the seemingly impossible situations. If you leave the farm then Avram marries Sarai and you will be forgotten. If you stay you will prevent the marriage and bring on the resentment of the very person you wish to placate. What should you do? I have a rule which I follow. When I don't know what to do I do nothing. Avram did not tell you to go. Then why hasten the final rupture? This thing may adjust itself ultimately."

"Mother, next time you go to the city please take me along. I must tell my troubles to Zaradan. He may have some suggestion. After all he is responsible for my dilemma."

"I have little confidence in the good faith of that high priest," declared Davarah. "I am sure that he will advise you what is best for himself. Yet I believe you should see him. He may disclose his intentions toward Avram, who is more or less in his power."

"Mother, did Avram disclose the source of his information about me? I am burning with curiosity to know who told him."

"He did not say and I thought it unwise to ask him. In any case, to know will help you very little."

"I wonder if Sarai had anything to do with the disclosure. She is the only one who could benefit by it. Besides, hurting me would give her great pleasure."

"Now Zirru, stop talking nonsense. How could Sarai find out a secret that only you and the priest shared? Is it to his interest to tell anyone? And how could Sarai reach him?"

"I don't know, but I feel certain that she is at the bottom of all this."

## III

"At last you are here," exclaimed Zaradan as he took her in his arms. "Why did you stay away so long? I missed you so much that I wanted to send you a message." He tried to kiss her but she turned her head so that his lips barely brushed her cheek. She slid out of his embrace with the words, "Please. Not today. I feel too unhappy." She then proceeded to inform him of the change in her life since seeing him last.

"Who could have told him?" wondered the priest. "Only two people know. The *kadosh*? I am quite sure he is faithful. Besides, what motive would he have? As for

Habliya, I wouldn't say that she is incapable of doing something slimy. But how could she reach your husband? Does he ever come to my temple?"

"Not to serve the gods," answered Keturah. "But he might come for business reasons."

"I could question her but I know she will deny it with a most injured expression of innocence."

"What shall I do? I don't want to lose Avram. Nor do I wish to see him marry Sarai. I love him too much. You are a wise priest. Tell me what to do."

"I can send for him and command him to fulfill both of your wishes."

"How will you force him to obey?"

"A trial for blaspheming or denying the gods would bring him around quickly. They are very serious charges, as I told you before."

"Oh no, I don't want a hair of his head injured. Besides he won't obey you. He does not fear you or the gods."

"Shall I put him to the test?"

"No."

"If you tie my hands I cannot help you. I am afraid that you will have to let things run on as they are." He sat next to her on the divan and took her in his arms. "Come, let's have some love. I haven't enjoyed you for a long time. Come kiss me."

"No, I won't," as she wrenched herself loose and got up. "Never again. I was foolish to believe you the first time you uttered these threats. Avram said to me, 'Why did you take it upon yourself to solve such problems? The least you could do was to consult me?' I shall let him handle his affairs himself. He is far wiser than I will ever be."

"But you can remain my sweetheart."

"No, I won't be foolish any more."

"You won't? Don't trifle with me, you harlot." The priest grabbed her by the hair and raised his arm to strike her when he suddenly remembered that she was the daughter of the former high priest Sabbattu, now high in the counsels of King Hammurabi.

"I lost my temper. I didn't mean to ill-treat you. Now you may go. But you will be sorry."

## IV

On the farm everything went on as usual. The *Shabbat* service-feast was attended by ever increasing numbers. On one rest day a Habiru reported to Avram that several evil-looking men had been loitering about making remarks that he did not understand but judging from the expression of bystanders they were not complimentary. Avram deputized six stout Habiru to circulate in the crowd, preserve order, and use force if necessary. On the following *Shabbat* the Habiru spotted four men talking to various visitors during the prayers and discourse. They ordered the ruffians to keep quiet out of respect for the service. When the rowdies laughed scornfully the Habiru took and conducted them by the arm out of the farm with the injunction never to return.

The incident led Avram to suspect that trouble was brewing. He drove to the market stall in the city and brought back iron daggers, knives, spears, swords, and gave them to selected strong Habiru with instructions to order all trouble makers out peacefully and not to use the arms unless absolutely necessary. On the following day of rest about ten hoodlums began laughing, jeering, and shouting while Avram was on his knees uttering his prayer; they succeeded in breaking up the service. The vagabonds became defiant and laughed derisively. When the Habiru ordered them off the farm they drew hidden weapons out of their clothes and began mocking and imitating their way of talking. A fight started. Other Habiru handed iron arms to their kinsmen and in the melee two hoodlums were killed and three wounded before they fled. Several of the Habiru were also hurt.

When the feast was over Avram drove his wagon to Haran, gave a full report of the near riot to the city guard and requested that the dead be removed and the wounded attackers taken away. He also demanded an investigation as to the instigators of the violence that led to the killing. Three days later an armed guard came to the farm, arrested Avram, and confined him in the city jail. Davarah immediately contacted Nahor and Sanu-Rimmon and begged them to do everything possible to get Avram released on bail. The captain of the city guard explained that since this was a special case he had no authority to release the prisoner who awaited trial for inciting to riot and murder. He advised them to apply to a judge of the criminal court or to a high priest for temporary release until the trial.

Nahor and Sanu-Rimmon decided to apply to the high priest of the Temple of Szin, the moon-god they both worshiped. They brought liberal offerings and Zaradan listened as if he knew nothing of the arrest. He informed them that years ago he had warned Avram of the danger he ran in bringing the worship of his unknown god to Haran. In fact, this arrest would have taken place long ago had he not used all his influence to prevent it.

"My only interest stems from friendship with the former high priest of Nannar whose daughter has married Avram. The neighboring farms are highly incensed against Avram for bringing a new religion into their midst but chiefly, I gather, for preaching to their laborers to cease work each seventh day. I really can do nothing since this case is totally out of my jurisdiction. It has no religious issue since you tell me that someone was killed in a riot. The charge is probably incitement to riot or murder or both. It is therefore a criminal case and only the king can help you. Of course, if the king seeks my advice I shall do what I can to liberate your brother. This I would do for my friend Sabbattu who stands high as adviser to the mighty King Hammurabi."

Sanu-Rimmon then asked whether they might talk to Avram. Zaradan immediately ordered the *kadosh* to prepare a clay tablet signed and properly sealed that would admit them to the prison. Two guards brought Avram into the room for the reception of prisoners by their families or friends. An armed guard remained throughout the visit. Avram asked the reason for his incarceration and was astonished to hear of the charge against him. Apparently relieved he saw no reason to worry since he had nothing to fear from such an absurd charge. He wondered when Eleazer and Hankas would return. Their presence would be helpful, he thought. The visitors left some food and wine and tipped the jailer with half a silver shekel.

That evening Avram lay reclining on the straw pallet again looking through a small square opening near the ceiling that revealed a patch of blue by day and a star or two at night. He mused on his strange destiny: the second prison and still in his twenties. For the first incarceration his guilt was quite patent. He did smash the idols and that offense was evidently against the law. But why in jail now? Wasn't it quite clear that here was a trumped-up charge? Did it not seem absurd for the owner to incite a riot on his own farm especially during a religious feast which he considered sacred? It seemed puzzling why the ruling power did not utilize the crimes of blasphemy and heresy.

All of a sudden Davarah's story of Keturah's latest meeting with Zaradan flashed into his consciousness. Was it possible that the priest did not want him convicted? The charge of complicity in riot and murder would no doubt frighten Keturah out of her wits. She would then fall on her knees, plead for his life, and offer to pay any price which the priest might demand. According to Davarah, Zaradan wanted only the enjoyment of her body. Avram hoped that Keturah would not fall into the trap again.

But was it a trap? He asked himself if it were possible that Keturah's compliance saved him from arrest, persecution, and possibly death? The priest has just demonstrated his power for evil. If so, was he, Avram, fair in his treatment of Keturah? Was he doing the right thing? Again the dilemma arose to plague him. He forgot about his immediate trouble. Again he wavered between a stern sense of duty and the compassion that lay deeply imbedded in his heart. What should he do? Take her in his arms again? That would be only too delightful, too indulgent, too ecstatic. By her own confession she was a woman who had sinned. Should he forgive? Could he ever forget? Would El Shaddai approve of such a course? Wouldn't it be too much like a compromise with sin?

He lay buffeted about between moral obligation and a desire to forgive, between tarnished honor and gratification of the senses, between the rocky road of virtue and the temptation toward ease and comfort. Worn out by the struggle his eyes closed as he fancied himself in a narrow cove on the Sea of Reeds described on one occasion by Eleazer. Lying in the water he was trying to reach the south shore of the inlet that was flat, grassy, inviting, and over which the sun was shining. But high, powerful waves were pounding him closer and closer to the north coast which was rocky, dark, and the butt of oscillating wind and water. Finally a gigantic wave billowing over the rocky shore landed him on a stony ledge which turned out to have a flat, smooth surface. There he lay listening to the stormy sea, the shrieking wind, the pounding waves. The sun soon disappeared and pitch-blackness descended over land and sea. Now he imagined himself lying on the wall of the Nannar temple in Ur waiting to be cast into the fiery furnace.

A sudden downpour, thick as a water spout, fell with a noise that obliterated every other sound. Strange he did not feel wet; while wondering he was virtually blinded by a flash of lightning that turned the darkness into noonday sunlight. Almost simultaneously a thunder clap of such cosmic power came crashing so close that his hearing process seemed impaired. Everything appeared so still that he feared he was now permanently deaf. A silence seemed to swallow every kind of sound from the patter of the heavy rainfall to the beating of his own heart. The death-like stillness made him wonder whether he was still alive. Yet the silence did not appear muffed, muted, stifled, or aphonic. Nor did the quietude suggest anything solemn, passive, somber, suppressed, or sepulchral. It was the mild, calm, serene quietness that preceded the two most joyous words ever spoken before the creation: YAHE OR (let there be light). It was the radiant stillness that precedes the luminous dawn. The quiescence was broken by a voice, stern yet kind, unlimited in power and infinite in love:

"Avram! Avram!"

"Henane, Eli" (Here I am, My God).

"Get thee out of thy country, from thy kindred, from thy father's house."

"Where shall I go, El Shaddai?"

"Unto the land which I will direct thee, toward the setting sun."

"Wherefore may I not remain here? Thy power is manifest everywhere."

"I will make of you a great nation."

"But my sons were born here."

"The offspring of Sarai, who shall hereafter be called Sarah, will give rise to nations; rulers shall issue from her."

"God of my forefathers! What shall I do with Keturah?"

The Voice became silent. Again Avram could hear the sea raging, the wind howling, the waves beating against the rocky shore.

# 24

# Sarai and Keturah

TWO DAYS AFTER AVRAM'S VISION THE HANKAS BOAT LANDED bringing the passenger Sabbattu besides a cargo of choice wares and merchandise. Hankas and Sipara went to the Terach house while Eleazer accompanied by four Habiru boatmen conducted the former high priest to the Temple of Szin. The four Habiru remained the permanent guard of the ex-priest during his stay in Haran.

Zaradan began to apologize for Avram's arrest before Sabbattu knew what he was talking about. The former assumed that the latter had come to liberate his son-in-law, not stopping to think that Sabbattu could not possibly have received the news and have hastened from Babylon to Haran in so short a time. Zaradan went into detail about his efforts to protect Avram for a number of years; that the hostile farmers finally reached the king who ordered the arrest as well as the criminal charges; that the entire matter was now out of his jurisdiction.

This piece of news was disturbing. Not that Sabbattu cared either about Avram's arrest or about his dangerous situation. Should Avram be executed he would take Keturah and her children with him to Babylon. But he had to face a practical situation that was important to him. For business reasons Avram and his group had become highly necessary. The danger of prosecution for stealing the temple treasure in Ur still hung over his head. He suspected that Hammurabi knew all about it and was waiting to utilize the Ur temple accusation should the occasion arise.

Meanwhile he had to live humbly and conduct himself as if in poverty. He did not want to display any ostentation that might betray his wealth; yet he wished to increase his silver. For this purpose the Avram group filled the need. To begin with they all were honest. Avram might be a religious fanatic but every ounce of silver left with him was as safe as in his own scrip. Thus due to Eleazer's business acumen his wealth was constantly increasing. He checked each submitted statement closely and was highly satisfied with the results. The chief reason for coming to Haran was to take back 2000 shekels in silver stored for him in a strong box of the Szin temple and registered in Avram's name. But here the first difficulty arose. According to the temple rules the priests could only release the iron casket to Avram in person. Should he die, the delivery would be held up until its contents could be ascertained. Then the temple would exact a fee in proportion to the amount in the strong box. It became quite obvious that he must effect Avram's release.

King Nimur-Adad received Sabbattu with the honor and ceremony befitting the emissary of the great ruler in Babylon. The envoy explained that he had several reasons for coming to Haran and thought he might as well seize the opportunity to acquaint the king with the urgency of signing the treaty of friendship and alliance while Hammurabi was alive. His son, Prince Amraphel, did not show any promise of following in the footsteps of his great father who combined the qualities of conqueror, statesman, builder and law-giver with the humane virtues of a humble man.

Amraphel would hardly grant so liberal a treaty to a neighboring small kingdom. On becoming king he would no doubt attempt to impress the world with his military prowess and start conquering the neighboring states. They were in no condition to withstand the powerful thrust of Babylon's war machine. King Nimur-Adad had had ample time to consider the proposed treaty and come to a definite conclusion.

The king of Haran admitted his interest in such an alliance but wanted to know what the tax would be. Would protection include patrolling the highways against robbers who plundered caravans? Sabbattu stated that he brought along several clay tablets formally signed and sealed by Hammurabi. They anticipated the questions raised and would no doubt suit the king of Haran, whose mere signature and seal would immediately establish the alliance that could greatly benefit his prosperous kingdom. Nimur-Adad expressed interest and wished to examine the tablets.

"And now, your majesty, may I take up a more personal matter? On coming to your kingdom I was amazed to learn that my son-in-law is in prison. It is truly inconceivable to me that Avram, son of Terach, the former image-maker of my temple in Ur, could be charged with instigating riot and murder. I am frankly astonished and cannot but wonder what is behind this accusation."

The king admitted knowing about the matter and declared that Avram had been a source of trouble for several years. His neighbors had been complaining bitterly about his blasphemies and his serving of a strange God, Who hated all the gods worshipped in Haran. They feared that Ishtar might in her anger blast their crops and curse their women with sterility.

"I heard their complaints yet took no action. But during his religious service when two outsiders were killed and three wounded, I felt that I had to take a hand. Riot and murder are crimes that cannot be overlooked."

"Isn't it possible, Adoni Melech, that enemies sent agents to provoke trouble at Avram's service? I do know that when accusations like blasphemy or false worship fail to move the authorities, then charges of riot and murder would stir them up."

"Possibly," admitted Nimur-Adad. "Yet doesn't this very incident reflect the danger of permitting the entry of new and foreign gods into our midst to undermine our religion? If the court fails to convict Avram then I am in favor of charging him with blasphemy and atheism. I cannot understand Zaradan's reticence all these years. He actually ignored the plaints of my subjects."

"With your permission, may I make this observation. We priests understand the consequences of persecution better than laymen. It is easy enough to start suppressing a religion, any religion, but one never knows what turn it might take. Once the principle is established that it is lawful and just to prohibit the worship of any god, then the dominant faith can use its power on its weaker opponent; and vice versa as soon as the lesser sect gains ascendancy it will start crushing its adversaries. This process goes on and on repeating itself."

"Does that mean that we should permit any new god to come into our midst and increase his worshippers until they outnumber the followers of our own great gods?" questioned the king.

"In an old city such as Ur we have had experience in persecution as well as in the practice of tolerance. We have learned by ancient experiment that toleration is the lesser of the two evils. Persecution is rigid while tolerance is flexible. The former eventually breaks its own perpetrators while the latter bends and adjusts itself to new conditions."

"I see," observed Nimur-Adad. "You mean that if the new god gets strong enough, that is to say, if he gets sufficient supplicants, then we must discard Szin or Ishtar and kneel to the new divinity whosoever he may be."

"Your majesty misses the point, I regret to say. Or perhaps I did not make myself clear. Under rigid persecution one must worship the newer or stronger god. One has no choice with the sword or spear at his breast. But under toleration one is free to go on serving his own god, regardless of whether he for a time is not strong enough to resist the new conqueror."

"Would you then give complete freedom," queried Nimur-Adad, "to every swindler to set up a temple so that he could draw away the followers of Ishtar or Szin to his own altar? With all the duplicity that exists in the world how long could we maintain the faith in our great gods unless we impose a strong discipline by armed force?"

"All I can do is to point to an illustrious example," maintained Sabbattu. "Hammurabi conquered Ur yet ordered that Nannar remain the guardian deity of the city. As everyone knows my king worships Marduk as the supreme head of all the gods. He could easily have imposed Marduk in the place of our moon-god. But he is too wise a ruler to interfere with the deepest instincts of a people.

Consequently no one in Ur thinks of rebelling for the sake of conscience in vindication of his ancestral gods. In this way Hammurabi ensures loyalty and cooperation instead of gaining the resentment that breaks forth into revolt as soon as the opportunity offers."

"That policy might be proper for an empire that rules over many different kinds of people with a variety of gods," declared the king. "But would it suit a single city such as my Haran? I tried out the stern method, which you call persecution, against the Hurrains who set up a sanctuary to their goddess Hebat outside of my city. The worship of Hebat was making headway until I took a hand. Soon all the new worshippers deserted and a priest had to come from Nuzu to sell the entire property, temple and all. The worship of Hebat ceased. I intend to do the same with Avram who, I understand, purchased the land and the Hebat sanctuary cheaply and on very easy terms."

"Now that is exactly what Hammurabi would not do," the ex-priest pointed out with a certain asperity which he endeavored to control. "My great king would never have disturbed the little rustic temple dedicated to Hebat and set up in the midst of farmers and serfs. He would have reasoned: Why antagonize a potentially strong nation, perhaps a coming power, because of a tiny sanctuary to an obscure goddess? He would rather have the good will of the Hurrains than their enmity. Now I wonder whether the great law-giver would enter into our proposed alliance if he were informed about this persecution."

"Would you give me the reason for your doubts, Adon ambassador?" questioned Nimur-Adad, nettled not only by the tone of Sabbattu but also by a vague suspicion that he himself was displaying rather poor statesmanship before the envoy of the greatest power on earth. "What possible connection can there be between the suppression of a petty nuisance and a treaty of alliance and friendship?"

"Like a truly wise ruler, my master weighs every contingency before entering a treaty. He once told me that he looked closely at the small things which escape the average person; great issues, he said, are obvious on their face. He thus regards an alliance as a grave responsibility, for should Haran be attacked Babylon must come to her assistance. Now we must always remember that people never forget nor forgive an insult to their gods. The hurt may fester for a long while but the time for revenge comes ultimately. Thus we should remember that the Hurrains feel anger over the humiliation heaped upon their goddess. Hammurabi knows that the Hurrains are numerous and in the event of an alliance with the Hittites they can become formidable. A war with both nations jointly can be a serious affair even for Babylon. I am quite sure that if I disclose this insult to their goddess, Hebat, my master will never enter this alliance."

Nimur-Adad became quite disconcerted. Was this former priest trying to intimidate him into releasing his son-in-law? But could he afford to ignore the warning of Hammurabi's envoy? Yet he must not surrender too soon. That would show weakness.

"Adon envoy, I respect the opinion and wisdom of the mighty king of Babylon. Yet I feel that one must adhere to his principles even if they seem undiplomatic. I firmly believe that the gods of my kingdom are supreme and must never be affronted or by-passed by the intrusion of any other god or goddess. I cannot forego my convictions even at the risk of offending the great Hammurabi. If this alliance cannot be effected then my kingdom must go on as heretofore. Now please understand that I want the friendship of your king and value highly any alliance with him. Nor do I wish to harm your son-in-law. You are a wise Chaldean or you would never be intrusted with the affairs of a great empire, the greatest in the world. Advise me, please, how I can be true to my religious policy without bringing injury to your Avram."

"Your majesty, I understand your dilemma and wish to be of assistance, if I may. As for my son-in-law, let me say that neither I nor anyone else can do very much with him. In the matter of his God he is stubborn, obstinate, inflexible; in short, a fanatic. I had trouble with him in Ur and it arose solely out of his belief in a lone God, Who has neither face, nor figure, nor form. For this unknown Divinity he is ready, nay willing, to suffer, even to die. He even has the strange delusion that when in danger this God will come to his relief. I am telling this for I do not think that your majesty will ever cease having trouble with him. I therefore counsel his expulsion. Avram is willing to leave any land which prohibits him from serving this God, Whom he calls El Elyon."

"Your friendly advice is highly welcome, Adon ambassador. Frankly, I was in a quandry for I would do nothing to displease you. If you have further suggestions please let me hear them."

"Avram has quite a household. Probably about several hundred people look to him for their bread. It will take time to harvest his crops and sell the farm. He is also engaged in trading and has capable, skillful associates who operate a caravan and a boat quite successfully. In fact, I am a partner in some of his ventures. It will also take time and effort to dispose of our joint wares. I would therefore ask your majesty to give him ample time to turn his property and merchandise into silver."

"How much time will he need in your opinion?"

"I can't say offhand. It is not easy to sell a landed estate. I would guess about a year, or perhaps longer."

"I shall submit your suggestions to my councilors and particularly to my tax collector. Such is my custom. With their usual caution they will no doubt recommend the agreed terms to be set out on a clay tablet to be signed and sealed setting forth his willingness to depart. This may take several days. Meanwhile I shall be pleased to read the tablets of the treaty submitted by King Hammurabi. Farewell until you come to see me in about six days unless I notify you earlier."

## II

On the day after his arrival Sabbattu sent a message to Keturah that she see him at the Temple of Szin. On the advice of Davarah she did not go but invited him to visit her at the farm. After the conclusion of the conference with Nimur-Adad he thought it too late to reach the farm but took the suggestion of Hankas to attend the *Shabbat* service the next day. The Habiru drove and the hired wagon came during the feast but in time for the service which Hankas delayed until his arrival. Of course everyone knew that the former priest had informed Eleazer of his high hopes that Avram would be released shortly.

Sabbattu watched the sacrifice of a goat and listened to the moving prayer of Hankas for El Shaddai to protect Avram and save him from all harm and danger. The fervent *so-be-it* of the kneeling worshippers impressed the priest who, accustomed to the formal, emotionless responses in the pagan ritual, could not but feel that here was genuine piety and veneration. Looking at the expression of reverence on the humble faces he wondered whether he was not witnessing the beginnings of a new religion that inspired devout faith stimulated by fervor.

Davarah led Sabbattu into the house then conducted him to the dining hall. Keturah and Sipara stood near the window looking out at the people gathered about the shrine to El Elyon. The ex-priest embraced his "daughter," kissed her lips then looked at her intently.

"My daughter, have you been ill?"

Her luscious, rounded form seemed to have shrunk to the girlish figure of a decade earlier. Her eyes looked troubled; her features seemed drawn and taut; an air of sadness and pain permeated her face. Before she could answer tears welled up in her eyes. Unable to control her feelings or master her emotions, she began to cry bitterly.

"Sipara, dear, please take her to her room and make her more presentable for so distinguished a visitor."

After the two young women left Davarah apprised Sabbattu of the reason for Keturah's grief. But she did not mention Zaradan. She merely intimated that someone insinuated to Avram about her relations with a high priest. Sabbattu could only infer that he alone was the cause of her sorrow.

"Davarah, I am willing, yea eager, to take Keturah with me. She will be well cared for, I assure you. Her boys will get the best education that anyone can obtain in Babylon."

"I am afraid you do not understand. Her heart is broken. She loves Avram. She has always loved him. How can she leave him? How can she give him up?" And tears filled Davarah's eyes.

"Well, I suppose she wishes to remain here," commented the priest resignedly. "There is no difficulty on that score, is there?"

"Please excuse me for repeating that a man simply cannot understand the feelings of a woman. She has loved

Avram since early childhood and always expected to become his wife. An accident beyond her control banished that hope. She resigned herself to second best and became his concubine. That position cost her many a pang. Now she lost even this station which is by no means an honorable situation."

The former priest began feeling annoyance. The bitterness in Davarah's words and in her voice were no doubt directed at him. Perhaps a sense of guilt brought a momentary twinge of remorse. But he was not given to self-reproach or penitence. Yet he felt a discomfort that began to approach impatience which was leading to anger.

"Just what are you driving at, Davarah? I am sure you see that I am offering to do all I can to alleviate her grief. If you know anything more that I can do, just say so. I hope you appreciate that I am not her real father."

"Oh, don't misunderstand. I know Adoni will spare no effort to make her life bearable if not gratifying. But I just could not help commenting on the expression, 'I suppose she wishes to remain here.' Does Adoni realize what it means for a woman to be rejected and cast aside? And to make matters more exasperating her chosen successor is her bitterest enemy, the person she hates most in this world. A man might dismiss all this as simple female jealousy. But jealousy is acrimonious, an emotion that can be as bitter as death itself. How can Keturah remain in this house and become the object of scorn and ridicule to a hateful rival as haughty and contemptuous as Sarai can . . ."

Her words were interrupted by loud shouts. "Hadad, Hadad, Yechi Adonanu" (Hail, Hail, Long live our Chieftain). Looking through the window Sabbattu and Davarah saw a wagon driving up. Avram sprang to the ground and helped Sarai alight. Eleazer followed. Amid the welcoming outcries Avram walked to the altar, knelt, and poured out his gratitude to El Shaddai for releasing him from prison and perhaps saving him from a violent death. The kneeling crowd responded with a thanksgiving, grateful so-be-it. Avram rose and addressed his auditors:

"My friends and fellow worshippers, this morning King Nimur-Adad sent to the prison for me. The king asked whether I liked Haran and wished to remain here. I answered yes. Would I cease to worship my deity and serve the gods of Haran? I answered no. He then informed me that I could not remain in his kingdom. The king allows me to stay here a year and two months to dispose of my land, houses, goods, and merchandise. Then I may go to whatever land pleases me.

"The God of my forefathers appeared and commanded me to get out of here and go to the land of the setting sun. Our faithful Eleazer, who has traveled far and wide, interprets this land to be Canaan; it lies near the great western sea. As soon as we are ready we shall depart for the land chosen by El Elyon. I wish to express my thanks to all of you for your faithful service. Whoever among you, free or bonded, who wishes to stay here is free to remain. I shall render you such assistance as I can. Whoever wants to go along with me shall be welcome." With one voice the people cried out, "We shall go with you."

Lot whispered to Avram that the high priest Sabbattu was in the dining hall with Mother Davarah waiting to speak with him. Taking Sarai along Avram bowed respectfully and before he could utter a word, the priest declared, "The last time I saw you in Ur you were a prisoner in the temple of Nannar. This time, years later, you are released from the prison attached to the Temple of Szin. I trust this practice will not become a permanent habit."

"I thank Adoni for his mediation with King Nimur-Adad, who made it quite clear that but for your intervention I would never have been freed. Allow me to present my future bride, Sarai, my half-sister and daughter of Terach."

"I trust the golden Ishtar will not withhold fertility from your most beautiful future wife. While on this subject, would it meet with your approval that my daughter and your children accompany me to Babylon?"

"Keturah may stay with me as long as she desires. But should she express the wish to go with her father I give my consent freely. This also applies to her children."

"If convenient I would appreciate seeing you at the Temple of Szin with Eleazer during the forenoon after tomorrow. There are some business matters to talk about."

"It will be a privilege to attend."

"I watched the ritual today. I really believe that you have started a faith which will endure."

"I thank Adoni for this observation."

At this moment Sipara came in and told Sabbattu that Keturah was in no condition to see him. But she could visit him at the Temple of Szin three days hence at noontime.

"May I now depart?" asked the priest of his host.

"It shall be my honor and privilege to accompany you to the wagon."

Keturah came into the dining hall expecting Davarah to be alone. Wholly unprepared to meet Sarai face to face she could not restrain herself and blurted out, "So you carried out your threat of years ago, when a little brat. By stealing my Avram you did succeed in making me suffer, I admit. But you will never know a day of happiness in all your future life. I have laid a curse on you which the demons have heard. My prayers to Ishtar, Nannar, Enlil, and El Elyon will not be in vain nor remain disregarded. Now you can go, you snake."

Without a word Sarai turned on her heels and walked out, holding her head high with a contemptuous smile on her lips. But inwardly, far from calm, she was more shaken and fearful than she would admit even to herself.

III

Later that afternoon Davarah came into Keturah's bedchamber and heard Sipara say, "After what I heard today I see nothing to prevent me from going with you to Babylon, that is if you will ever make up your mind."

"What's this you say?" demanded Davarah, surprised. "Leave your husband? What for?"

"You heard Avram declare that he intended to forsake this city. I asked Hankas what he intended to do. He answered: 'I intend to go along with him.' Here is what our conversation was like:

" 'Where to?' I asked."

" 'To Canaan. Didn't you hear him say that?' "

" 'How far must we travel to get there?' I asked."

" 'About 600 miles or so.' "

" 'By boat?' I asked."

" 'No, by caravan.' "

" 'That's too much traveling for me. What will you do with the boat?' "

" 'Sell it,' he answered."

" 'Hankas, you have always been a river man. What will you do way out there? I understand it's all desert. Become a nomad? I don't think I could wander that much. After all, haven't you some obligations to your wife? I would prefer living in Babylon. Surely you can get along there.' "

" 'I will go wherever Avram goes. If you want to leave me, I will not stand in your way,' declared my husband. So it's all settled for me. I do not care to live anywhere else but in Babylon. I can have a great time there. And so can you, Keturah, if you would only pull yourself together and think sensibly."

"Oh, I can't tear myself away from this place," whimpered Keturah. "I just love this old house and everything here. I call those cute lambs by the names the shepherds give them. Relinquishing this farm is like tearing a limb off my body and leaving it behind. You know something? I am losing my pride. I am thinking of going to Avram and begging him not to send me away."

"Zirru," explained Davarah, "it's not Avram who stands in your way. Sarai has asserted that she will never marry him while you are here."

"But, Mother, he will marry her and that means that I will be compelled to go. Do you know what I feel like doing? Remain and urge this marriage. I am told a man needs more than one woman. She can be his wife and I may be taken back to be his concubine."

"This is all hopeful thinking," commented Davarah. "But if that is in your mind, I must say that you showed little sense today. The wise thing would have been to greet her, wish her happiness in the marriage and try to make up with her. Women are vain. This appeasement might have soothed her vanity. But you kicked everything into the fire. I am afraid you lost your golden opportunity."

"I am going into Avram's room tonight and speak to him. I have nothing to lose. It's really up to him. If he insists she will give in. I know she will take no chances of losing this opportunity to marry him. What do you think of my idea, Sipara?"

"As you say, Keturah, you have nothing to lose. But why encourage such pride in any man? They are by and large pretty much alike. In Babylon you will find men far more desirable than Avram. He is, after everything is said, but a religious bigot who makes everyone suffer because of his nameless God. It is on account of this fanatic that I am leaving Hankas."

Before midnight Keturah tiptoed into Avram's sleeping room on the right wing of the house. Not yet asleep he lay gazing out of the open window contrasting his chamber with the prison and wondering whether Sabbattu really helped him with the king. On becoming aware of a presence he asked who was there.

"It is I, Avram. I want to speak with you." Avram sat up and saw Keturah standing near the bed fully clothed. "Avram," and she burst into tears. "Please do not send me away. I will do nothing to disrupt your marriage with Sarai. I will do everything to promote your happiness. Just let me stay. Please do. I just cannot leave."

"Keturah, I am not sending you away. Stay here as long as you desire. No one will interfere with you."

"I will do nothing that might produce the slightest discord. I simply want to remain with you. Let me be your servant, your slave. But do not banish me."

She got down on her knees, took his foot in both her hands and kissed the big toe.

"Do not humble yourself in this manner and please get up," he said as he got out of bed and stood up. "Why did you start quarreling with Sarai today? She did nothing to antagonize you. While sitting in the wagon we discussed our coming marriage. I told her of my attitude to you. She finally consented to marry and invite you to remain with us. In fact she was in the mood to forget all past feelings and be friendly to you. Then out of a clear sky you shattered everything and made all further relations between you and Sarai impossible. All of this makes matters difficult for me. Now I have to start all over again to get Sarai to marry and consent to your remaining with us."

Keturah got up and sat on the bed unable to cease crying. Finally she was able to say, "I don't see any prospect for me to live amicably in the same house with Sarai. I will therefore get out of your life and go with my father to Babylon. Will you please tell him this tomorrow. I am in no condition to see him the day after. Sabbattu will probably start out one day next week. My life is over. To me Babylon will be as dull as any other place. I hope Sarai will make you happy but I don't believe she will. This is farewell, I suppose."

## IV

The following morning Avram and Eleazer went to the Temple of Szin to meet Sabbattu. The three proceeded to the section that contained the locked boxes registered in the name of the depositors. Avram identified himself, signed a clay tablet, and received the heavy metal case which the Habiru carried to Sabbattu's apartment. Eleazer weighed 2000 shekels in silver and delivered it to the ex-priest. Avram weighed 500 shekels and informed Sabbattu that he was taking it to Keturah for her personal use in Babylon. The remaining silver in the box was carried back by the Habiru to the division in the temple whence it came. The three sat discussing their future plans. Sabbattu expressed satisfaction with their business transaction and his desire to continue this relation. He then asked Avram. "In which country to you contemplate settling?"

"I suppose it will be somewhere in Canaan."

"Why Canaan? It is not the most prosperous country I have seen. Nor is the civilization very high; in fact it is far below the lands you are leaving. In your place I would choose Egypt. That land is highly civilized, commercially developed, and by far the most delightful country in the world, I am told."

"That is true, Adoni. But Egypt is not suitable for me. One cannot farm there since the lands on the Nile are largely under government control. My wealth is chiefly in goats, sheep, and cattle. The Egyptians, who worship animals, regard shepherds with scorn and hatred."

"Then why not follow the occupation of a merchant? With Eleazer at your side you will, I am sure, do very well. We can develop quite a trade between Babylon and Egypt. With a skillful boatman like Hankas we can dispense with caravans and use the waterways."

"I believe Adoni is aware that to me the worship of El Elyon is far more important than gold, silver, or merchandise. In countries with strong governments the gods are upheld by the power of the kings. This we both know by experience. Egypt is a great Kingdom; the Pharaohs are all powerful; they enforce worship of the gods with their might. In a short time I will surely relapse into the same troubles that I fell into at Ur and here in Haran. No, I must stay away from Egypt."

"But are you not subject to the same difficulties in Canaan?"

"No, Adoni. I inquired closely. Eleazer was born in Dameshek and knows that part of the world. Canaan has no large cities. Each city has its own king and consequently no great power is concentrated in any single person or place. Phoenicia has three cities but they are not united. The same is true of the Philistines. Sodom, Jericho, Hebron, and Shechem are typical of the other cities. It is easy to move about from place to place with herds. The climate is warm and people can live in tents and therefore are not tied down to one place. I may even live out in the open myself and consequently expect no trouble on account of worshipping my own God."

The three decided to maintain the status quo until the

time came for Avram to depart. The former priest would then decide about going on with the partnership for the use of his funds. Sabbattu hinted that since he was in charge of collecting the taxes from the five cities of the plain he might need the services of Eleazer. Sodom and Gomorrah were not too prompt in their payments. But he would be in communication with them even after they settle in Canaan. He also wanted to investigate the possibilities of importing and exporting from Babylon via Ur to Etzion Geber at the top of the Sea of Reeds. Hankas would be useful with his experience as a boatman.

Eight days later all preparations for the journey to Babylon were completed. Sabbattu insisted on sailing in the Hankas boat. He felt safer under the direction of the skipper, who, together with the stout Habiru, would guard the treasure of 2000 shekels in silver. Besides, the boat could take back a cargo of wares and merchandise to Haran. The sailing day fell on the *Shabbat* so Avram ordered everyone present to do special honor to Keturah. He, himself, uttered a prayer to El Elyon to protect her and their sons from wind, weather, and dangers from men or wild beasts.

Hankas and Sipara came in one wagon. No one knew except Davarah that Sipara intended to remain in Babylon. Everyone assumed that she was taking the usual trip accompanying her husband. Avram supplied another wagon party to transport the baggage but chiefly to carry the group of boys who crowded the vehicles to send off their three friends. Avram, Davarah, Lot, Milcah, and Sipara sat in the wagon which Hankas was driving. Avram sat next to Keturah holding her hand to bolster her morale. He felt depressed. The farewell was touching. The women commingled their tears with Keturah's. All stood waving their hands until the boat was out of sight.

# 25

# To Canaan

IT TOOK SEVERAL WEEKS FOR AVRAM TO RECOVER HIS NORmal balance from the effects of incarceration, the decree of banishment, the departure of Keturah. His forthcoming marriage to Sarai he felt instinctively would be perhaps the most important step in his life. The day after Keturah left he ordered the Habiru to drive him to the Terach house. He found Sarai alone. Eleazer was out attending to business. The servants and slaves were either at the market stall or doing some chores. Avram insisted that Sarai come immediately to live at the farm. Keturah was no longer there to annoy her. Again Sarai pleaded lack of fear or of loneliness but nevertheless packed her belongings and went along.

Not having any notice of Avram's step Davarah felt somewhat irked at seeing Sarai permanently installed in the house. While her relations with Sarai had always been correct they were never too cordial. She could not suppress a feeling of resentment towards Avram's choice and felt that because of Sarai her foster-daughter was now exiled, to use Keturah's expression. Davarah expressed hesitation about remaining but Avram would not hear of her leaving, at least not until after the wedding, and even then he would prefer that she remain until the household left Haran. In fact he thought that Davarah and her son Lot might go along to Canaan since life on Nahor's farm could never be too pleasant even if Milcah loved her mother and brother.

Eleazer had driven over to discuss the purchase of provisions necessary for the seven-day marriage festival. At the evening meal the discussion centered on the various drinks, fruits, nuts, breads, vegetables, meats, and fish necessary for the occasion. The cost of the celebration seemed enormous.

"Why is it necessary to continue the custom of Ur in a foreign land? Instead of seven wouldn't three days suffice?" This question propounded by Sarai sounded revolutionary yet on second thought seemed sensible and even practical.

"Who ever heard of a three-day wedding?" cross-questioned Davarah. "This would sound like we are either poverty stricken or niggardly."

"It would simply establish a new custom," continued Sarai. "Coming from Avram it sounds quite authentic. After all he has defied customs of greater moment when smashing the idols."

"This idea has never crossed my mind," confessed Avram. "Sarai has come out with an excellent suggestion. Why perpetuate customs simply because they are old? What do you say, Eleazer?"

"I think it a wise suggestion and comes characteristically from our young mistress who is noted for her brilliant mind."

"It is too drastic," opined Davarah, feeling old-fashioned and becoming conscious of being displaced by the rising generation. Yet she sensed that it was necessary to compromise somewhere down the line. "I would reduce the number to five days."

"Why is five a better number than three?" argued Sarai, pleased and encouraged by Eleazer's compliment.

"What do you say, Lot?" queried Avram.

"Uncle Avram, I am for all seven days," answered Lot enthusiastically. "A wedding is so enjoyable that I can't get enough of it. In fact, I heard the Habiru talking about the wedding festival saying that they were looking forward to enjoying greatly all of the seven days."

"You have a point there, Lot," assented Avram. "Let us compromise and make it four days. That will make both sides win."

Later the same evening, after the others had gone to bed, Avram and Sarai sat in the open enjoying the balmy breezes. Sarai seemed lost in silent abstraction.

"What are you thinking about, my princess?"

The question broke into Sarai's cogitations and brought her back to earth. "Oh about the difficulty of changing established notions. If you cannot get agreement on such a simple thing as a change in the seven-day marriage festival, which on its face is unwieldy, then how will you ever succeed in getting people to worship a new, different, unknown God? I wonder whether you realize the magnitude of the task and the trouble you will run into?"

"I know it will be difficult but I do not despair. El Shaddai will never forsake me."

"What makes you so certain, Avram?"

"He saved me twice. In Ur I was in the gravest peril. I suppose you remember what happened. Here in Haran I was again in great danger. In both situations I did nothing to help myself. Assistance came from above. It will come again."

"How do you know, my Avram?"

"I have faith in El Elyon. I rely completely on Him and know He will save me."

"Do you have moments of doubt?"

"After He first spoke to me I did question whether it was not all a dream. But all doubt disappeared since escaping the burning furnace."

"Would you admit that there may be worshippers of Ishtar, Nannar, Marduk, or Shamash who believe just as fervently yet they act and feel altogether differently from you?"

"I haven't seen any who feel very strongly. Their high priests are formal and correct. In other words, they conform to an established code. They are far more interested in donations and offerings than in the kind of faith that calls for personal sacrifice. Would any of them give up their lives for their gods? I doubt it. If an enemy should take this city they would accept the new god with the excuse that he was the same deity they served but under a different name. Or they might maintain that they have room in their pantheon for any number of gods. In Carchemish I learned that the Hittites had 1000 gods. In India they believe in more than 3000. In such a scramble of gods men lose sight of morality, justice, or righteousness, the basic foundation for religion."

"You say, my beloved, that El Elyon spoke to you? Was it face to face? Did you see him?"

"I only heard his voice."

"How do you know it was not a dream?"

"He spoke to me only several weeks ago. He told me to fear nothing. He said that I would marry you and that your name henceforth would be Sarah."

"Did he say anything further about me?"

"Yes. Nations and rulers shall come from your offspring."

Sarai shut her eyes to comprehend more fully the implications of Avram's words. Somehow they did not stir or excite her. Was her future husband given to hallucinations? Yet could she brush aside a statement of such momentous import? Is it possible that this El Elyon is mightier than the gods of Sumer or Babylon? She heard herself saying quietly with closed eyes, "Avram, I would give anything in the world to have your implicit faith."

"Sarai, you look tired and sleepy. I think you should go to bed."

## II

After weeks of preparation everything was in readiness for the wedding. Avram declared a four-day holiday for all his servants and workers. Some of the men and women of the Habiru were required to help in the cooking and serving, chores which they joyfully accepted and fulfilled. Eleazer, assisted by the two servants and slaves of the Terach house, was there to direct and oversee. From Haran came Sanu-Rimmon, his wife, his son Amihud, Dulashish, his wife, and several prominent Hittites who came to inspect the farm which they heard was for sale. Nahor and his entire family came on the first day. Some of the neighboring farmers who had demonstrated a sincere friendship through the years were also among the invited guests.

Early that morning Avram and Sarai rode to the Nahor farm and took along wine, cooked food, bread, and fruit for the departed Terach and Emtelai, whose bodies lay in the chapel tomb underneath the house. The custom of Ur required the placing of food in the crypt for the dead who remained members of the family as during their stay on earth. The priests never could explain this mystery: how the dead lying in a tomb on earth could at the same time reside in the dark and dusty subterranean realm of Aralu. The food, the priests said, would be a welcome, refreshing change from the dust that the dead ate in the region below. Avram and Sarai felt it their pious duty to remember their parents on the important occasion of their wedding day. While the Ur custom did not prescribe any service or prayer for the dead it was considered highly appropriate to bring them part of the food prepared for the marriage of their children.

The Habiru workers on the Nahor farm cheered Avram and Sarai and wished them health, long life, and happiness. Avram invited all of them to the wedding. Since they could not all leave at the same time, they arranged among themselves to split into groups so that everyone could at different times be present to celebrate their chieftain's joyous occasion.

When the couple got back it was past the noon hour. The guests and other invitees were present and ready for the ceremony. Avram had been concerned about a fitting marriage rite. He rejected the elaborate Ur ritual which was interspersed with references to the gods. The center of the rite contained a prayer for Irnina-Ishtar to make the bride fruitful and a mother of many children. Avram decided to devise a new ritual which he and the worshippers of El Elyon could use.

He ordered the shepherds to bring a ram and a lamb to be sacrificed for himself and for Sarai. He slit the throat of both animals. The shepherds sheared the wool then skinned them. The horns of the ram were set aside to serve as trumpets. They cut away all edible flesh and gave it to the Habiru women to cook and broil for the feast. The remnants of the ram were placed on the altar. Avram uttered a prayer that El Shaddai accept the burnt offering of his servant. While the fire on the altar was slowly consuming the ram Avram and Sarai went into the house to change clothes. He donned a flowing robe of linen dyed in a color known as royal blue. Sarai's gown was of white silk from India strengthened and trimmed with cotton cloth. Her head and shoulders were covered with a thin veil.

Sarai led by Davarah and Milcah walked to a place near the altar and close to the sanctuary dedicated to El Elyon. Avram was conducted by his brother Nahor and the faithful Eleazer. By this time the fire had consumed the ram. Then the shepherds placed the head, bones, entrails, stomach, lungs, heart, and sinews of the lamb on the altar and after another prayer Avram lit the fire. Instead of waiting for the flames to consume the remainder of the lamb Avram and Sarai walked into the sanctuary, which after closing the door became dark as midnight.

Avram sat Sarai on a bench and stood near the eastern wall praying to El Elyon and invoking His blessings on their wedded state. To Sarai the prayer seemed endless. She could at the same time hear the noise of people talking and moving about as well as the spluttering of the flames consuming the lamb. But to Avram a deep silence seemed to descend into and to pervade the sanctuary. He could hear no hubbub whatsoever nor any other noise from the outside penetrating through the cracks of the shut door. The death-like stillness took on a positive potency that drowned out any possible sound. A familiar voice intoned, "Avram! Avram!"

*"Henane, Elohai Noach, Shem, ve Ever Avosanu."* (Here I am, God of Noah, Shem and Ever, my ancestors.)

Avram knelt and bowed until his head touched the ground his forearms resting on the blocks of dried earth that constituted the floor.

"You shall no longer be called Avram. Your name henceforth shall be Avraham."

"Wherefore is my name thus altered, Lord God?"

"Because you shall be the father of a multitude of nations. Such is the meaning of your new name."

"El Shaddai, I am preparing to depart for Canaan. Have I chosen the true land?"

"I will give that land to your offspring, and there I will make of you a great nation."

"Wilt thou bless my marriage with Sarah, Oh Creator of heaven and earth?"

"I will make your name great and you shall be a blessing to the nations of the earth."

"But, my great God, thou hast not blessed our marriage."

The voice spoke no more. The deep silence seemed to evaporate and Avram could again hear the buzzing and talking of the wedding guests. He rose and walked over to the bench upon which his bride was sitting.

"Sarah, did you hear anything?"

"I heard you mumbling, Avram. I could not make out a word."

"What did you hear, my dear? Tell me."

"I simply heard the crowd outside talking and the fire on the altar crackling."

"Didn't you hear a voice speaking to me?"

"I did not. You seemed to be lying on the ground, at least I thought so."

Both left the darkened sanctuary and entered the world of sunlight. Near the altar stood a canopy of sheepskins stitched together and supported by four wooden poles, each one held by Lot, Amihud, Bethuel, and another son of Nahor. This canopy was being used to shield the shepherds from rainfall or fierce sun rays while tending the grazing sheep in the open country away from the shade of trees. Avram, flanked by Nahor and Eleazer, entered the canopy and remained on the right while Sarah led by Davarah and Milcah walked from the opposite direction and stood on the left. Avram pronounced the prayer: "Blessed be thou, El Elyon and Shaddai, sole creator of heaven, earth, mankind, and everything in the universe. Thou hast entered into a covenant with me while the smoking furnace and the flaming torch passed between the animal parts. I agreed for myself and for my descendants to worship and serve thee throughout the generations. Bless the marriage which Sarah and I will now enter. Bless the fruit of her womb so that our offspring shall carry on thy covenant for evermore. As thou commanded, I shall hereafter be called Avraham and Sarai's name henceforth shall be Sarah. So-be-it."

The assembled people repeated "So-be-it." Then Avraham took the goblet of wine from the hand of Eleazer and declared, "Blessed art thou, God of our forefathers. Under this nuptial canopy we enter the sacred covenant of wedlock. Our descendants shall in all generations be hallowed by the rite of the nuptial canopy in the holy betrothal of matrimony. Let this goblet of wine be the symbol of joy and happiness throughout our married state."

Avraham drank a portion of the wine, then held the goblet to Sarah's lips. He placed a gold ring on Sarah's third finger and declared, "Be thou consecrated unto me by this ring. I will honor, love, and cherish thee as my wife."

The assembled people shouted "So-be-it." The four young men removed the canopy and the guests crowded about the newly married couple offering their congratulations to Avraham joyfully and vociferously. To Sarah they were formal and restrained. After Davarah and Milcah left her side to supervise the entertainment Sarah found herself standing alone. Lot seemed to have disappeared without speaking to her at all. On seeing Amihud and Bethuel alone and isolated she approached them and said, "Aren't you going to wish me happiness? I thought we were friends. Why are you so shy?"

They responded with their best wishes and she kissed them both on the cheek with the words, "This will teach you not to be bashful." She took each by the arm and walked about smiling to the people. The Habiru men responded with, "Long life and happiness to our new mistress." The women did not know how to regard her. They liked Davarah and were fond of Keturah but Sarah never came near them. They resented her aloof, uppish demeanor and did not know whether or not to address her. But when Sarah greeted them with, "I bid you welcome, my sisters," they also responded with, "Joy and happiness to the beautiful wife of our chieftain."

"Where is your father, Amihud?"

"He is near the pool, I believe, talking to some Hittites."

"Take me to him."

"I remember when after we left Eridu you joined our caravan." She smiled to Sanu-Rimmon and continued, "Amihud was then a little fellow."

"And you were a little girl, my lady. Now you are a beautiful woman." Together with the Hittites he wished her joy throughout a long and happy married life. Sarah and her two friends walked around inviting tributes from "her subjects." Finally Avraham found her and expostulated, "Where have you been? I have been looking for you."

"With the crowd milling about their sheikh I am sure you did not miss me." She tossed her head arrogantly and could not conceal her feelings, nettled over his apparent neglect. "My two friends were showing me off to your subjects."

"Come, we must sit at the large table and start the feast."

It was nearing sundown. Eleazer with Davarah and Milcah were finding places for everyone and ordering the servants to put lighted torches at every available spot. The feast lasted for hours. There seemed no limit to the capacity of the guests for the wine, the well-prepared foods, the nuts, fruit, honey cakes, and other deserts. Avraham and Sarah sat at the head of the table. In the midst of the gayety both seemed preoccupied. Avraham could not cease thinking about the words which his God spoke that afternoon. Sarah was irked at her unpopularity and wondered how she could antagonize people by doing and saying nothing.

The custom of Mesopotamia prescribed that the bride and groom leave the feast at its height and retire to their nuptial chamber. The couple walked away amidst the cheering and singing of the guests, who continued to eat and drink by the hour, some feasting and reveling all night. Instead of going to the bridal chamber Avraham led Sarah up the stairs to the rooftop of the building. Seated on comfortable cushions they gazed at the three-quarter moon and the innumerable stars, all the time being wafted by mild breezes. Entranced by the glory of the heaven, Avraham broke the silence:

"My sister and bride, El Elyon spoke to me in Ur and said, 'Look up unto the heavens and count the stars if you can. So shall your descendants be.' "

"He did not mention *my* children, did He? He said *yours* and you have children."

"Here in Haran when He spoke to me in prison He said

specifically, 'The offspring of Sarai will give rise to nations; rulers shall issue from her.' "

"Did He repeat it today?"

"Today He said, 'I will make of you a great nation. I will make your name great and you shall be a blessing to the nations of the earth.' "

"I wonder why I was not permitted to hear the Voice. Perhaps the people outside chattered too loud. I heard you talk but could not understand a word."

"That is strange," commented Avraham. "There was no noise whatsoever. A deep silence prevailed. The Voice was loud and strong. I could hear every word distinctly."

"I wish I could have heard. Then perhaps I might share your faith."

Both remained absorbed for what seemed a long time. The excitement generated by the theophany with El Elyon held Avraham in a state of exaltation. He had no doubt about his selection to bring the knowledge and worship of El Shaddai to all people on earth. But how such a supernal assignment might be implemented had not been revealed to him. Yet he did not question that such was the will and purpose of his God, even if as yet he had made but the slightest beginning in his mission. The results so far had been insignificant.

"My only genuine proselyte is Hankas. The Habiru follow me in worship as in other things. But they are not filled with fervor nor are they convinced of the truth to the extent of suffering for their faith. Should I declare for another god they would change at my dictation. The same might be said of Eleazer, only on a higher and more rational plane. He has no more conviction about my God than of the gods of Ur, Babylon, or Carchemish. Belief in a single God as against many gods is of little concern to him. Eleazer is perhaps a good example of the practical man everywhere. Not that he is hypercritical or dishonest. Far from it. He is simply a conformist to the prevailing code or the established mores."

But the indifference of his own family hurt most. His blood relations, his kith and kin, showed little faith in him or in his beliefs. Neither his father, mother, Nahor, Davarah, or their offspring had the slightest concern about the true God. Keturah really loved him yet was at heart an idol worshipper. And now his own sister-bride, whom his God had approved as the wife for him, betrayed the same skepticism about the messages he received from above. All of this was deeply mortifying, yet El Shaddai surely knew it all and continued to direct his steps. A thought suddenly flashed into his mind: "All of my God's directives dealt with the future. At no time did He mention the present except in the matter of leaving Haran and my father's house. Was it then God's will that His name and worship be spread in the future among all the dwellers of the world and by my seed only?" Avraham's heart beat fast as his spirit expanded. He felt the divine afflatus and was certain that this message came from the God of his forefathers.

While Avraham ruminated and talked to himself Sarah was occupied with her own thoughts. She was about to surrender her virginity, the crucial moment in a woman's life. "I have always heard that the operation was painful yet enormously exciting. But I am not at all excited. I merely anticipate a painful experience like pulling out a tooth. But women have assured me of the stimulating effect upon a girl who gives up her virtue to the man she loves. What is this thing called love? I am fond of Avraham but not thrilled by him. I am never enraptured when he kisses me. Then why am I so bent on marrying him? Is it the woman in me realizing my childish infatuation? Or is it that I just can't let that vile Keturah enjoy the satisfaction of being his wife or even his concubine? Perhaps so. My hate for Keturah seems to exceed my love for Avraham."

But did Avraham love her? She really did not know. She sat watching his face in the moonlight and starlight. He seemed immersed in some problem. "Am I in his thoughts? Hardly. At this moment he is unaware of my presence, of my very existence." His lips were moving. He was speaking and emphasizing with his hands. Was he talking to himself? She could only catch a word here and there. "Whom is he addressing? I know. He is talking to his God, that strange, formless, bodyless spirit that is only a Voice. Yet Avraham's feeling for this deity far exceeds his love for a woman, for a thousand women, for any human being regardless of how close he or she may be to him. He certainly loves this God far more than his sons, for he parted from them without a struggle or hesitation. Yet he did love that Keturah." And that realization made her furious especially whenever she recalled the tragic expression he registered on being informed about her infidelity.

Sarah doubted whether Avraham loved her nearly so passionately as he felt for Keturah. And that notion infuriated her. But she had the consolation of feeling that she was now Avraham's wife. It was therefore her duty to love him as strongly as she knew how. Instinct told her never to let on by word or deed that her love toward him was but lukewarm. She felt tired and was getting drowsy. Strange that a young man deprived of a woman for over half a year should not rush an attractive virgin to his bed. Ordinarily this would be evidence of lacking love for her but his rapt, beatific expression indicated that he was still thinking about, if not talking to, his God. He was—he was —and she dropped off to sleep.

Avraham became aware of regular and somewhat deep breathing mingled with mild snoring. "Oh, the poor girl is so tired. She has had a hard day." He felt conscience-smitten for becoming unaware of his bride on her wedding night. He bent over, awoke her with a kiss, then gathered her in his arms and walked down the stairs. She entwined her arms around his neck and kept her mouth glued to his lips until reaching the bedchamber. He laid her on the couch and she covered her face and eyes with her hands waiting stoically. She felt his hot, passionate breath and braced her loins for the tribulation as his strong arms tightened about her. Only once did a cry escape her shut-tight lips when she felt a sharp thrust of pain. But the ordeal was over rather quickly she thought when Avraham took her in his arms and whispered in her ear how beautiful she was and how much he loved her. He was soon fast asleep and she disengaged herself gently from his embrace.

"Is this all?" she asked herself disappointed. "Why did the women lie to me? They assured me that to be in a man's arms is the most gratifying experience a woman can ever have. I found it flat and vapid when not actually painful. A man must be different, I suppose." She sat up and looked at her sleeping husband whose expression appeared pleased and satisfied. "But how can he slumber so peacefully after the exciting pleasure he seemed to have experienced? How can he become so indifferent to the girl who so delighted him? I rather liked it when he pressed and squeezed me in his arms and whispered in my ear. Yet almost immediately he fell asleep. But why didn't I react? Was it that I didn't respond to his love?" Then came to her mind a conversation when Emtelai had tried to enlighten her about the facts of life. She recalled "her mother" saying that a girl might be cold to a man's embrace especially on the first night. But later she would respond, particularly if she loved her husband. "Is it possible that I don't love him?" she kept repeating until she fell asleep.

The next morning Sarah awoke in Avraham's arms. In a happy mood her husband kissed her and said, "I enjoyed your love so much that I can't fondle you enough. I suppose you are feeling quite sore. I know that my darling little wife was an innocent virgin, something rare in Haran I am told."

They dressed, went to eat breakfast, and received a noisy welcome. The established custom permitted friends to "razz" the newlyweds. It was considered in good taste to embarrass the bride with questions that could make her blush or stammer. Insinuations that might be coarse or bawdy were accepted good naturedly. The jokes were in the main crude and foolish. The guests could show off their cleverness by entering a contest to carry the ball pitched by one of them, all at the bride's expense. The pleasantries, some dull, some sprightly, some stupid and others smart, went on by the hour.

After abstaining for the period allotted to women for the cleansing of impurities Avraham went eagerly to Sarah's bedchamber expecting the transports of tempestuous passion with which Keturah had always received him. But he was destined to suffer disappointment. Sarah tried hard to comply with her wifely duty in making her husband feel the happiness resulting from the union of male and female. But she did not realize that the passion which seizes the man must also be met by desire normally lodged in the woman. Try as she would she simply could not ignite within her the spark of passion. Was it possible that she had no sex feeling? Did inborn, inbred frigidity inhibit her from feeling the warmth and glow imbedded in the normal female when embraced with passion by the man of her choice?

When Avraham lay silent at her side she sensed his disappointment. A feeling of self-pity gripped her. A consciousness of failure in the most intimate relationship with a man filled her with despair. She tried desperately to control her emotions but tears gathered in her eyes. She could not prevent Avraham from hearing her sniffles.

"What is wrong, my sweet bride?" He turned on one side and took her in his arms. "Why are you crying?"

"You know what is wrong. I can feel your disappointment."

"Oh nonsense. You are young. You will get over your embarrassment and act as other women."

"Do you really think so? I do hope what you say is true."

She buried her face in his breast and had a good cry. He held her in his arms until she went off to sleep. He then lay on his back thinking. Did he feel as confident as his words of comfort indicated? Of course he sensed the deficiency in his wife and could not but contrast her frigidity with the burning passion in Keturah. Could a man truly love a woman who did not respond to him? How long could he conceal his disappointment? Yet Sarah was the wife approved, nay selected, one might even say, by El Elyon. Didn't his God promise that she would be the progenitrix of many nations? Then came a flash of insight. He knew it descended from above by reason of the excitement engendered in the pounding of his heart. He pondered:

"Did the Almighty Power purposely choose Sarah because of her defect? He understands the weakness of men. He knows how they can be enslaved by passion, how a woman can exert an influence for evil upon her husband. My ancestress in the Garden tempted the first man to eat the forbidden apple and thus brought misfortune upon her descendants. Excessive love for a woman can detract a man from the true God; she can even lead him to false gods. El Elyon has surely selected me to spread His name and worship among all people. This must be my sole aim and purpose. No woman should have the power to wean me away from my God. He is far more important than wife or child, than father and mother. My duty to Him comes first. My love for Him must not be disputed by any woman. I must sacrifice the love of woman for the love of God."

Avraham removed the sleeping Sarah from his bosom.

## III

About a month after the wedding Hankas returned. To the surprise of everyone he was alone. No one except Keturah knew of Sipara's intention to leave her husband although she did mention it to Davarah. But Davarah had dismissed her words as mere woman's gabble not to be taken seriously. Hankas reported that Sipara refused to go with him to Canaan and therefore chose to remain in Babylon with Keturah and her boys in a house leased and furnished by Sabbattu. He did not mention some gossip relayed by a recently acquired slave of the household that the former high priest occupied the same house and slept alternately with Keturah and Sipara. This he refused to believe.

The final year in Haran turned out to be hectic. The last crop had to be planted, harvested, and sold. The goods and merchandise at the stall in the market place were disposed of. The cargo that Hankas brought was bartered for iron which he immediately transported to Babylon together with 1000 shekels in silver for Sabbattu. The last cargo that he brought back had also to be turned into silver or traded for such wares as could be carried to Canaan.

The hardest trading centered on the sale of the farm. The Hittites who accompanied Sanu-Rimmon to the wedding showed interest in acquiring the property for a sanctuary to their god Teshub. For months Eleazer fenced with them about the purchase. He demanded 6000 shekels in silver and the Hittites offered one-half of this amount. The bargaining went on until they raised their bid to 4000 and Eleazer reduced the purchase price to 5000. On hearing from Eleazer that the deal would be consummated Avraham told Sanu-Rimmon to notify his associates that they should first obtain permission from the king or the high priest of Szin to erect on the land a temple to a foreign god. The Hittites had already received the permit but utilized the well-meant advice to beat down the price. To the disgust of Eleazer they would now pay only 4500 shekels, which sum he was forced to accept. On the down payment of 1000 shekels a contract was entered into and sealed requiring the balance when the owner could deliver possession of the property.

The arduous task of organizing the caravan was of course delegated to the indispensable Eleazer. He procured about 30 covered wagons each drawn by two oxen or asses with ten additional animals in reserve should any become disabled. He filled about 20 of the vehicles with food, water, fuel, tools, weapons, and tents with poles; all of which should suffice for about three months, the time he computed necessary to reach the Negev in Canaan, considering the slow progress of the herds. Several additional strong wagons carried the gold and silver, withdrawn from the metal boxes stored for safety in the Temple of Szin, and other valuables consisting of wares, merchandise, and Sarah's finery. The itinerants numbering about 200 souls consisted of men, women, children, and disabled oldsters, the majority being of Habiru tribes.

Of Avraham's family only Sarah and Lot went along. Davarah, pleading advanced age, remained with her daughter Milcah on Nahor's farm but her son insisted on joining his uncle, for whom he had a strong affection. Hankas having sold his boat in Haran selected the stalwarts among the Habiru, who, armed with iron weapons, proved formidable guardsmen capable of protecting the lives and property of the caravan against any attacks by roving bandits. The faithful band devoted to their chieftain started out on the trek early one morning in the late autumn to escape the summer heat. The men walked alongside of the wagons while the herdsmen led their sheep, goats, and cattle.

Chapter 12 of Genesis states that "Avram departed as the Lord had spoken to him and Lot went with him. . . . Avraham took Sarai his wife and Lot his brother's son and all the substance that they had gathered and all the souls that they had acquired in Haran and they set out for the land of Canaan." Avraham no doubt felt that his journey, as commanded by El Elyon, was highly important. But he little suspected that this trek would ultimately change the course of human history.